THROWN-AWAY CHILD

Books by Thomas Adcock

Thrown-Away Child*
Devil's Heaven*
Drown All the Dogs*
Dark Maze*
Sea of Green
Precinct 19

*Published by POCKET BOOKS

THROWN-AWAY CHILD

A NEIL HOCKADAY MYSTERY

THOMAS ADCOCK

POCKET BOOKS
New York London Toronto Sydney Tokyo Singapore

This book is a work of fiction. Names, characters, places and incidents are products of the author's imagination or are used fictitiously. Any resemblance to actual events or locales or persons, living or dead, is entirely coincidental.

POCKET BOOKS, a division of Simon & Schuster Inc.
1230 Avenue of the Americas, New York, NY 10020

Adcock, Thomas Larry, 1947–
Thrown-away child : a Neil Hockaday mystery / Thomas Adcock.
p. cm.
ISBN 0-671-51985-9
1. Hockaday, Neil (Fictitious character)—Fiction. 2. Police—New York (N.Y.)—Fiction. I. Title.
PS3551.D397T48 1996
813'.54—dc20 95-49314
CIP

First Pocket Books hardcover printing April 1996

10 9 8 7 6 5 4 3 2 1

Printed in the U.S.A.

For my mother in-law, Violet Sykes, née Converse . . . who hears the sweet notes where she is

ACKNOWLEDGMENTS

I am indebted to my late mother in-law for at least a hundred things, among them: coffee she made on early mornings we spent together in her kitchen in New Orleans—"coffee so strong it'll make you want to get up and go slap your grandma," as Violet Sykes declared it; stories that were stronger yet, which like a thief I stashed away in my notebooks; and the spirit and title of this novel. Of course, I would never have got to that wonderful kitchen if not for my wife, Kim Sykes. Nor would I have got much of anywhere else lately without her support and sufferance. Encouragement and critical guidance from Gloria Loomis, my urbane literary agent, are continuing treasures. So are the past fifteen years of Saturday morning breakfasts at various Manhattan greasy spoons with my pal Thomas Gifford, novelist and raconteur. Somebody new to this cast of characters has likewise aided the cause: my fine and caring editor, Peter Wolverton.

A dog starv'd at his master's gate
Predicts the ruin of the state.

—*William Blake*

PROLOGUE

Sister sat alone on a bench at one side of the altar, opposite the choir loft and baptismal pool. She was dressed in white satin, something Miss Hassie or some other old fat church lady might wear. Underneath, though, Sister was as slender as any teenage girl, not so much bigger around the hips and bust than a clutch of bayou reeds. Her long skinny fingers were laced together, settled atop a spray of yellow calla lilies resting in her lap like a floral wreath draped over a crypt.

Sister's eyes were closed. Her delicate face, strong coffee colored, was uptilted to an oval window picturing a stained glass Jesus. Circled doves formed a plumed halo around the head of the Son of God.

Despite the commotion all around her—the junior preacher's bug-eyed harangue, finally ended; the stamping feet and impromptu *All rights* and *Tell it nows* and *Amens* of the assembled; the tambourines and rhythmic songs of the praisesayers, which was what Minister Tilton called his choir; the caterwauls of God-terrorized children; the passion flower aroma of Sabbath body oils escaping through the pores of overheated souls—Sister betrayed not the slightest expression. Sunlight streaked through the windowed eyes of Jesus and shone down upon her, as if the Son of the Holy Father had eyes only for this skinny girl sitting in a plump cloud of church-lady satin.

She had been like this for two hours: back straight, face to the heavenly sun, hands folded and still, her lanky form motionless. But Sister knew no discomfort. She was in a beatific trance, gone to visit Glory for a while, and listening for ancient voices across the divides of time and tide, life and death.

But quite suddenly, she was . . .

Possessed?

How was it he had explained this duty? *You do your part right, girl. You make them all know you are purely seized by the Almighty spirit!*

Sister trembled, and swooned for them all. And this so strongly resembled something not necessarily divine. That first time, what had he called it? *You just met up with the sweet-assed tremble, my lady-child.*

Then as suddenly, Sister collapsed into a kind of serenity. The serenity of someone in a casket set out for viewing.

Minutes passed. The congregants held their breath.

Finally, Sister rose from the bench, her body moving as smoothly as water. Calla lilies slid down her thighs, scattering at her sandaled feet in two abstract yellow bouquets. Her eyes, shiny as brown creek pebbles, fluttered open. But she saw nothing of the people in front of her, for she had been trained by a master.

She snapped her neck left and right, tossing back beaded plaits of black hair. Her face glistened.

Sister raised her hands to shoulder level, ivory palms turned outward to the agitated congregation. Her eyes dropped shut again behind heavy lids. And she chanted, in *français africaine:*

"Danse Calinda, boudoum, boudoum
Danse Calinda, boudoum, boudoum . . . !"

Lights burst full from circular fixtures in the floor and ceiling, forming a white-hot column of illumination at the center of the altar. Then, in great bursts of silver gray mist shooting up from steam jets built into the floorboards for just such very moments of high religious drama, Minister Zebediah Tilton made his entrance.

Ascending on a hydraulic lift from a pit below the raised altar stage, he was resplendent in a black satin robe, trimmed at the neck and sleeves in sable and covered with gris-gris—tiny dolls made of feathers and wax and kinky human hair, pigs' ears, snakeskins, withered crab legs, dried-up rooster hearts. Beaming at the fevered assembly below him, Minister Tilton turned and knelt before the altar table as Sister's chanting grew in volume and urgency.

He crossed himself, in the Catholic fashion, then stood and again faced his flock. He rapped the floor with a gold-topped ebony cane. And when the worshipers hushed, he reached into his pocket for a silver Tiffany lighter. He fired the wick of a single candle on the table. The candle was huge, shaped like a crucifix, black as Minister Tilton's robe.

This ceremonial task complete, Minister Tilton joined now in Sister's chant. He tossed back his Jheri-curled head and sang the old words. As he sang, in a voice that clapped like thunder, the dark wattles below his neck quivered to the stamping feet of the worshipers.

After a few minutes, Minister Tilton's forehead was beaded in sweat. He stopped and raised up his arms, heavy as a pair of hams. He commanded his people, "Ladies and gentleman, at this *hear*-uh church of ours . . . this *glow*-ree-us Land of Dreams Tabernacle . . . we show an open door to everybody! Yes sir, yes ma'am—yeah, you right. I'm talking about every-*body!* Doubters and pouters, shouters and shiners . . ."

A-men!

"But whosoever shall *be*-uh with us upon this beauty-ful morning . . . Oh La, please—you must understand!"

Understand!

"You all got one big *dew*-tee in common today, don't you know."

That's right . . . Tell it, brother . . . !

"You all got to join me, hear-uh? We must lift up our voices all together-uh . . . in a mighty, mighty call—to those whose spirits . . . whose *spirits* . . . !"

Yes, Lord!

"Whose spirits live with the *Lord*-uh!"

Yeah, you right!

Bodies swayed in time with the cadence of Minister Tilton's beseechings, and the oaken pews of the Land of Dreams Tabernacle groaned. And then the mass chanting began again, rolling and rolling in throaty waves, pulsating the liquid air of a warm, dank November morning.

"Danse Calinda, boudoum, boudoum . . . !"

Three hundred pairs of black hands clapped in syncopation. Three hundred pairs of shoes pounded out the downbeat.

Violet Flagg's eyes surged with tears. Reluctantly, then helplessly, she slapped her hands together along with three hundred of her friends, and stamped her feet, too.

She was so tired, so tired.

None of it was real. Violet knew that. Anybody in the church could recite Violet's sentiments down through the years on the subject of Zebediah Tilton. *That low-down greasy-headed black-assed humbug—he ain't nothing but a big old flabby pile of jiggery-pokery.*

But in the long nights preceding Ruby's arrival—her "prodigal daughter" she would say—Violet had not slept well. And in these past long years, she had grown lonesome in all the ways a widow knows how to be lonesome.

And so on this stifling, exhausting Sunday morning Violet Flagg gave way to the strength of a believing crowd of friends who were so powerfully sure.

She would hear her man. She would believe! And maybe somewhere in all that silvery steam up on the altar Violet would see Willis, at least in the prism of her tears.

Did it matter if sound and sight were not really, truly from beyond death? Did it matter if an image conjured in steam was no more real than all the times she saw Willis in her nephew Perry's face?

Oh—but what would Willis say of Perry now? Would he send him away from her? Would Willis, too, throw the child away?

Sister stepped forward to the front of the altar. Her bare toes, brown on the tops and ivory on the bottoms, curled over the edge. Her arms flapped like a pelican snatching up a speckled bass off the blue-gray Lake Ponchartrain. She switched from *français africaine* to the *canga* of a Creole patois:

"Eh! Eh! Bomba, hen! hen!
Canga bafio, te,
Canga moune de le,
Canga do ki la,
Canga li . . . !"

Minister Tilton and all the others joined this new chant, their massed voices gathering to a storm of pathos and yearning. A yearning for what?

Fatherly advice? Motherly love? A piece of the American dream? A ticket north? A view from the top? An even break? A day without fear? One more chance?

There was a narcotic swing to it all: to Minister Tilton's thunderclap voice, to Sister's rapture, to the old Creole words. Especially the words; Violet Flagg, devoutest of all doubters, felt them cut deep inside her.

"Sis-*tuh!*" shouted Minister Tilton, rapping his cane, addressing his pretty angel acolyte. His yellow-green eyes bore into her; he knew well the sweet girl-flesh hidden in the billowing satin, and thought now of its pleasure, his loins stiffening. Sister felt the heat of his impious eyes, and felt her own secret shame as well.

The storm of yearning voices faded, enough for Minister Tilton to be heard over his boisterous celebrants. "Sister, prepare!" he commanded. "Prepare for the *dance*-uh—the *danse calinda* of your revered-uh *voudou!*"

Sister moved to the altar table. She picked up a leather-bound flask of brandy next to the crucifix candle, opened it, and poured some of the liquor over a sprinkling of brick dust lining a black ceramic bowl. She set down the flask and bowed in the direction of Minister Tilton, then backed off from the table and returned to her bench.

Dropping his cane to the misty floor, Minister Tilton picked up the bowl with both hands. A shaft of sunlight glinted off one of his diamond cuff links. He lifted the bowl to his lips, and drank down the gritty mixture of brandy and brick. Slowly, he began rotating his hips and shuffling his feet backward, then forward. His movements accelerated as the congregation lifted voice again to the *canga,* now minus Sister, whose face was once more uptilted to her stained glass Jesus and heavenly doves.

Missing not a step of his dance, Minister Tilton poured the rest of the brandy into the bowl and ignited it with his Tiffany lighter. The bowl flamed up high over the altar table. Minister Tilton passed his hands through the flame, and quickened his dance steps as the *canga* picked up tempo. And soon his powerful voice soared above all the others:

"I call out Willis Flagg!" he shouted. *"Eh! Eh! Bomba, hen! hen!* I call out Willis Flagg! *Eh! Eh! Bomba, hen! hen!* Willis Flagg, speak through me . . . !"

Silence, or nearly so, as the congregants waited.

Violet cried softly.

A tall man in a scarlet robe, his head and face concealed by a hood, called from the rear of the church: *"Bomba, hen, hen! . . . Bomba, hen, hen . . . !"*

Minister Tilton was as startled as if he had just swallowed a fly. Grasping the gris-gris in both his hands, as if he sincerely believed in its power, he asked feebly of the man in scarlet rushing toward him, "What—?"

But there was no answer from the man running crazily up the center aisle, whirling and leaping and howling until he reached the altar's edge. Until a stunned Minister Tilton tripped over his cane and fell to his knees, and gasped, "No, you mustn't come up—!"

Disobeying, the man vaulted over the railing. He scrambled to the altar stage and took Minister Tilton's place in the column of light, then turned to the confused congregation.

He pushed back the hood of his robe. His head and face had been greased, and heavily caked in talcum. The hair was African, the hawkish features European. The camouflage of sticky white powder absorbed the light, deadening it, casting the intruder's face in a chalky pallor.

He undid the laces of his robe, allowing it to slip from his shoulders. Beneath, his sand brown skin was oiled and glistening.

He was nearly naked. Women screamed but did not avert their eyes. Not even the old ones with the lacy fans and their heads covered in *tignons,* for the figure before them was a perfect masculine beauty.

He raised his hands, clenched in huge fists, and cried out over a church fallen to deathly quiet:

"I am Willis Flagg! I *am* Willis Flagg!"

From a pew near the widow Violet Flagg, a trembling Miss Hassie stood up, and shrieked, "Jesus, Mary, Joseph—it's him! Oh La, it's *him . . . !*"

ONE

You do not crap where you eat.

This and some other counsel I tried to impart to inspector Tomasino Neglio the last time I saw him. Which was yesterday at noon when the two of us had it out in his office downtown over the little matter of how in God's name I can do right by anything holy in staying with a department that contains the likes of Sergeant King Kong Kowalski, who has an arrest warrant face, meat breath, and fingers like rolled quarters. (Which is to mention only one choice example of a wrong number who carries the NYPD-approved 9-millimeter semiautomatic while I myself am still twisting slowly on the rubber gun squad because I have been overly fond in the past of a certain Mr. Johnnie Walker.) I mention God because the department chaplain, Father John Sheehan, was also on hand for yesterday's unpleasantness.

After speaking my piece, I might have been slightly out of breath and wild-eyed. This I figured from the suspicious way Neglio and the padre looked at me, like maybe they were thinking they ought to toss the net and hustle me off to the puzzle house. When all I did was say what needed saying for crying out loud.

"Let's all go to lunch, someplace nice with tablecloths and clean forks. It should be a big change in your life." This the inspector suggested to me by way of changing the subject on my mind. "Afterwards—you want, I can get my driver to take you uptown. You can see my own family doc. He'll give you some pills. Make you feel better, make you all loose and lovely."

"The good father being here," I said, waving a thumb toward Sheehan, who sat cross-legged in a chair by a potted date palm clipping his nails, "I won't mention the graphics I am thinking of. So you should imagine for yourself exactly where I would tell you and the family croaker you should insert the good-time pills."

Neglio sighed. He got up off his maroon wingback leather chair and stepped over to one of his two banks of windows overlooking the New York harbor from twenty floors above the ruckus of Manhattan. These windows are the kind that actually open, the big tilt-in jobs that make it easy for cleaning, and also for jumping. Neglio yanked open one of the windows. There was a rush of harbor-soaked wind, and he said to me, "You know, I got this bona fide concern about your state of mind."

"How's that?"

The inspector did not exactly answer me. What he said was more in the way of a challenge.

"If you don't lighten up," Neglio said, looking out the window, then back at me, "you should give the department a freaking break and go ahead—do the brain dive."

"What do you make of this?" I asked, turning to Sheehan. "Inspector Neglio here, he's one of us. I don't mean a shamrock, but anyhow Catholic. A good Catholic suggesting suicide? Isn't that a cardinal sin?"

Sheehan said nothing. Instead he brushed a pile of little crescent-shaped cuttings from his puffy lap, then started on his cuticles.

"Father?"

"I heard you, son." Sheehan straightened his black horn-rimmed glasses and looked up at me. He sighed and stroked his beard, too thin to cover up the dimples. "A lot of devout Catholics can't honestly regard the idea of suicide as being so terrible. For instance, on rainy winter Sundays when there's a lot of boredom a man may be well advised to carry a gun. Not to shoot himself, but to know exactly that he's always making a choice."

"A very life-affirming sentiment," I said. "As a priest, you'd make an excellent grave digger."

Sheehan only shrugged. Then he went back to his self-inflicted manicure.

"Let's get down to it," Neglio said, highly impatient now. He closed up the window. He went back to his desk and lifted a crisp cuff to consult his Rolex. I also own a brand of wristwatch ending with the letters *ex*. Mine, however, I selected from a plastic display case on a little rotating stand on a Lamston's counter back in the days when there was such a thing as Lamston's. "I want your decision before you take off down south for the holiday."

My decision.

Only a couple of days ago, I made a splashy murder case with the collar of a society lady up in the same East Side neighborhood where Neglio and his Rolex live. Before taking her down, a sizable part of New York's population was panicked by this woman's idea of a memorable Hallowe'en: the systematic killing of low-rent homosexuals as a cover for whacking a bigger fish—namely her husband, a Madison Avenue big shot whose feathers she tried tarring with a lavender brush. That way, she figured, the homicide detectives would not be inspired to do what they are paid to do. Cop reasoning in this case being, What's the big deal about another fag bumped? King Kong Kowalski saw to it that such reasoning was paramount.

With the considerable help of Davy Mogaill—my rabbi in the ways of the department, who was himself forcibly retired and who is currently reduced to working as a licensed New York peep—I saved this husband's neck in the absolute nick of time. Also I made the case under considerable personal strain. Number one, I had just graduated from a six-week sentence at the Straight and Narrow, which is an actual intersection of streets over in Paterson where some priests run a rummy tank for New York cops who have had way too many. Number two, the reason I wound up in this Jersey tank from being overly thirsty had to do with some recent and very ugly discoveries about my Irish family that broke my heart. And number three, my brand-new wife, Ruby Flagg, was practically ready to dump me as the biggest mistake of her life.

Never mind, that is all another story. But in that story, I did what I had to do—in spite of King Kong Kowalski's many irritations. And what was my thanks for all this? Did the inspector take me off restricted duty? Did he give me back my Nina so I did not have to walk around with a naked holster? No, and no.

And these are not the only things that now cause me bitterness, that have me lying awake nights thinking over the option of hanging it up and taking early pension checks from the city every month for the rest of my days. Another thing is the unfinished business of Kowalski himself.

Joseph Kowalski belongs to the Holy Name Society of Our Lady of the Blessed Agony Church in Queens. Also he is the overnight desk sergeant at Manhattan Sex Crimes who freely exercises a famous habit of torturing homosexual perps. This habit he regards as a moral crusade, and squad room entertainment.

Because I have squawked loud about this, the word is out that I am some sort of champion of homosexuals. I am an unlikely champion. Two guys kissing on the lips creeps me. But then, the whole psycho-pathology of romance between men and women likewise creeps me. Anybody who ever read a history book knows that the things people do in the name of love, not to mention religion, are not nearly so noble as they are pathetic and dangerous.

Along these lines, as a human being and a cop I specifically object to some gay blade having his bold fellow walloped for the sake of some precinct station house sport. Which is Sergeant Joseph Kowalski's meat, so to speak.

He says to some frightened homosexual perp, after he has inked his fingerprints onto the standard FBI forms, "Come on now, queeny, drop trou and plop your lolly-johnson up here on the pad so's I can take your dickprint." Just routine, Kowalski says. Then instead of being routine like with the fingers, the sergeant goes into a drawer, brings out a braided sap, and smacks the guy. For this holy sport, and because of his gorilla girth, he is called King Kong Kowalski.

So I wrote out a formal complaint about the big ape and filed it with Inspector Neglio. Also I made a couple of things very clear: the department is not big enough for both Kowalski and me; and if it was me who had to walk, then I would go down in tabloid flames by spilling everything I knew about Kowalski to my pal Slattery at the *New York Post.*

In other words, I broke a pair of unbreakable cop rules. Number one, I made things personal. Number two, I ratted out another cop. (For this second heresy, I was awarded the usual recognition by my colleagues in blue. Somebody hung a half-dozen dead sewer rats on my locker at the station house. Also somebody used a set of picks one day to get into my apartment building, whereupon he decorated my door with an arrangement of more dead rats, sweetly spelling out what everybody calls me—Hock.) The fact that I committed these sins as a cop on restricted duty after an enforced dry-out did nothing to aid in my bargaining position.

So now something has to give. Me or this love-it-or-leave-it New York cop fraternity.

"You really should flee it, and without looking back." This according to Davy Mogaill when I sought his advice on my troubled place in a fraternity that includes the likes of King Kong Kowalski. "You're a man more interested in justice than police work, Neil, which now you see can be opposing forces."

There was an ace in the hole to go along with Mogaill's

advice. He offered me a partnership in what he proposed to incorporate as Mogaill & Hockaday, Private Investigations.

By the way, I am Detective Neil Hockaday of the New York Police Department's elite SCUM Patrol, which is an acronym for something that does not sound too elite—Street Crimes Unit—Manhattan. Along with the TNT (for Tactical Neighborhood Teams), the SCUM patrol is one of the few remaining acronyms in a department that was for many years letter crazy. The enthusiasm for this sort of thing evaporated fast when somebody had the bright idea of forming the Special Homicide Investigations Team and was laughed out of town when people started figuring out the shorthand sound of that one.

Inspector Neglio, being in charge of all of Manhattan's acronyms and assorted other specialized squads, is the boss I was about to leave in the lurch for a while. He will get over it sooner or later. And Mogaill has all the time in the world, since he is a bachelor and a peep with only a few clients. Of my own time and chances, I am not so sure.

"All right then, let's get down to it," I said to the inspector, agreeably. "First, what are you going to do about Joe Kowalski?"

"What—you think I just sat on that beef or yours? Let it go through the regular drill? No, Hock. I called out the lepers on this wrong cop right away."

"Internal Affairs? Don't make me laugh." I laughed. "Kowalski isn't one of your garden-variety wrong cops out there charging a little off-duty taxation on some drug dealer. Not that the lepers from IAD can deal with that even. Kowalski's rabid."

"As in rabies?"

"As in a guy with a gun and a badge and the idea that people ought to behave themselves according to his personal lights. Rabid, as in foaming at the mouth."

"Kowalski's being handled."

"Not like *I'm* being handled. I got drunk too many times, so you tanked me. You take away my Nina, you put me in charge of paper clips. All right, I see the point. But who did I ever hurt besides myself, and my wife? You knock me down to the rubber gun squad for boozing, but King Kong Kowalski, who is running a torture chamber down at Sex Crimes—him you let alone."

Sheehan piped up. "I'm not hearing penitence from you, son."

I have been around priests my entire life, ever since choirboy days at Holy Cross Church in the Hell's Kitchen neighborhood of Manhattan's West Side. Which is home to this day. Never have I seriously thought about decking a priest until now. (Neglio, on the other hand, I have often thought about decking.) But at that moment as I considered giving Father Sheehan a clout, it occurred to me why he was there with the inspector that day: to make me think twice about what might otherwise come naturally. A variation of the good-cop, bad-cop routine.

Anyway, Neglio and I argued back and forth for another half hour or so until we both realized there was no percentage in talking any further. Neglio wanted me to make my choice: stay with the department, or take early retirement. I wanted his personal commitment that Kowalski would be made to walk, one way or another.

"If I had a real choice, I'd go back to the street where I belong," I said. "I've had enough of your furloughs, your Straight and Narrows, your restricted duty, your rabid cops."

Neglio thought otherwise. Father Sheehan thought I was obsessed with King Kong Kowalski, which he said was evidence I was still "in denial," which is an expression I have come to seriously dislike.

"What I have decided," I said to all this, "is that the department has more wrong numbers in it than any time I remember—"

"Pills," Neglio interrupted. "I'm telling you, Hock, all's you need is pills."

"Loose and lovely," Sheehan said brightly. All over again, I felt like clobbering a priest.

"Listen to me, Inspector. Kowalski's not the only one foaming at the mouth. He's not the only cop making things dirty for the rest of us. For the love of God, can't somebody besides me see that? You do not crap where you eat. You do not let anybody else crap there either . . ."

So that is how I left the inspector, not to mention Davy Mogaill. With no decision about my future.

Like I said, that was yesterday.

TWO

Today, I am riding an Amtrak train. The Cresent line, from New York City way down yonder to my wife Ruby's hometown of New Orleans. And I am thinking how good it is to be out of town a little while.

Ruby wanted us to go by train, a journey of twenty-eight hours. This was to impress upon me exactly how far she had to travel all those years ago when she left home. I am only happy she did not choose to impress upon me the discomforts of her original means of transport: the Greyhound bus.

It is midmorning and we have returned from a meal in the dining car. Eggs scrambled with mushrooms and peppers and onions, toast and blueberry jam and coffee that was not too bad. The cots are folded back up into the wall of our sleeper compartment so that now we have couches. Which we are sitting on, drinking post-breakfast coffee in paper cups and staring out the window at blue-green pines high up in the Great Smoky Mountains.

"Will you look at all those trees? Christmas is coming." This Ruby says with a dream in her voice. She has been dreaming and talking of home and the South and the past for a long time. Not all her dreams have been sugarplums.

We have talked, ever since pulling out of Penn Station back in Manhattan, about the years not so long ago when our marriage was a crime in most states; about the first time somebody called her "nigger," when she was a little girl walking down the street with her braids and schoolbooks; about why she had not been home in all the years since leaving for New York, and telephone arguments about that with her mother; about certain delicate problems some of the family might have with my face, which is as fair as County Dublin.

There is one thing we have not discussed, though. That would be how close our short marriage has come to collapse due to the pressures of my job, and also due to my boozing.

No matter, Ruby slips her arm into mine as she looks at the trees rushing by. I consider myself lucky beyond measure. I have no doubt that Ruby has days she is sorry she ever took up with me. I have no doubt she would do it all over again.

"I remember the Christmas my daddy got sick for good and there wasn't any money," Ruby says, sort of absently. "Mama had to tell us there wouldn't be any toys that year."

We ride along for maybe twenty minutes without a word passing between us. Every so often, Ruby daubs her hazel eyes and her caramel brown cheeks with Kleenex. But there are no tears to wipe. I believe she is trying to cry, or that maybe what is inside her head at the moment is so sad she naturally thinks she has been crying.

Ruby has been like his for a week or so, on the edge of some raw emotion I cannot read—something I am guessing to be peculiarly feminine.

She starts singing after awhile, very softly as we watch the miles and miles of timberline. Her voice is low and sweet, and this surprises me. I have never heard her sing before. Ruby was an actress for a lot of years, but she never said anything about musicals. Her song is like the best songs of all, beautiful and mournful at once:

"Toyland . . . toyland, little girl and boyland;
While you dwell within it,
You are always healthy there.
Childhood, joyland, mystic merry toyland;
Once you pass its borders
You may ne'er return again."

"Are you all right?" I ask her, now that she has finished singing.

"Of course I'm all right. I'm on my way home to see my Mama, and the rest of my family. It's going to be wonderful. Oh, it is, I promise. Everybody's going to love you . . ." Ruby is speaking very fast, as if trying to persuade herself of something. "Just you watch your waist line, Irish. They're all going to want to feed you. And you're going to be fed the very best meals you ever had in your life. You're going to eat food cooked by colored people, with love."

Ruby does not look at me as she says the last of this. And her voice trails off, but the Christmas trees do not.

Anybody can tell that memory is pressing her. And so I ask, "Tell me about that one Christmas?"

Violet Flagg, standing in this place with her head bound in a woollen scarf and the wind being kind enough to blow away her embarrassed tears, looked up at a leaden December sky. Her thought was, Oh La—will it ever come easy for me? But she did not dare ask such a thing aloud, for fear of losing heart in front of the children.

Here, at the railroad tracks—at Elysian Fields, where Paris Avenue cuts under the viaduct, right near Henrietta's Wigs & Weaves and the Popeye's takeout chicken stand—was where people came by night and dumped their throwaways for as long as Violet Flagg had been in New Orleans. Which now, in 1960, had been almost two decades since saying good-bye and good riddance to St. Francisville.

She remembered her first visit to the dump, in the 1940s, and how everybody used to come take a close look at the trash—maybe pick a little some. You never know but that something useful would turn up, which you could not otherwise afford. But then the times got better in the 1950s—for Negroes, too—and only the tramps would come to pick, white and black alike. The tramps and also trashy women who were not too picky about men. Nobody respectable came here anymore.

Yet here she was on this raw day, Violet Flagg with three children following along after her like ducklings. At home, her husband, Willis, was in the big bed upstairs, swaddled to control his incontinence, slipping in and out of delirium. This was the worst bout of Willis's long sickness. He had not worked in almost ten months. The people at the clinic had no name for what ailed Willis, and they assured Violet that even the fancy doctors down on Canal Street probably had no better diagnosis. Nobody said he was dying, but Violet knew he was.

And so the black dogs of sickness and poverty were again, in 1960, the central facts of Violet's existence. Just as they had been in St. Francisville during the Great Depression of the 1930s. But Violet was determined to prevent at least one replay of those grim days. Christmas was coming! Money or no, it would not be like it was when she was a girl. She would not wear her own mother's scared brave face and tell a lie to her young ones, "Christmas is just another day." No! Her children—her little daughters Janice and Ruby, and Rose's boy, Perry—would have their presents. Her husband, Willis, too. If it meant picking trash, then so be it.

Violet stood back from the mounds of refuse. The cans and bottles, the soggy bags full of old clothes and household junk, jagged bits of lumber, broken furniture, rusted car parts. The children circled around her. The girls held fast to their mama's hands, warmed by an old pair of their daddy's brown cotton work gloves. Perry clutched at Violet's skirts, wiping a runny nose on the sleeve of one of Willis's khaki shirts. Violet let loose of Janice's hand for a minute. Violet shaded her eyes and surveyed the dump, to make sure it was free of trampy men. Tramps were different now than they were years back, more likely toward violence. Satisfied she had the trash mound all to herself, Violet then moved ahead, towing the children along with her.

"I'm freezing cold!" Ruby hollered, her breath frosting in the wind. And it was true; her little fingers were ice in Violet's hand.

Violet prayed silently to God for the gift of a child's mittens somewhere in the mean landscape. Ruby further complained, "Why we come here to this nasty place, Mama?"

"For a little knobby-kneed skinny thing, you got a awful big mouth," Violet answered her daughter.

Violet took off her floppy man's gloves and gave them to Ruby to wear, then shooed her off along with Janice and Perry to go find whatever they might find. She said to the three of them, "Go ahead, run around. But don't be straying far from me, and if you see something move—well, just don't be stepping on it . . ."

Ruby stops her story. The train slows to a crawl, to cross a long trestle bridge spanning a narrow and muddy river. The pines of one mountain riverbank give way to another and the speed resumes.

"I take it your mother found everybody a Christmas present there by the railroad tracks?" I ask.

"Yes. We just about froze to death that day, and I kept telling Mama I was ashamed of us being there. But Mama wouldn't leave that trash heap, not until she had all the presents she needed."

"I like that story."

"I don't."

"What was your present?"

"A little boy doll with a lot of dents and no clothes. He had pink skin and blue eyes and he was missing some of his hair—just like you, Irish." Ruby gave a laugh that I did not mind. "Mama sewed him a little jacket and pants out of a scrap of something she had lying around. I named him Tommy, and I loved him."

"Do you still have him?"

Ruby turns from me, and looks out to the plumes of dark fog in the hills. The miles and miles of Christmas trees appear to be on fire. Ruby says, "Sometimes, I think all I have of home is stories I don't like."

THREE

"Before long, you'll know all the family tragedies," Ruby says, sighing. "The cottage . . . how Daddy got sick . . . Perry and his Mama Rose, and Toby Jones . . ."

Ruby turns away and stares out the window for a while. Then she says, "You're going to see where I mostly grew up, Hock. I don't like it there. We didn't always live in the projects."

"It doesn't matter where—"

"No, it matters." There was no debating Ruby. "I should tell you another story now. When I was a girl, Mama told us all the story—and taught us how to pass it along. She said we shouldn't ever forget. It's about where we started out, and how nothing lived happily ever after."

Then Ruby told me a tragedy.

It was a cedar-sided cottage of four narrow connected rooms raised up on stubby hurricane stilts, with a high pitched roof, batten shutters over the windows, and French louvered doors on either end. In appearance and infirmity, the Flagg cottage was nearly the same as the forty or so others crowded into a rut-filled dirt lane between lower Tchoupitoulas Street and a levee almost crumbled away from years of flood and neglect. But Willis and Violet would make it the neighborhood showplace.

Every morning before going off to work, Willis scrubbed down the front steps with a mixture of steaming hot water and brick dust to keep demons at bay. His people raised him in such belief, and although he did not speak much of these things, he felt obliged to maintain the customs of his bloodline. The back steps led to a small fenced garden. Willis kept the grass thick as a new carpet and clean of kudzu. He planted a big chinaberry tree in the middle of the garden and lilac bushes in the corners, a bed of namesake violets for his wife, and a row of morning glories to climb the fence.

Despite the pretty Flagg cottage, the neighborhood was one that tourists were not encouraged to visit. It was one of many of the city's hidden lanes, where pain and fears from the hard past overlapped an insecure present. Some—Willis and Hassie Pinkney from next door included—said it was a haunted part of New Orleans, bedeviled by avenging African ghosts from slave times.

On most afternoons, people in the lane would go to the levee for the coolness of the river breezes, or to catch themselves a dinner of Mississippi catfish. Aged black ladies and gentlemen—the women with *tignons* covering their hair, Madras kerchiefs favored by *voudouiennes,* tied with seven points carefully twisted heavenward—would talk until dusk of the island days, and the old-time religious ways.

Violet and Willis were fiercely proud of their house. It was truly theirs, free and clear—and no thanks to any Jim Crow bank or mortgage company. It was a cottage bought and paid for with the saved-up wages of a yard man and a cleaning woman whose ancestors had once been shackled to posts in the public square above Canal Street and sold as slaves. But on the twenty-first of March in the year 1948, a sunny day in New Orleans, Violet and Willis Flagg took title to a little wood cottage and became the first of their respective families to own their home.

It was a long way up in a perilous, hostile world, and Violet and Willis were pleased to be gracious about their ascent. Everybody in the lane, with but one exception, shared generously in their reflected joy. The one who did not was Miss Hassie, who had a generally sneering horse face and a fondness for predicting disaster and spreading sour news.

When she learned that the Flaggs had up and bought the cottage, Miss Hassie wasted no time in rushing next door to tell Violet, "Ain't going to be no comfort to you or nobody else down here to be buying out your place when it's the last one here ain't yet owned by Minister Tilton."

"Who you talking about being a *minister?*" Violet asked. She took God seriously, and therefore believed that self-glorifying preachers of the gospel were no more anointed by the Lord Almighty than circus clowns. "Zeb Tilton? That chubby little hoo-doo man?"

Miss Hassie, eyes bulged and her body stiffened with the shock of Violet's sacrilege, said, "Well now, he *is* the Most Reverend Zebediah Tilton!"

"Ask me and the bartender up to Shug's and even the Lord Himself, and we all tell you the same: Zeb's the least reverent *Most Reverend* anybody ever did see. Minister Tilton—shoo! He ain't even got a church, Hassie. 'Less you call that ratty little root shop of his a church."

"He'll have his proper church one day."

"When pigs fly. Meanwhile, Zeb's nothing but a pork chop learned how to walk."

"Oh, La! You best keep a respectful tongue. Minister Tilton, he knows the mysteries."

Hassie's eyes rolled as she said this. Violet wanted to laugh straight in her horse face but she did not, for she was charitable with ignorant people. Especially Hassie, poor homely thing. Violet felt sorry for her living in the back room of the cottage the way she did, arguing all the time with her sister.

"Zebediah Tilton aims to have this whole lane some fine day, one way'r other," Hassie babbled on. "He's going to get you yet, my sweet Miss Ma'am—one way'r other."

Violet thought, Wait 'til Willis hears this! She would make a whooping joke of it all, mocking the way Miss Hassie's eyes grew round as plates and how her voice trembled and how she waggled her bony hands when she said, "He knows the mysteries." But then she thought again, realizing how her husband might not appreciate the joke. And so Violet kept it to herself.

But anyway, one day Miss Hassie bumped into Willis up on Jackson Avenue and was pleased to hang the black crêpe all over again. This rattled Willis so badly he had to slip into Shug's and have a few drinks to calm himself. Then he went home and had a tiff with Violet over her deliberate failure to relay Hassie's sentiments on their real estate holdings.

"I don't know why you want to be paying mind to that ugly-hearted toad," Violet said in her own defense. "Hassie a miserable woman. She got nothing to do but spread poison about everyone around her, even her sister and that man she want to marry. If I was her sister I'd get out of that miserable cottage right fast. Day that happens, then Hassie be miserable *and* lonesome."

"Gott-damn, but the woman's right, ain't she, Vi? We never took account of Zeb Tilton."

"What's he got to do with it? You telling me you spooked by Zeb?"

"Ain't spooked. Only saying now we got our pride we don't need trouble from nobody."

The pride of the Flaggs was brief.

One Saturday morning in July of 1948, the Orleans parish assistant tax assessor came calling. He was a huge, slow-moving, sweaty, talkative young white lawyer with the florid name of Hippocrates Beauregard Giradoux.

Giradoux wore a panama hat and an unpressed seersucker suit with an oval of perspiration on the back of his open coat and two more circular stains below the armpits. His shirt collar was unbuttoned because his neck was too fat. His necktie advertised eggs for breakfast. He had a runty red nose and blue eyes set deep beneath an almost prehistoric brow. Belying his bloated and generally decrepit appearance, Giradoux owned a sunny disposition; he was courtly and he smiled quite a lot, and the smiles seemed genuine.

He stood at the top of the front steps insured against demons, smiling as Willis Flagg came to answer his lightly insistent knock. Giradoux explained himself in a chicken-fried drawl, "Just a trifling matter of some homeowner business, sir." When Violet appeared at the door behind her husband, Assessor Giradoux removed his hat, which in the year of 1948 in the state of Louisiana was as rare a sign of respect given to a Negro lady as calling a Negro gentleman *Sir.*

But Giradoux had done both these respectful things. And now for several seconds all that Violet and Willis Flagg could manage was to stare at the smiling white fat man on their doorstep, holding his panama and sopping his forehead with a seersucker sleeve.

Finally, Assessor Giradoux was invited inside, where he shook Willis's hand just as easy as he would a white man's and said "Thank you so kindly" to Violet's offer of lemonade. Violet motioned for him to take the best chair in the parlor, the one with the padded seat and back fitted with slipcovers she had embroidered herself while riding the bus back and forth to house-cleaning jobs.

Exactly two other white people had been inside the Flaggs' immaculate cottage. First was a crewcut salesman for the Fuller Brush Company. Second was a bald bill collector who came around to talk about Violet's sister, Rose Duclat, and how she had run away up north leaving a stack of unpaid markers. Both these white men had pulled out handkerchiefs and wiped off the good chair before perching on it. But Hippocrates Beauregard Giradoux gave no such offense. He plopped down his milky big behind in the chair, as if he was home in his own parlor.

"Oh my, Missus Flagg, but you keep a mighty pretty house," he said.

"Thank you, sir," Violet said. She looked at Willis, who seemed as confused as she was.

"And this lemonade!" Giradoux lapped noisily. "Divine . . . divine!"

"Thank you again, sir."

"Might's well call me Hippo like they all do down to the courthouse and city hall." Giradoux spoke to Violet and Willis both. He patted a belly that overlapped his belt. Violet imagined his naked belly looking like a batch of yeasty dough. "My daddy, he's Doc Giradoux, you know."

"Is that so?" Violet asked.

"Oh yes. He wanted so very bad for me to follow in his footsteps. That's how come he named me after Hippocrates, the great Greek physician. You ever heard of Hippocrates?"

"I believe I have, sir," said Willis.

"My daddy's a good man—good to colored and white alike, you know—and I feel bad about wasting his money on every medical school between here and Shreveport. Well, but then Daddy finally give up on me and let me go free." Giraudoux patted his doughy belly again. "Daddy'd say to his friends, 'My young Hippo he took a different path—straight to the ice box!' "

Hippo and the Flaggs laughed together.

"No, I ain't like Daddy or that old Greek," Hippo said. "I become a lawyer eventually, not much of a trick. As a doctor's boy, I am a strong disappointment. Why—don't you know I sometime shop down to Cracker Jack's drugstore on South Rampart?"

"You talking about that root shop, sir?" Willis looked over at Violet, raising his eyebrows. *A white man in a root shop?* Violet shrugged.

"The very one." Hippo finished off his lemonade. "I drop around every so often and talk to the old smokes, you know? Real interesting. Buy me some money-drawing incense, or boss-fixing powder, or gris-gris balls of salt and saffron and feathers and dog dung. Hell of a thing for the son of a man of science, wouldn't you say, Mr. Flagg?"

"Well, sir, you never know."

"I figure the exact same way."

Willis and Violet could not help but like Hippo. Everybody did, white and black. Everybody said Hippo was a good and friendly talker. So good it hardly mattered if he was truthing or lying, it was just such a pleasure to listen to him. Everybody said that made him a natural-born Louisiana politician. That and the fact he somehow managed to find a college willing to grant him a law diploma.

Hippo was there with the Flaggs that Saturday morning of 1948 with some important papers for signing, papers that would bring paving to the little dirt lane off Tchoupitoulas Street. Cement curbsides and street lamps and a sewer hookup, too.

Willis and Violet did not understand all that the sweaty young white man was saying, nor could they completely follow the tiny print on his papers. But since he had been respectful and amusing, they felt they should trust him. And so the Flaggs proudly signed as property owners, on the dotted line where it said "Freeholder."

Then about a year later, when Willis and Violet had fallen impossibly far behind on the special surcharges levied against them for the modern conveniences—all in accordance with Hippo's important papers—the Flaggs' home was seized by the Orleans parish sheriff and put up for sale in tax-forfeiture court.

At the auction, there was but one bidder—the Most Reverend Zebediah Tilton. At last, he owned every cottage in the lane.

Minister Tilton wasted no time. After putting down cash money to retire the delinquent surcharges, the good minister drove straightaway from the courthouse to call on the Flaggs.

He arrived in his big maroon Packard motorcar, one of the first postwar models off the Detroit assembly lines. When the neighbors saw the Packard roll in from Tchoupitoulas Street they ran to their homes and shut the doors and windows until Tilton drove out again. All the neighbors, that is, save Hassie Pinkney. Hassie sat on the front steps of her cottage, straining to hear the sorry conversation going on next door.

In the parlor of the newly dispossessed Flaggs, Zebediah Tilton was polite and sympathetic. After all, he had no reason to be rude when he bought someone's home out from under them. The law made everything so easy and polite.

"Now, I know you can understand that our church has many missions," he said in his creamy preacher's voice.

"What in hell church is that?" Violet asked.

"The Land of Dreams Tabernacle, Mrs. Flagg. Although we are temporarily conducting services in Bynum's pharmacy over on Dauphine Street, we do have our Deacons Building Committee searching for a permanent location." Zeb Tilton's beefy brown lips widened into a smile, and Violet could see clear back to his gold teeth. "Among our churchly missions is providing what we can in the way of housing for our poor, unfortunate brothers and sisters."

Willis sat in a cane back chair in a sort of shock, still as a stone as Minister Tilton talked. Willis seemed as if he heard nothing. For days before the court sale, he had spent almost no time at home, instead sitting up at Shug's with his cares, hiding from Violet so she would not see him crying in his beer. But he could no longer conceal his sorrow. Willis's eyes looked as if they might rust away from grief. Violet sat next to him, holding his big calloused hands.

"Now, I surely don't want to see good people like you having no place to live," Tilton went on, soothingly. "But you see, the problem here is that we must serve our members first. So, I've been giving this predicament of yours a lot of my thought and my very most powerful prayer. And I do believe I have come upon a solution . . ."

When at last he was finished, Minister Tilton had collected twenty dollars on account toward the first year's tithe to the Land of Dreams Tabernacle. And the church's two newest members, Violet and Willis Flagg, signed some important papers their new pastor happened to have with him, pressed inside a Holy Bible with a red leather cover. They signed where it said "Tenant."

After scratching his name to Zebediah Tilton's lease, Willis rose angrily from his chair, tearing himself away from Violet's grip on his shirt. He stood towering over the pastor. The resignation in his eyes gave way to rage. His hands, made thick and hard from his work with shovels and stone and earth, clenched into dark fists.

Violet thrilled to the sight of her husband's anger. She closed her eyes and silently prayed, Oh, La, won't you bless all poor black men for what little arrogance they dare show the world?

Willis, his voice sounding as if it was a thousand years old, said to Tilton, "I ain't an educated man, and I ain't well spoken like you. But it don't mean I'm simple. Because I sure can figure you just done something crooked here. I'm going to think hard on this, long as it takes. I'm going to figure some way to bring you down for what you done to me and Vi—and most likely other poor folks beside."

Minister Tilton smiled. Then he stood up, his chunky physique no match for the tall, lean Willis Flagg. He folded the lease into his red Bible and said, "No need for being vexatious. I know you're a troubled man this day, and I'm sorry for you. Truly I am. But you'd best not be threatening your landlord, hear? There's plenty other tenants would love to be in a cottage as nice as you made this one."

Minister Tilton put on his hat. He waited for Willis to say something by way of an apology, but Willis maintained a silence that was now as threatening as his clenched fists. Tilton looked to Violet, finding no comfort in her cold glare.

"You'd best not take an adversary's tone against a man who knows the mysteries," he said, turning back to Willis. "You understand what I mean, don't you, Brother?"

Willis understood. Since boyhood he had been warned of the abilities and powers of a master *voudou:* how he could call forth the dead from beyond, and serpents from the rivers and the sea; how he could "fix" an enemy, how his power came from the hearts and fangs and claws of God's most ferocious creatures.

And Willis felt something cold on his neck, something like a wet breeze.

Minister Tilton smiled again at the discomfort he saw in Willis. Then he left the Flagg home. Violet watched him as he stepped over to where Miss Hassie sat, and said something to her. Hassie and Tilton looked up once or twice and noticed how the neighbors were watching from their windows. So they went inside Hassie's place, where Tilton stayed for a half hour. Then he came back outside and drove off in his Packard.

Later in the night, silent save for the skitterings of spiders and chameleons on the window screens, Willis awoke from a nightmare. He had a violent fever, and pains that shot through his chest and neck.

That was the start of it.

Convinced that mortal danger lay waiting for him in the alleyway—in the form of water moccasins or copperheads or cottonmouths, slithery agents of the demons—Willis began a new daily protective ritual. He would mix up a batch of quicklime and cayenne pepper into the boiling water left over from scrubbing the front steps. He then poured this potion in two parallel lines along the inside of the fence enclosing his garden. One of the *voudouiennes* assured him he would now be safe, backyard as well as front.

He started drinking several evenings a week at Shug's, and told anybody who would listen to him that Zeb Tilton had slicked him somehow, that something ought to be done about it. But the only thing that ever came of all Willis's boozy complaints was the occasional whispered advice from the bartender that what he was saying constituted "dangerous talk."

One early August morning in the year 1950, Willis sat on a step out back after his boiled quicklime and cayenne rituals, smoking a pipe of tobacco. Violet was getting ready to go over to a mansion on St. Charles Boulevard where she had a job cooking and cleaning for old Doc Giradoux.

Willis's left leg dangled off the side of the pine steps and his bare foot swung back and forth, toes brushing through the dewy grass. Suddenly his body was convulsed by a spasm so overwhelming it threw him to the ground, where he twisted around for a few seconds in mute pain. Violet found him there when she returned home in the afternoon. He was sprawled on his back in the grass, his face covered with bits of blossoms, the white and purple petals fallen from the chinaberry tree.

Violet ran to the confectionery shop up on Tchoupitoulas Street where there was a public telephone and rang up the mansion on St. Charles. Doc Giradoux, the only white physician known to make house calls on Negro patients, came speeding over to the lane in his Buick. The doctor examined Willis right where he lay, and after a minute or two pointed to a blue-black welt on his left ankle.

"He's full of venom, that's clear," Doc Giradoux told Violet. "Good thing I got here when I did. Another hour or so, and your Willis'd be a goner."

That day was the beginning of the end.

The lane was never paved, lighted, curbed, or connected to the city sewer line. Nor was it ever so much as named. Nor was there any explanation from the parish assessor's office.

During this period, the Most Reverend Zebediah Tilton somehow had the wherewithal to buy up more ragged neighborhoods of New Orleans, building his rent rolls and multiplying his church membership. Then after a series of storefront efforts, he finally built his very own house of worship—the Land of Dreams Tabernacle.

Willis's health declined in direct proportion to Zeb Tilton's rising fortune.

Each year he grew a little weaker, until eventually he was unable to do a day's work the same as other men, until everything fell on Violet's shoulders. Violet cleaned more and more white people's houses up on St. Charles Boulevard. Willis stayed home and cared for the cottage and the garden—and little Perry.

Sometimes Willis fell down doing simple tasks such as scrubbing the steps and hacking out kudzu from the grass. He kept this a secret from Violet as long as he could.

Violet eventually found it impossible to be off at work all day worrying about her husband falling down. The cottage needed a strong man's care. Violet applied for a row unit in one of the new city housing projects going up across town, figuring this would be easier for Willis. Which it was, but only physically so. Moving day broke their hearts.

FOUR

"Serious now. How you expect folks want to put out the long money with all that dangerous trash lying close by their doorsteps? Good folks, the right kind of folks."

"I admit we got a little problem on that account."

"Well, we best take care fast as possible. Bad enough to be having our own dollars blowing in the wind. We got to protect our investors."

"Like I say in the first place, it's going to take us a subtle mind to solve the problem."

"Subtle as dynamite soup."

"There you go again, talking all disturbed like. Look at you, scratching your head like some old mama fuss about her wayward boy. What you fretting about?"

"Scheme you come to me about the other day is what."

"You ought to get a load of your puss. I swear to God, anybody see you right now they'd say you're about as embarrassed as a priest with his pants down."

"I'd say embarrassment's the least of our worries."

"Sit back. Relax. Pull your damn self together."

"I need a drink."

"Lately you've been awful needy."

"Never you mind about that. Just give me a reasonable answer to the question I put."

" 'Bout our little problem?"

"Little problem that's needing a big answer."

"Else a solution old as wickedness."

"Any wonder I'm drinking? Give me that bottle there by you if I got to consider all this grotesquery again."

"Here now, go ahead, suck down your whisky. Drunk or sober, you hear me loud and clear."

"God help me if I do."

"You know what we talked about before—why, it's your scheme as much as mine. And you know what I'm saying's purely clean and simple."

"I highly doubt you on speaking terms with purity."

"Considering what an evil bastard you are, I'll forget you said that."

"Of course you will."

"I'm willing to forget your insult. And now I will tell you the most important thing you already know."

"What'd that be?"

"To make folks behave according to your liking, you must understand human nature."

"A less philosophical man'd probably just come straight out and declare what's on his depraved mind."

"Killing's not necessarily depraved."

"Well, murdering to keep folks in line—what the devil you call that?"

"Here now, there's murder and then there's killing. Only thing they got in common's death. Your civic leadership types—preachers, politicians, po-licemen—they can tell you the difference."

"Them and the philosophical type."

"Listen to me close, because killers got to be close if they keep themselves alive."

"I'm listening."

"Folks are naturally docile and obedient. *All* folks I'm talking about, including the high-classed ones who been to schools where they trick you into believing you know what time it is."

"Ignorance is most democratic."

"My exact point. You and me, being philosophers and longtime students of human nature, all we got to do here about this problem we're facing is twist up what folks been variously trained to believe. Twist fast and loose so nobody sees our own hands on the wringer."

"I need another drink."

"Twist good enough, and before you know it, things go to chaos. That's when we got folks halfway scared to holy hell."

"Scared folks they'll listen to any fool thing."

"Especially when it's reassuring. For instance, law and order."

"Just goes to show. Folks take their foolishness real serious."

FIVE

The master bedroom upstairs where Perry stayed was "nothing but a damn slum the way he keeps it," according to his Aunt Violet. That was one of a long list of complaints she had against Perry. He was also too smart for his own good, he had no interest in looking for a job, and he would steal everything but a red-hot stove.

Chief among her grievances was that Perry Duclat was past forty years of age and still utterly lacking the inclination to live on his own.

But Perry was family. So Violet loved him in her abiding way, which she worried was doing him very little good. And now with Ruby on her way home—her prodigal daughter, married to a white policeman, no less—Violet had a whole new set of worries about her nephew.

"God bless you in heaven, Rose . . ."

Violet would say these words often, right out loud, in hopes the Lord would oblige and look after her dead sister somewhere up in Kingdom Come. She prayed now, standing at the foot of the stairs.

"But that boy of yours up there . . . Oh, Rose, now you got to help me with him—some*how.*"

Though she had ceded the master bedroom to Perry, the rest of the narrow row house belonged to Violet. What did she need with that big old room upstairs anyhow? That room where Willis had spent all those years dying? The little bedroom next door, where Ruby and Janice slept as girls—that would do just fine for Violet these days. It held all she needed: a closet full of stored-up things anybody else probably would have junked long ago; a cherry-wood chifforobe, her mother's handed-down treasure that was plenty roomy enough for her few clothes; the matching cherrywood bureau and bed, the bed she and Willis shared.

But mostly, Violet did not sleep in that marriage bed. It held memories of Willis too strong to bear on an every-night basis. And so Violet and Perry had fallen into a sort of upstairs-downstairs routine.

Every night after dinner—which Perry usually cooked, she had to give him that—they would go their separate ways. Violet would settle into the couch in the parlor with a cup of tea, a paperback book, and her store-bought spectacles. She would take off her shoes, find something tolerable on the radio, and read. Eventually she would doze off right where she was, usually still dressed in her blue polyester maid's uniform. Perry would be upstairs, meanwhile, smoking and drinking and watching TV until the purple dawn.

A few weeks ago on one of these routine evenings, Hassie Pinkney had come visiting, without the advance warning of a phone call. There stood Miss Hassie at Violet's door, wearing lace gloves and a flowered dress with a hat to match and holding a leatherette Holy Bible. Miss Hassie and her big nose, Violet thought—broad and bumpy black as an overripe avocado rind, and always stuck someplace where it had no business being stuck.

"You miss three Sunday preachings in a row, Vi," said Hassie, staring at Violet's wilted uniform, then down at Violet's bare feet. Violet thought, For somebody with an avocado nose the magpie got an awful superior look. Violet kept her own face carefully blank. "Minister Tilton he tell me to come by see that you still alive."

"Tell Zeb I'm breathing fine, thanks kindly."

"You mind if I come in sit for a while, Vi?" Hassie looked past Violet into the parlor, suspicion and disapproval flooding her face. She cocked her head toward the droning sound of Perry's TV, drifting down the stairway.

"I'm busy reading."

Hassie sniffed. She lifted her Bible and pressed it righteously against her bosom, and said, "This here's the only book I ever be needing to read."

"That figures."

Hassie scowled and changed the subject. "What's that nephew of yours doing upstairs with his no-account self?"

"Boozing, smoking, frying his brains on TV."

"Ain't all he do. The nigger be up to something."

"What you dreaming?"

"Ain't dreaming. Perry be all the time coming round the levee by me. Like he some sorry lost dog. He sit down back of that old cottage you and Willis had, and he write and write in some book. And he peep at me, too."

"Sounds like you're the one peeping."

"I ain't here to argue, and maybe you don't want to hear about none of this." Hassie waggled her head, her way of sneering. "Vi, how come you take in such a nasty man?"

"I read in the Scriptures once how we all supposed to do good unto others, how we supposed to love the least of God's children as good as the best."

"Well, I don't know." Hassie squeezed her Bible and ignored Violet's Christian sentiments. "I guess you going to be all right around here."

"I get a little bone tired of some folks is all."

"Your spirits got the need of lifting."

"Maybe so."

"We be seeing you down to church anytime soon?"

"By-and-by."

Then by-and-by Hassie was gone. Violet watched her

march down Gibson Street with her gloves and floral Sunday clothes. And her Bible clutched tightly to her chest, as a shield against the taunts of sidewalk heathens. *Yo, mama—I got something right here in my pants do you better than God do you . . . Where you get that fine dress? . . . Tell me all about how Jesus love my black ass, church lady.*

The impotence of idling men on street corners making crude passes at women also made Violet Flagg bone tired. She closed the door and locked it, then sank back down into the parlor couch. Billie Holiday was singing "Don't Explain" on the radio. Violet skimmed through the final chapters of a paperback novel with a cover that featured a chesty, golden-haired maiden in the middle of a jungle wearing lipstick and an off-the-shoulder blouse and being tenderly ravished by a golden-haired muscleman wearing a leopard print loincloth. Violet dropped the book to the floor and shut her eyes.

Like most nights before drifting off, she saw Willis in her sleepy mind, and remembered the early days and being young with him.

She remembered especially the cottage in the lane, and a long-ago day when she and Willis fought about Zeb Tilton and Hassie Pinkney and the mysteries. And then later, when they sweetly resolved their differences.

"Shoo, you scared as a tied-up billy goat. Tell your little Vi how come you be so scared, big man." Violet's voice grew breathy. She moved in close to her husband, pressing herself against his wide chest, straddling her own soft legs over one of his hard thighs. She whispered, "You a fine and handsome rock of a man, Willis Flagg. You my lion, hear? I'm with you, and I'm not fearing nothing or nobody. So why you scared of Zeb on me? Don't you know it's a sin to be scared of anybody but God?"

Locked together in embrace, Violet and Willis sidled over to a couch where Willis was reassured about his power and his manliness. And in the tender afterwards, with their differences beside the point, Violet and Willis reminded each other of their love and their pride in how far they had come as a yard man and a cleaning woman.

She remembered, too, how her lion thrilled her so when he took heed of words she had put in his heart—*Don't you know it's a sin to be scared of anybody but God?* When he dared to face down Zeb Tilton the day their pride was stolen.

I'm going to figure some way to bring you down.

As Willis Flagg said those angry words back in 1948, a pretty young black woman lay on her back in a grimy bed, across the river in Toby Jones's coal yard shack, behind the Algiers Iron Works & Dry Dock Company.

She was great with pain and misery and shame. Toby stood by her side, weeping and mumbling a prayer. Next to him was a scowling midwife pulling a pair of rubber gloves over her hands.

The young woman was Rose Duclat, who had drifted back home from New York City, unbeknownst to her sister or the bald bill collector. She felt she could not call on Violet for help. And so Toby Jones had taken her in. God help him, Toby wanted Rose to become his wife.

As a result, the midwife now pulled a squawling infant boy into the world from between Rose's splayed legs.

In a matter of days, Rose would disappear. Again she would head north, leaving behind her baby, and more debts.

"Perry!"

No answer.

Violet called up the stairway again. "Perry—now you talk to me! I know you're up there. I hear that damn TV set."

Still, there was no answer. And so Violet climbed up to the second floor, steeling herself for the sight of Perry's room. She pushed open the door.

Indeed, the little black-and-white portable television set with the wire coat hanger antennae was running. But no Perry. Violet shook her head. *Good thing I check on him after he's done cooking dinner, he'd burn down this place forgetting to turn off the stove before he goes off wherever he goes.* She walked into the room and clicked off a TV soap opera.

Perry's room reeked of cigarettes. Violet wiped her nose in disgust. *Tobacco companies pushing cancer on black folks, they might's well be wearing sheets and burning crosses.* The bed was a mess of pillows and blankets, books and Dixie beer cans. The cans were bent. Perry liked to crush them after drinking. Lots of other books were piled in wobbly stacks against the walls. There were drawing pads and some spiral-bound tablets on top of the dresser. And overloaded ashtrays everywhere—on the bed, the dresser, the windowsills, the floor, the nightstand.

Violet sighed. *How's Perry live up here like this? A man so helpful about keeping things neat and clean in return for his room.*

So long as Perry was around, Violet never had to touch a broom. Of course, she had to do the shopping and bill paying. But with Perry handling dinner, she had to cook only breakfast—and lunch if she was home. This was as easy for two as it was for one. Easier, really.

Every morning, Violet and Perry would sit down at the kitchen table together with coffee and buttered rolls and eggs and grits and the *Times-Picayune.* After which Violet would go off to work or shopping or visiting with her friends. Perry would straighten up the kitchen and do the dishes, and anything else that needed doing: dusting, sweeping, mopping, window washing, laundry—whatever. He would then take a long nap afterward, since he had been up all night watching television.

Most often when Violet returned home in the afternoon, Perry would be gone out someplace with his TV set left running—like today, the day Ruby was coming home.

SIX

He would sit for hours staring at the mud brown Mississippi. He used to talk to the old-timers, but Hassie Pinkney had whispered it around that Perry was an escaped convict. And then everybody avoided Perry, leaving him to stare at the river alone. Nobody in the neighborhood needed additional troubles.

It was true that he had been a convict. But not an *escaped* convict. In forty-seven years of life, Perry Duclat had yet to escape any of the calamities and sorrows that had come his way.

On days not spent by the levee, Perry stopped by the little cottage in the no-name dirt lane where his Aunt Violet and his late Uncle Willis used to live. When he was a boy, his mother had left Perry in the cottage for days and weeks at a time. An old man with a wooden leg by the name of Newcombe was the tenant now. Perry would do a few chores for Newcombe in return for a little money and, more importantly to Perry, permission to sit out on the back steps of the house.

Perry might spend a whole afternoon reading a book on the back steps, or writing. Always when he sat on those steps, he was reminded of the stories Uncle Willis and Aunt Violet had told the family about their losing title to the cottage to Minister Zebediah Tilton; he remembered happiness here as a little boy, tagging after his faltering uncle. Hassie Pinkney, who considered writing and book reading highly suspicious, would spy on him from her neighboring kitchen window. Perry sensed it. He would look up quickly every so often, and laugh when Miss Hassie ducked out of sight.

This particular afternoon, Perry was at the levee, waiting for somebody who said he would be there at two o'clock. Only now it was ten past three. Not far away, at Edward H. Phillips Elementary School, the kids were letting out for the day. Their rambunctious voices were drawing nearer.

Perry was smoking cigarettes and staring at the river as usual, figuring the meeting with Cletus Tyler was off. He sat in his customary place—a jetty of concrete as pocked and smoky yellow as the stone walls of the Louisiana State Penitentiary up at Angola, where he and Cletus had been cell mates. *Nobody but us brothers caged up there in a prison town named for an African country. Coincidence?*

And was it coincidence that brought Cletus into Shug's that one day about a month ago?

Under the rules of parole, Perry was not supposed to knowingly fraternize with ex-convicts—definitely not with ex–cell mates. The same went for Cletus, of course. But the two ignored the rules that day. Up at Angola, they had also regularly ignored the rule about conversation in the cells after lights-out time. Inmates had one hour for chatting in the dark. But Perry and Cletus would go on whispering far longer than that. Usually, it would be Perry telling Cletus about the latest book he had read. Cletus was nearly illiterate, and so he was interested in hearing about most anything Perry had to say.

Like many convicts, Perry was obsessed with the subject of luck. One night after their bunk talk had died down to whispers, Perry said to Cletus, "I bet nobody on the outside has a clue how close they are to lying right here in the dark with us."

"Don't know as I follow that."

"A basketball player jumps higher than an insurance man." Perry pronounced it *in*surance. "Am I right?"

"You right."

"And one basketball player can jump higher than another one."

"That's true."

"But there's a certain height no man's ever going to jump. When you think about it, that height's pretty low, really."

Cletus thought about it. Perry could hear him scratching his head in the dark. "Yeah, I guess," Cletus said, with a hitch of confusion in his voice. "You saying all luck is bad luck?"

"Luck is probably an incomprehensible thing, that's what I'm saying. I know for certain luck is an inconsequential thing. What I mean is . . . well, you know, Clete, I don't have to tell you how bad and good have a way of changing places on occasion."

Cletus was quiet, then said, "Yeah, I do know that." He meant he understood about the shifty nature of bad versus good. He had been momentarily dazed by *incomprehensible* and *inconsequential*, these being book words.

"People say you make your own luck," Perry went on. "Like it's something always there for you—same as water under the ground if you dig through the dirt long enough. Water's always water. Lady Luck, though, she's nothing but a rumor."

On the day they met at Shug's, Perry was a lucky man by the dim lights of some people. He was flush with a twenty-dollar bill, recently stolen from his Aunt Violet's purse. Thievery offered Perry no real satisfaction. It always made him sick when he had to steal something, and more often than not stealing drove him to drink. Which was why he was at Shug's the day Clete happened by. Perry sported for beer, the least he could do for a cellie recently freed.

Although likewise a thief, Perry was not nearly so outgoing about it as Cletus. Perry had never taken anything directly from a person, for instance, as he wished no dangerous confrontation; he was a burglar, not a robber. He carried a knife, but had neither intent nor occasion to use it as a weapon. Perry had never touched a gun in his life, whereas Clete had just been sprung after eight years of an armed robbery stretch.

The cellies were as different in physical appearance as they were in criminal temperament.

Cletus Tyler was short and thickset at the neck and waist. His skin was dark like an African's. His nose and forehead were broad and his eyes were too small for his face, like a pig's eyes. Cletus's profile was bashed-in flat, as if someone had hit him in the face with a shovel.

Perry Duclat, on the other hand, was tall and slender. He had his mother's bright complexion and straight features, and his mother's hair—black and wavy, with red tones. He generally wore a peaceful expression, like his mother's. Perry had not taken after his father, Toby Jones, a coal yard worker over in Algiers who had long ago disowned him. Cletus, who had not the slightest idea who his father was, looked more like a son of Toby's than Perry ever would.

"How long you think they going to let us stay on the outside?" Cletus asked Perry.

"What makes you think I'm going back to the trap for a third time?" Perry answered, annoyed by the question.

"Seems the natural way of things these days for a black man." Cletus shrugged. "No decent jobs. Even the army turnin' down niggers 'less they Colin Powell–type niggers."

"So you expect to go back, Clete?"

"Can't say no, can't say yes."

"That's just pitiful."

"What?"

"You got no expectations, Clete."

"Who you think *you* is?"

A good question, Perry thought. Like Cletus, Perry had no money and no employment prospects for the short or long term. Like Cletus, he was pushing fifty and had a prison record. Like Cletus, he was living with and stealing from family, and knew that something had to give. And then where would he go?

Cletus drained his glass of beer, and slyly laughed at Perry, the same way Perry laughed at Miss Hassie in her kitchen window. Then the humor went out of Cletus's pig eyes, replaced by the kind of edge that distinguishes a robber from a burglar.

"You the same as me," Cletus said coldly. "Ain't neither one of us pre-homeless niggers got one lick of a promise, 'less you want to call Angola the promised land."

"Hell no."

Cletus laughed again. It was a sullen laugh now, a more hopeless sound than anything Perry had ever heard, including late at night up at Angola when the cell blocks moaned. But then came something even darker.

"They got them a plan for us," Cletus said. He moved close. Perry heard a shudder in Cletus's voice. "Oh my gawd in heaven, they sure got them a *plan*."

Perry bought another round of drinks and with it a change of subject. Cletus seemed as anxious for the change as Perry. And so they spoke the rest of that afternoon of absent friends and beautiful women and missed opportunities and lost youth.

That was a month ago.

Between then and now, the cellies had seen each other maybe half a dozen times, in the street or at Shug's. On only two of these occasions had they spoken, though. The first time was at Shug's.

"I don't want to chance it," Perry said.

"Your overseer snap the whip, did he?"

"My parole officer, he just happened to mention the law—"

"Don't be telling me about no damn law. Law's as useful to a black man as teats on a boar hog."

Perry could not disagree. He had no more respect for law than Cletus, but he did have considerably more fear. At the least, Perry did not want the crowd at Shug's talking as if he and Cletus were partners. That was the very kind of talk that would float around Jackson Avenue just waiting for a breeze to blow it on over to the Poydras Street offices of the Louisiana State parole board.

And so he walked out of Shug's that time, leaving Cletus at the bar laughing a robber's laugh. Perry stayed clean away from Shug's after that, but it was no use. He ran into Cletus Tyler anyway. Of all places, they met in the dirt lane off lower Tchoupitoulas Street.

That was yesterday, the second time they spoke—and the same day Aunt Vi told him that his cousin Ruby from New York City was coming home. Ruby and her white cop husband.

Perry was painting the front window battens of old man Newcombe's cottage yesterday when Cletus happened by, carrying a blue-and-white striped suitcase. "What are you doing around here, Clete?" Perry asked him.

"This your place, brother?" Cletus set down the suitcase in the dirt. He wiped sweat from his flat forehead with a handkerchief. "Maybe you got a spare room, hey?"

"I only help out the old crippled man stays here." Perry wished he had not passed this information about the vulnerable Newcombe to Cletus. "Family throw you out, Clete?"

"Shoo, I ain't got no family. It's no money that throw me out."

"Where you headed with that bag?"

Cletus nodded his head in the direction of the levee. "Figured I'd stay down there awhile. I know a little place where maybe nobody bother me for a while."

"How long's a while?"

"'Til the man come say I got to be homeless someplace else."

"Take care."

"'Course I will." Cletus picked up the suitcase, took a step, then set down the bag again. "Say, Perry—it ain't likely the overseer'd hear about us getting together by the levee of an afternoon."

"I guess not." And so Perry agreed to see Cletus the very next day at two o'clock.

"Don't fail me," Cletus said. "There's something I just got to tell somebody. Got to be somebody I can trust. Somebody like you, smart from books and all."

"I'll be there."

And so here he was, smoking, staring at the river. No way could Cletus have missed him.

Seagulls honked. Noisy schoolboys from Phillips walked along the lower path by the levee, just down from where Perry was sitting. A tugboat chuffed by. Perry watched the surface of the water bunch up in its wake, and the first of the waves creeping across the river his way.

A boy screamed.

Perry would have sworn it was a little girl screaming, so high was the pitch. But he was sure it was boys he had seen on the footpath. *Guess they haven't got the change of voice yet.*

Another boy screamed. Then another.

Perry jumped up from the jetty so fast a cigarette fell from his mouth to his lap, burning him.

He looked over the top of the levee and saw a boy down on the footpath with schoolbooks spilled on the ground next to him. The boy was looking up at Perry, the first available adult, and shouting, "Mister—you got to help us!"

"What is it?" Perry asked the boy.

"There's a man, he's—!"

Another boy interrupted with a shrill, "Get the police!"

Perry lowered himself down the jagged levee wall to the footpath, skinning his wrists in the process. Three boys waited for him.

"What is it?" Perry asked.

All three boys, frightened and crying, pointed to a gap in the side of the levee where a black man lay in a bloody heap, facedown and dead. Next to the body was a blue-and-white suitcase.

SEVEN

Bless me, Father, for I am a shitheel. I make this confession:

That priest I mentioned how I wanted to deck—John Sheehan, the department chaplain—was good enough to officially marry Ruby and me last April when we got back from the other side. After which I proceeded to honor my bride by making a weeping, drunken Irish slob of myself for the next several months in a number of New York saloons that cater to weepy Irish drunken slobs whose middle-aged hearts have been variously broken by dear old accursed Eire. As I also mentioned, this was the sloppiness that landed me in the Straight and Narrow for those six horrible weeks when some other priests laid into me about how the boozing is a sign I have been ungrateful to pretty much everybody in my life, including myself.

Yet here now I sit comfortably: a shitheel in a cozy Amtrak roomette compartment, on a fine leather seat by the window, watching the Alabama countryside speed by.

Dusty brown rivers, lined with groves of cedar and ash, webbed in Spanish moss; back alleys of grim small towns, crowded with milky-faced kids and skinny dogs with drooling ribbon lips; the old gray treeless hills outside of Anniston, weary from strip mining, topped with gigantic wood crosses erected by some nameless zealot in the cause of Christ the Lord; ancient billboards with paint peeling off the tin—hawking catfish dinners, chewing tobacco, peanut brittle, the depravity of communism and the glory of life insurance. My personal favorite sign features a square-jawed Aryan in a denim shirt adorned with a flag pin, muscular arms folded across his chest, and the caption: BE A MAN, JOIN THE KLAN.

Ruby's curly head is rested on my undeserving shoulder. She gently sleeps this way, beauty nestled against beast.

New Orleans, where I have never in my life set foot, looms in my imagination as I listen to the rhythmic clacking of the rails.

Boozy-smelling music halls on Basin Street, above-ground graveyards full of mossy crypts with French names cut in stone, old black men playing jazz at funerals, people out on their lace iron balconies throwing beads down on Mardi Gras revelers. And saxophones, and a streetcar named *Desire.* I have never heard of a subway named Desire.

New York City and all that I know for certain grows so very far, far away.

And I am thinking, ungratefully, that I do not miss home. Everything that has happened in New York since I met Ruby has distracted or sorely tested our slow-dance together: my own obsession with the cases I work, these having mostly to do with meek souls driven to maniacal deeds; Ruby's cash troubles with her struggling little way-the-hell-off-Broadway theater; the pain of an Irish heart; and not the least, my difficulties with Mr. Johnnie Walker.

I count on one hand the number of sober evenings I have spent with my bride. And for the thousandth time I consider the improbability of the two of us as an item, let alone a married couple. So I hopefully tell myself, It's good for us to be going far and far away. Far from New York City with its never-ending palpitations and the suffocating fraternity of cops. And the burlesque of Ruby and me.

Not that I oppose the more wholesome aspects of burlesque. The art form was a great and illuminating pleasure of mine back in sweet boyhood days when I would slip past the dozing stage door guard of the Roxy Theater on Seventh Avenue. There inside—in that dim palace of female illusion, reeking of talcum and ammonia—I thrilled to the abundant charms of Cowgirl Sally and her world-renowned twin forty-eights, Lolabelle the Snake Lady, Valerie Valentine and her famous onstage bubble bath, and the angel of my adolescent dreams—Pooh-Pooh PiDieu, all the way from Paris, France.

I especially remember the Roxy's house comic. He called himself "Scurvy" and was doubtless the world's worst comedian. When the audience of Times Square mutts and skels was in a polite mood, they would merely yawn at Scurvy. But woe upon Scurvy if the crowd grew restless for the matinee meat, which often happened. Sodden missiles would then be flung from all corners of the dark house, making Scurvy's career a matter of bobbing and weaving between the gags. It is old Scurvy with his wild red hair and his baggy pants who I am thinking of as I now consider the burlesque of Ruby and me. I, of course, play the role of Scurvy.

On our wedding day, was it not Ruby herself who saw the farcical tone that colors us? Father Sheehan pronounced us husband and wife, and I kissed my bride, and then Ruby looked around at our guests—mostly cops, including the inspector and Davy Mogaill, of course—and she cracked, "So, I see what this marriage is: a friendship recognized by the police."

Funny thoughts, these.

Ruby now awoke. She shook, as if something with scales were wrapped around her neck.

"I was dreaming about Rudolph Giuliani," she explained, by which she meant Hizzoner the mayor of New York. "In the dream, I am having lunch with the mayor, who is dressed in one of those aluminum gray sharkskin suits he wears. I'm in the middle of a bite out of my lettuce and tomato sandwich. Guess what the mayor does?"

"I don't want to guess."

"He unhooks this weave on his head and sets the hairy thing down between us."

"Some table manners." I patted the tiny field of skin at the back of my head, a reflexive gesture of sympathy for a balding brother. Never mind that Giuliani did not get my vote. "The mayor wears a piece?"

"Men should never wear those stupid rugs, especially politicians."

"You can't fool all the people all the time. But here we are rolling along to the New Orleans. Who wants to talk about a bald-headed New York pol?"

"You're right. So, Irish—what were you thinking about while I was dreaming?"

Burlesque I should tell her about?

"I don't know . . ." I felt myself going a little stupid. I could picture stupid happening: drops of black ink falling into a glass of clear water and making it go all dark. Then I even heard myself going stupid. "I guess I was thinking, I don't know—guy stuff . . ."

"What's guy stuff? Nails in an old coffee can?"

"Not exactly."

"I hope it wasn't booze you were thinking about." Ruby opened her pocketbook and fished around until she found lipstick. She daubed maroon on her light brown lips, and said brightly, "By the way, you know why guys never refill ice trays?"

"I suppose not."

"Because they don't put ice in their beer."

"You're cute."

"I know."

"In answer to your question back there, I was thinking about the troubles we've had—and will have."

"You're planning something awful?"

"I don't have to plan. Awful stuff finds me."

"Who am I talking to here—little Neil Hockaday wearing his short pants and his necktie on his way to Holy Cross School? The place where he first learned to believe that upon his choirboy shoulders rides the whole wide world? God Almighty, Hock! Those nuns really did the number on you, didn't they?"

"Well, there was Sister Bertice. She'd keep me after school and have me write a hundred times on the blackboard: I am personally responsible for the agony of Christ . . ."

"Sister Bertice. Please—I'm supposed to believe this?"

"I would steal from you, but I would never lie."

"Very clever. Just like your Uncle Liam used to say. This is the usual load of Irish codswallop you haul out when you want to hide your thoughts."

"Put it this way, sweet—I have to wonder if I'm the best guy for your plans."

"Now he tells me." Ruby waved a hand in front of her nose again.

"What smells?"

"Self-loathing. It doesn't become you, Hock. You've got troubles, more than your share. That's like all the best people."

I had to pause for a second to figure out how to express myself in order not to sound like the Holy Cross kid of my lost youth that Ruby somehow knew so accurately. She is scary that way. Finally I came up with, "You've seen people in those gyms working out on those exercise gizmos?"

"StairMasters? Rowing machines?"

"Like that, yes. Those contraptions where you're already *at* where you're supposed to be going."

"What's it to you, belly boy?" asked Ruby, looking at my thickening waist. "You're no gym rat."

"No, but I am a cop. Meaning I am supposed to battle against crime. By the way, what I happen to have is a virile paunch."

Ruby rolled her eyes. "So you're a crime buster. So what's that mean?"

"It means I'm on a treadmill. Like all those people on their StairMasters and whatnot. See what I mean? Sometimes I think hamsters all over America are laughing their asses off at me."

Ruby said nothing. She probably thought up another choice crack, then decided against letting me have it on humane grounds. She just sat there next to me, quiet and a little concerned, as if she suspected me of getting ready for a heart attack, or at least for throwing up. She looked particularly intelligent and beautiful in that still moment. I pictured us strolling through the French Quarter of New Orleans, Ruby in a lacy dress.

"This cop universe," she said, tenderly now. "It's in you deep. Like you once said yourself, about Ireland, it's in you deeper than you know."

"Deeper than I'd want you to know."

"Why? Because it's not what I'd plan for myself?"

"That's a good way of putting it."

"Since when do you think I ever planned on hooking up with you in the first place? But here we are anyway—married in the eyes of God, and duly witnessed by your cop universe. So deal with it. And listen to me very carefully: things you plan in life usually turn out to be meaningless, things you accumulate without knowing it become your real treasure."

"Quite a philosophy."

"It's the human condition. Love it or leave it."

"Do I deserve you."

"Of course not."

"Tell me what's deep inside of you, Ruby. What's in you deeper than you know?"

"Being a black woman in a white man's country." Ruby did not have to think about this for more than a second or two. "Or any color woman for that matter."

When I made no response, she asked, "Did I shock you, dearheart?"

"Not really. The Irish have a certain history of being on the outside of things."

Ruby smiled at what she doubtless took as naïveté. Sister Bertice used to give me this sort of smile when I said something goofy in her class and she happened to be in a nonviolent mood.

"Back when I was in Madison Avenue," Ruby said, warming to some lesson she wanted to impart, "I used to do a lot of lunch at the Twenty-one Club. Nice place."

"So I hear."

"Funny. I almost felt like I belonged. Right up until the year the agency threw a party for all the clients in a private room upstairs at Twenty-one. The Hunt Room, it's called. Very masculine chic. You might like it. The walls are covered with Frederic Remington paintings."

"Fox and hounds, that sort of thing?"

"Right. But Remingtons actually cover up this big mural, which is definitely masculine but hardly chic. All you have to do is look under a few of the paintings to get the idea."

"What's the idea."

"The mural is a series of tableaux of white soldiers raping Indian women."

"Small wonder they covered it up."

Again with the Sister Bertice smile. "That's the way it all is. Everything's nicely covered up these days."

"So now I know what Ruby Flagg carries in her bones."

"Love it or leave it."

"You see me going somewhere?"

"No. I see a jerk on a treadmill."

"I'm a jerk?"

"Yes. But you're my kind of jerk."

"You're kind of a jerk yourself, Ruby. The kind who imagines we're opposites who attracted."

It was now Ruby with the look of the class dunce on her pretty face. And me with the patient smile.

"What you really and truly carry in your bones is the sting of poverty," I said. "It's mixed up with race and sex to keep us confused, but it's poverty we're talking about just the same. And being taught to be hated because you're poor. Taught so well they can tell if you've ever been poor when they do your autopsy."

Ruby kissed my cheek, and whispered, "You jerk cop, I love you so." And then her hazel eyes went big and teary, the way they do when we make love. This always makes me slightly nervous. Which I cannot help, being that I am from a tribe that scoffs at most displays of physical affection and what I have grown up knowing as dreaded *emotional talk.* And so all I could manage in return was, "Me, too."

"Make us a bed quick, why don't you?" Ruby suggested. She stood up and started slowly taking off her clothes. Meanwhile, I pulled down the window shade and locked our roomette door and yanked on the couch until it spread full out. I mashed a finger in the hurried process.

When we lay down together, naked, Ruby said, "People like us who've had it hard should turn soft whenever we get the chance."

I kissed her eyelids, tasting tears. I cupped her face in my hand, and asked what I had been wanting to ask since we left Penn Station in New York. "What's the matter, babe?"

"Everything's changing, Hock . . . Everything."

"What—?"

"Never mind. Make love to me."

We then slow-danced pretty much through the rest of Alabama. And sometimes Ruby softly cried.

EIGHT

"Well—here lies one less . . ." The laughing detective in the sweat-stained brown polyester suit was about to use a rude word, especially so given the race of most people present at the murder site. He stopped to edit himself. "One less African-American in the fair city of New Orleans."

The detective's name was Mueller. He had a full moon face the color and texture of cottage cheese. He was speaking ill of the dead with an equally pale and poorly tailored partner named Eckles. Detective Mueller hitched up trousers that kept slipping down around a protruding underbelly.

"Yes, sir, Ricky Ray," Mueller said to Detective Eckles, loud enough so all the neighborhood folks milling around behind the yellow crime scene tape could hear. "This here unfortunate fellow, he ain't going to be doing no more of his old bad bidness 'round Tchoupitoulas Street."

Ricky Ray Eckles used the pointy toe of a snakeskin boot to poke at the soggy lump of the late Cletus Tyler, whose body had been dragged out from beneath the jetty and was now sprawled faceup on the walking path along the river. He said to Mueller, "Butt ugly ain't he, Paul?"

Some forensics officers, all of them white, were crouched

inside the tiny cement crevice where Tyler had spent his final night in mortal violence. They flashed lights around the dank black hole, searching the dirt and gravel for homicide clues. They did not appear to be especially interested in what they were doing.

A mobile unit TV news van was busily setting up for live coverage via satellite. A male reporter with a microphone in his hand was having a female assistant spray his corn-colored hair. Next to the van was another vehicle, this one belonging to the Orleans Parish medical examiner. A doctor with a black bag and two beefy morgue workers with a gurney waited for stage directions from the television field producer before stepping down to the corpse to give it the usual going-over.

Up above the jetty and the walkway, Officer Claude Bougart of the uniformed squad stood with the neighbors who had clustered around the levee for a look at the dead body. Like the lookers, Officer Bougart was black.

One of the lookers, an angry young man whose head was covered by a flat-topped *kufi* in the pan-African colors of red, black and green, demanded of Officer Bougart, "How come you stand here let that pig talk his trash right in our faces?"

Bougart turned his back to his white colleagues so as not to be heard. He pressed fingers to his lips and said to the young man in the *kufi,* "Keep it to yourself, my brother. You make an issue about what these cops are saying, it's not going to help me or you in the long run. I'm trying to work this my own way. Follow me?"

The young man shoved his hands in his pockets. He kept quiet, but Bougart knew it was not likely to last. He had seen a lot of hotheads in his police career. And how cops like Eckles and Mueller took pains to needle hotheads—outspoken black men being particular favorites—into giving them an excuse to haul out the leather saps.

"Stinks real bad, too," Eckles said of the late Cletus Tyler, needling hotheads with big ears. "Somethin' far and away beyond the usual. He stinks awful as a month-old boiled cabbage."

"Naw, I haven't met the cabbage ever reeked so bad's this one." Mueller put a handkerchief over his nose and mouth and knelt down on one knee next to Tyler's body.

Tyler's deflated neck had been slashed along two parallel tracks. So deep were the slash wounds that it appeared his head could fall off at the slightest manipulation, like a loose drumstick on a roast turkey. The flesh between the wound tracks had become a raised abrasion the size and shape of a night crawler. The blood that filled his mouth and nostrils was gelled, globs of it halting further flow from these orifices. Somewhat fresher, brighter blood trickled out from his earlobes and tear ducts. The coup de grâce, so it appeared, was a high-velocity bullet hole that had ripped open the left half of his chest, from heart to his shoulder blade.

A third wound reddened Tyler's abdomen, which was covered by his blood-soaked coat and shirt. Mueller asked Eckles, "What in hell you suppose's under the shirt?"

"Only one way of finding out. Tear it back, let's have a gander."

Mueller removed a pair of surgical gloves from his pocket and put them on. Then he pulled the coattails away from Tyler's drained body, along with the bloodied shirt. Wet buttons skittered across the walkway.

"Hoo-whee!" Mueller whistled. The lookers could see only the mess of blood in the area of Cletus Tyler's waist, but not the small black wound enveloped by his navel. Mueller called up to Officer Bougart, "Hey there—Booger! Come on here for a minute. Want to ask you something."

The hothead tore off his *kufi* and thwacked it against his leg in disgust. He grabbed Officer Bougart's sleeve, and hissed, "You hear what that cracker called you?"

Of course Bougart had heard it. Everybody had. Bougart pulled himself free. "Go home and chill. Unless you got a nice clean record so's you can afford to have me run you in today on incitement charges."

"Haw!" The young man raised his voice. "Nigger, you must love it."

"Say what?"

"*Booger* I say." Several in the crowd in back of him laughed at the taunt. "My oh my—you must just love it to pieces bein' a motherfuckin' black in blue."

"You also eat with that mouth of yours?"

"Least I don't eat the shit straight out of white assholes like you do, Booger *boy.*" Now a chorus of bitter laughter from the crowd. The young man turned and grinned, acknowledging his audience.

Officer Bougart moved up close to his antagonist, close enough to coldcock him, with complete assurance that no white cop would pay heed to a black comrade brutalizing an agitated black civilian. The younger man fell flat onto his buttocks, lost his breath, and was now sputtering. Laughter at Bougart's expense quickly died down to nothing as the crowd realized the same, and took a collective backward step.

Bougart stooped over the downed man and ripped the *kufi* from his hand. He eyed the label inside, laughed at the words he fully expected to find: MADE IN TAIWAN. He jammed the crumpled *kufi* up against the young man's lips. "Okay, let's see how you eat, garbage mouth. Take a big old bite of your phony hat."

Spitting helplessly, the young man turned his head away. He struggled to his feet. Bougart let him, but snarled, "Best you leave right now—*boy!* Else I'll bop you so hard your kinfolks in Africa going to feel it." Bougart threw the *kufi* after the young man as he slinked off.

The matter ended, Officer Bougart stepped down to the walkway where Mueller was kneeling over the remains of Cletus Tyler. "Looky here, Booger," Mueller said, pointing a latexed finger at Tyler's navel. "He's got some kind of tattoo. See there, where it's all welted up into letters?"

It was not a tattoo. "The man's been branded, like he was

livestock," Bougart said, sniffing the heavy, sour odor rising off Tyler's body.

Mueller asked, "Ever seen a tattoo like this here?"

Bougart looked closely at four letters Mueller pointed out with his latexed finger. Seared into Cletus Tyler's stomach, more than likely with a white-hot iron poker, were the letters MOMS.

Moms. Officer Bougart knew at least one meaning for these letters. But he decided against sharing raw information with the likes of Mueller and Eckles.

"No, Detective."

"Well, I was hoping you might help me on that one. Thought it might be one of them insider colored things."

" 'Fraid not."

The television producer cued the medical examiner. Klieg lights followed the man in the white coat and the gurney bearers off the levee to the walkway. The lacquered blond reporter, deeply blue-eyed with a suitcoat to match, stood in the foreground mouthing in urgent baritone to a hand-held mic, "Literally on the banks of that Old Man River, we have exclusive pictures of a little wheel in local crime who will no longer keep rolling along . . ."

Down the walkway from Officer Bougart and Detectives Mueller and Eckles, meanwhile, a second team of white detectives had finished questioning the schoolboys who had discovered the body. Detective Hartman, wearing a clip-on tie and a short-sleeve shirt with sweat rings under the arms, climbed back up onto the levee and started randomly quizzing the lookers. His partner, Detective Jimmy Fontana, strolled up to Detective Mueller and talked to him from notes he had made in his leather-bound case pad.

"Them little black kids back there," Fontana said, his thumb indicating the three schoolboys. "They was walking along on home and come across the dead man. They say they smelled something funny, else they never probably would've noticed anybody in the hole."

"The boys drag out the body?" Mueller asked.

"No. They tell me there's a black male loitering around here. Supposed to be good-looking. Older guy, they say to me—meaning my age, which is only forty-seven for Christ's sake." Fontana shook his head. "Anyhow, this so-called older guy, he come down off where he was sitting on the jetty, right up overhead the dead man, just smoking a cigarette like he's got all the time in the world. The boys say he's the one hauled out the dead guy."

"Where is this interferin' Negro?"

"The boys, they say he run off."

"Get a description?"

Fontana consulted his notes, then started to speak. He stopped when Hartman walked up behind him and tapped his shoulder.

Hartman was accompanied by a large black woman in a green-and-blue polka-dot dress and a wide-brimmed straw garden hat. She was somewhere in her sixties with a boxy figure, a stern expression, and skin as wine dark as the river on a summer's night.

"I think we maybe got us a witness," Hartman said, grinning at the other detectives. He ignored Officer Bougart. Hartman used a handkerchief to wipe perspiration off the back of his neck.

Then he said to the detectives, "Gentlemen, this here's Miss Hassie Pinkney. She lives right up over the levee in the lane off Tchoupitoulas." Hartman said to Miss Hassie, "Now, tell these men just what you told me, mama."

"I ain't your mama."

"Sorry, Miz Pinkney." There was a smirk in Hartman's apology, the kind that would take another generation of Hartmans before possibly disappearing.

" 'Pology accepted. Now, I seen that devil Perry Duclat run out of here like he was bein' chased by all the angels of Christendom." Hassie Pinkney waved her long fingers as she said this, then stepped around the blocky Detective Mueller for a gawk at Tyler's corpse. She took her time gawking, then said, "La yes, I see it right from my window.

Perry come barrelin' up from the levee, pass my house, and disappear down around to Tchoupitoulas Street. Next thing, everybody's down here nosing 'round."

Mueller asked, "You know where we might find this Perry Duclat, Miz Pinkney?"

"Well, he stay by Miss Violet's."

"That'd be exactly who and where?"

Miss Hassie happily provided Violet Flagg's address in the St. Bernard housing project. Detective Hartman noted it down for Mueller.

"What's this Duclat boy look like, ma'am?" Mueller further asked.

"Ain't a boy. He's a man."

"Sorry, ma'am."

"Shame y'all have to be 'pologizing so much."

"Suppose you just tell me what Perry Duclat looks like."

"Well, he's one handsome fella with no right to bein' handsome. Tall, somewheres between forty-five and fifty. Got a straight nose and a thin face and nice wide shoulders. Built gorgeous, like Billy Dee. He got the good hair, too."

Mueller turned to Fontana. "Sound like what you got off those kids?"

"On the button."

"All right, I think we know what we got to do now to close up," Mueller said to the other detectives. "Thanks for the cooperation," he said to Miss Hassie. To Officer Bougart, he said, "See you around, Booger."

The crime scene mop-up would be handled by the Orleans Parish medical examiner's crew, along with the listless detail of forensic cops. Detectives Mueller, Eckles, Fontana, and Hartman had their own routine to follow. And so they left, with purpose in their step if in no particular haste.

Claude Bougart, for whom fate had perhaps finally assigned a shapeless intent, had no such clear idea of what he would do next. Only that something needed doing. At long last, something.

NINE

"How many times I done warned you?"

"Oh, many times, Miss Hassie. Yes indeed, many times. That is certainly not at issue." Reverend Zebediah Tilton laughed, and tipped back his drink until the glass went empty of Scotch whisky. He sucked an ice cube into his mouth, savoring the trace liquor.

"I tol' you!" Hassie Pinkney said. She looked away from Tilton, disgusted by his evident pleasure in demon liquor. "He's been peeping at me with them two devil eyes of his."

"Well now, I don't expect you got to worry about that anymore now that he's flown the coop." Tilton winked at the girl in the white robe sitting to the right of his desk. Sister Constance Ritchie gave him no reaction. Her coffee-brown face remained impassive, her hands remained folded together in her lap. Tilton turned away, and asked Miss Hassie, "Just how did you say Perry was spying on you?"

"Every time I come by the window to take me a look over to Mr. Newcombe's, right there he was! He be looking up at me, laughing like a fool."

"But, what was he *doing* exactly?"

"Loitering all over the back porch is what. Writing in a

pad. All the time writing. Or drawing. Else he's reading a book. Never the Good Book!"

"Sounds like to me he was minding his own business."

"Devil business!"

"Yes . . . Well, I see how it must have been most troubling for you."

"What'd you think if you was to see a convict in your own neighbor backyard?"

"More importantly, what did Newcombe think?"

"Oh, that old cripple, he a fool. Three-quarters of the time, he just about half-delirious. I got to run over there look after him, take him to church on Sunday and all." Hassie shifted in the chair opposite Tilton's desk. She uncrossed her legs, then recrossed them. She cast a disgusted look at Sister Constance. Sister returned a look in kind, then went blank again. Hassie said to Tilton, "Mr. Newcombe be delirious on account of all the painkillers he always swallowing."

"For his leg."

"Use to be a leg anyways."

"Regardless, I don't recall receiving a complaint from Newcombe himself. As a matter of fact, it's my impression that Mr. Newcombe depended on Perry Duclat—for all the work needed doing around his place."

"See, you been tricked! I just knew it!"

"Who do you think's able to trick me?"

"Satan! Ain't no shame to confessing that."

"Miss Hassie, you're beginning to irritate me."

"I'm only trying to make you do the right thing."

"Which would be?"

"You got to deal with Miss Violet now. She know where that nephew of hers be hiding. You got to make her give up Perry Duclat to the po-lice. He the one kil't that Cletus Tyler, that other Angola no-account."

"Cletus Tyler," said Tilton, repeating the name. He wrote it down on a desk pad.

"It's what the man say."

"How are you so sure Perry's the killer?"

"Just am, that's all. And we got to do what we can toward catching him."

"Miss Hassie, now you know if a squad of white men with guns and badges are looking for a black man . . . Well, they're going to find them a black man." Tilton removed a silk handkerchief from his breast pocket and daubed his forehead with it. "I don't see where I can—"

"You can call up the fear of the mysteries, that's what you can do. Mysteries been keeping things the way they ought to be for a right long time now."

Tilton turned to the girl. He clunked his empty liquor glass on the desktop and said, "Sister, I believe I'll have another round." Constance Ritchie rose from her chair. Wordlessly, she stepped around to the credenza behind Tilton and picked up a crystal decanter. She poured him a drink and sat down again.

When he put away half the Scotch, Tilton said to Hassie, "Tell me, how's this police manhunt for Perry Duclat any of your concern?"

"I don't got to tell you nothing, Zeb. You just go have a talk with Violet Flagg." Hassie stood up and walked to the door. She turned and said, " 'Less you do, I be telling everybody about you and Miss Thing. Hear?"

Tilton laughed. The girl was expressionless.

"Maybe the mortal truth of girl flesh ain't enough to bring you down," Hassie said. "But you best know I know the Lord's truth about you . . ."

Tilton laughed straight through her threats.

"Anything happen to me, it ain't going to prevent the Lord's truth from being told. I got to remind you how I got a certain tape recording of a conversation you and me had? Tape I got locked up somewheres for posterity?"

Tilton stopped laughing.

He clunked his glass on the desk again.

Miss Thing's eyes went wide.

Tilton asked, "What are you saying I'm supposed to do, Hassie?"

"Call out the spirits, I'm saying. Call out Willis Flagg, and he put everybody straight on that murdering, trouble-making Perry Duclat."

"What kind of trouble is Perry Duclat capable of causing anybody?"

"Maybe he got ideas he fixing to spread around. Elsewise how come he spy on me—writing things down and all?"

"We surely don't want folks getting wrong ideas."

"That's what I'm telling you!"

"Wrong ideas can upset everything."

TEN

The first spooky thing a Yankee such as myself learns about the city of New Orleans is that a November afternoon can be a steamer. Not always, Ruby claimed, but sometimes.

November, and hot? I mean sidewalks hot enough to light you up like a Lucky Strike. I mean air so thick and tight it seems as if it is drawing in on itself in preparation for a siege. This was how ungodly hot it was as we came to the final destination of Amtrak's Crescent route.

Ruby was a little sleepy, but otherwise showed little wear after the long rail trip. The heat brought a sheen of dew to her face, nothing a cool breeze could not relieve if there was any such thing. I myself was not so freshly arrived. My Yankees cap was sponge heavy on my head, and every time my shoulders moved I felt sweat flow down my back and dribble into my boxers. I needed fresh clothes, something in a glass over shaved ice, and a short nap in a tall tub of cold water. All of which made me more anxious than usual to escape the train station.

Train travel these days is a stone pity, by the way. Saying that makes me sound like a codger, I know, but I am only stating the obvious. I remember as a kid seeing New York's glorious old Penn Station for the first time—the real one with columns of sunlight in slanted beams streaming across a marbled floor through delicate windows arched high above a graceful web of iron rafters. I thought I was inside a cathedral. Passengers owned intelligent faces, and they all wore hats and carried books or newspapers to read. The huge station clocks were works of art, the announcer's voice was as exciting as anything heard on the radio serials.

Then one infamous day came the striped-pants boys. Ever in grubby quest of profit, they had a cathedral of transportation torn down. In its place, they slapped together a vast stall full of mooing and oinking. There are not so many intelligent faces around the new Penn Station.

So this train station in New Orleans was every bit as inhuman as the dump that replaced my Penn Station of a fonder day. There was not a lady in the place with a decent hat on her head, although quite a number were pleased to be showing off multicolored plastic hair rollers. White Southern gents were the worst spectacles with their raggedy mustaches, golf shirts, gimmie caps, shorts, and hairless legs. The only reading matter I saw anybody carrying around was *USA Today*, which is to journalism as Robert Waller is to literature.

Outside the station, the fetid air and the exhaust of idling taxicabs did nothing to encourage a better mood. We climbed into the back of a taxi equipped with air-conditioning vents so puny they failed to put out sufficient breeze to lift the grass skirt of a plastic hula dancer dangling down over the dashboard on an old string of Mardi Gras beads. The driver, on the other hand, was full of breeze.

According to the Orleans parish hack license framed in tin and bolted to the back of the cabbie's perch for us passengers to see, his name was Hugh P. Louper. Into the edges of this frame were inserted little calling cards for the taking, one of which I did, since a mackerel pedals a bicycle about as well as I drive a car and Ruby is no help, since she does not even own a license.

"You call me Huggy if you want, sir, ma'am," the driver said to us as we settled carefully into a backseat of sticky vinyl. From "Huggy" I would receive a foretaste of the second spooky thing a Yankee such as myself learns about New Orleans.

He asked us where we wanted to go, and Ruby told him, "The St. Bernard projects—3810 Gibson Street." Hugh P. Louper seemed to know just where to head.

"Where y'all from?" Louper talked like he had a catfish sideways in his mouth. He used the rearview mirror to give us the once-over. I gave him back the same, and thereby saw that Hugh P. Louper was a wiry, pasty-skinned guy of about sixty with a pair of cords on the back of his fuzzy neck that stood out in a number-eleven formation.

"New York," I said.

"Man-o-man, that's a far piece. How come y'all didn't fly down on the aero-plane?"

"My wife prefers the scenic route."

"You two . . . you married?"

Ruby touched my arm and shot me a warning look that said something along the lines of *Don't rile him, he's probably a Kluxer.* My damp boxers bunched.

"Married, right."

"I had myself a wife once't upon a time." Huggy Louper sounded sadder but wiser, which did not strike me as the way a Kluxer would sound. "It all come to a poor end, though."

"How so, Huggy?" I had to ask. As Ruby has pointed out, I always have to ask.

"Well, sir, now there's a story." Louper fired a cigarette, and the dead air of the taxicab clouded up in a pale blue stink. "Ain't a long story. Marriage gone lousy don't never take much time to tell."

"Driver?" Ruby had a hand to her throat and was coughing. "That cigarette . . ."

"Ma'am?"

"Would you mind losing it?"

"Oh, a'course I will, pretty. Pardon me all over Dixie for making you choke." Louper held the cigarette out the window and tamped out the lit end against the yellow-and-blue taxi door, then tucked the dead butt up over an ear for later. "Disgusting habit. Honest to gawd. Trouble with old Huggy, I got a lifelong habit of being disgusting."

Louper had himself a raspy smoker's laugh at this. Ruby thanked him for his consideration and she coughed once again, lightly. I looked across the seat and noticed, again, her tiredness.

"You were saying?" I asked Louper. "About your lousy marriage?"

"Oh yeah, my missus . . . Orangadade Terrell." Louper pronounced this Oh-RANG-ga-dade.

"Unusual name."

"Yeah, it come inspired by a billboard. Orangadade's mama, she could only read and write some. The day Mother Terrell's pregnant belly burst some men happened to put up a sign in a vacant lot in the neighborhood, over to Gretna. The sign was for a kind of soda pop. Mother T's in her birthing bed spitting out her little girl, and the view out her window's that billboard. She thinks it's mighty beautiful what she sees—a big old picture of happy people prancing through a grove of orange trees."

Ruby guessed, "Drinking Orangeade soda?"

"That's right. Only Mother T, she don't pronounce it quite right."

"Your wife," I asked, "did she have any trouble with that handle?"

"Kids are cruel little bastards. They used to call her Orangatang. You know, like the hairy ape." Louper shook his head with true sympathy. I decided the man was no Kluxer.

"What did you call her, Huggy?"

"Called her Ory."

"Nice."

"She was a sure enough big blonde beauty, by the way." Huggy Louper whistled. "And didn't she know it!"

Louper had to stop the car for a red traffic light, which served as a natural pause in his story. We were passing through a neighborhood of frame bungalows in various stages of disintegration. There were starved palm trees in the front yards, and dogs lying in heaps under falling-down porches, too tired to snap at the flies swarming around their snouts. The light turned green. We rolled through the intersection. "Yes, sir, Ory was a razzle-dazzle beauty. My soul, but didn't Huggy catch himself the beautiful fever . . ."

Louper paused. I glanced out my window. Over toward a corner newsstand was a group of rail-thin young black men hanging around with nothing to do but suck beer bottles. Their female companions wore shorts and sandals, and little cotton blouses that bared their navals and provided only the scantest coverage to breasts with nipples as big and hard as carpenters' thumbs. Louper swiveled his head around. "Sure you can handle hearing about the fever, mister?"

I said I was sure. Ruby lay her head back and shut her eyes. She folded her hands across her stomach.

"Us two was sweeter'n peaches and cream there for a month or two." Louper turned back so he could watch where he was driving. "Then a'course after the burning heat passed there was lots of days I'd only say was barely toler*a*table. Then the whole thing just went all dismal like."

"Meaning what?"

"Turned out, Ory was loose as my teeth after a taffy apple. You know how that'll craze a man to ferocity." Louper looked into his rearview mirror, and offered Ruby something by way of an apology. "Ma'am, I am only speaking the Lord's truth. We're just animals, after all. Us men are savage, snorting beasts. Nothing personal, but women ain't so much better. Give you a simple telltale sign of what I'm talking about: men and women don't run around on all fours these days, right? But we sure as hell get around *with* all fours. I mean, you ever in your life seen anybody walk without swinging their arms? Animal nature, see my meanin'?"

Ruby mumbled something that I took to mean that she wanted no part of a dialogue on the animal kingdom.

Huggy Louper reached for the dashboard and clicked on the radio, recessed below the plastic hula dancer. I heard part of the local weather report, enough to know that a storm was rolling in off the Gulf of Mexico. Then a lady announcer with a magnolia-soaked voice said, "Hello, my dear sugars, wherever y'all are. You're listening to WWOZ—New Orleans Jazz and Heritage Radio, coming sweetly to you from our studios right here in Congo Square, in good old Louis Armstrong Park." Then she played a record of a guy with a gritty washboard of a voice, singing something called "Baby, I'm Itchy but I Don't Know Where to Scratch." Louper laughed again, only now it was more like a sneer. He said, "Well, ain't that just the appropriate tune for this particular discussion?"

I listened to the music as Louper took the taxi for a turn onto slow-as-molasses St. Bernard Avenue. We passed by a lot of crayfish stands—spelled *craw*fish—and little stores selling Jax beer in cans to big-bellied men, and Sno Balls and Moon Pies to barefoot kids. I assumed we were someplace near the housing project with the same name as the avenue. My boxers bunched up some more.

Like I said, the taxi's air-conditioning was useless. Maybe this was what had seized up Ruby's tongue. So I finally rolled down my window in hopes of a breeze. But this only made me feel crowded in a strange way, like I was in a casket with damp earth packed in close.

"If you want to hear," said Louper, "I don't mind telling you how things come to a bad end for Ory and me."

"Go ahead."

"I kil't her."

Silence in the taxi, until I asked, "You murdered Orangadade Terrell? Your big blonde beauty . . . ?" I was in New

Orleans for innocent purpose. I had not bargained on hearing somebody's criminal confession.

Ruby opened her eyes.

"No, huh-uh—I'm saying I *had* to kil't her." Sure enough, the lady DJ with the magnolias in her mouth then played another appropriate tune, Leon Redbone's rendition of "Your Cheatin' Heart." Louper now turned the taxi off St. Bernard Avenue to Milton Street.

Ruby sat up straight, dug her fingers into my arm, and whispered, "We're almost home." She sounded tense, which was not like her. But then Ruby was not sounding so much like Ruby lately. Maybe now it was because of what Huggy Louper was saying about killing his razzle-dazzle wife.

"My lawyer, he explains to the jury how legally speaking it wasn't no murder involved," Louper carried on. "See, one horrible day I walk into the house unexpected like—with all fours, I'm walking, according to the beast in me—and how d'you suppose I catch my wife and my ex-buddy Elmo right in front of my face?"

"Flagrante delicto?"

"Yuh . . ." Louper was a little stunned, as if I might have been his only passenger that day to say something to him in the language of ancient Rome. "Being that you know Latin, you some kind of lawyer up there in New York? I guess you ain't a priest since you're married."

"No, I'm not an attorney. I don't even understand the law the way I'm supposed to. It never made any sense to me why a rich guy and a poor guy are equally forbidden to steal bread."

"Oh, I see." Louper yawned. "Anyways—my lawyer he says to the jury that exact same Latin gibber you just said. This was after I testified in detail as to how I seen it was with Elmo and Ory that horrible day."

"Compromising?"

"I sure's hell guess so! Elmo's still wearing his khaki bus driver shirt and his rubber-soled shoes, but there's his pants flung across't my TV chair and he don't have no drawers on his pink ass. And oh my God, my Ory's just plain buck naked—'cept for these little blue panties snagged 'round one of her ankles. What's the Latin what-do-you-call for that again?"

"Flagrante delicto."

"Yuh. Or like we say 'round here, Elmo was taking the skin boat to tuna town."

"So, under the circumstances—?"

"Well, godammit, I run to the front closet, took down my squirrel rifle and commenced to blasting . . ." Huggy Louper stopped to sniffle, sounding as if he at least half-regretted doing what he did on that compromising day. Then he continued. "Ory's yellow hair flopped down back of her shoulders like she was a tin duck at one of them carnival shooting galleries. That's all she wrote. Elmo survived, but he don't walk right these days, since he's missing half his hind end."

"And you were acquitted?"

"Sure I was."

"That's some lawyer you had."

"You best believe it. He's powerful damn good. Hippocrates Beauregard Giradoux—*esquire.* Hippo they call him, on account of his size."

Ruby and I looked at each other. I seemed to be asking and she seemed to be answering: yes, the very same Hippo who foreclosed on the cottage.

"Hippo don't take on a whole lot of cases, what with parish politics he's involved in up to his elbows. But I'm a shirttail relation of his, for which I thank my lucky stars." Louper chuckled. "Boy-o-boy, I remember a case of bigamy Hippo argued years back. This was on behalf of my cousin Darryl."

"What happened then?"

"Well Darryl, see, he got two wives conspire to haul his ass into court. Charge of bigamy. But don't you know Hippo won the day?"

"How?"

"Simple. Hippo proved Darryl wasn't no bigamist."

"But there were plaintiffs—the two wives."

"That's right. But Hippo called up a surprise witness for the defense. And them two gals just about had a couple of calfs."

"Who was the witness?"

"Darryl's third wife. See—Darryl wasn't no bigamist. He had him *three* wives."

"Very shrewd."

"Shrewd's got nothing to do with it," Ruby said, the old steam returned. "It's Louisiana law, written by Louisiana politicians—a gang of men with garrulousness and the mob on their side."

"Also," I said, "let's not be forgetting the age-old corruption of inventing the forgiveness of sins with Latin phrases."

"You can pull up right there, alongside the double oak tree, the one my daddy planted," Ruby told Louper. We had just turned off Milton to Gibson, a block of dreary brick row houses—the St. Bernard Project. Ruby leaned across the backseat, kissed my cheek, and said, "I love you, Irish. Ready or not, it's time to meet your new family."

Louper brought the taxi to a stop. While Ruby and I gathered our things, he took the cigarette from his ear and put it between his lips. He did not light it, though. He stuck his head out the driver's-side window and craned his neck to look up at the big moss-draped oak limbs.

"Okay, Huggy, here's what I owe you, plus a couple dollars more." I pushed several bills up over the seat between us, fluttering them for Louper to hear. But the tree held Louper's fixed attention for several more seconds.

Finally, he tucked his head back inside the cab. He twisted around, took the money, and thanked me. "You don't mind me mentioning, sir, you got a sort of gift," he added.

"What gift?"

"The knack of pretending to be stupid before you're wise."

"Thanks, I think."

"Mind if I put a question to you?"

"I don't mind."

"What's better: living with a bad conscience, or knowing the peace of mind that comes from being hanged for what you done?"

"Nobody's wise enough to answer that. Or dumb enough."

"Yuh, I suppose that's right."

Ruby and I stepped out from the taxi with our bags. We stood on a sidewalk cracked by the oak roots sprawled beneath the concrete. Up in the little front window of Number 3810, I spotted an eager face that looked like Ruby's own, only older, and an almond-skinned hand holding back a white lace curtain.

"Did you nice folks take my calling card?" Huggy Louper asked, tapping the back of his seat. I told him I had. Then before pulling away, Louper said, "Whenever you need a lift, the dispatcher'll have me to you—Huggy-on-the-spot."

I thought Ruby might go running up to the door of her mother's house, or else maybe her mother might come flying out. One or the other. Instead, Ruby stood where she was, as if she were glued to the sidewalk. I stood beside her, sweat streaming down my back.

Ruby looked up and down the speckled sun-and-shade of Gibson Street, avoiding a glance up to the window where the eager lady held back lace. Neighborhood noise surrounded us. Ladies chattered as they walked along with paper grocery bags in their arms, bicycles whizzed up and down the street, boys chased after dogs, babies screamed because their teeth hurt, radios played on windowsills.

"I could stand here all day long, nobody would recognize me." Ruby seemed as if she had lost something important. "There was a time I used to be a part of all this sound and motion."

"It's still a part of you."

"Oh, I don't know anymore. Look at the street, then look at the two of us."

"We're different, obviously. So?"

"It's more, Hock. It's like I'm in a time bend. You and me, we're like a couple of hour hands in a crowd of second hands."

While I thought about this, my attention was drawn to four little girls just across the way. Two of them were at either end of a pair of jumping ropes, twisting them up and down. The two others were in the middle of the flailing ropes, skipping double-Dutch routines. They were all singing out some rhythmic jumping song, which we could not hear at the moment because of a car with a broken muffler rounding the corner from Milton Street. Ruby spotted the girls, too.

"I used to do that," Ruby said. I pictured Ruby with no hips yet, wearing plaid shorts and a T-shirt and tennis shoes. "I used to make up jumping songs, too."

"Let's hear one."

"Cinderella, dressed in yella, went downtown to meet her fella . . . How many kisses did she get? One, two, three, four . . ."

The car finally passed us by.

And now we heard the four girls across the way singing:

"Jill, Jill
forgot to take her pill
How many babies did she have?
One, two, three, four . . ."

"Time marches on," I said.

Ruby began to cry. She turned from me, embarrassed for some reason. She wiped at tears with the backs of her hands.

"Huggy Louper and his late wife . . . ," Ruby said, the halting start of an explanation. She turned and faced me. "That story of his upset me. I don't know why."

"Well, it was disturbing."

Ruby took my hand and we walked toward the front door of her mother's house. Along the way, she said, "The thing is, I can't remember a family gathering that didn't involve death."

In that moment, as Ruby spoke from pain somewhere in her heart, I came to my first understanding of the other thing that spooks the land of dreams. And in the days ahead, I would see its many levels: jazzy New Orleans, city of dead markers; a polished brass funeral urn set atop a flowered grave, under which a box is rotting.

ELEVEN

The screen door flew open, and there stood Ruby's mother, arms held wide from her sides. Her head was joyfully tossed back. Her hazel eyes looked much younger than they were, free of care and time's wreckage, at least briefly. But then Violet Flagg trembled some, and I recognized the brave Christmas smile Ruby had told me about.

I wondered what lay behind the tremble and the brave smile at this occasion of family reunion. This is my nature. I have been a cop for too many years to be able to ever go off the clock.

As I wondered, Violet Flagg called to the daughter she had not seen in so many years, "Come on up here and give us some sunshine, little one of mine."

Ruby's hand had been hooked in my arm. But now she slipped away. She took a tentative step past me, paused, and then galloped to the porch and her mother's embrace, as if she were a gangly twelve-year-old again. The two women stood clasped together, quietly and tearfully; all mother-daughter grievances seemed forgiven. I believe anyone passing by at that moment would have had a hard time saying who was Violet and who was Ruby. I have noticed that at a certain point, no matter their ages or relationships, women become mothers to one another.

"La, we been waiting on you all day, Ruby," Violet said, breaking from her daughter, brushing at her eyes. She gave me a quick up-and-down appraisal as I reached the porch myself. Then she looked back to Ruby, and added, "Waiting for the both of y'all, I should say."

I set down our bags and stuck out my hand. "Hello, Mrs. Flagg," I said.

Mrs. Flagg stared at my hand and screwed up her face, as if I was showing her something dead. "What's wrong with you, boy?" Her own hands were spread flat on her hips now. "Don't I look sweet enough to kiss?"

A vision of my own mother came to me: her auburn hair gone early to gray, her work-lined face, hands chapped raw from dousing glasses in scalding water every day of her barmaid's life, the beer and cigarette smell of the pub clinging to her like a shroud. My mother, who always turned her face away from a kiss, in the chaste Irish way.

Or did my mother think of herself as unalluring, unworthy of a kiss? I have been told that once, in Ireland, Mairead Fitzgerald Hockaday was a great beauty. I myself have no memory of her that way. Anyone in Hell's Kitchen who would remember her as such is now long gone.

My mother was neither angry nor wistful about her loss of fair looks. Nor did she begrudge physical beauty in others. She had a ready and extravagant compliment for handsome women, always the same one. Hearing the echo of my mother, I said her own words to Ruby's.

"Mrs. Flagg, you're lovely as spring's first blooms along the cool, blue streams of Galty."

I then took my mother-in-law's shoulders, drew her to me, and kissed a warm cheek. Her neck smelled lightly of orange. She turned the other cheek for equal treatment, then gave me a kiss of her own—on the lips.

Violet cast an approving glance at Ruby, and asked, "Girl, this one always talk so flowery?"

Ruby answered, "On the blarney meter, Detective Hockaday gives good value."

In hearing this from her daughter, there was a catch in Violet Flagg's voice. Only a cop would notice. She recovered quickly and smiled at me. "Come along into my parlor, Mr. Po-liceman," she said. "Have some lemonade. Bring along your pretty wife."

"Thank you, Mrs. Flagg."

"You best call me Mama like all of them do." Violet said this as we followed her through the door. There was no hallway or foyer to her house, just a simple, square parlor with brown-and-beige linoleum tiles and a round braided rug and a pair of windows looking out to the street. At the back end of the parlor—behind a partial wall of family photographs dominated by a yearbook portrait of Ruby that could have doubled for Angela Davis circa 1968—was a staircase. Ahead of where I stood was an archway to the kitchen. In the middle of the parlor, Violet stopped. "Oh, it's going to be so nice with the whole family here."

"Everyone's coming over?" Ruby asked. "Tonight?"

"Sure this evening. Going to be enough Negroes around here to make a Tarzan picture."

"Janice is coming, too?"

"Of course Janny be here. Your sister and all of them coming, unless . . ." Mama's voice trailed off as she crossed over to the foot of the staircase. She peered up the steps and cocked an ear, listening for something. But there were only the three of us in the house to make any noise.

This peering and listening took but a second. Then Mama cut a look to Ruby. "Janny's coming here with all best intentions. I want you to be good to each other. Hear me?"

"Yes, Mama."

I asked myself questions. Ruby and her sister, Janice, were on the outs with each other? What other little family secrets lay ahead? Could this be why Ruby's been acting so strangely?

"I don't want to even hear no hurting words," Violet added to her warning. "Least you girls can do is put aside your squabbling and teasing and just enjoy what I've been cooking up." She was through with Ruby and looked my way now. "We going to have a party so fine, with much good Creole food, it's going to be dangerous being a chicken around here. What you like being called? *Neil?* But then you got a nickname, too, so I hear."

"Hock," Ruby answered for me. "That's what all his cop friends call him. Also his so-to-speak clients. Sometimes I call him Irish."

"I believe I call you Neil." Mama motioned for us to sit down on a couch under the lacy windows, which we did. She smoothed back her linen skirt and patted her marcelled hair and sank into an easy chair next to an oak lamp table spilling over with photograph albums. She shook her head up and down decisively. "I like Neil, it's a pretty name. A real *fly* name, like the youngsters say."

As for me, I liked Mama's cottony voice and Louisiana accent. *Pretty* came out *purdy, with you* was *witch yew,* and *Lord* was *La.* Her sound was soothing and natural. I imagined her in moonlight, sitting out on the steps with a paper fan, nodding and calling out hello to neighbors as they slowly passed by.

Mama's soothing voice made me feel a very long way indeed from the snarl of Manhattan. I enjoyed the distant feeling. But that soon passed as she popped me a question as straight and hard as a New Yorker's elbow at rush hour.

"Now that you gone and married my daughter, now that you part of my family—suppose you tell me all you know about us Negroes."

"Mama, for God's sake—!"

"Hush, Ruby, else you ain't going to hear Officer Neil say what he thinks about the sweet brown berries of the world."

"He's a detective, Mama."

It was comforting of Ruby to clarify my rank, less so to see the skeptical smirk on her face as she waited for me to answer her mother's blunt question. I was struck stupid and speechless, with blood rushing to my face to make me pink as the heart of a Paddy's fried steak. Also I was being stared at by two nearly identical sets of African eyes, reduced from ebony to hazel down through the years of an American heritage involving rape somewhere along the rude line.

"Come on now, boy. You surely know some about talking." There was the snap of historical accusation in Violet Flagg's voice, leavened by affectionate mockery. And in the case of the stricken white man she had invited to call her Mama, a special note of clemency. "Let's hear some more of that Irish tongue of yours."

But I could think of nothing to say.

"What do I got to do to make you speak, boy? Shake you 'til you go bald?"

"I could talk, Mama," I finally said. "But it doesn't mean I know."

Violet smiled, as if I had passed some test she hoped I would pass. She slapped both her knees and said to Ruby, "The man talks honest as he does gorgeous. You done yourself all right, even if he is the po-lice." Then she asked me, "How'd you like me to tell you the story about black folks in America, sweet land of liberty?"

I said I would like that.

"When you was a kid, you ever catch bugs in a jar on a summer night?"

"Fireflies. In the summertime, up in the Catskills."

"White folks love doing that. Very seldom do you see black folks going after bugs. Neil, you ever give a little shake to your jar full of fireflies?"

"Sometimes."

"Negroes is like bugs trapped in a jar. White folks holding on to the jar, of course. And oh La, white folks love shaking us up! Then sometimes one of us Negroes figures some way to get free. I mean free and clean out the jar. Then the white folks is left looking at all the other Negro bugs still trapped. And you know what, Neil?"

"I can guess . . ."

"Don't mean you'd know." Violet smiled kindly on me,

her acknowledgment that we had established affinity. "The white folks holding the jars, they be giving us the cold eye. You hear me?"

"I do."

"They upset and confused about how many Negroes still trapped. And how we all angry-like. Buzzing around so bad we bashing and killing each other to get free, too. Now then, that's one of God's true lessons in American history. But you never hear about that in any schoolroom, did you?"

"No, I never did. You mentioned cold eyes, though. That's something I do understand."

"What you know about it?"

"I know what it is to have your people's grief buried deep. How sometimes you feel a crucifixion of the heart, which can't help but show. And how people around you—by which I mean *others*—don't trouble themselves to respect your grief; how they insist on believing the old gag about time healing all wounds. And how the others look at you sometimes . . ."

"Go on, boy," Mama said when I paused.

"When I was young, I could tell how the others looked at my mother and me—"

Ruby interrupted, explaining to Mama, "Neil's mother raised him alone. She was an immigrant." Mama nodded, and I continued.

"The comfortable ones would see Mother and me, and turn away. Mother told me they were afraid of the hard memories in back of us. Afraid of life in mud cabins with no windows, afraid of gassy women with their bellies full of children and their sweaty husbands with no teeth left in their despairing heads. Mother, she'd say, 'No matter it was them that reduced us to this lowest peasant state; no matter it was them consigned us to famine, forcing us into contorted thoughts—forcing us to flee our own land. No matter—' "

"Say it!" Violet clapped her hands together, in a churchly way, as if encouraging the cascading locutions of a preacher.

"And I would think, even as a boy, No matter that the Irish

came to New York and learned the city ways, and had a few of our own sitting with the men in the fine suits. No matter! They saw Mother and me in our used clothes, purchased twice a year from the Holy Cross bazaars. They saw Mother's tired and shapeless hair, a poor woman's hair. They saw from her hands and her creased face that hard work was using her up. Myself they saw as only another red-faced neighborhood Mick with the possibility of becoming a donkey for the pier bosses so long as I didn't show up drunk at the hiring hall. They looked at us both like it was our own fault . . ."

"That's all right now." Mama daubed her eyes with a flowered hanky pulled from a sleeve. "All right, Neil."

"They looked at us with the cold eyes," I said, finishing. "Cold as a ditch in the rain."

For a little while then, Violet was struck as silent as she had made me a few minutes earlier. I had moved her to tears, and there was something in my own eyes, and we were each of us contented by this. For a little while, the cultural barriers between an old black southern lady and a cop from New York with a map of Ireland for a face seemed no thicker than a dragonfly's wings.

Ruby broke the quiet. "Mama, you told me always to remember the terrible way that white woman looked at us that time."

Mama finished with her hanky, tucked it back into her sleeve. "Time was that?"

"The Christmas when you took Janny and me and Perry over to the city dump off Elysian Fields, and then we caught the bus back home . . ."

Arms full of discarded treasures, Violet Flagg and her three shivering ducklings stumped out from the piles of trash back up to Paris Avenue. They sheltered themselves from a sharp wind at the bus stop, and waited for the L. C. Simon coach that would carry them home to the St. Bernard Project.

Scattered around Violet's feet was a Christmas bounty. There were prayed-for mittens for Janny, which Violet would clean with a Woolite soak and repair with a few stitches around the raveled cuffs before wrapping them up with some paper and ribbons. For Perry, a little tin circus wagon attached to a miniature tricycle, with flecked pictures of Happy Humphrey on it, from the Joe Palooka comic strip. Violet would fill in the paint flecks with ink and crayons. The present for Willis was nearly perfect: a wooden box lined in red satin, torn only some at one edge, containing a small leaded decanter and three out of four matching shot glasses. Violet felt badly about what she managed to find for Ruby, a banged-up white boy-doll with no clothes and not much hair. But Ruby seemed happy enough.

Ten minutes went by as they waited for the bus, ten minutes that seemed like sixty. "I hate the cold, Mama, I just hate it so!" Ruby said. Janice agreed. "Me too. When I grow up I'm going to buy me a big old fur coat." Perry stamped his feet. Violet drew the children around her, and rubbed their hands in hers, one after the other.

A long black car pulled up alongside the bus stop. Thinking at first it was a funeral car, she pulled the children back. Violet made an X over her heart with a chilly finger, and said under her breath, "God kiss, the devil miss." Up in the country, people said that whenever a hearse passed by.

It was a Cadillac car, all right, but not the kind with the long sprays of waxy lilies sticking out the back over the casket. Same as a hearse, though, there was a colored man in a leather-brim chauffeur's cap sitting up front. And did she recognize that man? Why, yes—it was Matthew. Violet relaxed some.

A back window whirred down. A lady in a delicate chapeau of purple felt pushed her head partly out the window. She held on to the chromed window edge with one hand, which was protected from the elements by a contrasting purple glove. Tufts of lacquered gold hair showed beneath her daintily cocked hat. Behind a scrim of millinery gauze was a vanilla pudding face, with wafer lips and dimpled cheeks liberally rouged.

"Yoo-hoo!" called the pudding puss from the window of the purring limousine. "Why, Vi—is that you there?"

Violet stepped in front of the children. "Oh let me see the shiny car," Perry said, tugging at her skirt. "Who that is?" She pushed him off toward the girls. Ruby and Janny peeked around the sides of their mama's coat to look at the lady in purple riding in the big black car. Hand held to her mouth, Violet whispered sternly to the children, "Shush!" Then she stepped toward the back of the big car and bent over a bit, in a sort of bow. She said, "Yeah you right, it's me, Miz LaRue. What you be doing out Paris Avenue way today?"

"Well, being that it's Tuesday I'm on my way over to your very own church—the Land of Dreams Tabernacle, of course. Now you know that, Vi."

"You right, Miz LaRue."

"Can you believe it? Here it is, Christmas near upon us." Mrs. Hippocrates Beauregard Giradoux—or Miss Ava LaRue, as Hippo's wife preferred to be called, this being what she referred to as her stage name—spoke with an excited rush. She stroked her forehead with the back of one of her soft gloves. "Oh, and my charity committee's got ever so much to accomplish yet in working out details with the Negro ministry and all. You know, the poor families of the city must have their holiday baskets—and proper gifts for the little colored children . . ."

She stopped talking then, taking note of six big, inquisitive eyes belonging to three shivering children that Violet held back behind her.

"They yours, Vi?"

"Just the girls. The boy, he belong to my sister."

"Well now, aren't they just cute as three little bugs." Miss LaRue winked at the children. Violet looked up to the front of the car, exchanged a sigh and a silent greeting with Matthew, the driver. Miss LaRue said to Violet, "Come on over here on your own, Vi."

Violet felt awkward but did as she was asked and stepped over toward the car. When she was out of the children's earshot, Miss LaRue asked her, "Tell me, what can my committee get for those three adorable children?"

"Pardon me, but no thanks," Violet said, retreating from the car, trying but failing to hide the insult she felt. "I am providing

Christmas for my own family." She returned to Ruby, Janice, and Perry, who clung to her.

Miss LaRue looked hurt, at first. Had she not meant well? But then something else crept into her face, something not so charitable. Ruby saw the change. Miss LaRue said nothing more to Violet. Neither would she look her way. She spoke a few words to Matthew, though. Matthew tossed a wink at Violet, and the Cadillac quickly pulled off.

"Who was that?" Ruby asked her mother.

"Just one of them ol' damn St. Charles Boulevard women." Violet made a spitting sound. "Made a fool of herself out to Hollywood, she did. Then she made a damn fool out of the rich man who married her."

"She the white lady you work for?"

"Used to, I expect."

"I don't like the way she looked at you, Mama."

"You noticed that, child?"

Ruby said she did. And she said she would never forget the look.

"Best you don't forget," Violet told her daughter. "Best, too, you never get the airs to be giving that look to anybody else. Way Miz LaRue looked at me now, it surely don't have nothing to do with Christmas. Way she looked at your mama—made me feel like two cents waiting for change."

"Two cents waiting for change," Mama said. She trembled again. "I got a widow's telephone call make me feel like that, just before you two come by."

"What are you talking about?" Ruby asked.

"Minister Tilton call me up. He tell me to come by Sunday for sure. He say your daddy going to be called from beyond for testimony about certain troubles . . ."

I soon learned the nature of these troubles. It came in the form of two white men in bad suits hammering at Mama's front door with the wooden butt ends of their .38-caliber police specials.

TWELVE

"Afternoon, Mama," said the loud one, stepping through the door and right past Mama, scanning the small front room, drawn revolver in his hand. He looked straight through Ruby, as he had her mother; as if the two of them were windows instead of women. He was less cocky when he spotted me. In fact, he smiled and reholstered his .38, reassured by the presence of . . . what? Someone from his own gene pool? He motioned the other one through the door, then addressed Violet with too much courtesy to have meant it. "I'm Detective Mueller, ma'am, and this here's Detective Eckles."

Mama folded her arms and stared at the two cops, saying absolutely nothing. I had the idea she felt the same as I did about the courtesy. Also I had the idea that her silent treatment was a useful technique that had come to her with time and much experience. The cops were reliably dazed for a couple of seconds.

Detective Mueller fumbled with the cheap brown suitcoat draped over the shoulder of his short-sleeved yellow shirt. His flabby sides were wet from perspiration, from his armpits clear down to his gunbelt. Detective Eckles looked at the pointy toes of his snakeskin boots, like he was a smart-alecky school kid waiting to be disciplined by the principal. Mueller flicked his eyes over me again, deciding I was no ally after all. Maybe it was the way I looked back at him, like he was a sick person's former lunch.

"Ma'am?" Mueller's voice turned soft as funeral parlor talk. "You know why we're here?"

Mama was having none of Mueller's new tune. "What you mean by mangling on my door with your damn gun and calling me your *mama?* And how come you suddenly got a case of the nices?"

"How's that?"

"You deaf, too? I know your eyes is poor. You haven't got the first idea what your ownself looks like."

"Ma'am, I—"

"Elsewise, you know I'm not ugly enough to be your mama. What's your real mama name?"

"Florence—"

"Poor Flo. I bet you was her ugliest child."

Detective Eckles had a spasm of laughs. Mueller cracked an elbow into his partner's ribs. Eckles accidentally chomped his tongue, which took all the humor out of the situation for him.

"Look here, ma'am," Mueller said, hand resting on his gun, "we'd like to have a little talk with your boy."

"No boy staying here, sir. Only a grown man—name of Mr. Duclat."

"That's just who I'm talking about. Perry Duclat."

"You had a mind, you could to learn how to talk respectable about a black man."

"Respectable's got nothin' to do with the bidness we got with Perry Duclat."

"What you think Perry done?"

"Where is he, ma'am?"

Mueller drew himself a step toward Mama. So did Eckles. Which brought me off the sofa and to my feet. I moved in on Mueller, warning him, "You want to gear down some, Detective?"

"Who in goddamn hell are you?" Mueller drew out his gun again, holding it barrel-down to the floor.

"Put it away."

But Mueller kept his gun where it was. Eckles now drew his piece as well, dangling it the same as his partner.

"Don't sound like he's from 'round here," Eckles said, having difficulty with the letters *d* and *s,* on account of his injured tongue.

Mueller pressed me. "I as't you a question, Yankee-boy."

"I asked you to put the gun away."

"You best answer me first."

"I'm family," I said, smiling.

"Oh, man—that's choice!" Mueller laughed hard, expecting me to join in the joke. When I did not, he took a second look at Ruby. This time he did not look straight through her. He turned back to me, eyes lowered like a couple of broken sunshades. "Now ain't this just special. The pretty one, she your missus?"

"That's right."

"Where y'all from, Yankee-boy?"

"The gun, put it away."

" 'Fraid I can't accommodate you. Not until I got me at least a name."

"I've got identification." I pulled open my coat, slowly, so that Mueller could see the inside breast pocket. "There's all the ID you need in my pocket. Come and get it, Detective."

Mueller gave his gun a shake, directing Eckles. "G'wan over there, take it off'n him, Ricky Ray."

Eckles removed what he naturally thought was an ordinary wallet, opened it and whistled at the gold shield he found inside. He handed the wallet over to Mueller, whose lips moved as he read my name off the shield.

"Says here your name's Neil Hockaday," Mueller said.

"I know that."

"Says here you're a detective up there to Jew York City. Hoo-whee! A po-liceman, just like me."

"I don't think so."

Mueller returned the wallet and shield, and ignored me for the time being. He put his gun away, though. So did his trained seal.

"Say now, Mrs. Pretty," Mueller said to Ruby, shifting his lopsided bulk. I said to myself, Now that's a very unwise manner of addressing Ruby. As I had not warmed to Mueller, I decided he was on his own. "You down from Jew York to visit some ol' Louisiana kin for a spell?"

"Listen up, you ignorant peckerwood. What I'd like to do is cram a rat in your mouth and sew your lips shut. But I'm going to be polite instead." Mueller might have preferred being in a dentist's chair than having Ruby drill her eyes into him the way she was. "State your fool *bid*ness. Then kindly move your big ass out of here."

Mama added, "Go, girl!"

Mueller and his red face exploded. "Missy, I just ain't accustomed—!"

"No, I'm sure you *ain't!*" Ruby looked like she might leap up from the couch and grab Mueller's fat neck. Mueller took a step back. "A cracker like you pisses in my face, I do not call it rain—I call it piss. Have we established an understanding, Detective?"

I broke in to advise Mueller, "In the interest of being professionally helpful, I'd take things from the top if I were you." I nodded to Eckles, including him in my counsel. "Take a little beat, fellows. Then make like you're actual gentlemen."

The two of them sputtered for a couple of seconds. After their feathers were smoothed down, I asked Mueller, "Now then, Detective, what do you want with Mr. Duclat?"

"Got a few questions."

"About what?"

"None of your affair, Detective Hockaday. We ain't up north right now, we in New Orleans. But I don't mind tellin'

Miz Flagg here." He turned to Mama, and said, "Little matter about a friend of Perry's, ma'am—by the name of Cletus Tyler."

"Mr. Tyler, as I understand it, was a cell mate of Perry's up to Angola," Mama said to Mueller. She explained to me, "That's the penitentiary—Angola." She turned again to Mueller. "Now you know my Perry's not going to be taking up with Cletus Tyler. That'd be a violation of parole, wouldn't it?"

"You happen to know Cletus, ma'am?"

"None of your business," Ruby said to the detective. "Unless you're fixing to arrest my mama for whatever trouble you've got with this Mr. Tyler."

"Of course I ain't going to arrest your mama. All the same, I thought she'd like to know about poor Cletus." Mueller looked from Ruby back to Mama. "Fact is, Cletus got himself dead."

"La, no!"

"Oh, yes. I got to say, ma'am, when we found Cletus Tyler he was deader than a deep-fried palmetto. That's about as gruesome a corpse as I ever want to see. Got him shot up with a dumdum, got his neck whacked so bad his head pretty near rolled off."

"Oh, La . . . Oh, La . . ."

Ruby left the couch to stand next to Mama, taking one of her hands into her own. Mama looked up at me, hazel eyes beading.

"Must of been somebody familiar with the prison ways got to poor Cletus," Mueller continued, unmercifully. "Yes, ma'am, somebody whacked him—Angola-style."

I had to ask. "What style is that, Detective?"

"Them little rascals up to Angola, let me tell you. Always innovatin'." Mueller laughed wetly. "Latest thing, somebody gets him a nice stiff wood club for whacking. But before he does the job, he sinks razor blades into the club, along a couple of parallel lines—about a half-inch apart.

That way, there ain't enough stitching surface between the wounds so a doc can sew the skin back together proper."

Detective Eckles added, "Leaves a big old snaky scar."

"Take a man down Angola-style, every time he looks in a mirror he's reminded about it. Unless 'a course it croaks him, like our boy Cletus." Another wet laugh from Mueller, who I began to see was rabid, like King Kong Kowalski. Even worse, Mueller came with chimes, in the form of Ricky Ray Eckles.

"Haw, Cletus got him whacked real good!" Eckles said. "That Cletus, boy—he's really, truly dog dead! Got him shot through the heart, and creamed in the gut."

Mama's head fell. I could not see her face, but I knew she was crying.

I had a decision to make, fast. Should I do what I had to do and get these two thugs out of the house? And what would it take to accomplish such a feat? I should sic Ruby on them? Or should I encourage the usual predilection of rabid thug cops to shoot off their mouths? But to what advantage? And why was I thinking like a cop so far south of my jurisdiction?

"How do you mean Cletus Tyler also took injury to his *gut?*" I asked Eckles.

Eckles tried to say something, but another one of Mueller's elbows cut him short of breath. "Ricky Ray, you ought not to be blabbing like some old gal with a dryer on her head."

Mueller had a warning for me, too. "Obstruction of justice ain't a particularly pleasant thing, 'specially when I'm the obstructee. Don't be getting any strange notions about messing around in my case, Detective Hockaday."

"I imagine notions around here are strange enough as they are."

Mueller's pasty face was a study in wrinkled confusion, which did nothing to improve his appearance. "What exactly's your meaning?"

"Skip it, Mueller. Say, didn't you come here looking for somebody in particular?"

Mueller turned to Violet, whose uptilted face had become calm. She brushed her eyes with the backs of her brown hands. Violet's hands were large as a man's, but they moved in a delicate and purely feminine way. Mueller asked her, "All right now, where is he?"

"How'd I know where Perry at?"

"Ma'am, I as't you nice as pie."

"I answered the same. Trouble is, you didn't hear what you want to hear." Violet trembled again, but not from fear. Again there came the brave Christmas smile. She raised her eyes to the ceiling, and I wondered if it might be somebody up in heaven she was really trying to see, somebody mortal. "Trouble is, nobody ever want to know where Perry Duclat is bound to go."

"Ma'am, for the love of Christ—please!" Mueller was close to boiling over. Slow-witted people and overheated kettles are alike that way. "Do you suppose I might get one straight answer to one simple question before I leave?"

"I suppose you could leave easy enough. Being just a little old colored woman, I don't suppose too much otherwise."

"Godammit to hell—!"

"Don't be talking ugly. I'm a church woman."

"Sorry, ma'am."

Violet laughed at him. Mueller was smart enough to know he had been made a fool fair and square, so he said nothing more for the moment. I had a fleeting thought as to how a rabid cop like Mueller might express himself later that night, after some drinks. Maybe there was a Mrs. Mueller he could punch around.

"All right," Violet said. "You want it straight and simple? Perry ain't here, and I ain't got a clue to where he at now. Okay? But I know where Perry been. That I do know. You want me to tell you where he *been?*"

"It'd be real nice." Mueller smiled, not from friendliness.

He reached into a sweaty shirt pocket and took out a Woolworth notebook and a ballpoint pen. He clicked the pen.

"Been up to Angola a time or two."

"Ma'am, we already know that kind of thing. Perry Duclat's a thief. Now, you said something about where Perry'd *been?*"

"My Perry been in a place much different than you ever going to know about. Remember when you was a little boy?"

"Ma'am?"

"Probably you had nothing more to worry about than Mickey Mantle's batting average. Probably you played in the street all night with your little white friends, and the sound you dreaded most was your mama calling you home to supper. That's not where my Perry been."

Violet stopped. She looked at me for a moment before turning back toward Mueller. What she had to say was meant for my ears, too.

"Perry mama Rose left him, and his daddy Toby wouldn't have him. My late husband, Willis, took a shine to Perry and looked after him some when he was little. Then Willis took sick from a snake bite and couldn't even look after his ownself. I did what I could, but the street got hold of Perry. The street's like quicksand, you know. Anyhow, all the little street boys he run with? They either dead or up to Angola, same as dead. All his life, Perry lie awake at night thinking on all this. Thinking on what he is—nothing but a thrownaway child. Understand me?"

I doubted that. Detective Mueller had the dazed, stupid-looking face of a fat man whose own snoring had roused him from a nap. He closed his notebook, stuffed it back into his shirt pocket, and said to Eckles, "Come on, there's nothing here but time to waste."

Mueller handed Violet an embossed New Orleans Police Department business card with his direct-dial phone number on it. "Now, ma'am, we got us two ways of catching Perry Duclat—with you, or without you. You want to give up Perry to me, I'll see things go easy on him. But I don't extend no such guarantee otherwise." Mueller tossed a sneer in my direction. "Ask your blue-eyed family boy if I ain't talking fair and reasonable like."

"Neil . . . ?" Mama looked up at me.

"Oh, I'd say the detective's a fair man," I said. "I picture his daddy before him—persuading a mob to give a man the sporting chance of a head start before they run him down for a lynching."

Violet ripped up Mueller's police department card, dropping the pieces to the floor.

Mueller grunted at me, and said to Violet, "Just you remember, ma'am, we going to get that boy, one way or another."

He's going to get you yet, my sweet Miss Mu'um—one way'r other.

Violet glanced heavenward once again, then said to the back of Mueller's sweat-streaked shirt as he stamped out her door, "First thing y'all do, you come steal our bread. Then you want us to butter it for y'all."

"What'd she say to you?"

"Just get in the damn car."

Mueller eased himself behind the driver's wheel but did not start the engine right away. He gazed up toward the row house instead and stared at Violet Flagg standing defiantly at her door, flanked by her daughter and her white son-in-law.

"Now look it here—"

"You want to worry some, Ricky Ray? Worry about that goddamn New York cop."

"Why?"

" 'Cause I been to New York is why. Only city in the world you can get run over on the sidewalk by pedestrians."

THIRTEEN

Ever since that day in Harlem, Perry Duclat had drunk himself toward the sunshine of oblivion whenever the opportunity arose. But never could he quite make it through the shadows cast down around him by that single day. He could not forget, he could only remember.

He drank anything he could get his hands on. When he was still too young to walk into liquor stores under his own steam, he would buy vanilla extract or rubbing alcohol or camphor oil or hair tonic. In those days, he was partial to Vitalis. He preferred drinking alone, even when he was running with the gangs, and so the times he would share in a case of stolen beer were few. Once he reached his majority he could buy whatever he wanted, of course, providing he was on the outside; providing he had the money, or reasonable access to an unguarded purse or wallet.

On the inside, he drank mushroom tea when the screws ran out of whisky to sell to the inmates. Most cons drank the tea at one time or another, and also some of the screws. Some prisoners shot silver into their veins. But Perry would not associate with them, certainly not after what he had seen in Harlem.

Two cups of mushroom tea and most men would see beautiful, sunny things above all else. They might become a little weepy over these pleasing mushroom visions, but the suffering of their present and the waste of their past seemed to belong to somebody else, at least for a while.

Like all the other tea drinkers, Perry had seen beautifully imagined things. But no matter how much he drank, he could not escape the destruction of his personal history. There was one day in particular that was inescapable—its memory stronger than prison bars, stronger than booze, stronger than mushroom tea.

Even now, the memory was sure to come, and Perry knew he was helpless against it. The guilt of memory was not his to bear, that he also knew. Had he not once whispered to Clete, "Guilt and persecution and innocence, it's all the same thing for the luckless"?

But now Clete was gone—gone so terribly. Perry knew the police had to be hunting for him. Which was why he had come to this place: a rotted shed, where he could hide himself in a dank-smelling patch of secret shade.

In flight from the levee, he had had the presence of mind to buy cigarettes and a quart bottle of whisky. And now he would smoke and drink until the safety of darkness. He listened to his booming heart, and considered the next move in his sorry-ass life.

The shed was a lean-to at the rear of Nikki's Dockside Club on Chartres Street between Piety and Desire. It was made of corrugated steel, twisted and discolored from a fire that rushed through Nikki's some years back. As a matter of fact, it was the same year Perry had been serving his first burglary stretch. In a manner of speaking, Nikki's was likewise incarcerated. The club had lost its customers, and so the owner closed up and had all the doors and windows covered with iron bars. Everybody assumed the place was torched for insurance money.

In the fortunate years, Nikki's was virtually the neighborhood parlor, always full of stevedores who worked the bustling Governor Nicholls Street Wharf. Sometimes there was entertainment, and sometimes it was good. A piano player, a zydeco band, a pickup jazz combo . . .

Sometimes a pretty girl named Rose, who pinned a gardenia in her hair and sang dreamy songs while men bought Coca-Colas for her little boy, Perry.

Nikki's was a friendly and unassuming place, as natural to its humble surroundings as the sweet smell of fresh-cooked praline candy cooling on window ledges. Nobody in the neighborhood had reason to believe they stood in the way of progress.

But then one day—that was all the time it seemed to take—the Governor Nicholls Street Wharf was not what it used to be. Cargo containers and huge semitrucks decimated the manpower needs of the waterfront, resulting mainly in two things: bigger profits for investors in the moneyed parts of town, and a crime wave for the immediate and newly impoverished neighborhood. Nikki's, for instance, was robbed about once a week toward the end of its life.

Residential blocks fanning off from the wharf were wounded, dying or altogether deceased. Working men in denim and khakis used to crowd these blocks, swinging lunch buckets on their way back and forth from the docks. Their jobs had left them with thick, rough hands and fingers as big around as rail spikes. Such hands were not needed in the new low-wage computer jobs, which was about all anybody could get in the way of a job. And so these men had nothing much to do beyond mining the alleys for redeemable bottles and cans; either that or stay home, drinking beer and fighting with their wives. The only people making serious money were hard-faced young men who carried beepers and dressed in cashmere sweatshirts with attached hoods and hundred-dollar sneakers, and rode around in Mitsubishi Monteros with heavy-tint, bullet-proof windows.

The neighborhood children had to make do with angered parents, temptations of historical proportion, schools that would not teach them, and politicians yapping about traditional family values. Children who could not cope were on their own. Children like Perry Duclat.

From inside the blackened shed, hidden in shadows with his diminishing bottle of Duggan's Dew, Perry shook his head. Anybody who had ever been locked up would have recognized the hollow sound of his laugh. Those who had never been imprisoned would have thought he was crying.

Perry saw beyond the shed wall through a rusty hole the size of a peach still green on the branch. He had an unobstructed view of the landmark next to his birthplace—a black-and-white billboard on the other side of the muddy river: ALGIERS IRON WORKS & DRY DOCK COMPANY. Behind the sign was a coal yard, and in it the shack where Perry was born, where his father still lived. He laughed because he believed not in God, but in Irony.

"Old dried-up nigger's probably sitting over there in his hole drinking, just like I'm here in my hole drinking," Perry whispered. He might as well have spoken in full voice. Only the weeds pushing up through the dirt floor could hear. He took a swallow from his bottle. There was precious little whisky remaining, and at least an hour before sundown, when it would be safe to venture out for more.

Perry set the bottle down carefully in a corner, where it was least likely to tip over. He lit a Pall Mall and pulled his knees up to his chest and hugged them, his habit when the helpless vision came.

Which now it did. The vision of Harlem—and a ghost floating before his drunken eyes in blue-gray curls of cigarette smoke.

"Cutie, you don't got to be peeking at me from over by the door." She waved the frightened boy into her drafty room with a handful of lacquered fingers, red with silver sparkles. In her lap was a brass clock with a bell on top. She picked it up and wound the stem, setting the time. She placed the ticking clock on a chair

next to the bed and said to the nervous boy, "Come on here. You be next."

"Mama?"

"Whoa, little darlin' . . ." Her slitted eyes fluttered wide, slowly focusing. A cigarette fell from her rouge-caked lips, landing in the cleft of her black lace push-up brassiere. She picked the glowing butt from between her breasts—casually, as if she was used to being burned—and crushed it into an ashtray by the clock. There was an open Te-Amo box on the chair, too, containing no cigars. The boy looked at the contents of the box, knowing just enough to fear the things he saw inside. He jumped when she spoke again. "Who you calling your . . . ?"

She quit speaking, for the fog of time and neglect and guilt and grief had now lifted. She simply knew, and understood there was no place to hide anymore. Mother and son stared at each other, recognizing themselves in their opposite faces.

Rose Duclat had skin the color of a yellow August moon, and eyes as soft and green as pine forest shade. Perry's African tones were a few shades closer to the surface than his mother's. He was built lanky like Rose, with her own straight features and wavy brown hair with a cast of red to it. Mother and son were both young, less than twenty years of age between them.

Rose's beauty had not completely faded, but it had been harshly used. Her attraction to men was now increasingly dependent on paint and hasty eyes, or darkness, or the right price. Her pride was altogether gone, to a bed in a room that rented by the quarter hour. Her boy was very handsome. He might have been surrounded by adolescent friends and exuberant times if not for the cares that crowded him. Perry usually wore the expression of a dog vaguely suspecting he was about to be cuffed. This caused people naturally to shy away from his company.

Rose Duclat pulled up a sheet to cover her nakedness.

The alarm sounded. Time! Perry turned his back to Rose, as much to hide tears as to heed the hallway commotion.

A heavy woman of fifty years or so with a honey-blonde wig and skin dark as a blue plum stood at the whore's portal, rapping a steel-tipped cane against the jamb. She had a pocked face and dressed in a sporting man's clothes, a pale blue suit and silk shirt to match, and an orange ascot and white patent-leather shoes.

"Nigger, you done used up more'n your time," she barked at the frightened, embarrassed boy. She squeezed the bridge of her flat nose and took aim at the hallway floor, hawking snot from flared nostrils. "You want to stick around and dick around, that's all right by Madam. But you do got to pony up extra." Madam wiped her nose with a finger, then stepped inside Rose's room. "I see you ain't even managed to drop your drawers. Well, don't matter, you got to pay to play, whatever's your game."

"I don't got the money to spare," Perry said. He rubbed a sleeve across wet eyes.

Some of the roughness left Madam's voice. "Aint' no reason to fuss. We only engaged here in a little enterprise old as time. Nothing personal, nothing special about it. You understand?"

Perry said nothing. Nor did he make a move to leave, which peeved Madam. "Now go on, you got to vamoose!"

"Give us a little minute, won't you?" Rose asked her. "The boy he's kin of mine."

"I'll give you half a little minute. And don't never be bringing no family here again." Madam stalked back out into the hall. She turned and glared at Rose and Perry, and hawked some more snot before moving down the hallway.

"Mama—"

"Perry, Perry . . . Why'd you come here?"

"To be with you, Mama. I can't stay with Toby, I just can't! Please can't I stay with you?"

The words were fists pounding on Rose's ears.

Perry reached inside his jacket and pulled out a small box wrapped in foil and ribbons. He walked to the whore's bed and handed the gift to his mother. "I brought you something from down home, from Bynum's. Your favorite."

Rose sat up straight as she undid the wrapping and opened the box. Inside was an ounce of Evening in Paris brand perfume in a bottle shaped like the Eiffel Tower. She held the Eiffel Tower in both her shaky hands, pressing it to her black lace chest.

"Mama, I'm going to take you away."

"Been trying my whole life to get took away. Finally got myself up north, figuring I could be one of them what-we-call passant blancs. That's New Orleans French for colored folks think we can pass. Understand?"

"Yes, Mama."

"I could've passed, too, if I only could've somehow lost my mouth. I got this black-bottom accent that's tough as moss to shake. Looks ain't all, I sure did learn that."

"How'd you wind up here?"

"Oh, baby boy of mine . . ."

Rose's voice trailed off to a mix of weeping and laughing. She set the perfume down on the chair and lit up another cigarette from her pack on the bed, dragged on it, settled it into the ashtray. Then she picked up a length of rubber tube from the Te-Amo box. She coiled this tightly around the bicep of her left arm, holding on to one end with her left hand, securing the other end with her teeth.

"Mama—?"

Rose reached for the needle in the box with her right hand. Her voice was muffled by the tube in her mouth. "Mama don't feel so good."

Perry cried. "Why you got to do this?"

"People come in three types. There's the ones who make things happen. There's ones who watch things happen to them. Then there's the ones wonder what the hell happened. I know my type. What's your type, boy?"

Rose plunged the needle into her arm, and shot down on the syringe plunger. She got herself taken away, to where there was no escape.

But when his mama's ghost cleared from the cigarette cloud, thick and motionless in the shed, Perry only saw more. Now came Uncle Willis in the smoke, dead face covered in chinaberry leaves . . . Now came Cletus Tyler, his head beaten clear off with a razored club, the branded flesh of his belly stinking.

Perry thought, People I'm closest to are dead. What's that make me?

He heard Cletus again, *They got them a plan . . .*

Sure as holy hell they do!

Perry thought about his old cell block, and the likelihood of his having to go back there again, this time for something he did not do. This time without Cletus to talk to at night.

He thought about the Angola night.

Early morning, actually. The only time Angola is truly quiet—for an hour, sometimes two. Everybody fast asleep, guards included. Then suddenly, all up and down Perry's row of cells, rats swarming and swarming up through the lidless cell block toilet commodes. Hundreds of frantic rats, somehow rudely disturbed from the prison sewers, scuttling through the humid darkness. Fleeing something. Rats squealing, running a gauntlet of thrown shoes, broomsticks, bleach bottles, dirty underwear. Cries filling the cell block—Oh, my gawd, git—git! Rats running stupidly into walls, scrambling over bunks full of flailing arms and legs. Rat teeth tearing at anything in the way. Caged men screaming until sunrise.

In his remembrances came the beginning of an answer to what he might now do with the rest of his fugitive life. Perry grabbed his whisky bottle and pulled it to his lips, the drinker's reflexive confirmation of a decision made.

What's your type, boy?

Perry set down the bottle. Then he mashed his cigarette into the damp ground. He shuddered at the foul smells that filled his hiding place—his whisky breath, the smoky stench of his clothes.

"That'll be just about enough," he said aloud. He kicked at the liquor bottle. It went flying into a dark corner of the shed, glass breaking.

"Enough," he repeated.

Perry Duclat was drunk, his pocket contained stolen money, he was sought by the police in connection with the murder of his Angola cell mate. In spite of all this, he had a sober realization of what he was now experiencing: self-pride, of all improbable things. For a new question occurred: am I going to settle for being one of them—just another of them sorry-ass MOMS?

A sorry-ass is a prisoner of the worst of his past. Perry could hear himself saying this now; he wished he was sitting at Shug's and saying it, with Clete sitting next to him, alive and listening. He heard himself talking like a preacher to a church full of sorry-asses:

Haven't we done our time, sisters and brothers? Hadn't we best now look for the way out? Way out of what, you say? Way out of being a tourist in your own life! People say you make your own luck. Now y'all know that's fool talk, like I already say. But now I'm saying there's something you can make, low-down as you may be. You can make your *future!*

Perry laughed again, and thought, That's close as I get to religion! Private religion, real religion—as far away from Jesus-pumping Sunday services down to the Land of Dreams Tabernacle as Zeb Tilton is from going heaven when he dies!

He thought about his Aunt Violet going to those Sunday services. How he had argued with her about Minister Zebediah Tilton, how she had argued back. *Don't you know a woman's got to get dolled up once in a while so she can feel like somebody? You tell me some good man want to take me someplace respectable in my good dress, and just watch how fast I quit on that church. 'Til then, sometimes I just got to go, and Zeb Tilton be damned.* And Perry thought about how much his aunt enjoyed it when he would get up early on a Sunday and go to church with her, how it cost him nothing but time and an understanding of needs that had nothing to do with his own.

He thought about whisky, then cast it out of his mind.

He thought about that pretty girl he always saw at Zeb Tilton's church, up there in the choir with the Praise Sayers—Sister Constance. And what was it Vi said about her living in the lane years ago?

He thought about his late Uncle Willis, as he had every day up at Angola and every day since. He thought about the house in the lane, and the little backyard where he had been happy once.

He thought about poor Clete. And how he died.

No! Perry Duclat would not settle for being just another ratty sorry-ass.

Again, Perry laughed the prison laugh, and said aloud, "Every coffin has a silver lining."

Then, as he looked once more through the green peach hole in the shed wall, he saw a white man walking around out there between him and the view of Toby's coal yard shack . . .

A white man wearing a baseball cap.

FOURTEEN

"He didn't do it, Neil. That's God's truth."

Mama's back was to me as she said this. I was looking over her shoulder, watching Mueller sneering at me from his car. He started up the engine and peeled away, leaving plenty of rubber and resentment.

Mama turned. She looked tired and saggy, as if she had somehow lost a lot of weight in only a few minutes.

"But it doesn't matter if Perry's innocent, does it?" I asked her.

"Likely not." Mama's voice was resigned.

My own mother would become overwhelmed like that sometimes. She would come around when she noticed me worried about her. I remember her saying once, *Nothing defeats us quicker than the ever-present thought that we're defeated, son. That's what fear is, and shame for who you are. Resist living in fear and shame. Believe in a rich imagination of yourself. And if you never hear another thing I tell you, hear me now: belief is stronger than reason.*

And that was how I decided that Violet Flagg was right: Perry was innocent of what two armed crackers said he had done. Standing in her doorway, watching a pair of rabid cops, Mama had spoken the hard, simple truth. I believed her. Anybody would.

Then she told me a harder truth. "No black man can hide in New Orleans for long."

Ruby took her mother by the elbow and steered her back to the easy chair. Mama sank down into it like she wanted to be dead. She sat still and silent for almost a minute, hardly breathing. But then she roused herself, and looked around the room after something.

Mama's eye fell on her purse, sitting on the floor next to the table under the front window. "Listen, you two, now I got to run a couple little errands before this house starts filling up." She stood up and smoothed her skirt. "Ruby, y'all going to be sleeping in my room. The small room, that is. Take your things on up there now. Have yourselves the nap you sure must need."

I tried telling her, "We don't want to throw you out."

"Better than half my nights I doze off right here in this room," Mama said. "Tell your husband I ain't lying, Ruby."

"She isn't lying."

"You want to feel better, tell you what," Violet said to me. "Go on out to the kitchen and fetch my easing pills. I left them on the table or somewheres about."

Uncertain of exactly what sort of medication Mama had in mind, I nonetheless went off to the kitchen. I started back for the parlor after finding nothing, but stopped when I heard Ruby and her talking about me.

"That white man good to you, child?"

"He's very good."

"He bring any of them man-troubles to your house?"

"He used to drink. He still eats too much."

"What you mean about drinking?"

"He's a recovering alcoholic, Mama. I'm learning to take a day at a time, so is he. I'm satisfied he's doing all right. You want to know more about his boozing—how he used to drink—ask him straight-out."

"Maybe I will." Violet dropped the subject. "All right now, Mr. Neil seems to be an intelligent man."

"He doesn't think so."

"Only proves he's smart."

"Also he doesn't think he's good-looking," Ruby said. "He worries about his bald spot."

"Where that man going baldy?"

"Top of his head, in the back. He's got a little Friar Tuck thing happening."

"My, my—just like my Willis."

"I kiss his bald spot sometimes."

"Same's I kiss my Willis head, child . . ."

I heard Violet cry softly, and then Ruby moving to take her mother in her arms. Ruby asked. "All these years gone, and you still miss Daddy so bad?"

"He was my lion. Oh, I know I'm a weepy fool."

"No—"

"Time was short for us . . ."

"Mama, I understand."

I waited a couple of beats before walking into the parlor. When I finally did, Violet was holding her open purse in one hand and a hanky to her eyes with the other. And Ruby looked at me in a moony way, like she was a teenage kid waiting for me to pin a corsage on her first spaghetti strap.

Ruby is not the moony type. I doubt she ever went through the stage as a girl. But then she had been breaking character ever since we boarded the train in New York.

"I don't find a bottle of pills anyplace in the kitchen," I said to Mama.

"Don't be fussing no further then." Mama flicked the hanky away from her eyes back into her purse. "Well, what do you know. I got me a tin of Bayers right here in my bag."

"Why not let me run your errands?" I asked.

"I'm only walking over to the jot-em-down store."

"Got your list, Mama?" Ruby asked. She said to me, "Mama's always got her list."

Sure enough, Mama pawed around inside her purse until

she found a recycled envelope, one side full of pencil marks. "Right here it is."

"Be careful out there," I said. I wondered why I said that.

"Funny you worry about your mother-in-law's welfare. Mr. Willis Flagg, he used to be always clowning about his mother-in-law. My Willis he'd say, Every time a mother-in-law dies it's 'cause hell needs a fresh devil."

"Oh, Mama!" Ruby said.

"Now, y'all go upstairs for your lie-down like I told you." Mama's orders. "When I come back, I'm going to be storming around my kitchen."

Ruby crossed through the parlor to the stairs. She turned to me. "Coming?"

"Go ahead, I'll be up in a minute." I had the feeling Mama wanted to say something private to me. Ruby continued up the stairs. After I heard a door open and close again, I asked Mama, "Do you have an idea where Perry might be?"

"Now you heard what I told them other po-lice."

"And you know I'm not like either one of them."

Mama looked me up and down. She was not eyeing a son-in-law, she was taking measure of a cop. "Suppose I tell you where Perry might be at. What you going to do?"

"Better I should find him before Mueller and Eckles do. Perry's got the right to be afraid. But somebody has to tell him you make mistakes when you're afraid."

"I know you right."

"Where's he hiding?"

"Only'd be a guess, but I'll tell."

After she did, Mama crossed the room, opened the door, and walked down the steps to the street. I watched her through the window, and saw a switch in her hips as she walked along, like she was a young woman again, with a lion in her life . . .

This woman bearing the lonesome sorrow of widowhood, and now the sorrow of her nephew. How do such women sleep? Sister Bertice, who was not all bad, knew the answer. One year she made me memorize a Yeats poem about the muttering Moll Magee, tortured by her little girl's death. *But always, as I'm movin' round, Without doors or within, Pilin' the wood or pilin' the turf. Or goin' to the well, I'm thinkin' of my baby and keenin' to mysel.' And sometimes I am sure she knows: When, openin' wide His door, God lights the stars, His candles, and looks upon the poor.*

Upstairs, where I had carted our suitcases, I found Ruby lying flat out on her back in a high bed that dominated a small room with pink walls and the smell of sachets buried in bureau drawers. The bed looked like a Macy's display of pillows and lace. Ruby had stripped off her clothes and dusted herself with talcum in attempts to drop off into a cool nap. But she was still awake.

I set the suitcases underneath the double window over the back alley. I glanced out the windows, and pictured Ruby as a girl again—playing down there in the alley in another day in shorts and sneakers, going off to Sunday school in braids and a polka-dot dress and Mary Janes and white anklets. Then I looked back at Ruby lying naked in the big bed, and thought of her soft grown-up breasts pressed against my chest and her breath in my ear and her brown legs entangled in my own . . .

Then came the grim visage of every nun I have ever known in my life, a whole coven of them chanting at me in Irish, *Peaca súil*—sins of the eyes. This quickly changed the earthy ideas coursing through my mind and emboldening my middle extremity.

"Do you think Mama likes me all right?" I asked, thinking this a wholesome line of conversation.

"Like? I think she wants to adopt."

"Damn, I'm sweet!"

Ruby yawned. "We're going to need some rest before the onslaught of Janny dearest, and the rest."

"You and your sister have problems? I've never even heard you mention her."

"No, you haven't." That was all Ruby had to say for now on the subject of Janice.

There was a photograph hanging in a wooden frame over the bed, and a crucifix tucked back behind it. In the photo were two people in church robes—Violet Flagg and a heavy-set, dark-skinned man with a big smile.

"That's Mama with a voodoo con artist," Ruby said of the picture. "You know, the Most Reverend Zebediah Tilton."

"The one who scammed your mother and father out of the cottage?"

"Same one who telephoned and made Mama feel low by saying he'd be calling out Daddy from the dead this Sunday. Damn him!"

I sat on the edge of the bed. Ruby ran her hands over the lace coverlet. "This is the bed I was born in," she said. "Also the bed my daddy died in."

I looked to another photograph. It was the centerpiece of the bureau, a hand-painted wedding portrait. Violet Duclat in a silver bridal gown with yellow flowers in her hair. And the groom, Willis Flagg, a handsome young man in a black suit and a red boutonniere.

"The chifforobe over there," Ruby said, pointing to a cherry-wood wardrobe closet that matched the bureau and bed, "and the other pieces, they all belonged to my grandmother. Mama had them shipped down from St. Francisville when she died. Of course, it all fit better in the big bedroom. Which is Perry's now."

"What was this? Your room?"

"Janny's and mine." Ruby turned her head to the window. "Out there is where we spent all our time."

I got up and looked out over the alley again. A skinny black dog lapped up oily water from a puddle. A cat watched from beneath a rusting car. A few units down the line, a pair of pregnant girls shared a crack pipe.

"The neighborhood could use a ball field," I said.

"This is the projects, Irish. What we need are parents and social workers and condoms and sanitation crews and smaller classrooms and vaccinations and medical insurance and credit. And jobs. I mean real jobs with futures to them, not those casino jobs."

"Casinos?"

"Oh, that's the newest thing around here. It's supposed to be the economic salvation of New Orleans."

"You don't see it that way."

"Gambling promises the poor what property performs for the rich. That's why politicians and preachers rarely denounce the scam."

Where I should have seen kids playing there was instead an expanse of weeds and broken glass. "Still, a ball field couldn't hurt," I said.

"There used to be one. With wooden bleachers and Astroturf and everything. It was a gift to us kids from some rich ladies' club."

"What happened to it?"

"My friends and I tore apart the seats and set fire to the Astroturf." Ruby paused. She had a hurt and angry look on her face, as if she was trying to start a fight. "Are you shocked, dear heart?"

I lied and said I was.

"In a thousand years, those ladies wouldn't understand why we wrecked their ball field. What about you? Do you understand?"

"The rich don't need to be tough and rude. They don't understand that these are social skills poor kids have to practice."

"Not bad for a blue-eyed choirboy."

"Your choirboy never saw Park Avenue until he was a grown-up cop."

FIFTEEN

The detective trade has taught me that a man in need of disappearance, given the briefest running time, will generally make quick and skillful choices about his burrow. Such determination is second nature to human beings.

In our work as children, we play games meant to serve us through life; among the most vital is hide-and-seek. Maybe our biggest weakness as adults is that most of us have mastered only half the game. Hiding is instinctive, requiring virtually no thought. Few of us become seekers because most adults would sooner drop dead than think.

I suppose I should be grateful. The New York Police Department pays me to find people who make themselves scarce, almost always for socially unacceptable reasons. Since I am not the brightest in my business, I do not need competition from any more thinking people than there already are.

My mother-in-law, I deduced, was a thinker—therefore, a natural-born detective. Nobody had to tell her that a case is solved when a cop finds the sweet spot—that vulnerable place where hiding and seeking is one in the same. Mama just knew that.

"Like I say, Perry spend a lot of nights laying bug-eyed awake, wondering how cheating-heart people able to show their faces after they gone thrown away somebody." Mama said this to me after Ruby had gone upstairs. "Anybody got imagination, they can see Perry Duclat is a man who lost his way from searching. Somebody lost like that ain't too difficult to scare up. All's you need to do is respect what he's after, and get close to it."

Mama suggested I begin at the beginning, a little place in the tired-out part of town. An old neighborhood that gave Perry early memories of his pretty mother. Mama said, "Rose used to sing at this one saloon . . ."

So I waited until Ruby fell to sleep, then changed my clothes: dry boxers, chinos, sneakers, T-shirt, and my Yankees cap. I took Huggy Louper's card from my wallet and rang up his number from the kitchen telephone.

True to his word—*Whenever you need a lift, the dispatcher'll have me to you, Huggy-on-the-spot*—Louper and his taxi with the dashboard hula dancer soon came to collect me. While I waited for him on Mama's front porch, I spotted the slogan on Huggy's card, printed beneath his name: NOT HONEST, BUT RELIABLE. If Hugh P. Louper were a politician, I would vote for him.

Huggy dropped me at the corner of Chartres and Piety streets, which according to his tone of voice he considered suspicious. "Peculiar destination for a tourist." He lit a cigarette as I stepped out of the taxi and surveyed the pot-holed street with its commercial lots gone to weedy craters, some ragged men off in the distance picking up cans and bottles, the occasional passing Jeep. Huggy asked, "Want me to wait on you?"

I told him no. Huggy shrugged his shoulders and drove off. I stood there looking for several minutes, trying to imagine a saloon now gone with the wind.

There was something that looked like a cage on the bleak horizon. Twisted steel bars that contained the burnt lumber of an old building about the size of a suburban garage. Nobody had to tell me. This was Perry Duclat's burrow.

I walked around the side of the caged building, and a sloping steel shed came into view. As I neared the shed, I swore I could feel a pair of desperate eyes boring in on me. I have learned to trust such instincts.

I stopped. We were all alone there in the scabid range of a cast-off precinct of New Orleans, and so I called out, "Perry, I'm Ruby's husband—Neil Hockaday . . . Your Aunt Violet sent me . . . I won't harm you, I want to talk."

Nothing.

I called again, "Perry, I can help . . ."

Behind me, some two hundred feet off, there was the sound of a vehicle idling at the curb. I turned and saw faces in a Jeep. Two faces, maybe three, blurred by a shimmer of haze in the setting sun. Whatever, nobody seemed to be paying attention to me.

I walked clear around the building toward the shed, until the Jeep was gone from sight.

I was close enough to whisper now. "Perry?"

"Don't come no closer!" The voice came from inside the shed. I saw a small opening between corrugated steel panels. On the other side of that hole was a frightened eye. The voice held as much fright as the eye, and warned, "Back off, I got a gun."

"I only want to talk."

"Going to shoot your motherfucking white po-lice ass you take one more fucking step!"

So he knew me. And knew that I was a cop.

"It's only you and me, Perry. If you had a gun, you would have used it by now."

Big talk. I stayed right where I was.

"Going to fuck you up, motherfucker!" Perry's rising voice told me I had won the bluff. "Fuck you up real good!"

"How? You plan to hurt my feelings again about my mother and me?" If I was dealing with an armed man, I should have heard a gun cocking by now. Which I did not, and which gave me much relief. "Your Aunt Violet says you didn't kill Cletus Tyler, and I believe her. A couple of cops came around looking for you. Pigs, both of them. Know what I mean, Perry?"

"All kind of pigs already mess up my life."

"I'm not a pig."

"What you want, man?"

"Violet wants to know what you're up to."

"Tell her I'm sitting here in the hole of time."

"Doing what?"

"Tell me what *you* doing married to a black woman."

"One day I told her I loved her, she said the feeling was mutual. We did what lucky people do in that situation. You're not so lucky. So what are you going to do about it?"

"Try to resolve two things pressing my mind."

"You want to come out of that shed and talk to me face-to-face?"

"No."

"What do you have to resolve?"

"A duty to remember that's agitating against my longing to forget."

"Sure you can afford the time for philosophy right now?"

"Pigs going to find my ass sooner or later. They going to claim I done my cellie for some reason they make up. Then they going to fry them another nigger. So what? See, I don't worry about that. I use my time to resolve a certain piece of old business. That's what I decided after a lot of thinking."

"You need a lawyer?"

"Shoo! Lawyer's nothing but a white man sitting in the toll booth at the bridge where anybody want justice got to cross."

"All right, all right." He had a point about chasers. "What's this old business?"

"Just you go on back to Gibson Street. Tell Aunt Vi I'm going to do something about Zeb Tilton to square what he done to Uncle Willis and her. Tilton one nigger ain't no better than a damn lawyer in a toll booth. You got that?"

"Zeb Tilton, toll booth. Got it. Anything else?"

"Tell Vi I ain't about to check out like Clete, I ain't going to die a zero. What I do going to leave a mark."

"I wish you'd—"

"What's that coming?"

I turned at the sound behind me, hearing it a split second after Perry had.

A speeding engine, ratcheting gears. A Jeep with three men crowded into the front seat, bearing down on me like I was a target. Something wrong with the jouncing faces, something untrue about their colors.

On instinct, I looked down from the faces in the windshield to the Jeep's front bumper, where a license plate should have been. I looked back at the faces, trying to figure out what was wrong. . . .

I had no time to make sense of it.

Not with gunfire.

SIXTEEN

"His weekly press conference is fixing to close, looks like to me. Either that or the bourbon's finally run out."

Having thus informed the surprise visitor, the ball of blonde frizz sitting at the reception desk glanced through the open archway where a mahogany door used to separate an outer office from private quarters. Miss Frizz turned back, cheerfully snapping her pink wad of chewing gum and waving a handful of Press-on Nails in the direction of some chairs and a table full of old magazines. "You want, officer, take a load off while you wait."

"Thanks just the same," Claude Bougart said, "but I got a fine view of the proceedings right where I'm standing."

"Whatever bones your crawfish."

Under less pressured circumstances, he might have responded to Miss Frizz's colorful remark with a friendly laugh. He could surely use a laugh now. Claude Bougart was as tense as a shackled man in slippers and a shaved head on his way to a plug-in chair.

But he could reveal no anxiety.

He had to appear confident and controlled because something had to be done . . . *at long last, something*. Claude Bougart was the only person he knew who could make it even begin to happen. He wished he knew for certain what *it* was. He wished he could employ the oldest cop trick in the book, knowing the answers beforehand to the questions asked.

But Officer Bougart was in a most unfamiliar darkness. And so nervous he wondered if he was actually something far beyond nervous; he wondered if he was out of his mind for being where he was, sure of so little, gambling so much.

He could be certain of only two things—dead certain, so to speak. The first was, nearly nothing murky about New Orleans escaped the closely held knowledge of Alderman Giradoux. Second was, the only way to operate at an advantage with a man aware of the fact he knows something useful to nearly everybody was by means of the second oldest cop trick in the book: namely, Bougart would have to hide his own motivations by making Hippo strut.

To do that required being slightly impudent with a powerful white man. Which is why Bougart now had to question the state of his sanity, and the odds of all that could happen to his career in the next few minutes. Which is why he was stricken, standing where he was in Miss Frizz's outer office, gazing in at the circus of Hippo's press conference.

He beheld a vast inner sanctum of New Orleans political might, amassed over four decades. A stage designer at the Saenger Theatre over on Canal Street could well have arranged such a setting, worthy of an opera about the Kingfish himself, Huey Long. An enormous desk with ornately carved oak elephants for legs occupied a sort of thrust stage. Behind this was a thronelike chair with red velvet backing and broad arms that ended up as elephant heads for handles, with genuine ivory tusks pointing halfway down to the Oriental rug on the floor. This stage was surrounded by a sort of political cabaret, with circles of little chairs huddled around small tables, hospitably cluttered with liquor bottles and highball glasses. Floor-to-ceiling leaded-glass windows were heavily draped. The walls were laden with hundreds of ribboned citations, and signed photographs of high-profile pols and low-profile operators. Potted magnolia trees were everywhere, as were all the flags ever flown over the state of Louisiana—Spanish, French, Union, Confederate, and Union again. Everybody in the place seemed to be smoking cigars the size of kitchen pipes.

Center stage was the great man, Alderman Hippocrates Beauregard Giradoux. He usually sat behind his imposing desk, alternately pounding the top with his chunky fists or leaning back in his throne. If his mood was folksy, he would perch atop the desk on half his formidable rump, dangling a leg off the side and chatting with his audience. On formal occasions, such as announcing for reelection, he would stand rigidly in front of his desk with his tree trunk arms flapped out from his sides, fat fingers in Churchillian V-for-victory formation.

Today's format was folksy. Hippo sat for the press in his striped shirtsleeves, responding to the last of the raised hands.

"Say now, Hippo," one of the reporters in the audience asked, a smirk covering his florid face, "what you got to say about these here complaints you been overly familiar with the girls on your campaign staff?"

"Who that been complaining on me?"

"Oh, you remember, Hippo. All started back last New Year's Eve at your fund-raising bash?"

"Look here, all's I said was something a little risqué like in a whole room full of folks. You know, just something to keep the party rolling. 'Up with skirts, down with pants!' What's so bad about a fat man saying a fool thing like that after he's had a belt? Come on, it ain't like I inspired everybody to some big old Roman orgy . . . though from looking down at all your sad-sack pusses, most of y'all would be considerably more sprightly if you'd have such an unholy experience—"

A roar of male laughter.

Alderman Giradoux resumed the entertainment. "Why,

my own dear missus, Ava LaRue, she like to bust a gut when I say what I said. And best I further recall, it was lusty giggles all 'round from members of the fair sex, 'cepting some little gal went off crying. Might've been her time of the month, you know?"

Male laughter kicked up again. But then a woman rose from her chair, a TV reporter with her cigar-free hand waving in the smoke-laden air, shouting for recognition.

Claude Bougart recognized her, even way off from where he was in the outer office. Janice Flagg, little sister to Ruby Flagg. Back in his school days, Bougart had a brief crush on Janice. This was to be eclipsed by his later devotion to Ruby.

"Mr. Alderman, Mr. Alderman—!"

"All right, girl, all right." Giradoux pointed to Janice. "Ain't you the cutie from the morning show on WDSU?"

Klieg lights flipped on, heating the air. Janice Flagg stepped squarely in front of the camera and, like the beautician she once had been, patted down some errant hair. Then she asked the lens, as if the lens were Hippo himself, "Alderman Giradoux, are you saying to the women of New Orleans that you are *not* sympathetic to feminism?" She turned to face the alderman, which was his cue; reporter and politician knew well their co-dependent roles. Hippo likewise looked past his questioner, straight into the lens. When the red light clicked, he delivered forth a sound bite.

"Missy, you're obviously a very smart and pretty African-American lady. And so dang young it hurts me. It's because of your youth that I'm obliged to overlook the frivolity behind your question. Now, I can't help it, I just don't understand men calling themselves feminists. No more than I understood when old Hubert Humphrey was down here running for president back in '68 and telling your people he was a soul brother."

"But, the women's vote—" Janice sputtered.

"Don't matter none who's filling out the ballots, honey. Only way old Hippo's ever going to get voted out of office is if I wake up in bed some morning with a dead girl or a live boy."

Thunderous laughter drowned out Hippo as he asked the camera lens, "Now ain't I right?"

Under cover of laughter, Hippo whispered to a nearby aide, "Tell that pretty black TV gal to come see me after, I'll give her a little exclusive, ought to please her."

Addressing the crowd, Hippo asked, "That going to be about all, ladies and gents?" He stood up from his desk and blew kisses to everybody, this being the customary gesture that drew an end to the proceedings.

Over the heads of the departing reporters, Hippo spotted a uniformed police officer in his outer office. "See y'all next week, folks," he said to the reporters, as if offering up a benediction. "Until then, keep your eye upon the doughnut and all that sort of happy horse crap."

When the press corps had shuffled out, most with bourbon bottles tucked under their arms, Officer Bougart walked through the archway into Alderman Giradoux's auditorium of a private office. Giradoux resumed his place behind the desk. He held an iced tumbler of Maker's Mark to his sweating brow, and motioned for the policeman to approach.

"Step right on up here, Booger." The alderman moved the tumbler to his plump lips, and sipped noisily. "You know I maintain an open-door policy, this time of day anyhow."

"There's no door at all, sir."

"That's the stuff."

Bougart walked up to Giradoux's desk and stood in front of it. He might have been offended by Hippo calling him "Booger" but instead was glad. It had made him angry, and his anger was calming.

"What can I do for you, son?" Giradoux pointed to a leather club chair at the side of his desk. Bougart declined.

"You and I ever met, sir?"

"I believe not."

"How'd you know they call me Booger?"

"I make it my business to know all sorts of things."

"So I hear."

"Big stories are made out of little scraps of hearsay most folks would count as nothing at all." Hippo sipped more bourbon. Poker-faced, he studied the policeman in front of him. Without the aid of bourbon, Claude Bougart was doing the same with Alderman Giradoux. Both men realized it of the other, and how their words had a contested quality.

Hippo said, "That's how come I'm in the habit of listening around. Little bits of chatter and gossip and resentments, they do have a way of accumulating."

"I'll remember that. It's good philosophy for a policeman."

"You want a drink, son?"

"Another day."

"Later it shall be."

"That was quite a performance."

"My little old weekly press conference?"

"Don't you ever worry those reporters are going to catch on that all you're giving them's just a bag of wind?"

"Son, I could take that as an insult. But I'm going to slough it off and pass along something helpful to you."

"What's that?"

"Never worry about reporters wising up. If reporters were acrobats, they'd all be dead."

"I'll remember that, too. Thanks."

"You're most welcome, Booger. Now, you care to state your business?"

"Police work, sir. You know—life and death, good and evil."

Hippo said nothing. He finished off the tumbler of bourbon, opened a desk drawer, pulled out a fresh bottle, and poured himself another drink. *What in blazes is this boy driving at?* He looked up.

Bougart was staring hard at Giradoux, hard enough to force an expression on the alderman's face he knew to be close to the surface. It was only there for a heartbeat, but

Bougart saw it. He had seen it since boyhood: the way a white man crinkles his eyes in even the mildest confrontation with a black man, an expression of combined confusion and contempt. Any halfway observant black man knew when he had a white man on edge.

Further calmed, and pleased with himself, Officer Bougart changed his mind about sitting. He lowered himself into the club chair, took off his stiff-brimmed policeman's cap, and set it in his lap. "Know what I wonder about sometimes, sir?"

"No, I do not."

"Well, how do I say it? By a policeman's lights, the world's a very sick and crazy place."

"I expect lots of folks see by that light."

"Yes, sir, probably so. For instance, you ever notice the violence in a lot of your respectable faces?"

"Look here, Booger—"

Bougart interrupted by tossing his head back and laughing, so long and deep that Hippo could see the little brown freckles that splotched the pink roof of Bougart's mouth. When he was finished laughing, Bougart said, "I wonder if we can truly know whether or not at this very minute you and I are sitting in a madhouse."

Alderman Giradoux rolled his eyes. "Sometime fairly soon, you want to come to the point?"

"All right, Hippo." Bougart saw the crinkle in Giradoux's eye again. It stayed there longer this time. "We found us a murder this afternoon, sir. Down by the Tchoupitoulas Street levee."

"You calling that an unusual occurrence for the neighborhood?"

"That's a funny question."

"Who's laughing, son?"

Bougart thought, There it was—the edge to Hippo's voice to match the uneasy expression. He asked, "You ever heard of a con from Angola name of Cletus Tyler?"

"That'd be the dead man?"

"Know him?"

"Know *of* him anyways. That boy hangs at Shug's over to Jackson Avenue, along with about a thousand other criminals I've known of."

Claude Bougart let the *boy* pass. "So you're familiar with Tyler because you listen around at places like Shug's?"

"I listen anyplace there's talking."

"Listen to this. Clete Tyler got it bad. Got his head just about sliced off at the shoulders, and got his stomach branded."

"What call you got to come here telling me about some jailbird comes to a gruesome end?"

"Supposing you saw the word *moms* spelled out in capital letters. What's that mean to you?"

"Moms? Like in mother?"

"Could be. That's what they branded on Cletus Tyler's fresh-burned belly—*moms.*"

Hippo wiped his lips with a sleeve. He wore the labored expression of a drunk in deep thought. "Who's your commander to this here case, Booger?"

"I'm not exactly assigned."

"Why's this Cletus Tyler any concern of yours?"

"Can't even answer that myself. I'm like you—looking for little scraps."

"You come up here in your damn uniform to pester me when you ain't even been told to snoop?"

"Consider the valuable advice you've given me."

"I got some very supreme advice to impart right now. Don't be po-licing 'round where you ain't been assigned. Hear?" Hippo said this with a calming anger of his own. Then he stood and retrieved his suitcoat from where it was hanging over the arm of his oak and velvet chair.

"Time to call it a day, sir?"

"Oh my, yes." Alderman Giradoux slipped on his coat and waddled toward the archway. Claude Bougart followed. "I'd say it's quitting time for both of us."

"Nice talking with you, sir."

Hippo stopped, turning to face Bougart. He thought for a moment, then spoke carefully.

"I like you, Booger. Truly I do. I want you to enjoy a long and rewarding po-lice career, and I surely would not want to hear about your doing some fool thing that'd imperil your pension. So far you been doing real good, that's what they tell me. But now you come here like this and I can't help but feel trouble's coming for you."

"What kind of trouble?"

"Let's just say, it'll pay you in the long run to wisely remember about fences."

"Fences?"

"Jump over the wrong fence, Booger, and soon you'll be the sorriest kind of cop there is."

"How's that, sir?"

"You're liable to wind up like a country dog in the city. Run, and all them other dogs going bite your ass. Hold still, they going to fuck you."

SEVENTEEN

Their faces were rubber, not skin.

I dropped to the ground, rolling and twisting on my belly through weeds and glass shards as bullets slammed around me and ripped open the top of Perry's shed. And this is what ran through my mind, like a cartoon nightmare: rubber masks . . . children's rubber masks.

Serpentine, you motherfucking morons! This, too, ran through my mind: the bad dream of a U.S. Army drill instructor at Fort Dix in the summer of '65, barking at us draftees slithering down a clay field in Jersey. *Serpentine!* Good old basic training.

I rounded the protective corner of the caged building, my elbows and knees on fire. A bullet pounded into the dirt somewhere behind me. I heard another one slash into steel. Then the sound of the Jeep, fading as it drove away . . .

. . . and away.

I scrambled to my feet for a look at the retreating Jeep, which was kicking up dust and moving fast. No license plate on the back bumper either.

"Perry . . . !"

I called his name as I ran toward the shed.

"Stay back, man—stay the gott-damn hell back!"

I froze. He was right. I was the target, not Perry. Who knew he was hiding in the shed besides Mama and me?

"You're okay?" I called.

"I ain't hit. Ain't that lucky?" Perry laughed, but there was nothing funny about it. A flap of thin steel was sticking up where bullets had struck the shed. "How about you shut up now? Maybe somebody still watching. Maybe listening, too."

He was right again.

I wiped dirt off my clothes and rubbed my limbs where they hurt. My chinos had kept my knees from bleeding, but one of my elbows had not fared well. I picked a broad leaf off a clump of unfamiliar weeds, hoping it was not poison ivy or something like it, and sopped blood off my arm.

I spotted my Yankees cap a few feet from the shed. I went over to pick it up and noticed where two bullets had plowed into the ground nearby. After taking a full-circle look around for the sight of any Jeeps, of which there were none, I picked up a stick from a pile of rubbish. This was the handle from an old paintbrush, actually. I used it to dig down into the bullet holes.

I recovered a pair of 9-millimeter expandable hollow-points, still warm, and shoved them into my back pocket. Somebody was firing slugs that could have opened up spaces in my chest the size of volleyballs.

"Come on out of there, Perry," I called. I looked from the shed back out to Chartres Street, knowing I should leave fast.

"Hell no! They after a white man like that, I ain't about to leave here 'til it's full dark. Go on with you. You got your business, I got mine. Go on, just go tell Vi what I say."

"What about you? Where are you going?"

"That's my worry. Looks like you got a worry all your own."

I had to leave Perry with something to chew on before

walking off, and maybe myself as well. "You say you want to square accounts with this preacher?"

"That's what I say."

"Then you and me, we're on the same side."

"Shoo, what you talk about?"

"Think about it, Perry. Call me at the house sometime."

EIGHTEEN

When Claude Bougart experienced his first jazz funeral he was six years old and living with his family in the dirt lane off Tchoupitoulas Street, ten houses down toward the levee from the Flaggs. On a hazy Thursday August afternoon in the 1950s, a musician neighbor everybody called Smoke was afforded the greatest dignity available to a black man in those days.

Did not Claude's own daddy say as much? As he held tight to his little boy's hand throughout the moaning, musical procession, the elder Bougart wept openly, unashamedly, like all the other black men. And he said to his boy, "Your finest day is when they lay you away."

To Claude, young as he was when he first heard them, those words sounded historical. As a schoolboy, Claude loved history class the best, especially African history. He would eventually read about Ile Gorée, off the coast of Dakar, where his father's father's father's father's father was shoved aboard a ship, in chains; where his people were robbed of their lives, to begin their zombie existence of work and sleep and whippings, and pitifully few fineries—among these jazz, the music of freedom, and the blessed day of death. These lessons absorbed, Claude Bougart fully knew the curse of his father's words; how they connected a black boy in New Orleans of the 1950s with ancestral slaves minted at Ile Gorée in another century.

Neither did Claude Bougart forget the other details of that first funeral day.

Two sable-colored horses, draped in white lace that surely cost Smoke's widow twenty dollars at least, pulled the hearse up Tchoupitoulas toward Jackson Avenue to a little storefront church that Reverend Zebediah Tilton had started up. Driving the hearse was an old man with dark, rough skin. Everybody called him Joe Never Smile due to his reliably cheerless disposition.

Joe Never Smile lived alone in a small house near Basin Street, adjacent to St. Louis Cemetery Number One, which he naturally found convenient. He was always hired for jazz funerals because his horses were so impressive.

"Look at them horses," said Claude's daddy, pointing to the laced team. "See how they crying?"

It was true. As the hearse carrying poor old Smoke passed them by, Claude and all the mourning neighbors and friends saw four big horse eyes streaming with tears. Very impressive. Of course, Miss Hassie and her flapping mouth told anybody who would listen that Joe Never Smile had smeared onion juice in the horses' eyes. Some people believed Miss Hassie, others did not.

Out of respect for the family's loss, the musicians walking along behind Joe Never Smile's hearse doffed their derby hats to the widow in her black veil and all the other family members and friends and neighbors by her side. They gave a solemn wave with their instruments as they stepped along, never cracking a smile nor blowing a note in praise of Smoke's life until the proper time, the moment when Reverend Tilton would bring a close to his service by saying, "Brothers and sisters, now we've reached the end of a perfect death . . ."

After which the music and food would come, in great abundance and exuberance. All this was quite gaudy and high-spirited and brimming with raw emotion. But, still, everybody knew it was a dead man lying up there on Joe Never Smile's hearse, and that his widow was hurting bad that day, and that she would hurt for some time to come. Claude Bougart's first jazz funeral was of the old school, which was to say a family affair.

But now it was different.

Now a grown-up Claude Bougart left City Hall, his arms and legs shaking off the nervousness he had managed to postpone. He crossed over to where he had left his squad car in Poydras Street, and found himself in the middle of what the New Orleans jazz funeral has sadly become: warped by popularity into a means of free mass entertainment—meaning, of course, titillation for tourists.

Joe Never Smile was still the man in charge. But he had changed with the times. He still had his sable horses and his hearse, but in the name of tourism he now wore a tasseled jester's hat and curled-up clown lips. Poydras Street was swarming with out-of-towners lugging video cameras and bitching about the heat and shelling out dollar bills for neon-colored snow cones and pointing and laughing at cute colored kids hanging off traffic signs and tree branches.

Instead of going to his car right away, Officer Bougart walked after the funeral procession as the mourners and gawkers rounded the corner to a storefront church that reminded him of Zebediah Tilton's early days on Jackson Avenue. Bougart walked along sort of absentmindedly, following a tourist whose Budweiser shorts were creeping down into the crack between his buttocks. He thought, So that's why old Joe is smiling now.

At the church, the crowd was pushy. They whispered too loudly and snapped pictures with their disposable Kodaks. A family uniformly dressed in sneakers and jogging suits hooted merrily, pointing at the wasp about to land on a fat lady's hat. Those who had not managed to hog their way into the church waited outside at the curb and picked carnations off the floral wreaths decorating the hearse—souvenirs of their trip to New Orleans, with the bonus of witnessing a bereavement peculiar to the Crescent City. Their counterparts inside the church presumed to stand all too close to family members. None of them troubled to bow their heads as the preacher prayed.

Way up in the front of the church, at the foot of the coffin, one of the lady mourners let her self-control slip ever so slightly. Bougart could barely see above the sea of tourist hats kept resolutely atop of tourist heads. But he clearly understood that a woman had simply given in to the emotional burden that fate had loaded on her. She moaned, then cried, again and again, "Oh, La, no—don't leave me yet! Oh, La . . . !" A detail of amply built usher board ladies dressed in starched white uniforms and armed with feathered fans and smelling salts helped the poor dear. Meanwhile, the gawking crowd passed quizzical glances among themselves, as if such fundamental expressions of loss and sorrow were out of place.

The service was short, if not sweet. When the church emptied and the coffin—a small coffin—was loaded back onto the hearse, Bougart stood watching as the crowd followed the boisterous musicians and the umbrella strutters back to Poydras Street and out of sight. The tourists could go home and gush for years about what they had seen that day in New Orleans.

"Don't seem at all proper, do it?"

Bougart turned at the question. He faced a small, finely featured old man with a red-brown face, silver curls, and a clerical collar. "Hello, Officer." The old man extended a hand. "I'm Pastor Hearn." Bougart gave his name, and the two men shook.

"When I was a kid, these funerals still belonged to us," Bougart said. "You're right, Pastor, it's not proper the way it's gone today. How do they find out about it anyway?"

"Oh, the bellhops and doormen and all, they keep an ear to the ground. Good tips are paid for information about where to find a jazz funeral."

"Yeah, I suppose." Bougart thought about the smallness of the coffin. "Who was it died?"

"Just a boy nobody seemed to know. About twelve years old he was, look more like eight by the size of him. He used to entertain around here for the tourists. Played the banjo and the harmonica. Also he danced some."

"Well, somebody knew him. You had a lady carrying on pretty good up there I noticed."

"No kin of his. She's just one of our members shows up regular at funerals. Some people, they like the feel-good times. Others they like the feel-bad times."

"Who arranged the service?"

Pastor Hearn shrugged his narrow shoulders and started back inside the church. Bougart stopped him and repeated the question.

"Just some other kids nobody know. They come around a few days ago and gave me a little money to open up, and something in the way of a fee, and that's how it was." Again Pastor Hearn shrugged. "Like I say, don't seem at all proper."

"No . . ." Bougart paused as a New Orleans Police Department cruiser drove slowly by. There was a uniform driving. A white man in a suit stared out the passenger window at Bougart. The cruiser came to a stop at the corner of Poydras.

"Officer?"

"Sorry, I was distracted."

"Time was, babies were having babies. Now comes babies *burying* babies."

"I see what you mean."

"Is that so? Then what you going to do about it, Officer Bougart?"

Bougart was further distracted. The white man stepped out from the police cruiser, crossed the street, and headed determinedly in his direction.

"Where's the burial?" Bougart asked the question hurriedly, making Pastor Hearn jumpy. Bougart had to grab him before he could lock the church door behind him. "Where is it?"

"I got no idea what they going to do with that mutilated body."

"Mutilated. How do you mean?"

"That boy had something burned into his belly, like he was nothing but a farm animal."

"You talking about he was branded?"

"That's right." Pastor Hearn crossed himself. "Tell you a little confession, Officer. I know I should've asked, but I was plum afraid of the answers I'd get."

"I guess I can understand that." Bougart turned for a look at the man approaching him and recognized him as one of the deputy commissioners. He could not think of his name right away, but he had a fair idea of what he was about to be told. "Pastor, could we speak again?"

Hearn could see the white man stalking up toward the church. He looked from him to Bougart. "All I did was a job of work here. I don't want any po-lice trouble."

"It won't be official business. I just want to know something about this kid you sent off."

Pastor Hearn crossed himself, and slowly closed the door. "I don't suppose you read poetry, Officer."

"Not on a daily basis."

"Ever hear of Edna St. Vincent Millay?"

"Sure I have."

"She wrote something worth your thinking over."

"What's that?"

" 'Childhood is the kingdom where nobody dies.' "

Bougart had neither time to think nor respond to Pastor Hearn. The white man was on him now, sweating and puffing after his walk over from the cruiser. He flashed a silver star, and said, "Deputy Commissioner R. D. Geary." Bougart smelled tuna on his breath. "You the one they call Booger?"

"I'm the one."

"I want a little word with you."

Pastor Hearn slammed the door of his church.

NINETEEN

Ruby's sister, Janice, was not among the early arrivals. "She loves making her entrance, and she hates seeing a head-sucking mess." That was Ruby's cryptic explanation. Mama added, "Janny got appearances to keep up."

This was how I learned that Janice Flagg was a television reporter, and therefore a local celebrity who naturally took her own sweet time about gatherings of any kind, family included.

The meaning of "head-sucking mess" would dawn more gradually. For the time being, I was happy to be back in Mama's house with all my in-laws to meet, which would be enough to keep me from buckling at the knees whenever I thought about the alternative.

Back on Chartres Street, I had managed to flag down a taxi after being ambushed. I returned home while Mama was still out shopping at her jot-em-down store and Ruby was still snoozing. I had managed a bath in the clawfoot tub set against a wall full of schoolgirl crayon drawings by Ruby and Janice. Also I had myself a cat nap and somehow managed not to dream of three men in a Jeep firing dumdums.

By the way, what was I going to do about that? Call a cop? *You're a man more interested in justice than police work, Neil, which now you see can be opposing forces.* I felt like ringing up Davy Mogaill back in New York. Beyond that—and deciding to keep quiet about the ambush with Ruby and Mama, who had worries of their own—I had only a hazy idea about how to ride the situation. I felt more like a rookie cop on the beat than a seasoned detective. Besides which I was not even walking my beat, I was sleepwalking.

Speaking of sleep, I wished I could have had more. But while I was trying to let something shrewd float into my dreams, Violet's kitchen was filling up with pungent Louisiana cooking smells, which ended any further rest. I left Ruby where she was and went downstairs.

As pleasant as her parlor had been, save for the intrusion of New Orleans' worst, the kitchen was clearly the sweet, warm heart of Mama's house. I watched her for a moment, wielding a long wooden spoon and tending her crowd of steaming pots and pans atop a massive four-burner Magic Chef range. She wore a terry cloth band around her perspiring forehead.

Violet dipped the spoon into the largest of the boiling pots and agitated a school of screaming crustaceans. At least I imagined them screaming. There was besides this a pot full of red beans and rice, redolent of cumin and peppery hot sauce, a skillet overflowing with onions and Creole sausage, chicken jambalaya, and a filé gumbo. Mama had stocked the adjacent sink with the refrigerator's overflow of sodas for the children and Dixie beer for their parents, the bottles wedged into place with plastic bags of ice.

"Whoa!" Violet yelped in surprise at my entrance. "I'm sorry, Neil. Am I making it too hot down here for you to sleep up there?"

"Too fragrant actually." I helped myself to a paper towel from a rack on the counter wall and daubed at my face. "But don't worry about it."

"How's my child?"

"Ruby's getting the sleep she needs."

"That's good. Sit down at the table. Want a beer?"

God, that sounded good.

I took an armless side chair at the long table set beneath a double window that looked out onto a back stoop, a tiny grass yard with a clothesline and a bed of roses and sunflowers, and the alley beyond. A window fan big enough to chill a shop floor gave out an ocean of coolness at the table, near as it was to the busy stove. Except for an empty coffee cup, a pencil, and a copy of the *Times-Picayune* folded open to the crossword puzzle, the table was thickly covered in newspapers anchored at the edges with adhesive tape. I started to ask about this but decided instead to deal with the question of my drinking sooner rather than later.

"Mama, I can't drink."

"Yeah, I know that." She nodded her head. "It's what Ruby say about you."

"Then how come you offered me a beer?"

"Just testing the deviltry in you, son." Mama turned and laughed at me. She made me like it, the same as when Ruby laughed at me. "I know lots of mens have no business drinking, but don't they just guzzle anyhow? Soon's a good lady's back is turned, that is."

"Not my style."

"Glad to hear."

Mama walked slowly across the kitchen toward a tall antique cabinet of painted pine and tin. Next to this was the refrigerator. She opened it and took out a pitcher of lemonade, then took a tumbler down from a cabinet shelf, and poured me a glass. I had the feeling during all this that Mama was considering how best to ask me about my old drinking life.

There are not too many available euphemisms in inquiring about such an unsubtle thing as drunkenness. Mama eventually concluded as much. She set down the glass of lemonade in front of me, and straight out asked, "Why'd you finally decide to quit your nasty drinking style?"

"It came to me that I couldn't drown my problems in drink. Which wasn't so hard to figure, since I noticed my problems knew how to swim."

"You all right, Neil. That's about as good and true as a tough answer gets."

"Thanks." I emptied half my glass.

There was a knock at the kitchen door. Through the heavy screen, I saw the outline of a figure on the stoop, somebody the size of a Buick in a dress, with a boxy purse dangling off one arm. I smelled a cigar and figured my nose was having a little fun with me.

"Vi, you there?" The figure on the stoop called through the screen. The voice sounded like the bass section of a church choir. "Am I the first to drop by?"

"No, it's just like all the damn time—you the second thing attracted to all this food I cooked up," Violet answered. She crossed over to the door and unlatched it. "First thing's the flies."

About the cigar, it turned out I was right. The smoky cheroot rode into the kitchen clamped between dark brown lips that looked like a horizontal pair of roasted kielbasas nestled below a curly black mustache, which matched a headful of close-cropped hair. Also I was right about the dress, a dark blue cotton number sheathed in pale blue organdy. What I thought was a purse turned out to be a plumber's toolbox.

"This is Uncle Bud," Mama said. The introduction did nothing to explain the matter of a burly cigar-chomping plumber dressed for a date with the ladies' bridge club. Uncle Bud stuck out a calloused paw, and we shook.

"So you're Neil Hockaday, our little Ruby's new husband." Uncle Bud puffed some clouds out of his cigar, then removed it from his mouth, lifted a leg and tamped out the butt against the soggy bottom of a rubber-soled boot. He stuffed the cigar down the front of his dress for later. "Vi told me some about you. Says you're a po-liceman up in New York."

"That's right. And you're a . . . plumber?"

"Finest damn plumber in all New Orleans."

"Bud's half-brother to my late Willis," Mama said. She patted Bud's grandly protruding stomach "Bud's what you call a cook's fright."

"Now come on, honey—I'm a cook's delight." Uncle Bud's weighty box of screwdrivers and steel washers and pipe wrenches clanked as he set it down on the floor. He pulled out a chair, lifted his skirt, and sat down at the table, smoothing newspapers under his sturdy forearms. "What's for starters, Vi?"

Mama dished up beans and rice and set this down in front of Bud, along with a fork and some chewy French bread. "Where your wig at?" She asked this of him as if it were a perfectly ordinary question.

"Ain't a comfortable day for the topper. I be like a worm in hot ashes if I's to run around under that wig today. Got it over there in my toolbox, though. You know, case of emergency."

"What color's the wig?" I tried sounding nonchalant.

"Chestnut brown," Bud said politely. "With highlights of honey blonde."

"Ruby hasn't told you much about the family, has she?" Mama asked.

"She left out some episodes."

"Maybe you want to tell Neil about the dress and all?" Mama suggested to Bud. She shot me a quick roll of her eyes that I took to mean that by-and-by all would become clear. Mama took an iced bottle of Dixie out of the sink and gave it to Bud. He flicked off the seal cap with a thumb, like it was nothing more than a penny resting atop the bottleneck.

Uncle Bud drank down the better part of his beer, then told me, "Well, you know, bein' a po-lice. A man got to feel safe and sound."

"Nothing like a dress for security."

" 'Specially when the Klan's out for you."

"The Klan?"

"Bud had a little run-in one time up to Mississippi," Mama said.

"Little run-in she call it." Uncle Bud rubbed his neck with the cool Dixie bottle. "My throat's still warm from the rope they put 'round it."

"You escaped a lynching?" I asked Bud. I looked over at Mama. She shrugged.

"I had them ofays trippin' all over they sheets chasin' after me through the woods." Bud was drooling beer slightly. "I run away so fast my legs near melted. Ran clear down to here from Hattiesburg. They still be lookin' to find ol' Bud."

"So the wig and the dress? That's your disguise?"

"Well, they ain't caught me yet." Bud picked up his fork and started in on the beans and rice.

"Maybe you living on borrowed time," Mama said darkly.

"What's that s'posed to mean?"

"You be eating so much you liable to lose that girly figure of yours."

Bud, his face stricken, dropped his fork.

"Shoo," Mama said, "if I thought of that some years ago I could have saved me a boatload of grocery expense."

"I got to go rest, Vi." Head in his hands, Bud lumbered off into the parlor, where I heard him fall into the couch like a freshly axed tree.

"Uncle Bud's story, it's for real?" I asked Mama.

"Ask him more about it if you want. Bud don't take up the rest of your life telling you his lynching tale, he'll start in on the night the Martians came swooped down from the sky and took him for a ride in their funny plane."

"I get your drift. Tell me something, though. Don't his customers think it's a little strange when their plumber shows up in a dress to unclog a drain?"

"Honey, this here's New Orleans. Nobody's going to pay no mind to a trifling thing like that."

The subject of Uncle Bud seemed at a natural close, besides which we could hear him snoring contentedly. So I asked Mama to further illuminate another family legend, namely that of her sister, Rose, and Toby Jones.

"Well, I'll tell you if you sure you want to hear." Mama picked up a bowl full of cooked crabs she had cooling off in tap water, and came over to sit down beside me at the table to shuck them. "Going to use the meat for an étouffée," she explained. I studied her technique for a few minutes, and then we shucked together.

"Poor Rose—bless her, God." Mama shook her head back and forth. "That girl went to church every day, and prayed for the impossible dream."

"What was that?"

"She want to pass."

"For white?"

"That kind of sorry business, that's right. Down here black folks want to be uppity class about it, they call it by the French—*passant blanc.* That's from back in the old days of what they call the New Orleans *gens de couleur.*"

"People of color."

"Shoo, what you know about talking French?"

"*Cela n'a pas d'importance.*"

"Whatever you say, I guess. Anyhow, we got regular American names for gals like Rose. Briquet, yalla, red, mariny, bright. Redbone, too, but that ain't considered polite. Some old Creole folks, they say mulatto or quadroon or octoroon. All them terms, ain't it terrible?"

"How so?"

"It's depressing for us Negroes being all churned up on the insides on account of what shade we born with on the outside. It's a sickness."

"Uncle Bud's got it bad."

"Yeah, you right. I'd say Bud and Rose, they was cursed the worst."

"What happened to Rose?"

"Rose was a yellow gal, pretty as Lena Horne. Thought she had talent to go along with the looks. But honest, she wasn't no eye-popper in either of them departments. Pretty enough for St. Francisville, even New Orleans, and Rose'd carry a tune. But New York and Hollywood? I'm telling you, Rose was the only one ever thought she'd travel well."

"She lived in New York?"

"Mostly she died there, thanks to some high-stepper come down here at Mardi Gras and dragged her back north. He was white." Mama Violet stopped shucking and gave me a look I had to believe was for the white man who wrecked her sister's life. "Ruby never told you about that ugliness with Rose up there in New York?"

I thought, So maybe this is what has Ruby on her emotional loop-the-loop? The inescapable ghost of Rose Duclat? Here was Ruby, after all—back in the projects where she started; a colored girl, as she would say, dreaming of show business in New York; a colored girl mixed up with a white man.

"Not in so many words."

"Don't that just figure?"

"Anyway, what about Rose?"

"Well, she just thought she was good as biscuits in the morning. Used to tuck a gardenia in her hair—"

"Like Billie Holiday."

"That's right. And like I told you, she'd sing all Billie's tunes at Nikki's Dockside Club. Wasn't a professional engagement, though."

"She didn't get paid?"

"All Rose ever got was free drinks and disgusting propositions. And like I also told you, she always took little Perry with. Rose, she let the mens buy soda pops for the boy so long's he never told Toby about Rose singing at Nikki's."

"What did Toby think Rose was doing?"

"Oh, just some little conjure tricks for the old ladies in Algiers. That or else over to Jackson Square singing for coins. Now, Toby don't mind his Rose being a backstreet *voudouienne,* and he don't mind her singing little songs for fool tourists. But any otherwise, he don't want Rose shaking her stuff or such-like."

"He was a jealous man?"

"Ain't you all?" Mama laughed. She touched my arm affectionately. "But serious, Neil—that Toby Jones, he wasn't just ordinary jealous. Brute mean is what he was. I'll give you a for instance. Perry didn't like calling him Daddy, he call him Toby. So Toby he put cigarettes to little Perry skin until the boy'd show respect by saying Daddy."

"I'd like to meet this guy in a squad room."

"Wouldn't do no good now. Anyhow, my Willis more a daddy to Perry than Toby ever was. Perry even grow up looking like Willis."

"This Toby's still around?"

"Toby too evil to die."

"At some point Rose left him for good?"

"Year Perry turned seventeen's when it was. Like I say, this fancy white man come through town one Mardi Gras. I can't tell you his name, or how Rose and him met up. All I know, one day I get a letter from Rose saying how she's living the Manhattan high life."

"But it turned out to be the low life."

"How'd you know?"

"It's an old story I've seen play out a few times."

"I give Perry money for the train to go see his mama up in New York. I say *give,* since *loan* is a word Perry never heard about."

"He found her?"

"In a Harlem whorehouse. The boy come back here hurt as bad as I ever seen anybody hurt. Perry he didn't talk to nobody for months. Then we got this letter. The New York City health department writes me as next of kin, saying Rose Duclat's about to be buried someplace called Hart Island unless I claim the body."

"What was the cause of death?"

"Overdose of heroin." A tear rolled down Mama's eye. She wiped it away. "With my husband sick like he was, we didn't have a spare dollar in the house. No way I could fetch home a body from a thousand miles up in New York, not even for my onliest sister. Poor Rose. Well, that's a old story, too, I suppose."

"I suppose."

"What's that Hart Island place?" Mama asked.

"Potter's field, New York style."

We looked up from our crab shucking to the window. The sky rumbled from somewhere far off. "Rain's going to be coming faster than you imagine now," Mama said. "That's Louisiana style. Be a little gray and windy for a spell, but that don't last long. Things grow still as a dead dog, then the sky go fiercely black. Then the rain come down hard as a Bible story."

TWENTY

Perry looked up at the darkening sky through an open flap bullets had made in the shed roof. He laughed, and sighed, "Every coffin has a silver lining."

Rain came, as fast as the thought of rain.

Perry scooted across the ground on his haunches, out of the way of a cold stream that shot through the roof like tap water pouring out from a broken spigot. The dirt floor quickly soaked up the rain, until it grew overly saturated. Perry watched silted water rise slowly, spreading higher and higher through the shed.

He could not sleep here. Worms would be drawling up from the damp earth below to get air from the surface of the soil, and this would attract rats. Perry would sooner face gunfire again than rats.

But where to sleep? No point in crossing over to Algiers. If Toby had heard the news of Clete's murder, he would call up the police and turn in his own son. Aunt Vi's house? The police would be watching the place close.

. . . Wait! Why not the least likely place?

Perry waited until the last light of day gave over to the purple shadows of a New Orleans night, and until the rain eased into a fine drizzle. He then pushed open the shed door and crawled outside.

One good thing about the rain. Most people would be settled into their homes and unlikely to venture out for the rest of the evening. This made walking the streets as a wanted man ever so much easier.

He started walking west along Chartres Street toward the Quarter. Perry figured the police had posted everything from Tchoupitoulas Street north along the levee. He was shaking from the need of a Pall Mall and a pull of whiskey, but he kept moving along, shaking off cravings. He crossed through the French Market and up along Esplanade to St. Bernard Avenue.

Nearly an hour later, Perry had reached another shed. This one was in the back parking lot of the Land of Dreams Tabernacle. He knelt to the pavement, lit a match, and peeked under the shed door. Sure enough, Reverend Tilton's car was still there—his prized Rolls-Royce Silver Shadow.

Perry waited, hidden behind the shed. Fifteen minutes passed and then Tilton appeared in the back door of the church, his heavy shoulders cloaked in one of those high-priced raincoats with brass rings on the belt. Next to him was that skinny acolyte girl, Sister Constance.

Tilton stood at the top of a small porch leading to the parking lot. Perry could clearly see the minister and the girl, standing for a moment under a yellow light hanging over the door in the shape of a half-moon. Sister Constance looked up at the light, not at Tilton. Perry saw how pretty she was, especially now, standing in the artificial moonlight. He thought of her in a protective and fatherly way, something new to him. And thinking this way caused him a rush of regret for the wasted years of his life.

"Give us a kiss, then," Tilton said to the girl.

Sister turned her cheek. The fat preacher man planted his mouth on her neck, like he was a vampire. Perry heard smacking against girl flesh. His fists clenched.

Tilton stepped back. The girl relaxed, free of Zeb Tilton's

embrace. But then Tilton took hold of her thin shoulders, and in a voice hoarse from liquor he demanded, "Lips, my lady-child. Give your dear minister them sweet, young, ever-loving lips. Give us that pretty pink tongue, too."

Perry struggled against a choking anger by telling himself, again and again, It's no good to take him out now—no good! I got to beat him another way—got to beat him for once and for all!

After Tilton got what he wanted—how was Sister Constance to resist his needs?—he started down from the porch toward the shed. Perry slinked back around the shed, out of sight. Tilton took keys from a pocket of his raincoat, opened the shed, and started up the Rolls-Royce.

Sister Constance closed the door when Tilton and the Rolls had driven off. She started slowly back up the stairs, walking like an old lady with a backache. She turned when Perry stepped on a patch of gravel.

"Who that?" she called out.

It was Perry's intention to answer, but for a moment he could only look at the dark girl in the pale light, softened by the misty remnants of the storm. Constance put a hand up over her eyes and scanned the parking lot. Then she did something that Perry thought absolutely remarkable.

Constance sat down on the top step of the porch, pulled her knees to her chest, and hugged them. Just like Perry always did when the visions came. He wondered if she had visions.

"Sister . . . ?" he called.

The girl turned toward the sound of his voice.

"You don't got to be afraid."

"I ain't afraid, Mister Whoever-you-are."

Perry stepped from around the shed and walked into the light. "Perry Duclat's my name. You heard of me?"

"I don't know." Constance did not move, she did not even blink. "Should I've heard of you?"

"Well, you will soon. The po-lice looking for me."

"For what?"

"Killing a man."

"You do that?"

"No."

"Well, what you be doing here?"

"Came to see you, Sister."

"Who you s'posed to kill anyhow?"

"Man named Cletus Tyler. Me and Clete, we was up to Angola together."

"Now I remember, I seen it on the TV news." Constance shifted her hands from around her knees to either side of her hips, as if bracing herself in the event she had to jump up and run away from this hunted man who appeared from the shadows. Perry took no offense, it was only natural. "This Tyler man, he was killed bad the news say."

"That's right, but I didn't do him."

"How'm I s'posed to know whether you honest or not?"

"All depends on if you believe in the presumption of innocence."

"Say what?"

"A man's suspected of something, you got to figure he's innocent until he's proved guilty. Not that it matters where a black man's concerned, but at least that's what it says in the Constitution."

"It's something like respect?"

"That's a good way of putting it. I told you I didn't do what the po-lice think I did. I spoke the truth, but the truth is not respected from a man like me. Before I'm believed, see, the truth's got to come from a liar—which is whoever it was *did* kill Cletus Tyler. That's the way it goes. They ain't going to believe me 'til some lying killer backs up what I say."

"What if the liar never speaks up? What if they catch you, go ahead and hang the crime on you?"

"I know that I am not the killer."

"Like you say, maybe that don't matter. What if they set you down and give you the lethal injection anyhow."

"Then I would go to my death without begging for my

life. I would not humiliate myself that way. I will not let the man break me."

"Mister, you an interesting man to listen to. But I can't see why you telling me all this."

"You're a pretty girl in a trap, ain't that a fact?"

Sister Constance lowered her head.

"Don't be shamed, you can't help it." Perry took a step closer to the girl "You got no place but this place, do you?"

"No." The girl's voice was sad in the moist black night.

"What goes on with you and Zeb Tilton, it ain't your fault."

"I hate him."

"I understand."

"Oh, yeah? What you know about it?"

"Same as everybody owns eyes, ears, and a good heart knows. The question is, girl, what you going to do about it?"

"No idea."

"You asked me twice now what I'm doing here. I'm going to tell you." Perry stepped near the girl. He put out his hand and she took it. "I need your help, girl."

"Doing what?"

"Waking people up to things been wrong for a long, long time."

"You talking dangerous."

"I surely am. I'm saying no way folks should keep on forgiving those who trespass against them. I'm saying people got to pay what they owe. And Sister, I'm saying the debt is high."

TWENTY-ONE

Back when we were getting our asses whipped in Vietnam by a short old man with a stringy wisp of chin hairs who understood the contradictions of America—he venerated the Declaration of Independence, and was refused a haircut by a Boston barber—I mostly spent my R and R leave time in Bangkok. Which is the city where fleshpots were invented, not that I myself ever knew of such things.

There was I, halfway around the world in Indochina, a teenage harp from Holy Cross parish struggling mightily to obey the sexual code of the Church. It would be some years yet before I figured out that nobody should take sexual advice from nuns or priests—nor even His Holiness the Bishop of Rome, Vicar of Christ—for the simple reason that if these people knew anything about it, they shouldn't. Nonetheless, my indoctrination had been fierce. To this day my ears ring with Sister Bertice's earliest warning to us frisky boys of Holy Cross: *Touch yourself and the saints weep!* Hotly remembering this and other warnings, I was spared wicked congress with sloe-eyed femininity.

Luckily, Bangkok held other sensual attractions. The tattoo parlors I did not care about. But I did smoke a stunning amount of excellent hashish in the city's dope dens. And I may well have drunk enough booze to fill up the Gulf of Siam. Also in those days I became a gourmand, even something of an epicure. Both these qualities were impossible back home in Hell's Kitchen, a neighborhood of cabbage spiced with Colman's dry mustard, some thirty different ways of eating potatoes, bread and butter, and earnestly boiled beef. All that and Irish soda bread besides, prized for its throat-scorching dryness.

But, oh—Bangkok! Here was the city to cure my stunted Irish tongue. Noodles baked in the shape of birds' nests, doves' eggs spun into crisp confections, the spices of two millennia.

Once, a delegation of us Yanks found a back alley bistro specializing in what I had thought was the most exotic entrée there could ever be. A waiter brought to our tableside a contraption that appeared to be a four-foot-high oak stand upon which a fern plant might usually be perched. But instead of a leafy fern, the top of the stand held a device of circular wood blocks and leather straps. These blocks and straps held in place the head of a small monkey, dazed from a fresh clouting back in the kitchen. Clamped at the head, the monkey's hairy, quivering body hung suspended inside the stand. The waiter then produced a small saw, cut open the monkey's head, and ladled warm, bloody, living brains over the watercress on our plates.

I could not help but remember about Thai cuisine as I learned the meaning of "mess" in Mama Violet's New Orleans kitchen. For here was where a twenty-five-pound heap of crawfish had recently met their end in a vat of Zatarain's crab boil.

And now here was I, surrounded by the first wave of newly met in-laws and doing my part to devour the mound of steaming hot crawfish dumped into the middle of the newspapers spread all over the tabletop. Twelve grabby hands—two of them pale white, ten others various shades of brown—snapped up red boiled creatures that looked like miniature lobsters.

We ate, all of us, in greedy communion. The law of the swiftest was at work in this meal. Also I had to learn the art of cracking open brittle shells for the sweet specks of meat inside.

It was halfway into the mess when I thought about the unfortunate Bangkok monkey. This memory was interrupted by the bustling entrance of a woman wearing expensive sunglasses despite its being an hour into evening. She made it clear that she knew perfectly well what the man sitting on my left was about to do with the crawfish skull poised in front of his mouth, the man being Cousin Teddy the Torch.

Teddy slipped the beady-eyed delicacy between his lips, glistening red from salty crab boil, and inhaled. The woman in the shades pointed an accusing finger at him, and said, "Oh, ish!"

"What you . . . ?" This was all Teddy was capable of saying, since his mouth was full of something mushy as the mud from whence it had come.

"Head-sucking fool!" she hollered. "You want to swallow that mess of crawfish brains, you going to wind up being soft in your own damn head!"

"Well, there she is—my little sister," Ruby whispered to me, polishing off a bit of crawfish meat and poking my ribs with an elbow. She called out to Janice, "Hi there, Janny dearest."

Janice glowered at Ruby through dark glasses. She moved along to the opposite end of the table and busied herself by kissing everybody hello, leaving Ruby and me for last and Cousin Teddy for never.

Not only had she interrupted my monkey reverie, but Janice had also interrupted Teddy the Torch. He had been regaling the table with the retelling of a legend. Of course it was my first time hearing the story, one more of the family gems that Ruby had withheld from me. Everybody else had no doubt heard the story a hundred times, though it did not seem to diminish their enjoyment now.

Teddy was cousin to Ruby and Janice on the Flagg side. His head was an oil field of pomade, and he had a spongy face the color of peanut butter. I imagined if I was to touch his face it might actually feel like peanut butter, too. I have noticed that faces get that way when they are finally tired out from vices: too many cigarettes maybe, certainly too many days of liquor or drugs.

A lot of people must have observed the same about Teddy, so many that he had developed the habit of being the first one to comment on his appearance. Such as right after we were introduced, when Teddy said, "I got the kind of face where people who don't even know me come up and say, What's wrong?"

Teddy worked with some kind of computer at the dog pound. He told me what kind, but I understand nothing about machines that are smarter than I am. Anyway, the dog pound gig was a day job. His show business vocation had earned him the sobriquet Teddy the Torch.

"Don't do too much singing and dancing anymore, though," Teddy explained. "Just a little now and then. Still do choreography, and my good deeds. Like for instance, I'm trying to talk cousin Perry into taking the test for a job at the pound. Also I direct the choir at Zeb Tilton's church. Yeah, I had to cut way back on actual artistic performances—after the accident."

The "accident" was ten years ago on the Fourth of July. Teddy was the center man in a near-nude, five-man dance line at a Bourbon Street club called Boys! Boys! Boys!—Three-Bs for short—and that year he came up with the idea of ending the regular floor show with a patriotic pièce de résistance in commemoration of Independence Day.

"Go on, tell Ruby husband what you did, fool!"

Teddy's orders came from Mama's neighbor, old Miss Minnie Sue. ("Practically another sister to me," Mama said when I shook the old lady's spidery brown hand after being introduced. "Shoo—I'm old enough to be Vi mama!" Miss Minnie said. She had twin black warts on her chin, one of them sprouting a clump of gray hair. "I'm so damn old I count my teeth every time I got to bite the bullet.")

Quite the innovative showman, Teddy explained that part of his scanty costume included a dozen sparklers stuffed into his nether cheeks, which would be set ablaze by one of the other dancers when the attention of the audience was drawn to the slam-bang crest of the orchestra's drum solo. Then, as the drummer came down from his heights by tapping on the snare rims, the blue light would fall dramatically on Teddy. Teddy was to twirl around, bend over, and pull away a rear flap of silver lamé, surprising the audience with a festive burst of multicolored sparks.

"Didn't quite work out the way I planned it in my head," Teddy said. With a straight face he said this. People who wind up with what's-wrong faces tend to develop unusual logic systems. They do not laugh at the right places, for instance.

"Gawd a'mighty, I'll say it didn't work out!" Miss Minnie whooped, clapping her thin hands together, nodding yes to Uncle Bud when he held up the offer of a long-necked bottle of Dixie beer. "The Negro's asshole caught fire from them sparklers! That's why we all calling him Teddy the Torch!"

The table rolled with laughter, Teddy laughing as hard as anyone. I turned to Ruby during all this merriment and asked, "How come you never told me any of this stuff?" But she was laughing so much herself she could not make out the question. Which was just as well. It was enough to see the improvement in Ruby's mood.

"So they run Teddy down to Charity Hospital emergency room," Uncle Bud said when he could be heard. He popped the Dixie cap with his sturdy thumb and handed the bottle to Miss Minnie, who put it to her lips and slugged back the beer as if she had been drinking with sailors most of her life. "Teddy, he stay over in the burn unit a couple, three days 'til his rump healed."

"A harrowing story," I said to Teddy.

"Yeah, well, you know—all part of my wild years." Teddy sniffed, and wiped his nose with some fingers, a residual habit from white powder days. "I quit all that bad stuff—the drinking, the sex, the drugs. Especially the drugs. They started creeping me day and night."

"That can happen," I said.

"Sure, but I'm not saying all that excess wasn't fun. It was. I quit, but—big old *but* here—I never robbed anybody, never murdered or raped anybody. And never did I lose a job or show up late when somebody was expecting me. All those years of the drugs and all, I laughed my ass off and had a great time." Teddy looked up to Janice, who was finally approaching our end of the table, and asked her, "So where's my TV commercial?"

"I don't even want to talk to a head-sucker." Janice curled her lips and turned from Teddy. She took off the Ray-Bans and looked at me.

She was an attractive woman with a kindly face, her disdain for poor head-sucking Cousin Teddy notwithstanding. She was quite tall, taller than a lot of men, but seemed untroubled about that, since I noticed she was wearing high heels. She had big intelligent eyes the color of licorice, and cinnamon skin with freckles lightly sprayed over high cheekbones. After one look at her up close I would have wagered big money on a cop hunch that Janice Flagg was the type of attractive woman who draws wrong numbers for men pretty much all the time.

Teddy cracked open another crawfish and slurped down more cooked brains. Janice ignored the disgusting act. After giving me the once-over, she said to her sister, "Hello there, Ruby. You're looking real good. So's the new boyfriend. I could sit down in his lap and say hi—or else maybe you could introduce us."

Ruby turned to me, and said, "Any wonder now why I've kept my little family secrets?"

I wiped my fingers on the tabletop newspapers, stood up,

and offered a semiclean hand to Janice. "The name's Neil Hockaday." Janice took my hand and would not let it go.

"Well, well," she said, "you're surely different from all Ruby's other beaux."

"That's right, we got married." Janice let go of me. I sat down. Ruby laughed.

I certainly had not meant to fuel anything between competitive sisters, but that was exactly what my crack about marriage might have done for one cheap, fleeting moment. I regretted the marriage remark because I felt a little sorry for Janice. From experience I know a lonesome soul when I see one. Like her freckles, solitude also marked Janice's face. Solitude would be fine if only a person could choose the people to avoid.

"I hear you're some kind of policeman up in New York," Janice said. This was a statement, but Janice had one of those southern inflections where everything sounds like a question.

"Neil's a detective," Mama said. "He work for this special unit called SCUM something-or-other."

"It stands for Street Crimes Unit—Manhattan," I said.

Janice glanced at Ruby and smiled. If a cat could smile before snatching up a mouse, it would look like Janice's smile. She said to me, "Let's see now, I don't believe Ruby ever had particularly warm feelings for policemen."

"Janny, why you want to go saying a thing that?" Mama asked.

"Oh, I didn't mean—"

"Janny needs a man, Mama," Ruby said, calmly interrupting her sister. "We should try to understand her bitterness and overlook the foolish things she says."

"La, you two girls!" Mama said. "I can't stand it. Why don't y'all get it out of your systems—go back out to the alley and scuffle like you used to?"

"Vi honey, they grown womens now," Miss Minnie said. "Womens got eviler ways of fighting than rolling in the dirt. Besides, they entertaining us."

"My life's too busy for me to be fretting about boyfriends or husbands," Janice said, ignoring both her mother and Miss Minnie. She seemed to be addressing everybody at the table, as though they were an unseen television audience. Like any family watching television, everybody seemed to have better things to do. Janice looked specifically at Ruby, and said, "Besides, for your information I got me a BMW."

"She doesn't mean a car," Ruby said, turning to me. "She means BMW—black man working. A little dig at me for marrying whitey."

"No, it is *not,*" Janice protested.

"By the way, where is your BMW tonight?" Ruby asked.

"Well, right at this minute he's got things to do."

"He's real good to you?"

"He's a doll."

Mama asked, "How come I never met this here doll of yours, Janny?"

"Be patient, Mama. You will."

"I hope you'll bring him by while my husband and I are still here in New Orleans visiting," Ruby said in a butter-melting way. "What's BMW's name anyway, Janny? What's he like?"

"Oh, he's a very fine man, very successful. We got so much in common, you know. Haven't even had our first fight. Seems we agree on everything."

"Two people shouldn't agree on everything," Ruby said, sticking her sister unmercifully. "If they did, one of them would be unnecessary. Don't you think so?"

"I'm going to fix me a serving of Mama's good food, that's what I think." Janice picked up a plate from the table and huffed over to the Magic Chef range and helped herself to the étouffé. Then she found a spot to sit, as far from Ruby as possible.

"Still didn't get that fine boyfriend's name," Ruby called across the table.

Janice pretended to be interested in something Uncle Bud was saying.

"Janny?" Ruby persisted.

"Oh—what?"

"The name. Tell us your boyfriend's name."

"Let's just say, maybe he's Mr. Right."

Miss Minnie clapped her hands together again and whooped some more. "Janny, you remember that first time you said you tell us you found a dreamboat man?"

Janice groaned.

Miss Minnie turned to me. "She just a young thing with her first-time case of love. Nobody too picky when they got a case of the screaming thigh sweats. Janny sure as hell wasn't picky. It was right here in this kitchen, she say, 'I've found Mr. Right, only I think he might be an abusive alcoholic.' "

Teddy led the table in chortling over this latest remembrance. And eventually Janice, in spite of herself and her grand entrance shot to hell by Ruby, joined the laughter.

And this was how the grown-up sisters managed to get the inevitable scuffling out of their systems. So this is family, I thought. So help me, I loved it.

And so help me, I worried about the family member nobody joked about—Perry. I hoped he would call.

Over the course of several hours and several more arrivals, the whole twenty-five pounds of crawfish and nearly all the rest of Mama's spread vanished. Then when everybody was satisfied and variously slumped into sofas and chairs and rubbing their bellies and talking about all the food they liked that had not liked them in return, Mama opened up her photograph albums. She pronounced her collection "my treasure" and piled several albums into my lap, with the others set on the floor at my feet for later.

"You don't have to look at each and every one of these Negroes you don't want to," Mama said, sitting next to me on the couch and looking on. Ruby sat on my other side, and Janice had the easy chair. "Just page through and find the Ruby pictures. Oh, she and Janny they quite the little camera hounds."

Ruby was not so enthusiastic as I was when I would come across her kid pictures, mostly black-and-white snapshots tucked into tidy slots of the heavy photo album pages. I particularly enjoyed the picture of Ruby when she was a seven-year-old flower girl at a family wedding, marching up the aisle in a floor-length dress over crinolines and her famous cat-eye glasses. Her face was uptilted and those cat-eye specs were a glare of camera flash, and her little chin looked to be covered in butter.

"You take that picture home to New York with you if you want," Mama offered. Ruby said no thanks, but I snatched it off the album page and put it in my pocket. "I'll have it copied at a camera shop I know, then I'll return the original," I promised Mama.

"Well then, take any of them strikes you."

So I helped myself to three more. There was the one of Ruby and Janice mugging on the kitchen stoop in their blouses and jumpers, hands insolently on their hips, as if they were the models they saw in the fashion magazines. And a snap of Ruby at nine or ten in her Sunday-go-to-church clothes. And that high school graduation portrait, Ruby in her angora sweater and her Afro. The cat-eye specs were gone by then.

"Look at this one," I said to Ruby, pointing to another snap of her in her high school years. "What's this?"

"Nothing." Ruby flipped the page.

"Let's see." I turned the page back.

"Please, Hock. Enough!"

"Oh, that one's when Ruby went to her prom," Mama said. Ruby glared at her. "Don't she look gorgeous in that green satin dress, though? I like the way she done her hair for the prom. Wasn't like a bush."

"Gracious, big sister, you surely must have won all the

votes for the title of 'Miss Tits' that night," Janice said, recognizing the photo even though she was looking at it upside-down. Suddenly, a lot of Ruby's little boy cousins who had been wrestling on the floor became interested in the family album. "Look how you forgot about wearing a bra under that scoop-neck drapey thing. And who's that boy in the lime green thing with the big velvet lapels? Probably he rented it out of Petey's Tuxedo Emporium over on Claiborne at the overpass."

"Shoo, you ought to know Claude Bougart when you looking at him," Mama said. "That fine yellow boy they call Booger, he had the glad eye for both you girls one time or the other."

"Well, I called him Claude—and he was an awful nice guy." She said to Ruby, "Guess what happened to Claude."

"Just tell me why don't you?"

"He's a policeman."

"Where? Here in New Orleans?"

"That's right, Ruby. Your prom date is now Patrolman Claude Bougart of the NOPD." Janice smiled a mouse-snatcher smile, letting the irony sink in. She asked me, "Isn't that just a remarkable coincidence, you and Claude being officers of the law and all?"

"Remarkable I don't know," Ruby said. "But if Claude's single, maybe you should give him a call sometime."

"Why'd I do that?"

"Claude being a BMW and all."

"Oh, you!"

What happened next was a remarkable coincidence. This being in the person of the next guest to walk through Mama's front door. Not so much a guest as a family friend who had not been around to call in some time.

An older version of the Claude Bougart from the prom picture now stood in front of Ruby and me. Bougart was wearing neither a lime green rental tux nor police blue. Instead he wore a Saints warm-up jacket, a T-shirt, and neatly pressed jeans. He took off his baseball cap as he entered the parlor. I have to like a man who wears a baseball cap.

"Evening, Miz Violet," he had said, greeting the head of the house. He nodded hello to a few more whom he knew. Then he crossed the room toward Ruby, as if hypnotized.

He gave me a look of passing wonder. But it was clear to the point of awkward that Ruby was his true focus.

Ruby broke a weighted silence.

"It's been so long, Claude." Ruby held out her hands. Claude bent down and kissed the backs of her fingers. Janice let out a swoony sound at this. Ruby smiled at her, and something in code passed between sisters. "Tell me what I want to hear, Janny."

"I'm jealous."

"Thank you, Janny."

"All this time, Ruby . . ." Claude stopped. His voice did not crack, but maybe it would have if he had not paused. The poor guy sounded as if he had just run up and down Gibson Street about ten times. "I just want to say, Ruby—if pretty is a minute, you're a whole hour."

"Oh!" Janice said, clutching at her heart, obliging Ruby again. "I am *so* jealous!"

"Claude Bougart, you're still the charmer," Ruby said. "Tell me what's new in your life."

"Not so much."

"I hear you're with the police department."

"That's true." There was nothing close to pride in Claude's voice as he said this. Which I could understand after meeting Eckles and Mueller, which I could further understand, given the equally odious thought of King Kong Kowalski in my own department. "I know you're living up in New York. What else is new with you?"

"Well," Ruby said, taking my arm, "you see why we're here visiting."

"No . . ." Claude stopped talking then, frozen by the sad

truth that Ruby Flagg was spoken for. It was not hard to read Claude's mind.

The tension was thick between Claude and me. For as Claude Bougart stared at me—of all things, Ruby's husband—I realized one of those moments that African-American men know on a daily basis: that moment when a man knows full well that the only relevant thing about him, according to the other man staring at him, is the accident of his race.

Compounding my discomfort was the fact that all my in-laws had stopped talking to watch the prickly encounter between Claude and me. I caught sight of Uncle Bud with his plumber's fingers stuck firmly in his ears, like he was expecting something to explode.

Ruby said, "Claude, I guess I didn't—"

"How you doing, friend?" I said. Somebody had to interrupt Ruby, since she was hot in the face. "I'm Neil Hockaday." I put out my hand. If it had been anything other than somebody's hand that Claude took hold of now, he probably would have dropped it.

"I'm . . . Claude Bougart. Well, Ruby already said my name."

"Yes, I guess she did. Ruby and I were married earlier this year. Happy to meet you, Claude."

Janice greatly enjoyed the clumsy exchange. She moved to Claude's side, folded an arm into his, and said, "Did you know that Ruby's husband here's a policeman, too? Now isn't that just too much? He works for this unfortunately named outfit called SCUM. That's an acronym."

"He's a cop?" Claude turned toward me. "Where at, up to New York?"

"Detective, first grade. Street Crimes Unit—Manhattan."

"Claude, wait a minute," Ruby said. "You didn't know until right now that I was down here visiting with my husband?"

"No."

"So how come you happened to drop by tonight?"

Claude looked over to Mama, who was looking down at

her hands, which she held folded in her lap. He said to everybody listening, "I'm not in uniform."

Mama lifted her head. "But you come about Perry?"

Claude started to say something to her but then changed his mind. He turned to me, and said, "Mind if you and I have some private shop talk, Detective?"

"All right."

"I got my car outside."

TWENTY-TWO

I sat on the passenger side in the front seat of Bougart's car. Claude was at the wheel. It started raining seriously again. Bougart set the windshield wiper on intermittent. Neither of us said a word.

For a second or two, I considered mentioning the near fatal events of the afternoon, but then decided to let Claude take the conversational lead in any criminal subject. It was his town, after all. Instead, I wondered, What kind of car is this I'm sitting in while I'm waiting for my wife's high school heartthrob to open his mouth?

As a New Yorker and a cop, my knowledge of automobiles is limited to three basic models: beat-up yellow cars with checkered strips on the doors, suspicious meters, and drivers whose English is minimal; discreet navy blue detective sedans that might as well be plastered with NYPD decals in Day-Glo orange; beat-up blue-and-white cars that come with empty doughnut cartons crammed into the glove box and flashing red lights on the roof.

Claude's was definitely a cop's car. The clues were all over the place, beginning with upholstery that smelled like cigarettes and week-old chow mein. Definitely the scent of cop car. Visors were stuffed with extra pairs of sunglasses. The inside panel of the driver's door was fitted out with a custom shotgun holster, empty at the moment. The backseat and rear floor were littered with newspapers, empty pizza containers, and fifty or sixty crushed, coffee-stained Styrofoam cups. On duty or off, Claude spent a lot of his time in whatever make of car this was.

"First trip to New Orleans?" the old boyfriend finally ventured.

"Yes."

"How you like it so far?"

"I love seeing where Ruby grew up, I get a kick out of my family, I love my Mama Violet."

"How about otherwise?"

"Otherwise, I think your police department needs fumigating. Nothing personal."

"I don't take it personal. This department here ain't hardly got a personal mark of mine on it."

"I didn't think so."

"Let me ask you something."

"Okay."

"A couple of our New Orleans detectives most in need of fumigating probably called on my friend Miz Violet this afternoon." Claude turned from me and stared out at the rain. "You happen to be there at the time?"

"If you're talking about those humps Mueller and Eckles, yeah—I met them."

"Oh, man, I thought so." Claude turned to me again. "You ain't anything like them, are you?"

"It's Officer Bougart, is that right?"

"You right."

"My friend, you want to get out the bag someday? Wear plainclothes, carry the gold shield?"

"Sure, I'd like detective work."

"Okay then. Think twice about what you asked me. Let me know what you come up with."

Bougart considered the possibilities. Luckily, he was quick. I was not in the mood for any more small chat.

"Here's the way I see," Bougart said. "If you was some crap-for-brains redneck—like Mueller and Eckles—then Ruby wouldn't have married your white ass."

"Not so charming, but true. Congratulations, Officer Bougart. You just passed lesson number one in the Hockaday School of Detection."

"Thanks."

"Since you're at the head of the class, now I'll tell you the truest thing I know about the detective trade."

"I'd be obliged."

"Question everything, at least once. Including whether two plus two necessarily equals four."

"Mister man, I believe I've been doing that all my life." Bougart said this without the slightest trace of sarcasm. Nevertheless, I was made aware of how patronizing I had just been. "Stay around New Orleans long enough, maybe you learn to appreciate what I'm saying."

"Already I appreciate sitting here in your car with you like this. Getting to know you and all. And by the way, you must tell me what brand of air freshener you use." I cranked open my window all the way, which only let in more damp, dead air. "But, Claude—guess what?"

"Detectives don't guess, do they, Neil?"

"It happens I know from the drill. So—are you about all through feeling me out? Are you reasonably satisfied I'm not a Kluxer after my poor Uncle Bud in the dress?"

"Reasonably."

"Good. Let's cut to the chase. What's your piece of this Clete Tyler homicide I hear about from your colleagues, the two crackers?"

"I ain't got a piece of it. That's been made real official to me."

"What are you saying, Claude?"

"Up to City Hall, there's this alderman and lawyer and whatnot—name of Hippo Giradoux, who is something else.

He used to be the po-lice commissioner here, still runs the department to tell the truth."

"I heard about the guy."

"You should check out that office of his, Hockaday. Look like something from the Huey Long days."

"What did you see Giradoux about?"

"Just sniffing around, that's all. Hippo he told me a story about a country dog."

"Story about a what?"

"Call it a warn-off."

"A guy with the name of Hippo who's nothing but a squeak alderman—*that's* got you spooked off poaching?"

"Neil, let me suggest something. You teach me about detection, I'll teach you about southern."

"Sounds fair."

"Okay, but for now if you want official, here it is. This afternoon, an hour after Hippo tell me the story about the country dog—"

"By the way, I want to hear that story."

"Anyway, I finish up with Hippo and soon thereafter I'm officially told by Deputy Commissioner R. D. Geary—he's one of Hippo's hacks that run the department for him—to stay off the Tyler case or else, quote, 'Boy, your black ass is going to know a cop hell they going to write up in the ACLU history books,' unquote."

"That's putting it crude, but COs warn cops about poaching cases all the time." I thought, From personal experience, Hock, you ought to know.

"No problem with a warn-off. So long it's a clear out-of-bounds situation. Like one cop crowding another cop's collar, for instance."

"Which doesn't apply here?"

"You honestly believe Detective Mueller and Detective Eckles are serving this town as guardians of truth, justice, and the American way?"

"I don't know, Claude. What do you know?"

Bougart fell quiet again, but only for a second or two. He

had been sitting stiffly on his side of the car, hands gripping the wheel, his eyes mostly avoiding mine. Now he relaxed himself, allowing his lanky frame to slump in the seat. He even smiled.

I have smiled that inscrutable way many times myself, usually at some twitch I have invited to spend an afternoon inside of an interrogation room. I will drill the twitch until he struts, at which point he becomes helplessly helpful. At which point I smile at him, like Bougart just smiled at me.

"First place," Bougart said, "Cletus Tyler's body was disfigured. I'm talking real, real bad . . ."

I remembered what Eckles had said. *Cletus got him whacked real good . . . Got him creamed in the gut.* And when I asked what this meant, I remembered Mueller putting the muzzle on his partner, and snarling. *Obstruction of justice ain't a particularly pleasant thing, 'specially when I'm the obstructee . . . Don't be getting any strange notions about messing around in my case, Detective Hockaday.*

"Second place, sending around two walking pork chops like Mueller and Eckles to bring in a usual suspect like Perry Duclat! Hell—it seem like to you they was carrying out serious detective work?"

"No. It was more like Mueller and Eckles were trying to scare Mama into saying something to Perry that would be sure to send him underground, get him out of the picture."

"Could be. Also could be that Cletus Tyler ain't going to be alone in the way he got killed."

"You're talking serial killer here?"

"Somebody took a hot iron to Cletus Tyler, probably after they killed him. They branded him with something I know sure as my own name is a message to a certain underground."

"Message?"

"Moms."

"Moms what?"

The letters —*M, O, M* and *S.*"

"An acronym?"

"That's right. Like your SCUM squad up in New York."

"Let's have it. What's *M-O-M-S* stand for?"

"Nothing polite society want to know about, and that includes black and white."

"Don't make me guess, Claude."

"Mutants, Orphans, and Misfits."

TWENTY-THREE

Sister was saying how the rain gives no relief.

Rain comes up fast and furious after a low rumble, she was saying. It paints everything gray. Then it seeps into the New Orleans dirt. Not dirt like the kind in other cities up beyond the delta, not anything that could rightly be called by any other name—earth, soil, ground. Just plain New Orleans dirt, the kind that never stays around, the kind that slips through your fingers and toes and flies away in the wind.

New Orleans does not sit upon the dirt, Sister was saying. That would be unreliable and most impractical, the nature of New Orleans dirt being what it is. New Orleans is a city floating on the mouth of a river.

And see how the dead have no holes in which to rest in peace. See how their bodies are cremated every day—some of the rich and most of the poor. Oh, and then thousands of the rich and memorable are sealed up to rot in stately tombs. Many thousands more, memorable but not rich, lie in the mausoleums, each occupying a little steel box—each box part of a long tier of cupboards with marble doors and italicized names stamped into brass plaques.

But there are no holes in the dirt for the city's dead. Sister was saying, you do not bury the dead in the dirt of New Orleans, only the living.

That is why the rain is unrefreshing. Because it marries cloudburst and delta humidity and dirt that ought to be flying away into an overpowering aroma. It is on such rainy days that the general smell of New Orleans decay is so sadly strong.

Sister was saying, the smell of death comes quicker in a watery grave.

All this Sister Constance told him after Perry merely mentioned how it would be impossible for him to return to the shed behind Nikki's Dockside Club on account of his dread fear of rats coming after worms fleeing the rain-soaked dirt. He meant nothing untoward by saying so. She believed he was telling her the truth—which he was, for she had become his daughter; he, her fatherly avenger—and that no liar was required as guarantor of his own veracity. And so, having nowhere safe to stay the night, Sister provided him refuge in the Land of Dreams Tabernacle. And told him about rain.

And about the first time it happened to her.

It was back when Sister's folks were having hard times and had to live for a while in a house rented to her mama's old maid aunt, Hassie Pinkney. She was mostly called by her real name then, a name she liked—Connie. It was Auntie Hassie who eventually got her called *Sister*, dragging her to church all the time, telling people her little niece had demons inside of her.

Connie was ten. But if a stranger with something shameful on his mind saw her walking along up on Tchoupitoulas Street he would have thought she was old enough.

One day she heard her Great Aunt Hassie tell the ladies washing their clothes at the levee, There go little Connie, now ain't she just a piece of jailbait? Hassie said that right in front of Connie's face. Connie ran home—so fast she had to sit down in the kitchen and hold her sides until they stopped heaving—and told her mama what Auntie had called her.

Hassie just a old snake lady, Mama said. Connie and Mama made a pact not to tell Daddy about what Hassie said. Daddy's temper could be ruthless.

Never you mind now, Connie's mama said. And then she held her little girl's hands—hands that looked old enough to know—and with tears streaming from her eyes she told her daughter, Connie, I'm going to show you what you got to do and tell you what you got to say if it should come to the worst for you. Going to be disagreeable, and against the nature of your pure heart, but you got to do it. Connie, you hear me close?

In the passage of only three days, and with the arrival of her daddy's good buddy Larry from the army days, the advice and training was put to use.

Since Larry was a guest and deserving of a real bed, the household shifted around at night. Larry and Daddy used the twin bed and the roll-away in Auntie's back bedroom, and Auntie slept in front with Mama in her bed. Connie slept on the parlor couch.

One early morning, just before dawn, Connie was awakened by noise from the kitchen. Voices, she thought in her half-sleep. Auntie's liquored voice, laughing at rude sounds Larry was making like a fool on Hassie's old tape recording machine she always liked to play with. Connie turned over in the couch, and was soon falling back to sleep.

But soon more noise. Now it was Larry and Auntie arguing. Then Larry crashing around like he was chasing after Auntie, and Auntie saying, I ain't in the mood! You want some, whyn't you go do sweet cherry?

Connie opened her eyes. A man—had to be Larry!—stood in the archway between the kitchen and the parlor. Behind him was the faint light from the twenty-five-watt pantry bulb Connie's mama always left burning so people could see their way to the bathroom in the middle of the night. Connie saw Larry's shoulders were slouched, like he was ready to leap at something. She saw Hassie behind him, rushing back to her bed next to Mama through the faint light, wearing nothing but her panties and brassiere, which was hanging half off of her.

Connie wondered, Am I dreaming? But when she knew she was awake and seeing the slouched shoulders, and hearing and smelling the raspy beer breath, she cried out, Oh my God! and sat right up straight.

Then he was upon her, quick as a switch, pawing her away from the lamp on the table beside the cot, which was what she thought first of grabbing. Larry said, Little bitch, you best not turn on the light. Then Connie thought twice, and remembered what her mother had sternly instructed. She was glad that Larry could not clearly see her face, for she was so afraid.

He got up close with his stinky mouth and said, Little bitch, you holler on me and I slice your pretty throat with this. Then he put the cold greasy blunt edge of his army souvenir to Connie's neck. Only last night at supper Larry had been showing her daddy the same oiled bayonet. And now he said to a ten-year-old girl, You best not even breathe too hard, even while you about to enjoy Larry going to rock you every place a young girl needs rocking.

He slipped out of his socks without even bending over. Then he tore off his T-shirt, then he struggled out of his undershorts. Connie watched his every movement in the gray light, looked at every part of his body. Not because she had any interest in seeing that big thing he held in his hands—as he laughed at her, his hairy body hovering over her as he whispered, Oh, you sweet young cock-teasing bitch!—but to locate what it was mama explained would be hanging off a man, right below the big stiff thing.

Larry's sweaty body collapsed on her. He rolled around, trying to force open a ten-year-old girl's legs, slobbering her pretty face with his beery tongue. But then much to Larry's surprise—and final sorrow—sweet young Connie took the situation in hand

Six weeks later there was a trial. Minister Tilton took it upon himself to elicit privately the full details of little Connie's defilement, and a father's resultant fury. Then he listened again when the district attorney interviewed all concerned.

Minister Tilton, at great personal expense, so he informed his parishioners, provided lawyers to protect the honor and interests of Connie's family, and the criminal defense of Connie's daddy. After all, Connie's daddy was a rent-paying member in good standing—though not an attendee—of the Land of Dreams Tabernacle.

Little Connie, who had done exactly what her mama told her to do, held back nothing in telling of what happened after Larry's naked body came crashing down on top of her.

She said, I reach out and got him by his basket. I grab it with my right hand, and when I grab it I gave it a awful hard yank. And twist it round at the same time. I forgot all about that bayonet of his until I hear it drop down to the floor. Was I relieved! But then he go hit me one fierce across the head and I go dizzy. I don't know how long. Anyway, now I grab a-hold his basket with my left hand, too, and twist it round in the opposite direction.

Larry yelling now and we fall on the floor. He hit me a couple of licks, but they only light licks because he so weak just like Mama say. Well, we clump and bump over to the front door, making a racket. Larry trying to get away, trying to get loose of me. But I still hanging on with both my hands, twisting and twisting. I'm afraid I let him go he kill me. Which is what he yelling at me all the while—Bitch, I'm going to kill you!

See, I ain't got nothing to defend myself with, so I just can't let him loose.

Then all of a sudden Mama and Daddy they come screaming into the parlor, and the lights go up. I never did see Auntie Hassie, she stay in the back.

And I don't remember just how we wind up there, but anyways Larry on his back on the couch—with the afghan hanging over it my grandma knit for us last Christmas. Larry clutching his giblets and begging like. He say, You got me! You got me! Please—you killing me!

Mama, she step right up and say, Well die, you sonofabitch! Then Daddy he pick the bayonet up off the floor. Daddy eyes go wild. I know then to let loose of Larry. So I do. It ain't my fight, now it belong to the mens.

Daddy shoulders go slouch like Larry shoulders when he make his move on me. He don't say nothing. Daddy take up the bayonet high in his hands, then he bring down the blade on Larry bare belly. Whomp!

Once I seen Daddy take up a cleaver, chop a goat head clean off the carcass. That's what it look like what he done to Larry. A'course, the goat was already dead and Larry was still alive. But just the same, Daddy one mean and accurate man with a blade.

Right away after Larry die they's so much blood in that room it ain't never going to come clean. And parts of Larry they come sliding out from his insides.

But what do you know—that ain't enough blood for Daddy. He pick up that big knife and he plunge it down and down again on Larry, slice him six ways to Sabbath.

Larry just lay there taking it. I think he dead the very first time Daddy stab him swift and true.

When she finished her stories of rain and rape, Perry's heart was racing and his skin felt like it wanted to run away from the rest of his body. He realized his mouth was hanging open.

"Holy jump up and sit down!" he said. "How's an angel-looking girl like you learn about telling such unholy tales?"

"In church."

"This here church, I guess so."

Perry spooned up the last dab of Campbell's tomato soup that Sister had heated for him in the kitchen at the back end of the church dining room and social hall. She had also made him a sandwich of bologna and butter, and before that showed him in to Minister Tilton's personal dressing room, where he bathed himself under a steamy showerhead cast in twenty-four karat gold and afterward borrowed a pair of silk pyjamas and a matching silk robe.

"Every Sunday I sit there watch my Jesus window," Sister said. "I be at peace when the sun throw the colors of heaven through the pretty glass. I don't hear a word what Minister Tilton say. I hear it all before anyways."

"You think about bad things that happened to you?"

"Don't hurt to remember. Not with Jesus and the doves near me."

"What your mama mean calling Hassie Pinkney a old *snake lady?*"

"Oh, you know, Auntie she one of them believe in all that hooey 'bout the mysteries. She keep that old machine of hers and record folks talking tongues. She keep the hoo-doo snakes, too. La, them things stink."

"What snakes?"

"She snag up cottonmouths from the ditch and keep them

in glass tanks back in her bedroom. Feeds them worms that rot in they bellies. Auntie's room I remember it always smell maggoty and dead from wormy snake breath."

Perry was quiet for a few seconds, wishing he had his notebooks. He asked, "Sometimes, you think about hating Zeb Tilton?"

"I sure do." Sister crossed herself. "I like it if something happen to him."

"Yeah, for what he done to you."

"No, Perry. It don't matter about that. Reason I hate Minister Tilton is he poison Mama and Daddy on me, convinced them they got to cast me out since I was spoil't and unclean."

"Shoo!"

"Minister Tilton, he tell Mama and Daddy he been hearing things about me—very bad things Auntie Hassie tell him. He say if not for me, why Larry wouldn't be dead and Daddy never would've had to be locked up by the po-lice. Leastwise 'til the judge say to go on home, since he only defending his daughter girl. And he say Mama would've never gone a little round the fruitcake bend like she gone."

"Tilton right there to scoop you up, right? Take you in after your folks be so stupid they listen to a conjure man can't keep his pants zipped. Shame on your people for turning their backs on a little girl."

"Like I'm good-for-nothing New Orleans dirt!"

"Something heavy's got to come down. That's what I'm thinking."

"Perry, I don't want nothing to happen to Minister Tilton like what Daddy did to his army buddy. But something."

"Something." Perry stood up from the table. He took his empty soup bowl to the sink where he had seen his Aunt Violet wash up dishes after hundreds of Wednesday night spaghetti banquets and just as many Friday night bingo marathons. "Something," he said again.

"What about tomorrow?" Sister asked. "You got to be gone from the premises early. I be letting you back here come nightfall, but you can't afford to let Minister Tilton or nobody else find you round here by daylight. You got someplace to go for the morning and afternoon?"

"One place is my room at Aunt Vi's, long's it looks safe enough from the po-lice. I got to get my notebooks, to help me think."

"Yeah, think about *something*. I be worried for you."

"Don't fret on me, little Connie."

"A'course I will. You and me, we the same. I don't know much, but I sure know that."

"What you think you know?"

"Somebody throw you away, too."

TWENTY-FOUR

Over the last several years of my career I have been variously dragged into investigations of a number of very bad crimes. I am talking about crimes so bad and bowel-shriveling that the spillage of human blood and tabloid ink reached parity.

Back in '89 there was the murder of a flimflam Harlem radio preacher. This reprehensible character turned out to be weirdly connected to big money real estate, which in Manhattan is a sea of green swamping everybody with monthly ransoms instead of rents.

Then a couple of years later this squatter turned up one day in the park where I read the newspapers, an artist on the skids calling himself Picasso and jabbering about slaughter on Tenth Avenue. The jabber was considerably more than hot air, and I wound up on a roller-coaster ride through the dark maze of Picasso's sorrowful life.

After that, I thought I was pretty clever by leaving the country. I innocently went to Ireland to look up some of my own sorrowful family tree. Some innocence. My inquiries set off a chain of mindless political violence, ending with the discovery of the father I never knew—a man who had wasted his life on grand tribal revenge: a vision, as only an Irishman could see, to drown all the dogs of war.

The year after that—after marrying Ruby, by the way, and being furloughed from the department to rethink my relationship with Mr. Johnnie Walker—I one day innocently phoned up my wife at her ad agency job and asked her out to lunch. I never made the date. Instead, I wound up in the bachelor apartment of a Madison Avenue tycoon who was very bloody, very naked, and very dead on account of his being nailed down to the kitchen floor. This was quite another dark ride, with one stop I will not soon forget—a nightclub for gay necrophiliacs called Devil's Heaven.

But now, here am I—innocently out of town around Thanksgiving time, meeting my wife's big and colorful family. I am better than a thousand miles from New York, way down south in the land of dreams. Yet, still—I cannot look away. Not after what Claude Bougart has been telling me, not after learning about the cottage in the lane and the hard story of Perry and Rose. Certainly not after being ambushed.

And I know, I know. I am walking straight into the snake pit. *I hate snakes!* Where have I heard that before?

I have just spent half an hour in a car—funky with *eau de cop*—talking about a very bad crime somehow involving mutants, orphans, and misfits. And I am deep into it with a guy who is so much like myself I wonder if maybe we were separated at birth.

He is on the outs with his department; my situation exactly, due to this negative attitude of mine on the subject of King Kong Kowalski. We each have nicknames that could not be considered genteel. Mine of course is Hock, as in to spit up; his is Booger, as in . . . well, booger. We have the same taste in women, namely Ruby. (For once in my life I got the girl. I am not going to feel sorry for Claude on this particular score.)

Our business just about complete so far as it could go for now, Claude and I step out of the car. I think over what on earth I am going to say when I have to break it to Ruby that I am on a case somewhat outside my jurisdiction.

Then Claude lays it on some more, which right away I

know pretty much blows my chances that night for sleeping the sleep of the good.

"It wasn't just one guy dead today," Claude says heavily as I am about to go back inside Mama's house and the bosom of my new and colorful family. "It was two."

"As in two and counting?"

"Could be."

"What are we calling the second guy?"

"He's a kid, the type who can't afford a name."

It is late and my head hurts and I do not want to spend another half hour talking about bowel-shriveling topics such as kids too poor for names. I let the question pass for now, along with the one about mutants, orphans, and misfits.

"Perry's the lead on Clete Tyler's murder, but he's out of sight someplace," I say. "Any lead on the no-name?"

"Just one." Claude reaches inside his blazer and pulls out a notebook and a ballpoint pen. He starts writing. "All I got's a street and a name. Get to the street, ask anybody you see about the name and they point out the house for you. Meet me there tomorrow, early in the morning so we sure to catch him. Say about seven."

"Meet you? You can't pick me up?"

"Out of my way, Neil. Ain't you got wheels?"

There was always Huggy. "No problem." I take the slip of paper Claude tears out of his notebook. "The no-name kid. How was he killed?"

"Gunshot."

"Find out the caliber. Let me know."

"Why?"

"I have my reasons."

I leave Claude wondering and head up to the house.

But when I turn at the top of the steps and look back, now I can't help but feel sorry for Claude. He is standing there on the sidewalk by his car, watching me go inside the house where once he came in a tuxedo to call on Ruby.

As we are two guys apparently separated at birth, neither one of us cared to comment on the way the dice happened to fall on this score—me winding up in Ruby's bed, him in Mama's photo album. No sir, we said nothing about it. No doubt we shared the dread of emotional talk.

But I have to say something. Otherwise I will wake several times during the night from the hazy remembrances of nuns scolding me for being impolite. Claude beats me to saying something, though.

"Sweet dreams, Detective Hockaday."

"Not bloody likely."

As I walk through the door I look at the slip of paper Claude has given me.

Crozat Street, it says. Joe Never Smile, it says.

When I walked back through the door into the parlor, neither Ruby nor Mama asked me anything about my little talk with Claude in his car. Nobody else did either.

Down through his thieving years, Perry had squandered his capital of familial goodwill. Even now, with rabid cops one generation removed from lynchers on his tail, concern for Perry's travails was hard to find.

At one time or another Perry had borrowed money from everybody in the family, never repaid. He had made promises, never kept. He had stayed awhile at everybody's house, during which time the kind of merchandise found in pawnshop windows had a way of disappearing.

Sympathy was all used up on Perry, excepting for Mama's dependable compassion, which was regarded as something either saintly or weak. In any case, nobody wanted to hear about bad news Perry.

I stayed up until about midnight with Janny and Uncle Bud and Teddy the Torch, playing a card game I never heard of called pitty-pat. Then when everybody finally left the house (Uncle Bud took along a basket of leftover food), Violet shooed us upstairs to her bed. She would have it no other way. She slept on the parlor couch. Perry's mess of a room stayed empty.

Ruby and I lay awake in bed for twenty minutes or so. We spoke of small things I cannot now remember. I do remember looking at the softly curving outlines of Ruby's face in the New Orleans darkness. And I remember us both looking up at the window when we heard the night scratchings. Fast and graceful creatures with spiny tails and darting tongues skittered over the outside screen.

Warm though it was, Ruby snugged herself against me. She asked softly, in a voice strangely unsure, "You love me?"

"You know I do, Ruby."

"Am I everything you want?"

Ruby's breath warmed my shoulder. She draped an arm over my chest, and stroked at my skin with her hand, which moved slowly and gradually lower.

"I should turn on the light," I said. "You don't sound like my wife. She wouldn't like my being with somebody else."

"Tell me what I want to hear."

"I love you, Ruby."

"Are we going to grow old together?"

Maybe it was not the time to be talking about an old lady, feeling so elevated as I was with Ruby touching me warmly in the dark. But anyway I said, "Sometimes I think I'm going to love you most of all when you're old, Ruby. When we've had a long life together. One day years and years from now, when we imagine we've told each other all the stories of ourselves, you and I are going to be very surprised by something."

"What would that be?"

"That there's still mystery to us."

"I like that, Irish. Love me now."

And so I turned toward my wife and kissed her lips. Ruby slipped beneath me. There was urgency in the way she moved, in how she wrapped her legs around mine, and clutched my back.

But slowness and delicacy came in all that followed. And when we were through, perspiring and lying quietly, we heard the scratching sounds again. We watched something streak across the screen.

Ruby's voice was husky. "When I was a girl, that's what I wanted to be."

"You wanted to be a lizard?"

"A chameleon."

"Chameleons change colors."

"Yes, they do that."

I took Ruby into my arms and held tight to her, and knew that what I had just heard was one of the saddest things I know. During the next few minutes, we both shed quiet tears.

"Thank you," Ruby said, before drifting off.

"For what?"

"For crying. When men cry, women feel less alone."

I lay awake for an hour thinking about that.

And then from downstairs in the kitchen I heard the telephone.

TWENTY-FIVE

"So I'm calling you, man, like you ak'st."

Perry said this halfway into my own *Hello,* like he could see me answering the phone.

"Who is it?" Mama asked. But of course she knew. She was up from her couch and into the kitchen right after me, hair oiled and pressed in a cloth, robe belted tightly, snapping on the light.

"Perry's all right," I said softly, a finger to my lip. Mama's hands flew to her flushed cheeks. To Perry, I said, "Where are you?"

"Never mind that. I was just thinking . . . How you fixing to help me?"

I thought, Perry's come halfway to trusting me, and I was halfway to seeing the big picture. I felt a haze lifting, I felt like my old self again—like a detective.

"You want to square things with Zebediah Tilton?"

"Him and Hassie Pinkney, too. I just imagined what's been missing from the mystery. Hassie a snake handler, see. She's the one—"

"That day Ruby's father was bitten!"

"Had to be that old witch Hassie."

"Stay in touch, Perry. I believe we're all going to church on Sunday."

"What you got in mind?"

"Extracurricular justice."

"I don't follow."

"Church is a fine place for all hell to break loose."

TWENTY-SIX

Miss LaRue and her maid were in the backyard talking girl talk as usual. And as usual, Hippo sat up in the balcony off his bedroom, in a wingback wicker chair.

Hippo looked down and across an expanse of lush green grass to where his wife and the maid chattered. In this private setting, Alderman Giradoux was not his hail-fellow-well-met politician self.

As a matter of fact, there was more than a flicker of repugnance in his face, this being his general expression when pondering the circumstances of his wife's early years. He used to tell her, "Jesus H. Christ on a stick, you coon-asses up to Monroe—you're the shame of Louisiana. Don't even know how to wear shoes." Repugnance also showed in his face when he thought about his wife's show business career, a souvenir of which he sat upon nearly every morning.

The chair was a big one, even for Hippo. It was used in a movie called *Fu Manchu Risen from the Grave,* in which Miss LaRue—in one of her precious few Hollywood screen credits—played a bobby-soxer in a scene where a mystical gangster wanders through a California cemetery popular with romantically inclined teenage motorists.

Spread across Hippo's hairless, pillowy knees was the *Times-Picayune.* There was a celluar telephone on a table next to him, which also held a plateful of beignets, a glass of grapefruit juice, and a humidor full of Cuban cigars that were the real McCoy.

The newspaper had been read thoroughly, including the page-one item about an Angola drifter found dead and cryptically branded under the Tchoupitoulas Street levee. And now with the paper out of the way, Hippo cocked an ear to the conversation below, which inevitably turned from girl talk to something about himself. Hippo enjoyed pretending he was too far off to hear what was being said.

The alderman was dressed the way he usually was at that early part of the morning, before he went off to City Hall. Pin-striped trousers held up with his trademark fire engine red suspenders, nylon socks and Romeo slippers, and his sleeveless undershirt. His suitcoat, tie, and a striped shirt with white collar and cuffs were laid out for him inside. His trousers were unzipped so he could relax his belly while he went through the paper.

Down below, Ophelia the maid—Ophelia Dabon, big and thick-armed, skin dark and shiny as a piano case—was wearing her uniform. Black cotton dress, white apron, black support hose, beige hair net underneath a starched white cap. Also sensible shoes, which she bought two pair at a time every year during the mid-January sale at D. H. Holmes.

Mrs. Hippocrates Beauregard Giradoux—who was to be called Miss LaRue by everybody, save for Hippo, who was allowed to call her Ava—was wearing nothing.

Ophelia walked along the outer edge of the kidney bean–shaped pool. She pushed a broom in between the potted palms to sweep up the fallen detritus of the previous evening: Spanish moss, dead palmettos, drifted dirt.

Mostly Ophelia talked, but sometimes she sang little Cajun songs from an upcountry girlhood. Her voice was not sweet. She sounded like a Sunday morning hymn after a long Saturday night's drinking. But Miss LaRue loved hearing the songs all the same.

Ophelia started one now:

Jolie fille, jolie fille
Écoutes-toi ma chanson
T'es la reine
La lumière et le son—

"Ophelia . . . ?" Miss LaRue asked, interrupting the song, raising up her head some.

Ava LaRue was lying stark naked on her back on a rubber blow-up raft, floating at about midpoint of the pool where the sun was strongest on her skin, which was sand white and sixty-six years old. Miss LaRue held a purple parasol to shade her neck and face. In those regions, too much tan might burn open her surgically tightened throat, cheeks, and forehead, causing collagen leaks.

"Ophelia, what's that pretty song of yours mean?"

"You kidding me, Miz El. Don't you know?" Ophelia stopped her sweeping. She looked up toward the balcony, where Hippo was biting into a fresh beignet.

"Been a long, long time since I sang the old songs myself, Ophelia. I'm afraid I've forgotten."

Ava LaRue—née Ava Dubberly of Monroe, pronounced *Mon*roe by one and all of Ouachita parish—had made a life of forgetting things. Like many other pretty girls from dusty Louisiana towns, Ava Dubberly fled for Hollywood at the first opportunity. When she found out that Hollywood was overpopulated by pretty girls, she tried to forget that, too. And when she met a visiting fat boy from New Orleans one night on the Sunset Strip, where pretty girls might run across gentlemen willing to sport them to steak dinners. Everybody told her she made a lucky catch in the nick of time. The fat boy never let Ava Dubberly forget her luck.

"Well, you know I was singing a old *fais dodo,* 'bout a black man go to Paris and take up with a Frenchy girl,"

Ophelia said. "He think his little Frenchy's just 'bout as pretty as the queen of the world."

"You don't hear that kind of lovely song much these days. Sing me the rest of it, Ophelia, will you?"

Ophelia sang:

Jolie âme, jolies yeux
Tellement douce et gentille
T'es la reine de mon coeur
La raison de la vie.

When she was through, Ophelia agreed with Miss LaRue about the shoddiness of contemporary popular music. "Anymore, nothing sounds like what you'd want staying in your heart. And you surely can't hum any of that type of shit, you should pardon my French."

"You're quite right, dear. I see all these kids carrying radios big as an ice box—right up on their shoulder wherever they go, rattling the walls with that horrible noise they put in their ears. Most of them are deaf to a normal voice." Miss LaRue set down her parasol on the raft beside her, dipped her hands into the water, and paddled toward a shady side of the pool. "No offense, dear, but most of these kids with the big radios are colored."

"S'not my kind of music. Why'd I take offense?"

Miss LaRue shrugged her bony shoulders, and crossed her long legs at the ankles. She reached for her eyeglasses, which were usually on a chain around her neck. She had forgotten about them this morning.

"Tell me," she said, "what's my Hippo doing up there on the balcony? I can't see."

"Oh, you know—eating his beignets, pretend he ain't listening. Your mister, he sure do love the beignets."

"I swear, every one of them he ever ate is hanging on his belly and hips." Miss LaRue made a noise with her lips to express disgust. "Beignets are mostly lard."

"My Lucius, he the same way. He just love his butter.

Everything he like me to make, it go one stick of butter for this, two sticks of butter for that. Sometime he get a mind to pare himself down, all he got to do is lay off the butter and the flab going just melt clean off him."

"Hippo's never going to change."

"I expect not. Ain't nothing on earth more stubborn than a old white man." Ophelia resumed her sweeping. "No offense, Miz El."

Hippo's cellular telephone rang. Both the women heard, and looked up at the alderman in the Fu Manchu chair.

"What?" Hippo answered. Then he spent about a minute listening, after which he said, "I don't like hearing that. I surely do *not!*"

"What's he doing up there now? He agitated over something?" Miss LaRue was not so much worried by what she sensed as she was eager for details. "Sounds like he might have a gasket ripe for blowing."

"That is just not to be tolerated!" When Hippo pronounced the explosive *t* in *tolerated,* the powdered sugar on the beignet he was about to plop into his mouth went flying up into a little cloud. He went ahead and ate the naked beignet anyhow, and at the same time continued scolding his caller. "You so damnably dumb! Why, I'd do better having my old Ava and her hairy white crotch take over!"

"Ophelia . . . ?"

"I'm looking at him, Miz El, I'm looking."

"Looking's one thing. What's he saying?"

"Hush now, ma'am." Ophelia, irritated at missing a line, waved her arms, then remembered her place. "No offense. I'm trying my best to get a sense of it."

"Well . . ." Miss LaRue's voice trailed off. She paddled into a patch of sunlight.

Hippo barked, "You just take care of *bidness!* Hear me?" This time, Hippo's explosive *b* and *d* brought up a few particles of sugarless beignet that had not managed to make it down to the pit of his belly. He put a hand to his mouth and belched.

"Ophelia . . . ?"

"Miz El, I think we here." Ophelia staggered to a poolside chair and sat down. She pressed a hand to her forehead, wearily. "I believe we coming on the right time."

"Is it your knees?"

"Ankles, too. They all starting to ache up."

"When can we start, Ophelia? Tonight?"

"You sure that what you want?"

"Oh, I'm very sure."

"You remember what I say happens."

"I remember."

" 'Bout the sound he going to make, I mean. You can forget little Cajun songs, but once you hear it, you ain't never going to forget *that* sound!"

"I told you, Ophelia—I am *sure*."

TWENTY-SEVEN

"We got us complications. Godammit, I knew there'd be complications!"

"Everything's going to be perfectly all right according to the plan."

"Oh, yeah? What'd you think if I told you there's kin of some visiting New York City detective on the run?"

"I heard all about that. Don't amount to anything more vexing than toe jam. Anyhow, seems like to me that hanging one on Perry Duclat's a stroke of luck, like killing two birds with one stone."

"What you care about skinning some jailbird? And how you come by knowing his name? You holding something out on me?"

"Nothing of consequence you'd want to be responsible for knowing."

"Okay, but mind you don't mix personal business in with this enterprise of ours. Big money's riding on us making them neighborhoods empty. That's hard enough to do without extra troubles."

"I don't see troubles. What we got ahead of us is a simple job that takes simple tools, and the simple trick of finding the likeliest ones to . . . discourage."

"Some trick."

"Right, it is. We just find the ones that can get hurt real bad—like turtles without their shells—and we do it. Only thing onlookers going to care about when the bodies start piling up is clearing the hell out of the area. Easy-peasy, our work's done."

"Simple."

"Not to mention that killing's the cheapest form of urban renewal."

TWENTY-EIGHT

Having no idea where Crozat Street was or how long it might take to get there, I waited for Huggy at half-past five in the morning on the front steps under a yellow porch light that drew something I could only describe as flying cockroaches. I would later learn, to my horror, that my description was dead-on correct.

Back inside, I had quietly telephoned for the taxi and left a lie on the refrigerator door. This was in the form of a note as to how I was off on an early stroll, which Ruby knows is not my habit.

"Thanks for the repeat business," Huggy said as I slid into the dewy vinyl backseat of his taxi. At least I hoped it was morning dew. Huggy flicked off the radio and dumped a half-smoked cigarette out the driver's window. "You make out okay yesterday to Chartres Street where I took you?"

"Just swell."

"That's good. How's the missus?"

"Fine, thanks." But I wondered, How *was* Ruby?

Huggy turned fully around to look at me. Instead of asking my destination, he said, "Heard a good swifty from this DJ I was listening to."

"Oh?"

"What do you get when you cross an insomniac, an agnostic, and a dyslexic?"

"I give up."

"Guy who stays up all night wondering if there's a dog."

"That's real good, Huggy." I searched my pants pocket for the paper slip Claude had given me last night. "Crozat Street, that's where I have to be by seven o'clock."

Huggy looked at his wristwatch. "Why hell, this time of morning it's only ten minutes from here. What you call me so early about?"

"Just drive," I said, glancing back at the house. Huggy put the taxi into gear and crept slowly away from the curb, so as not to disturb the dozing neighborhood. When he had turned onto Paris Avenue, heading east toward the first slant of sunlight, I had a bright idea and asked, "Had your breakfast yet, Huggy?"

"No, sir."

"I'd like to talk to you about one or two things. The bacon and eggs are on me. Wherever you want."

"Well, there's the Hummingbird Grill. Place is never closed, and reasonably nearby Crozat Street."

So Huggy took us to the Hummingbird. This was on St. Charles Boulevard, but according to Huggy not the St. Charles tourists knew.

"See, for the polite crowd you got that there lovely streetcar goes through the better part of St. Charles, clear down to Tulane University," he said, stopping his taxi in front of the Hummingbird, just south of Canal Street. "This part of St. Charles, it's got the necessities of life for the downwardly mobile."

I glanced across the street. There was a Popeye's chicken shack, not yet open for business. Pigeons and skels shared the garbage bin menu in the parking lot. Farther down, next to the YMCA, was a Price Busters shop selling cigarettes and hot dogs. This was between a pair of bars, one called the Mardi Gras, the other Michael's C-Note. Thirsty ancient mariners and a few Harley-Davidson bikers were already stumbling in and out of both establishments.

"Thought you wanted bacon and eggs," Huggy said, tapping my shoulder, drawing my attention away from the bars.

"I do. Let's go."

The grill was on the street floor of the Hummingbird Hotel, the lobby of which was reached by climbing up a worn flight of red and gray linoleum stairs. Three windows of the grill were covered by greasy venetian blinds, the old kind with the chunky blades.

A blind man with a straw hat and folding cane walked into the grill ahead of us, and took his apparently regular booth at the first window. A tired waiter shuffled over and dropped a bacon, lettuce, and tomato sandwich without a word. The blind man felt around for a skinny bottle of Tabasco sauce, opened it, and lubricated his sandwich.

Huggy and I took the far window booth. Between us and the blind man was a booth full of musicians, all wearing very dark sunglasses: a Japanese guy in black jeans, earrings, and a Miles Davis T-shirt with about a twenty-eight-inch waist, which is what a seaweed diet will do for you, and three long-legged American girls with skimpy silk blouses, skirts slit up the sides to reveal black hose up to the knee and pale white thighs, and suede platform heels. The girls were applying Rocky Horror Picture Show makeup and looking increasingly less angelic.

A couple of good-old-boy bartenders at the counter were discussing various methods of skimming the till in saloons from New Orleans north to Baton Rouge. Shortchanges, overcharges, credit card edits—the usual grifts.

The waiter appeared. He wore a floppy blue-black hairpiece, wrinkled white skin, and thick spectacles, giving him a faint Roy Orbison resemblance. "Ready to grease down, gentlemen?"

"Eggs soft-scrambled and biscuits with maple butter for me," Huggy said. "No meat."

"Bacon, not too crisp, fried eggs over easy," I said. Remembering about the uniform ghastliness of bread anywhere outside of New York, I went with Huggy on the biscuits.

The food came in a flash. I had not remembered about grits being an automatic addition to anything ordered in the morning in a southern restaurant, so I pushed the dribbly eyesore off into a corner of my plate.

"Said you want to speak to me about something," Huggy said. He caught a biscuit crumb that fell from his lips to his hand. "Now, I know from picking you up at the train station that you ain't a lawyer and you ain't a priest—"

"And that I've got the knack of pretending to be stupid before I'm wise."

"How can Huggy help you?"

"I've been thinking about how you killed your wife."

"Oh, gawd."

"Her name was Ory?"

"It was."

"And your lawyer. He was Hippocrates Beauregard Giradoux."

"Shirttail cousin of mine. That's right."

"You know him well?"

"Know him good enough I guess." Huggy sucked cooled-down coffee through the spaces between his teeth, a sort of oral hygienic habit, repellent but effective. "Good enough to see through the joy-boy crap he throws up to everybody like a splatter of locusts on a windshield 'til you can't see the driver no more."

"You got something against him, Huggy?"

"Not really. He saved my behind when they put me on trial for Ory's untimely passing, that's for sure. I'm only saying I know the man's nature."

"Which is?"

"One thing, Hippo's got power now, and it's changed him. He's gone cold, 'less he wants something. He got a way of tipping his hat to you on a Sunday morning and saying How-do and making it sound like he just said Drop dead."

"What about another thing?"

"He's learned the politician's way of taking. He could steal sweetness out of gingerbread."

I took out a pad and pen from my shirt pocket and wrote down a reminder to manufacture some reason for a personal call on the good alderman.

"You ain't a lawyer, you ain't a priest," Huggy said, scratching at short tufts of orange on his otherwise scabby head. "Care to tell say what's your interest in all this?"

"Maybe I'll fill you in later, maybe I'll need some more dope only you can provide. I'll tell you then." I wondered about the load behind Huggy's question. *All this?* "Right now, I've got an appointment on Crozat Street."

Huggy Louper was confused and bedazzled by my mysterious manner and said nothing as we finished our coffee. I caught him looking at me several times in his rearview mirror as he drove me to where I would find Joe Never Smile. My guess was that Huggy had led a quiet and exemplary life since killing his wife, too quiet and too exemplary to suit his style.

Crozat Street ran south through the Iberville housing project west of Basin Street. The neighborhood's early risers—mostly old women with heavy-lidded eyes—sat on porches fanning themselves in the wet heat that had risen with the sun. Alleyways were clogged with hulks of broken-down, rusted, burned-out cars.

Oaks and sycamores had been planted in rows all through the project, sealing the decrepitude of poverty in shadows. This cover no doubt comforted busloads of tourists who came to see the famous cemetery on Basin Street. Tourists would not mind seeing decrepitude amongst the dead, but would surely feel uneasy seeing it amongst the living.

According to a smudged sign on the sexton's stone shed, it was ST. LOUIS CEMETERY NO. 1. The sun shone bright and full upon this necropolis of brick and limestone and marble. Row upon row upon row of tombs, some painted in colored chalks, some bearing garlands of flowers or dusty black-and-white photographs of the deceased encased within. As my taxi passed the cemetery, I read aloud the Latin blessing for the dead on a nearby tomb, *Requiescat in pace.* Rest in peace.

"That's one place I ain't never going inside of," Huggy Louper said, crossing himself as we passed by the cemetery gate. I felt obliged to do the same.

"Why not?" I asked.

"Ever hear about Marie LaVeau?"

"No."

"She just about run the life of half the people of this town once. Voodoo queen she was." Huggy gave a nod of his head toward the last post of the cemetery gate as we rounded a corner into one of the shady streets. "Her tomb's in there since just before the First World War. She still gets her regular visitors, and lots of tributes are dropped down in front of her tomb—chicken feet, hair tied up in string, tongues of dead cats, that sort of voodoo-hoodoo stuff. Some folks say, Marie don't like what you done or what you got away with she can still do you wrong, don't matter a lick she's dead all them years."

I heard Huggy's strange question again, the one he asked on the day I arrived in this strangest of towns. *What's worse: living with a bad conscience, or knowing the peace of mind that comes from being hanged for what you done?*

"Are you saying that you believe you got away with murder?" I asked.

"Don't it seem to you like everybody's haunted by something they don't talk about?"

"I've noticed."

"Well, here's Crozat," Huggy said, abruptly stopping the conversation, along with the taxi. He parked at the head of a long huddle of row houses identical to the ones in Mama's St. Bernard project, only worse off. Iberville's houses were all crumbled brick with bashed-in green fire doors and a street full of condoms and crack vials.

Huggy seemed anxious to get me to where I was going and to get himself out of the project. "Any particular address, or you just want the corner here?"

I pulled out Claude's slip from my shirt pocket. "I'm looking for the house where somebody called Joe Never Smile lives. You know where that might be?"

"I guess I sure don't know a house along this here street by the name of who lives in it."

"That's all right, I'll just walk along and ask."

"Mister, you got to be crazy." Huggy turned from the front of the taxi and looked me up and down, from my Yankees cap and blue chambray shirt to my creased khakis, clear down to my brand-new Nikes. "Lord a'mighty, I suppose you think we all just dripping molasses and saying howdy down here. Think you can go where you please when you please, so long's you smile and tip your hat to folks on porches."

I opened the taxi door and stepped out onto Crozat Street, saying nothing.

"Believe one thing Huggy tells you about New Orleans, my friend,'" Huggy told me, holding his hand out the window for the fare. "Things ain't always as they seem."

I assured him, "I believe anything but the obvious."

Then I headed down Crozat Street wondering about a guy called Joe Never Smile. I figured I could at least walk up and down until I spotted Claude's car. Or smelled it. I looked at my wristwatch. Twelve minutes before seven.

The only traffic on the street was a yellow school bus that slowed to a stop at the far end of the block to pick up a knot of waiting girls and boys. Then the bus rolled on past me, mashing transmission gears and exhaling a cloud of oily fumes. Earnest black faces filled the bus windows. I waved at the sleepy children, a few waved back.

I tipped my cap to the first old lady I saw on a porch, a large woman in polka dots sitting there with her legs spread wide and hose rolled up to just below her knees, drinking something with ice in it.

"Good morning, dear," I said. "Morning," she replied, sweetly. Then she slipped back inside her house when I had passed, and in the time it took her to make a few critical phone calls the curtains and blinds up and down Crozat Street began discreetly opening for a look at the stranger.

A boy of about eight years old came up behind me, shirtless but otherwise wearing a stiff white sailor cap, shorts, and sandals. He was pulling a wagon full of empty bottles and cans. The rattling made me turn around.

"You lost or something, Mister Man?" he asked. He was a good-looking kid, with dark brown eyes that matched his skin and a mouth on him that was ten years wiser than his age. His hair needed brushing. If I was his daddy, I would have made him take a bath.

"No, son, I'm looking for Joe Never Smile's house. Trouble is, I forgot the number."

"What for you want to see Joe?"

"You know where he lives, kid?"

"Where you get that fine hat?"

"Up in New York."

"That's where you from, hey?

"Does it sound like I'm from around here?"

"Sure it don't."

At last, the kid had not answered a question with a question. I would have been irritated with him except that he reminded me of myself about a thousand years ago.

"Okay now." I waved my arm up the street. "You want to tell me which one of these houses is Joe Never Smile's?"

"Well, I might know where Joe stay. Then, too, I might never get to New York."

"What's that supposed to mean?"

"Means I know what you want, you got what I want."

"Forget about the Yankees cap, kid."

"All right, Mister Man." He shrugged his skinny shoulders and resumed walking up Crozat, pulling his rattling wagon behind him.

Then of course it hit me, with the force of a powerhouse right thrown by Ali in his prime. Exactly why was I looking for Joe Never Smile? Because Claude Bougart and I were trying to get a lead on some no-name kid who was murdered yesterday—and branded. And what about this shirtless street kid who by rights should have been on the school bus? What was this one's name?

"On the other hand, kid," I said to him, catching up with the wagon, "maybe when I'm home I could just get myself another one."

I took off my Yankees cap and gave it to the boy. He held my cap by its brim, feeling the light wool, turning it around to check wear and tear in the sweatband and the tiny backside figure of a Yankee at bat embroidered in white against the navy blue.

The way this kid handled my cap was the way jewelers on West Forty-seventh Street inspect gold. Every so often, the shirtless boy whose hair needed brushing would look up from the merchandise, to see the way I was watching him. The jeweler and this kid, the same look.

"Authentic big league licensed merchandise, right?"

"What's your name, kid?"

"How come a New York white man be running 'round here asking a little black boy name?"

"You got one?'"

"Maybe it's Richard. I forget." No smart-mouth question this time. Now came the bald honesty—and tragedy—of a child who thought that forgetting his name was not particularly unusual. Or that standing in the middle of Crozat Street on a school day swapping a Yankees cap for some information was perfectly natural.

"Go ahead, try it on," I said.

The kid took off his sailor cap and wedged it between a couple of Jax beer bottles in his wagon. He pulled on the Yankees cap, snugging it down in back. It was too big.

"I'd have to take a pin to it," he said.

"That or a few stitches. Tell me now—"

"Joe Never Smile, he stay right over there," the kid cut in. He pointed across the street to a house two doors from where we were standing.

"Okay, thanks. What do they call you, kid? Rich? Dick? Richie?"

"Everybody call me Maybe."

"As in Maybe Richard?"

"Yeah, you right."

I spotted Claude Bougart's car turning into Crozat from up at the corner where the school bus had picked up kids with names. Bougart slowed to a stop in front of the house the no-name kid had just identified, stepped out, and gave me a wave. He was wearing his uniform. Maybe Richard panicked.

"You the po-lice, too?"

"Not in this town," I said.

"I'm out of here, man."

Maybe yanked his wagon and trotted down the street. A couple of Pepsi cans jiggled off the side, clattering to the sidewalk. Maybe did not bother retrieving them.

I crossed over to where Claude Bougart stood alongside his car and asked, "You see that kid with the wagon?"

"Sure I do."

"He's wandering around the city on a school day, doesn't even know his name." Claude and I watched Maybe Richard as he neared the corner. I asked, "Any idea where he's going?"

"Boy like that who don't belong, chances are he's headed for his day-time hiding place. Boy like that's got to sleep by day, make his way in life by night."

"Some life. What do you do about it around here?"

"Tell me what you'd do about it, Detective."

"Run him through juvenile."

"What do you know? That'd be the exact same thing I'd do. *If* we had a juvenile division cared about black boys being in school, such as schooling is. *If* I figured that boy had at least his mama at home . . . if I figured that boy even *had* a home."

Bougart's expression was a blend of amusement and long sufferance. At least he was not laughing at me. So why did I feel like I was wearing baggy pants and a rubber nose?

"Jesus, Claude—what chance does he have?"

"Same as the rest. The chance to pay us all back some day of reckoning."

Maybe and his clanking wagon turned at the corner. He never gave us two cops a backward glance. I watched Maybe and my Yankees cap slide into the shadows of Iberville.

"Shame on me," I said as the boy vanished. "There goes something I see every day and want to forget."

"What is it you want to forget?"

"The moral equivalent of a slow-moving car with a shooter riding shotgun."

"You shouldn't be putting something on your shoulders don't belong there alone, Neil. You ain't any blinder than most, and you ain't any stronger."

I wanted to reply to Bougart's flat view of myself. It somehow seemed very important to have him think better of me. But anything I thought about saying—such as, *But, I'm a cop!*—I wisely reconsidered.

"Tell you how I figure the truth of the boy's sorrowful situation." Bougart paused. He lifted a packet of Pall Malls from the pocket of his uniform shirt, opened it, and lit one for himself. I declined the invitation to join him. Bougart sucked in smoke and exhaled a cloud of blue. "There's all kinds of treacheries folks practice without believing they're doing any harm. Good and respectable type of folks. Like for instance, here I'm smoking this tobacco, knowing it's poison."

"As a nun you'd be lousy, Claude. At least the kind of nuns I grew up with."

"How's that?"

"You shouldn't be so quick to minimize treachery."

"For instance?"

"A boy's not the same thing as a cigarette butt."

"When he's poor he sure is."

And what could I say to that? The way he talked, Bougart was like a crack handball player: he stepped up to the line and served a lazy ball, at the same time plotting out his next two or three hard, lean returns to win him the score. I thought back to last night and the way he had talked then, spooning me bits and pieces of a complicated mystery, complete with a puzzling acronym, MOMS; the way Officer Claude Bougart, disenchanted New Orleans cop, finessed me into involvement in a case he had been warned off by Alderman Giradoux and Deputy Commissioner Geary.

Then it came to me: Bougart saw the opportunity of turning me into a tool, to do the work that he himself could not so easily do. I could not fault him for doing this to me. How many times as a cop have I myself made somebody into a shovel?

"By the way," I asked, "you were going to let me know calibers?"

"Ugly kind—nine millimeter, high-velocity expanders. You want to tell me why that interests you?"

"I went looking for Perry Duclat, three guys in a Jeep shot at me." Claude did not look particularly alarmed. "I picked dumdums out of the ground. Nines."

"They could have nailed you if they wanted."

"You figure it's a warning?"

"Sure as hell is. You ever hear about anybody in the path of a street-sweeper live to tell the story unless he allowed to live?" Claude took a last puff on his cigarette, then tossed down the butt. It sizzled out in some pavement beer. "I expect it's illustration to the dog story."

"How did Hippo's warn-off go exactly?"

"I guess you do got the right to know about all the red flags likely to get thrown down on this job. Hippo, he says anybody snoops around Cletus Tyler's murder going to wind up in a bad way, meaning a country dog in the city."

"That's a joke or a threat?"

"Your call, I guess. A country dog noses around fences in a city where he don't belong, that dog can't win, Hippo says. Country dog runs, the other ones bite his ass. He sits still, they fuck him."

"Charming advice from the people's choice."

I considered sharing the impressions I had of Alderman Giradoux by way of Huggy Louper. Then I thought better of it. Bougart and I were not quite partners. He was spoon-feeding me, which I would not call a gesture of full trust.

"Yeah, it's some kind of advice." Bougart gave a tired look up and down Crozat Street. "Street like this one's full of fences. You see them, Detective Hockaday?"

"I see the fences. They're invisible."

Bougart laughed, in a way that told me I had said the right thing. "As politicians go 'round here, just understand Hippo's about the best we got. So long's you stay on his good side."

"What's happening on his other side?"

"Hippo's a big man. A big man throws a lot of shade."

I glanced up at the house Maybe Richard had pointed out to me. "How about Joe Never Smile up there? Is he likely to lead us into the sunlight?"

"That's for you to find out, Detective. I'm going along with you to make the introductions. Then I got to report to my station house for muster."

"What's orphans, mutants, and misfits, Claude?"

"Old Joe can tell you better than me."

"How do I get in touch with you?"

"You don't. I'll be off duty by four, four-thirty. I'll drop by Miz Violet's after. I'll be trying to pick up on what I can during my tour, which ain't likely going to be much. So you pretty much in charge of things today, Neil."

"Making me the country dog."

"Well, being from New York, I'm counting on you to have a better nose than most for sniffing out truth."

"What's truth mean around here?"

"New Orleans truth is a rabbit in a bramble patch. Maybe you never going to spot that rabbit fair and true. Maybe all you can do is circle around them brambles and say it's in there someplace."

Maybe.

TWENTY-NINE

Ruby shifted her hips, expecting to press up against her husband's thighs. Nothing there. She threw back an arm touching only the cotton sheet. She did not have to open her eyes to know Hock was gone from bed.

Still muzzy from dreams during her first New Orleans night in so many years, and now feeling the viscous heat of Louisiana sunlight pouring through Mama's lace window, Ruby thought, This is how it is being a tin wife—isn't it? Half the mornings of your life, rising alone, trying not to wonder about too much.

Back in New York, Ruby was acquainted with a woman named Inez, tin wife to the late Patrolman Egidio Ignacio Maldonado of the plainclothes anticrime unit in the Thirty-fourth Precinct of upper Manhattan. Eddy he was called, before his young head was blasted off his shoulders one evening in Washington Heights by an even younger entrepreneur informally associated with the American pharmaceutical industry. Eddy's wake at Our Lady of Lourdes in West Harlem was the first NYPD funeral Ruby had attended.

It happened that Ruby and Hock (who wore his old

shield, cap, and tight-fitting blues for the occasion) sat directly behind the black-clad widow that windy January day. Ruby could not take her eyes off Inez Maldonado, imagining herself on some future windy day in the same circumstances: front pew center, with the mayor on her left and the commissioner on her right, and Hock in a box dead ahead.

Ruby sat up in bed, pushing aside the sheets and pillows and the lace coverlet. She rubbed her eyes and looked across the room to the clock on top of the bureau that said it was nearing seven.

After a quick shower in the hallway bath, Ruby dressed and followed her nose downstairs toward the fresh coffee and chicory in the kitchen. Mama was sitting on the parlor couch she had slept in overnight, drinking coffee and looking at television. Her bedding was neatly folded and stacked on one end of the couch, and Mama had bathed and fixed herself for the day, apparently a day of work. She was wearing one of her blue polyester maid's dresses and thick support hose.

Ruby leaned over and kissed her mother's cheek, which was smooth and smelling pleasantly of glycerine facial soap.

"Morning, Ruby girl. Coffee's in the kitchen, you go help yourself now. I'll be cooking some eggs and such right after my program here." Mama said all this without looking up from the TV set, which was filled with the empty face of a blond-headed news anchorman mispronouncing foreign names and places, and several on the domestic side as well. "By the by, your handsome husband gone off for a walk someplace. Left a note on the Frigidaire."

"A walk? Did you see him before he left?"

"He slip off too early, I never seen him go." The television distracted Violet from the anxious sound in Ruby's voice. "Coffee's done up strong. Hope you can stand it. Neil like it strong?"

"Yes, he does."

"Well, when he come back in you tell him I make coffee so strong he want to get up and go slap his grandma."

"I'll tell him what's what, all right." Ruby stared at her mother's uniform, and stockings that covered up over-worked veins standing out on her legs. She hated seeing Mama dressed like that. She hated it even more that she was embarrassed seeing Mama dressed like that. After all, cleaning house was worthier than the work Ruby did in Madison Avenue. "Where are you going this morning, Mama?"

"Oh, I still do some housekeeping, you know. Just two little days a week."

"For that Ava LaRue?"

"I spell her regular maid, this hoo-doo lady by the name Ophelia Dabon."

"How are you getting along with Miss LaRue after all these years."

"Fine, so long's I don't run into her damn husband Hippo." The anchorman flashed California teeth and said he would return after some important messages. "Go on, get your coffee while the commercials are jabbering."

"Hippo." Ruby said the name as if she were horking up spoiled food. "That greasy tax collector!"

"Well, he a big old alderman nowadays. Had him a life of politics since you been gone from town, including he used to be po-lice commissioner. Hippo got his big butt in a tub of trouble lately, though."

"Trouble?"

"Hippo be getting too flirty down to City Hall. Ain't that a kick? That white man think all he got to do is say How-do and all the sweet young ladies going to spread they legs. White mens got them some kind of arrogance."

"As I seem to recall, Hippo Giradoux is so fat it takes him three days to reach around and scratch his butt."

Mama laughed. "Oh, Ruby girl, I see you remember the dozens."

Growing up, Ruby and all neighborhood kids would "do the dozens," as it was called. Nobody ever thought about the name of the game, no more than anybody ever analyzed hopscotch. But then one day, Ruby's fifth-grade history teacher taught the class the roots of the dozens: during the slave trading days of New Orleans, white plantation owners deemed some Africans so ugly and undesirable that traders had to sell them off by the dozens.

Ruby ran home crying after this rude lesson. She told Mama what she had learned. And after that, Ruby and Mama reserved the dozens for the cold-hearted.

"Hippo Giradoux's so ugly his mama had to get drunk to breast-feed him . . ." Ruby's eyes were closed. She tried remembering her best zingers. "Hippo's so big his hips are in two different time zones."

"Hippo he so ugly, when he was a little his boy family set him in the corner, feed him with a slingshot," Mama said. She got to laughing so hard a piece of dental bridge fell out of her mouth. She wedged it back in with her fingers and snugged down porcelain with her tongue. "Go on, get your coffee. And hurry on back, girl. You don't want to be missing what's next after these commercials."

So Ruby went into the kitchen and found herself a mug, filled it halfway with grandma-slapping coffee, and stepped over to the Frigidaire. She read Hock's pitiful note taped to the door: "Good morning, ladies. Woke up early, decided to walk. Back later. Smacks—Hock."

A big fat lie, Ruby told herself. He's off somewhere with Claude—that sweet boy in the lime green tux. Whatever they're up to, it's got something godawful to do with Perry.

Ruby sighed and cut her coffee with milk and took her first sip of the day. And then—slap!—she thought of Princess Pamela back home in New York, proprieter of Hock's favorite Lower East Side chicken joint and jazz club. A sloppy, preachy old black lady with a red-blonde bouffant wig and ready advice about the meaning of Neil Hockaday: *He is a poor fool who can't help but bein' this all-day cop in a twenty-four-hour town. No more than he can help bein' the only cop who knows how every life's maybe not valuable, but how every life's a big deal. My friend Hock—well, he ain't a easy man, Pretty.*

Ruby thought, Where's Hock right now? Off somewhere with my old prom date—who after all these years carries me in his heart. *If pretty is a minute, you're a whole hour.* Most men would do the decent thing and become jealous of a sweet-talking beau. But not my Irish. No, Hock and old Booger, they go off gallivanting together . . .

Oh, he's a man of so many bad habits. He sleeps on his back with his mouth wide open, for instance. But I only have to nudge him, and Hock turns onto his side and his mouth closes up and the chainsaw stops, at least for a while. Likewise, haven't I nudged him along on a fair number of cases?

Well—slap!—that's it. There is no living with Neil Hockaday unless I'm actively involved in his sentimentality, his rare notion that every life is a big deal. If I have to sit between the mayor and the commissioner some day in a church pew . . . God help me, I want a part of myself to be in that box along with my Hock.

So—what's my part in this thing that Hock is helpless to ignore? This murder in the local news, down by the levee where Mama and Daddy were once upon a time the pride of the Flaggs, this terrible murder with cousin Perry somehow in the wings?

I can start by talking to Teddy the Torch, that's what I can do. If anybody knows about backstage New Orleans, it's Teddy . . .

Ruby returned to the parlor and asked Mama for Teddy's telephone number.

"Hush yourself and sit down here beside me, girl. Look what's coming up on the TV."

"Mama, you were never one for daytime TV." Ruby sat on the couch. "You'd always be in the kitchen in the morning, reading your precious *Times-Picayune.*"

Violet pressed two fingers to her lips, saying nothing.

"And now—welcome back to 'Good Morning, New Orleans,' " said a new but similarly empty face. This was a TV morning talk show host from central casting, a white male variety by the name of Jim: leading-man slender, brown hair carefully layered and lacquered, glassy blue eyes, square jaw dimpled, baritone TV voice utterly free of local color. He spoke from a raised camera set: shag carpeting, potted ferns, two wicker chairs with a table and coffee service in between, the GOOD MORNING, NEW ORLEANS logo as backdrop. Jim of the square jaw said, "All right, folks, it's time now for City Beat, with my co-host—Jan Flagg. Let's all give a big, warm welcome to Jan."

Ruby turned to her mother. *"Jan?"*

"The TV station think that name sound more classy—and white. But you talk to Janny next time, don't be making her feel bad and say I ever tell you that."

Cued to applause, the audience did its duty. Jim rose from his wicker chair as Janice Flagg flowed onto the set in a creamy silk suit, chunky gold jewelry, and blazing smile. She was greeted with "Morning, Jan" and a buss on the cheek.

"Well, well—there's a big leap for New Orleans," Ruby said, hands on her own cheeks, gaping at the televised interracial embrace, quick and juiceless as it was.

Violet shrugged. "That don't mean hell's froze over quite yet. You still never likely to see it the other way 'round on the TV. Shoo, I don't got to go back in my mind too many years to when a colored gent give some white lady a little no-account peck and they call it rape, haul him out to the woods, and string him up."

Meanwhile back in television land, *Jan* Flagg was taking her applause and close-up as naturally as a Hollywood movie queen sashaying down an aisle full of velvet ropes and paparazzi. When Jim sat down again in his wicker chair, Jan did likewise in hers.

"Coffee?" Jim held a silver pot poised over the cup and saucer on his co-host's side of the table.

"Oh yes, and thank you so much," Jan purred. Female

sighs could be heard from the studio audience. "Make it sweet and light."

Ruby asked, "They do this gooey-gooey bit every day?"

"Make you want to gag, I know. That's show biz."

Coffee and repartee complete, Jan Flagg flashed camera number two her cutey-pie, over-the-shoulder smile. Then she straightened her shoulder pads, swiveled around in her chair, and crossed her legs as the camera trolley advanced. She waited for the Teleprompter cue, then read the rolling script she had prepared for her "City Beat" segment.

"Add yet another deep, dark mystery to the story of New Orleans." She said this ominously. "What—or who—are *M-O-M-S?* It's not what you think, it's not about nice little ladies in checkered aprons baking cookies for when their kids come home from school. No. It's what police investigators are asking themselves in the wake of an ugly case of murder yesterday afternoon. Now, stay with me on this . . ."

"Oh, La—no, no!" Tears flooded Mama's eyes. Ruby put an arm around her shoulders. A chill shot through Ruby as she held her mother. *What is this?*

"At first glance, there's the killing of a homeless black man—a drifter whose severely mutilated body, wedged beneath the Tchoupitoulis Street levee, was first discovered by a group of frightened children walking home from school." Jan Flagg paused. "But the drifter had a name—Cletus Tyler—and a criminal past, here in his hometown of New Orleans. He was an ex-convict, recently turned out of Angola Prison after serving an eight-year term for armed robbery. That much is known, but little else. For starters, why was he murdered? A man with no known enemies. And the even nastier question—why was Cletus Tyler's body branded with a red-hot poker?"

Another dramatic pause. Then Jan Flagg reported, "Yes, you heard me—branded. *After* being stabbed to death. Branded like he was a sheep or a horse or a steer. What kind of psychotic murderer would first kill his victim, then afterward sear his body with burning steel? What was this brand? Did the killer want to leave some kind of sick, twisted message . . . ?"

Ruby thought, Here we go again—a cop job with Neil Hockaday's name all over it. She felt sourness in her stomach.

"Here's where I asked you to stay with me, folks. The four letters in the brand, remember, were *M-O-M-S.* What do they mean? A confidential City Hall source tells me the letters stand for . . . Mutants, Orphans, and Misfits."

The studio audience gasped. Mama covered her forehead with her left hand. "Oh, La!" said Mama, as if she was about to faint. She flattened out her right hand and fanned herself. "I never did expect nothing like this from Janny, that's the real truth! What the devil my baby be mixed up in? Sweet Jesus in heaven, please see us all to mercy!"

The camera slowly backed away from Jan Flagg until both TV personalities on the shag carpet set came into frame. Jim seemed to be fidgeting. A stage director gave him the cue for a solemn expression.

"That's quite a story, Jan. Not the most appetizing report you could bring us at the breakfast hour . . ." The stage director was waving wildly. "But nonetheless, a story of our troubled times that I for one think we all must know, and try to understand."

"Well thanks, Jim." Jan ignored the stage director. "There's one thing more. There are no solid clues thus far, according to my source."

"She knows they're after Perry," Ruby said. "Why didn't she mention that?"

"Don't you worry. Neil talk to Perry on the phone last night, and Perry—"

"Perry called here? Is that where Hock went this morning—to see Perry?"

"Can't say. Neil up to something, though. I just hope it's helpful." Mama's hands fell to her lap. She twisted her fingers into knots and sighed. "Oh, La! Minister Tilton, what he be thinking?"

Back in TV land there was Jim, with relief in his voice, saying, "We'll be back after this important message."

"Might's well shut that thing off now," Mama said.

Ruby got up and switched off the television. She crossed the parlor to the front window and gazed out at Gibson Street, blindly thinking, Maybe Hock's going to come walking up from the corner of Milton. She asked Mama, "So that's Janny's show nowadays?"

"*Was* Janny show more likely." Violet shook her head. Then she put her hands on her knees and pushed herself upright. She took a few seconds to shake the stiffness from her housemaid's legs. "Your sister, she begun to get all unexpectedly serious lately. They don't be wanting serious colored ladies talking on the TV."

"I never knew Janny had so much spirit."

"Prob'ly Janny didn't neither. Typical for a Negro, 'specially if she's a girl."

"What are you saying, Mama?"

"Facts of life what I'm saying. Most of us Negroes, we raised up with practically no appreciation for the heads God planted on our shoulders. That's how white folks want us—kept down, blind to our own black brains—because the scariest thing in the whole world to the man is the possibility that colored folks is just as smart as he is. No smarter, just the same. You see how terrifying that is."

"Yes."

"Facts of life go double for colored womens. You always got the mens to keep you down and not seeing too good, whether they white or black."

"So Janny . . ." Ruby's thoughts drifted off, and with them her words as well. She marveled at her mother's new and feisty spirit. When had Mama awakened? Ruby also tried to appreciate the impulses that lay behind her sister's on-air subversion; for maybe the first time in her life, Ruby imagined Janice not as the silly sister she could always wrestle to the ground, but as a grown-up woman who could no longer be flattened into submission.

"Janny still got her ditzy side, which you saw last night for your ownself," Mama said, picking up the drift as if she had just read Ruby's mind. "But she coming along. One thing, Janny don't settle no more for playing that pretty-face Negro TV lady. She somebody real like you now, Ruby. Like she up and moved on. Yes, ma'am, Janny Flagg is a late-blooming somebody."

Ruby wondered, again, Since when has Mama wanted either Janice or herself to be *somebody?* My little old mother has the capacity for change?

"She deliberately held back in her report on the Cletus Tyler murder . . . ," Ruby said. She was not so much speaking to her mother as she was thinking aloud, wondering about the new sensibilities of Mama and Janice, and how to test them. "She held back about Perry. Why do you suppose?"

"Less said about him the better."

"Have you changed your mind? Do you think Perry killed that man?"

"A'course not!"

"Mama, tell me what Perry's been doing since you took him in."

"Tell the truth, he mostly been a pain. He been all right about chores, and I admit it's good having a man around at night. But it all come at a price."

"Perry's light fingers?"

"Ain't just that. Just you go up and see that Negro's room with all them nasty cigarette butts he leave around—and bent-up Dixie beer cans, and them notebooks. He sit up there watching a old TV. Like he just waiting around his Mama Vi house for one of them knock-at-the-door jobs."

"Notebooks?"

"Well, when he ain't laying around here Perry be off to the old place off Tchoupitoulis Street. You remember?"

"Sure."

"Perry, he obsessed with it. He write down things about it in them notebooks. He even talk himself into a little work down there, just so he got business hanging around the neighborhood."

"What's his job?"

"Nothing steady like. Perry just do a little yard work and such for old peg-legged Mr. Newcombe."

"The tenant who took over when you and Daddy left."

Mama's eyes went blank. Ruby would sooner see tears in her mother's eyes than that blankness.

"About the notebooks," Ruby said, changing direction. "What does he write in them?"

"I don't know. Miss Hassie next door she all the time ragging on them notebooks. She say Perry spying on her, always peeping at her through the window when she in her kitchen."

"She complains to you?"

"It comes to me, by way of Minister Tilton."

"Mama, I will never in a thousand years understand about Zeb Tilton. You believe going to his little church makes you a good Christian?"

"Going to church don't make you Christian no more than going to a garage make you a car. I know that much, girl, even if I ain't *with it* like y'all in New York." Mama snorted. "I go to Zeb church on account of my friends. We all just stuck with Zeb is all. Zeb like glue for us. You understand?"

"Yes. I'm sorry, Mama."

"Don't be worrying about it." Violet found her purse and zipped it open, checking the contents. With Perry gone, there was all the money she expected inside. "All right, I got to off to Miz LaRue's. You tell Neil I'm very sorry I missed him this morning."

"I will."

When mama left the house, Ruby was upstairs in a heartbeat. She pushed open the door to the room her mother and father once shared, the room where Daddy died.

She spotted the notebooks, stacked neatly atop Perry's unmade bed. They were the red-covered Big Chief notebooks of her school days. As Ruby bent over to pick them up, she became dizzy, lost her balance, and fell to the floor.

THIRTY

Claude Bougart climbed into his car and waved at us. Joe Never Smile and me, that is, standing together just inside the front door of Joe's house on Crozat Street.

Joe waved back through the screen to the friend who had introduced him to a New York cop; had vouched for me, had said to old Joe, "Don't mind them blue eyes, Joe. Hock, he's all right. You tell him anything he want to know about how it really goes."

Joe sighed as he watched Officer Bougart drive off. Then he said, "Most of Claude type, I don't be paying no mind to. Break my heart so."

"What's his type?"

"Black-in-blue."

"What's heartbreaking about a black cop?"

It was not true about Joe Never Smile, for now he smiled. It was one of those patient smiles that told me answers to any questions I asked were likely to come outside the usual sequence.

"I was back to the kitchen drinking my coffee, son. You want to join me in a cup?"

I said yes and followed the ancient hearse driver down a

corridor that ran the length of his house. There was a parlor and two or three other little rooms off the corridor. These were darkened places that smelled unused, like mildewed trunks in an attic. The kitchen was where Joe Never Smile spent his time, lived his life. It was a room big enough for a round table surrounded by chairs, and full of sunlight from a wall of windows and a door that led to a back garden. There was a radio at low volume on one of two counters. Johnny Hartman was singing "Lush Life."

One of the chairs was pulled out from the table. This was the spot where Joe Never Smile had been sitting when the doorbell rang. A coffee mug rested in a damp ring on top of a newspaper.

"You want to sit down over there?" Joe Never Smile motioned to a chair across from his own. I sat. My host went to the stove and put some heat under a glass coffee pot. "How you like your coffee?"

"Black."

The old man turned around from the stove. He screwed his dark features into the same sour expression as the late and pink-faced Father Tim Kelly, a Holy Cross priest from my boyhood who likewise had no respect for black coffee. "Protestant coffee" Father Tim always called it.

"But I got me some very good farm-fresh cream, and nice raw sugar," Joe Never Smile said. "Now, you still be telling me you want your coffee straight?"

"Make it light with sugar."

"That's better."

Joe Never Smile made a turn around his kitchen, going after the coffee things. He moved slowly, for fear he might slip and fall and break a bone. When we were both settled at the table with proper coffee, I reminded him, "You never answered me about black cops."

"I'm a old, old man." He seemed to know I would return to this subject. "And I be dealing in the sorrow business all my life. You know what I'm saying?"

Yes I did, I said.

"I got to ask you a question of my own, son. Would you say it's a dangerous occupation being a po-lice?"

"I would."

"More dangerous now than when you first started?"

"Yes."

"And would you also say there's more Negro po-lices now than when you first started?"

"I know for a fact there are."

"Ever strike you strange how just when it became more dangerous in a city they hire Negroes to deal with it?"

Here I was expecting to interrogate a man on several matters: some no-name kid murdered and mutilated like Clete Tyler, the mystery of MOMS, the meaning of a shirtless kid on Crozat Street calling himself Maybe Richard. And here was Joe Never Smile, the kind of old man with answers that dwarf a younger man's questions, and most certainly a younger man's immediate concerns.

"I never thought of it like that."

"No, I expect not." Joe Never Smile wiped his dark forehead with a napkin. Not because he was warm, I thought, but to soothe something in his mind. "Whole world's more dangerous than ever before in my long life. That's how come it is you see most of the U.S. Army is black men nowadays. Yes sir, black men. Negroes all got us some great opportunities in these trouble times. We can be soldiers and we can be po-lices."

"Heartbreaking."

"Son, I don't mean it to sound simple as that. The heartbreak come in imagining the terrible logic hiding just around the corner. Terrible logic of a black-in-blue world, you might say."

"How would *you* say it?"

"Things going to get worse before they get better. Maybe the country slide into a horrible, violent depression. By then, probably just about all the po-lices and all the soldiers going to be black. Which by then, you got the hope of all the people riding on black men. See my meaning?"

"No."

"White folks, they going to reject that kind of hope. See—true heartbreak."

Now I saw.

At least two minutes passed without either one of us saying anything. We sipped coffee and thought our separate thoughts. Time-outs from talking are the natural results of a conversation that runs deep.

Joe Never Smile finally spoke. "Claude bring you round here about that young black boy I take on his ride to glory yesterday, over by Pastor Hearn on Poydras Street?"

"Did you know him?"

"No, I didn't. He just another tragedy folks don't want to give a name to."

"Why not?"

"Ain't easy to carry on if you got to be recalling sad names. Folks these days, they just live and let die."

I had nothing to say to that. Not that it mattered. Joe Never Smile had enough to say for us both. I figured he would eventually tell me anything I wanted to know, along with a lot of other useful things, so long as I allowed him his own pace. Trying to change Joe Never Smile's pace would be like trying to turn around the *Queen Mary* in shallow water.

Joe looked down at the newspaper opened on the table in front of him. "Back a couple of years, they run a story about another black boy here in New Orleans—name of James Darby, just nine year old. James and his class over to Mahalia Jackson Elementary School, they all write to the president about what's on they minds. James letter, it touched the big man himself—enough so he wrote him back. Which is how come it made the news."

"In New York it was news, too." I remembered the James Darby account in the *Times*. "The kid was obsessed about random violence."

"You right. James, he wrote 'Mr. President, I want you to stop the killing in the city. I think somebody might kill me.' I am never going to forget them exact words. The boy wrote the big man in April, you know. Then come May and little James, he got shotgunned to death walking home after a Sunday picnic."

"On Mother's Day it was."

"I bet you never heard of two other black boys shot dead here same day as James Darby."

"No."

"One was ten year old, the other two. The young one, he was a shield in a gunfight. Nothing unusual about either one of them two colored boys and how they go. They didn't write no letters to the White House. Know what I'm saying?"

"I know, I know." I was now rubbing my forehead. "I'm the same as you, in a sense."

"What you talking?"

"In the sense of the sorrow business. I myself have seen all kinds of kids stretched out on morgue slabs—teenagers to toddlers." My breathing came hard. "I've seen babies snuffed in dumpsters."

Silence.

There was something dear and fierce and protective in Joe Never Smile's lined face, something that made him the father of us all. He whispered, "National goddamn disgrace."

"I need to ask you something."

"Go ahead ask. Claude say you all right."

"It's about that boy you took to glory. After he was killed, his body was mutilated—branded with the letters M-O-M-S. There was a man by the name of Cletus Tyler who was killed, the same day as the boy, and his body was branded the same way."

"Yeah, I know about all that."

"I know what the letters stand for. But what's the meaning?"

Joe Never Smile sighed. Then when he started talking he sounded like a man making a deathbed confession.

"Mutants, orphans and misfits—that all go back to before the war," he said. "War Between the States I'm talking about. You know Congo Square?"

I said I had heard mention of it on the radio, when Huggy

Louper tuned in WWOZ in his taxicab. Joe Never Smile told me that today's Louis Armstrong Park is built around the old Congo Square, where slaves were allowed to gather on Sundays back in the plantation era, to amuse themselves and to dance the *calinda.*

"That's a old African voodoo dance by way of slaves arrive here to New Orleans from Saint Domingue and Cuba," he said. "Black folks talk about *danse calinda* anymore—that's the Creole French for it—they pretty much showing ignorance."

"How so?"

"They only know about it from church, and that's nothing. Lot of your Negro preachers they swipe *calinda* from schoolbooks. They take what been disrespected by white folks as nothing more than a immodest dance where the womens line up on one side and mens on the other and then everybody come together wriggling wild to the beat of bamboo drums, and they go turn it into just another simple black church holy-roly deal. Fact is, *calinda* mean more, a lot more."

"Such as?"

"Number of things. *Calinda* teach that mens and womens no matter what got the power to make new life. Even if they existing slave-dead the power's inside them. *Calinda's* the idea that lowdown divided-up folks got real power when they get all excited and come together—power ain't nobody able to deny."

"Some people would call that subversive."

"They be damn right. That's how come they just about clean steal away the memory of *calinda*—'cause it's subversive. That's typical, though. Black folks born and raised here in New Orleans been robbed of just about everything in life, starting with history class at grade school. Louisiana school teach the type of history that'd be a wonderful thing if only it was true."

"How did you learn about *danse calinda?"*

"There's certain ones keeping memory alive for those who care to know."

"Certain . . . misfits?"

"It start out years ago in Jim Crow days we had a little set-apart society during Mardi Gras. They don't want coloreds in they damn parade back then, see. Even today they only got these Zulu Aid and Pleasure Club fools wear grass skirts and bones in they noses. So we start up our little alternate festivities. Mutants, Orphans, and Misfits we call ourselves, sort of a sorry joke on history. We just get together at Congo Square like the slaves we come from, we drink beer and clown around."

"This MOMS outfit, it's still around?"

"Oh, yeah. It's still about mis-fitting, only even more so than years back. Now it's about a lot of our young black men realizing they sentenced to life on the outside of society with no options whatsoever—including help from black folks. Ain't enough they orphaned and misfit, now they been made into mutants, see. MOMS ain't a joke today."

"What is it?"

"Disease and true crime, I call it. Never going to be rubbed out by inventing a new medicine pill or building new prisons neither. Lot of prison cells already occupied by the exact wrong people. And even if they was a pill, it wouldn't be sick people need to take it. It'd be the so-called healthy ones need pills to turn they hearts human." Joe Never Smile paused to sip coffee. "You think I be talking riddles?"

"I think you're talking about the crime of poverty."

Joe nodded his head. Then he pushed himself up from his chair and crossed the kitchen to where he kept coats and hats and an assortment of walking canes pegged to a wall. "Come on with me, son," he said, taking down a cane. He chose the thickest one, the one with a curved handle wrapped up in a hundred rubber bands or so. Warm as it was, he also slipped on a coat.

He led me back through the hallway to the front porch. He locked the door behind him. Without a word, I followed the father of us all down off the porch to the sidewalk. We walked east along Crozat to the corner of Basin.

Joe chattered as we walked. "I can't never leave the house no more without a stick. Doc say I'm all-over brittle, like to crack up like a china vase if I was to fall down. He tell me, 'You got a crick in your git-up now, you surely ain't ought to be working with horses.' Say I got to give up on my funerals. Ain't that the shits?" He raised his big cane up over his head, like an Irish warrior swinging a shillelagh. "This here old thing with the extra rubber band grip, Doc say I got to take it with me when I got to go outside, lean on it like it was my leg. I calls it my clumper."

"Where are we going?" I asked.

"On a sentimental journey."

We turned north on Basin, keeping to the cemetery wall. Eventually, Joe Never Smile led me through the sexton's gate. This was after a twenty-minute stroll that would have taken five were I alone.

I sneaked a look at my wristwatch. Joe Never Smile apparently had eyes in the back of his head. "This about the last place you got to worry what time it is, son."

Joe started off toward some distant spot in the cemetery he knew well enough to ignore most of everything we passed. Everything but a certain two monuments.

I asked Joe about the first one, a tall marble tomb with Greek columns in front and a dozen people huddled around it, tourists in sneakers and crinkly Gore-Tex outfits. The tourists were chalking Xs on the sides of the tomb, crossing themselves like Catholics even if they were not, turning around three times and counting off in Spanish—*unos, dos, tres.* Joe Never Smile pointed at the tomb with his clumper. "That there is Marie LaVeau resting place. You hear of her?"

I told him I had.

"All kind of strangeness come around to visit that old dead voodoo queen," Joe said. "Heavy-metal musical types, they come by to worship her, like this cemetery a church. I ain't lying. Then you got your Bible crowd, also your motorcycle crowd. They convinced for different reasons that Satan live right in that tomb along with Marie. No lie. So all these fools they come 'round here throwing little gifts up top of the tomb."

Joe elevated his clumper. "Look up, see what I mean?"

I saw beads on strings drooping over the sides of the flat-topped marble slab—rosaries?—and also the heads and limbs of dead, moldering animals. Chickens mostly, also rats and cats and maybe a goat. I said, "That's got to be one disgusting mess up there."

"Prob'ly so." Joe shook his head. "Old bloody bones is laying up there, beads from Mardi Gras, coins, bricks wrapped in tin foil, hanks of dead folks' hair, cats been swung by the neck 'til they dead—and mouses eaten up by flies. All that stuff, the voodoo folks they call it gris-gris. S'posed to have powers. Shoo!"

Joe lowered his clumper, but raised it again to point out the very next tomb. This was less grand than the one for New Orleans' most famous *voudouienne,* but not by much.

"Dutch Morial lying cold inside of that one," Joe said. "That'd be Ernest Morial, first Negro elected mayor here. Looked white, but Jim Crow say if you got one thirty-second of African blood don't matter how you look—you black, that's it. I know Dutch when he was a young man bragging on how he pass. Then come the civil rights movement, so-called. And Dutch—oh man, he suddenly the ace of spades."

We slowly made our way through the rest of the cemetery. We were quiet about it, except for our shoes and the clumper making thick echoes in the narrow brick paths bordered by marble and limestone monuments.

Finally we stopped at a gray tomb the size of a refrigerator. It looked as common and unassuming as a refrigerator, too, until Joe raised up his clumper and motioned me to take a closer look.

There was a small inlay on the front, which was a stone door. The inlay replicated a hearse drawn by a pair of swayback horses, driven by a stern-faced black man. Below the inlay were a pair of chiseled words, JOE and MOMS. And at the top of the door, where chrome script on a real refrigerator might have spelled out Kelvinator, an inscription had been cut into the slate: IT'S THIRTEEN O'CLOCK—DO YOU KNOW WHERE YOUR CHILDREN ARE?

"What is this?" I asked, turning to Joe Never Smile. He crossed himself. I did the same, and felt thumping in my chest. And around us a crushing quietude, silence so complete I could hear the tourists counting in Spanish from halfway across the cemetery. *Uno, dos, tres . . .*

"This here where we come yesterday to put to rest the ashes of that tragedy boy," Joe said. He stepped close to the tomb and pulled open the stone door, left unsealed from the day before. Inside was a maze of cubicles—some empty, others occupied by cremation urns. The urns had metal strips stamped with dates, though not with names. "This here's where they all are, leastwise the tragedies come to my personal attention."

"In this tomb . . . ?" My throat went too thick for talking. And suddenly the waxy odor of lilies seemed as heavy and threatening as thunderclouds, though neither flowers nor clouds were anywhere in sight.

"Ain't too fancy, as you see plain," Joe said, not looking back at me, leaning on the clumper with both his gnarled hands. He sniffed at the cemetery air.

"Thirteen o'clock," I said, slowly grasping the unusual charity run by the father of us all. "Meaning time's run out?"

Joe's face brightened. He turned to me. "Not too many understand my joke."

"No."

"I had this tomb put here some years ago, intending it for my ownself when I'm called to glory. But with things the way they are nowadays . . . well, I figure it ain't fitting for me to be cold like all the rest."

"Cold?"

"Meaning the way folks shun the tragedy boys, even

when they drop dead. Folks just box them up, say some prayers, stash the ash somewhere, and move on."

"But Joe Never Smile, he takes them in."

"Sure I do. Even dead boys need they daddy."

All three of them—two in the front buckets, one sitting cross-legged in the Jeep's small backseat—were riding along the pot-holed street in the late morning. They wore combat boots, olive drab military fatigues, and plastic Hallowe'en masks. Guns bounced in their laps.

One man was a jolly pirate with a gold earring, the second a smiling hobo with a plastic cigar butt built into protruding plastic lips, the third a beaming faerie princess in a rhinestone tiara. Their dime-store masks were too small to span their foreheads and did nothing to cover up their jowls. Consequently, a lot of pale, puffy skin was showing around the edges of each disguise.

The driver (Hobo) slowed down to a crawl. A red-white-and-blue U.S. mail van raced past, operated by a man with a ponytail and a Walkman radio oblivious to a Jeep full of men in children's masks. Hobo swiveled around to make sure traffic was clear in both directions. Then he gunned the Jeep's engine and ran it up over the sidewalk, around to the back of a weathered building with a caved-in side wall. It took several minutes for all the dust to settle.

The collapsed building that hid the Jeep from notice by passers-by was once upon a time an upcountry-style juke joint. Its owners gave it an extravagant name, to impress the city clientele: *Di Moin Qui Vous Laimein,* which was Creole for Tell Me Who You Love. A musician called Antoine Domino used to be a regular.

After playing rhythm and blues piano and singing for tourists in the Quarter, Antoine liked to let his hair down among his own kind, in the black neighborhood where he grew up happy and well fed. And so in the tiny hours of most mornings, he would would drop by the *Di Moin,* as people called it.

True to his nickname, Fats Domino would order double and triple portions of his favorites: the house gumbo, the trout po'boy, the oyster roll in Tabasco sauce. Whenever he was around, the other patrons could tell what day of the week it was just by looking at the Cadillac out on the front curb. Antoine owned seven Cadillacs, which he alternated according to a daily color code.

For many people—including the three men now climbing out of the Jeep, racking their guns, sneezing through their Hallowe'en masks, brushing off dust—Fats Domino and his joyful music were the hazy innocence of long, long ago. Cadillacs had fins way back then; William McKinley was the last president somebody managed to kill, with probably only one person in a hundred able to name the assassin; and some noisy Negro up in Newark called LeRoi Jones was able to shock people by writing, "I am not interested in being a murderer, but then I am not interested in being a dier, either; I am not going to kill you, but I am not going to let you kill me."

The man who had occupied the cramped backseat (Faerie Princess) was last to emerge from the Jeep. Like his comrades, he carried a TEC-9 semiautomatic assault pistol fitted out with a barrel extension and silencer, encased in a hard plastic stock and butt for hip firing—the so-called street-sweeper, favored by drug gangs in the city's housing projects and terrorists elsewhere in the world and capable of firing thirty-six rounds of hollow-point bullets per magazine clip. Additionally, two bits of hardware dangled from his belt, like a pair of bulky swords. On his one side was a skinny two-foot length of steel with the bottom end twisted into letters, on the other a portable acetylene torch.

Faerie Princess said to Hobo and Pirate, "You boys about got your balls up and ready for this here?"

"Ready!" said the other two in gruff unison.

"All right then." Faerie Princess held up an arm, cocked as if he was holding up a checkered flag at a speedway. "Get ready."

Faerie Princess stepped out from around the old juke joint to where he could peek at the street again. He clanked as he walked. A couple of cars drove by. When they were gone from view the arm chopped downward, and Faerie Princess barked, "Move!"

Hobo and Pirate bent their knees and scuttled—serpentine-style, as they had practiced—across an open stretch of freshly bulldozed embankment, making their way toward a cinder block structure at the riverbank. Faerie Princess scrambled along behind them.

The target of the day for a trio of urban commandos was a discarded building—Substation No. 141, recently deactivated in favor of real estate development—belonging to the Louisiana Power & Light Company. Unplugged, as it were, the substation still appeared forbidding, deadly to the touch.

A low cement building sat in a small fenced yard of bleached gravel. The building and yard were caged in a dome of razor wire. Surrounding the building was a network of braided steel cables, red fuse boxes the size of doors, and corkscrew surge pilings. High-voltage warning signs—DANGER in block letters, red thunder bolts and black skull-and-crossbone figures on a background of taxi yellow—were bolted to the fence, inside and out.

The caged compound once emitted a constant buzz, the kind of sound that remains in the ear long after it has quit. Once there were frequent showers of white-hot sparks, rambling bursts of electrical current spouting through the cable runoff points. Even deactivated, not many would want to chance entering the compound.

But the LP&L design experts, comfortable professionals all, had not imagined an age in which desperation for shelter would make their impregnable handiwork a home. Which is what Substation No. 141 had become: home to a gang of distinctly unlucky squatters, more frightened by the perils of life in the open air than by the possibility of electrocution.

A flock of dozing seagulls perched on the razor wire blinked their eyes and cawed as the commandos neared.

Pirate, first to reach the torn part of the fence, looked up at the gulls through the eyeholes of his mask. He turned to his comrades, sniggering. "Birdies fixing to spoil our surprise."

"Shut your face," Faerie Princess said in a whispered snarl. "We got to catch them little niggers in their sleep."

Pirate pulled back a flap torn in the fence. Like their masks, the opening was too small for jowly men. Hobo pulled a wire cutter from his pocket and snipped a larger opening. Pirate pulled some more.

One after the other, the commandos quietly piled through the fence. They stepped lightly over the gravel toward a steel door at the front of the cinder block building. The door stood propped in its frame, hinges missing.

Faerie Princess barked, "Showtime!" He pulled the steel bar from his belt and used it to pry away the door. Then he powered up his acetylene torch, the blue-white flame providing a moment's faint illumination of the small space inside.

Black boys lay on cardboard mats that covered the concrete floor. Their bodies were entwined, like kittens, to increase warmth. Startled heads rose.

Someone screamed.

Pirate squeezed off half the magazine of his TEC-9. The silencer made it sound as innocent as a motorboat.

Another scream.

All three men now fired at the floor, sweeping the high-powered weapons in short but comprehensive arcs. They emptied the magazines, filling the dark space with smoke and the quick silence of the dead.

Putt-putt-putt-putt-putt-putt-putt.

They reloaded, and fired all over again.

Putt-putt-putt-putt-putt-putt-putt.

Faerie Princess powered up the torch once more. "Count up the coons," he ordered.

Hobo pulled a flashlight from his shirt pocket and shone it over the bloodied floor. His lips moved under his mask as he counted. Pirate counted, too, while Faerie Princess got down to business with the acetylene torch, heating up the end of the steel bar until the letters glowed red.

"Fifteen," Hobo finally said. Pirate added to the assessment, "Hoo-whee, that's goddamn good!"

"No time for bragging," Faerie Princess said. "Just hold your light steady for me, left to right as we go."

Hobo moved behind with the flashlight as Faerie Princess stepped from body to body, searing stomachs and buttocks and chests and limbs with hot red letters. Sometimes he branded a dead boy clear through his shorts or T-shirt or whatever raggedy thing he wore.

The smell of burnt flesh swirled in the smoke. Faerie Princess counted off the bodies. "One, two, three, four, five, six . . ."

Pirate kept watch in the doorway. He saw nothing to worry about, nothing but a wooden tug gliding along down on the river. What alarmed him was the odor behind his back.

"Holy shit, it's like burning tires in here!" Pirate's eyes watered and he coughed. So did the other two.

"Shut your face!" Faerie Princess shouted. He reheated the steel bar and continued counting. "Seven, eight, nine, ten . . ."

When he had finished up with the fifteenth branding, Faerie Princess led the way back to the Jeep. Hobo took the wheel again, waited for a clear view, and then did a spinout from behind Fats Domino's beloved old juke joint, over the sidewalk, back into the street.

The tugboat crewmen down on the river decided to investigate the peculiar activity they had seen up on the levee.

THIRTY-ONE

Picking herself up from the floor, Ruby felt puffed and weightless, as if she were a balloon on a slow rise toward the bedroom ceiling. She clutched hard at Perry's ink-stained notebooks—anchors that would keep her from floating off.

She took two wobbly steps around from the foot of Perry's sloppy bed and flopped belly-down across the mattress, covered in a pile of twisted sheets and blankets that stank of cigarettes and liquored breath. Ruby rolled over, holding her nose. The ceiling swirled crazily.

Flushed with heat, and an overwhelming guilt for leaving her family, Ruby closed her eyes. She had fled, she had tried to forget, she believed she had succeeded at both. Yet now the simplest wisp of memory—lavender sachet—held physical power, rendering her helpless to do anything but wait for a return of equilibrium. As she waited, she remembered more.

What was it Daddy used to sing to his babies that soothed them so? So long ago in the cottage, before Daddy grew so ill himself that he forgot their names—Ruby and Janny—and Perry, practically his son.

Tighter and tighter Ruby squeezed her eyes, imagining

her long-ago father; seeing his handsome profile; watching him putter in the garden, sweat breaking across his wide brown back, his hammer hands delicately working the soil and flowers and grass.

In sweet delirium, her father's hands now lay on Ruby's fevered brow. And then she heard his voice, its deep and stony rich timbre. Daddy was not a man who often spoke. But when he did, his talk came like rain held too long in heavy clouds.

Finally, her Daddy's comforting song:

Three little children lying in the bed,
One most sick and the other most dead;
Call for the doctor, and the doctor said,
Feed them children crackling bread . . .

Still more memory in Ruby's spinning head:

Mama out doors on a summer Monday—laundry day. All the neighbor ladies scrubbing clothes in tubs of steaming water set out on back porches, the sharp odor of Fels Naptha soap competing with the sugary bouquet of morning glories and snapdragons and periwinkles in the alley breeze.

And Mama taking her part in lively woman talk up and down the alley. Everybody else taking their turns at *tearing up some air,* as the women said. *Magpie chatter,* Daddy said.

Young Ruby, all ears and gangling arms and legs, receiving her first inkling of sexual mystery . . .

Mama making a fanning motion with a free hand, telling the other ladies, *My Willis—why, he thrill me to the thigh bone whenever he open his mouth. He got the sound of a African lion inside him, even when he whisper.*

The ladies all laughing in sisterly communion, husky laughs men are not meant to hear. There was no issue to take, for Mama had not bragged. The commanding beauty of Willis Flagg's voice was a simple fact, as attested by a next-door lady. *Oh, you so lucky, Vi. That man of yours could say night was day and we'd all be strapping on our sunglasses. If Willis was white—why shoo, he be at least the governor.*

Ruby opened wet eyes to the present.

The ceiling had stopped spinning. Now she could do what she had come to do—snoop. She propped herself up against the headboard and riffled through the pages of the first of Perry's four Big Chief notebooks, the one he had marked on the cover, "Thoughts from a Dirt Lane #1."

Perry's private voice was indeed thoughtful, strangely eloquent and innocent for a man of his unfortunate experience. It was an inner voice freed of harshness and male bravado required by the streets of Perry's life. His penmanship was likewise surprising, cleanly and artfully set onto paper. Perry wrote with a delicate and careful hand within the wide lines of what he clearly intended as a serious journal. His tiny letters slanted neatly rightward. Never once did his pen's black ink overlap the faint blue horizontal lines or the red margin line.

Perry had been a reader of books just as Ruby had, providing them both the ability to transcend rude surroundings. The fastidiousness of Perry's handwriting—a common trait among prison inmates, she remembered Hock once telling her—was certainly a contrast to Perry's sloppy room. Ruby kicked three empty, crushed Dixie beer cans over the edge of the bed, along with a dirty ashtray and a girlie magazine. Then she settled into reading page one of the ruminations of her thieving cousin Perry Duclat:

> *I remember a cracker from up to West Monroe always trying to get some politics going on inside of Angola. Warden be spreading it around this boy was a communist agitator and therefore unprofitable to be associating with. Communism is dead and gone. But damn if it's still a word like to get a jailer all frothy. Don't ever get any kind of rise out of a jailee though. Anyhow they take this cracker and lock him down in what the offi-*

cers call the coon wing. Cracker in the coon wing's supposed to shame a sorry white ass, but it don't really. Besides this here cracker he just about pure delighted to have us niggers all round him. They cage him just one trap over from Clete and me. I am referring to my cellie Cletus Tyler.

Oh my but this boy was a fright to look at. Yellow hair so wild you think his skull maybe on fire. Lumpy skin the color of old bubble gum. Had him a big mouth too.

Now some boys with the big mouth you don't remember a word they say even if they holler day and night. But this here one name of Rusty was smarter than he look I give him that. Real interesting to listen to. He made you recollect him because he had this way of putting across a big idea so even a man who been just about belittled to death can understand. Like for instance what he say about a fat man at the chow table.

He ask my cellie—You ever been to a great big old barbecue in your life? Clete he lie and say—Course I have, I got a family you know and we got us reunions in the summertime. Rusty say—Okay let me ask you would you let just one fat man eat up ninety pounds out of a hundred pounds of meat on the table? Clete say—I'd sooner eat a bug. Rusty look at Clete like a proud papa would and he say—That's right you'd make that fat man put back that grub he don't need.

Well that is a good lesson I hold in my mind now while I'm setting here after I finish chores for the cripple man and try to write my way to some sense out of a belittling life. I am referring to my own life and to the back porch of old peg-legged Mr. Newcombe place that when I was a young boy used to be my Uncle Willis place before a couple of good old fat boys come take it clean away by using tricks they don't lock you up for so long as you pull them on poor folks. I am referring to a couple of hogs whose time will come by and by.

What do you know about that! I just look up and see Miss Hassie Pinkney from next door peeping on me out her kitchen window. First I thought some old mule be peeping from a barn then I know it actually Miss Hassie scowling face in that window. Hassie spreading it all round the lane and down by the levee like I am Jack the Ripper dangerous. The woman don't own half the sense of a mule and none of the mercy of a ass either. Lucky thing for Miss Hassie lack of thinking ain't the same as lack of air. Elsewise when she start her ignorant yapping her head would blow out like a flat tire.

No matter what Miss Hassie say I am surely no danger to nobody. Truth is I am nothing but a fortysomething-year-old nigger can't figure how them decades pass or who done steal away my happy days—maybe just the thief of time or maybe people themselves.

You know I can think back in time and feel my Mama Rose touch on my skin? That sound crazy I know. Also I know Mama touch a lot of mens she got no business touching. But she never touch nobody true and tender like she touch her little boy. And oh my I remember that touch same as I remember five minutes ago. Sure I know what my Daddy Toby call Mama and what some nasty-mind others like Miss Hassie call her too. Don't take away from the fact Mama was a beauty and it was beauty touching me.

My Aunt Violet and my Uncle Willis they never say one hurting thing about Mama, even though she let me go. That is the worst thing people do, throw they kids away. My daddy Toby Jones is evil, so I expect he do the worst thing. But poor Mama not evil. I suppose I go to my grave trying to figure out why she let me go.

Uncle Willis he say he ain't a churchy man. He don't intend to lie by that. But all the same he is spiritual in a way. Uncle Willis always say about my Mama Rose something I think is godly-like—Before we blame we got to see if we can excuse.

I remember Uncle Willis setting right here where I am now. Setting on this porch smoking his pipe. I remember Uncle Willis and me horsing round this little backyard where he so proud of his grass so soft on his feet and so proud of his lilacs on the fence and his chinaberry tree.

No I ain't hardly a danger.

Actual truth is I'm too damn sad to be dangerous.

I am sad as a dead bird's birdbath.

Ruby's eyes were streaming as she finished this, Perry's maiden journal entry. She had touched the broken bits of a man's heart. And she thought, Shame on me for blaming Perry before excusing him, for betraying Daddy's faith.

She felt another nauseous wave. Ruby was glad to be lying down. The Big Chief notebooks spilled from her sweating hands, all but "Thoughts from a Dirt Lane #4." When she recovered, she turned to the last few pages, and read:

I see these boys and girls roaming round the streets of New Orleans. Hundreds of them living in shadows everybody pretend they can't see. Well it ain't hardly different for these children than for Clete and me up to Angola except for the fact that in the trap we all got us a place to sleep at night. These children they free but not free. They living but not living. They dead but not dead. They eat. They breathe. They suffer till they beyond suffering.

To my way of thinking it only going to be worse when these childrens grow older and wiser and meaner. Then they going to figure out what happened to them is a crime.

Somewheres they could be a war in some desert. Somewheres they could be scientists shooting up rocketships to Mars. Up in New York City they could be putting on a cock-a-whoop Broadway show like Mama always want to be in someday. A fine show with a orchestra and singing and dancing—starring Rose Duclat in a slinky mink and a spangly gown. But all that don't mean nothing to a child with no place to dream. Don't mean nothing to a child who don't mean nothing. See what I mean about crime?

I see the childrens everywhere. Mostly boys I don't know why. Down under the levee right here off Tchoupitoulas Street. And over by Chartres Street. Also back of the Di Moin *where they close up the power station. All kind of hiding places like that. Sometimes these dirty raggedy children brave enough to show they faces right in Jackson Square and the French Market. The polices chase them off lest they upset the almighty tourists.*

It troubles my mind all of this. Mushroom tea it helps.

As I have lots of leisure time I drop by the library up to Rampart Street most days. One time in the library I seen a magazine article with pictures to it all about childrens roaming the streets of Rio de Janeiro and Caracas and Mexico City and Calcutta and I don't know where all else. Plenty other places in the world though—oh my, plenty.

When I look close at the eyes of these foreigner childrens in the magazine pictures they look the exact same as the boys and girls getting thrown away right here in New Orleans. Most others see that magazine though they like a fat man at the chow table. They don't see nothing below they big guts.

Children who don't mean nothing might like to see that magazine. But it ain't going to happen. Them snotty librarian ladies they know the thrown-aways when they see them. And they ain't letting them in by God. I think if they could these snotty ladies would just go ahead and hang the childrens in advance of their eventual foul deeds that deserve the gallows.

How come I can see what I see but people born high and fat are blind fools? How come in this world one fool can make many fools but one wise man make only a few other wise ones? Anyhow that's the way it seem to go.

One time at the library I hear this snot with her arm held up like a traffic police say to a thrown-away child—You bring along your mama or daddy before you come in here, boy. Child just about shamed to stone. Oh my, I know shame. But snots and fat folks they don't. Blind fools.

Fools so blind they don't even respect the dangerous words they got waiting for the likes of me on they library shelves. Like these words I copy down from Dr. King who at the time before they went and gunned him down was thinking about Vietnam where we went and birthed a whole mother-lode of thrown-aways—

As I have walked among the desperate, rejected and angry young men, I have told them that Molotov cocktails and rifles would not solve their problems. They asked if our own nation wasn't using massive doses of violence to solve its problems, to bring about the changes it wanted. Their questions hit home, and I knew that I could never again raise my voice against the violence of the oppressed in the ghettos without having first spoken clearly about the greatest purveyor of violence in the world today—my own government. Violence is refusing to give up privileges and plea-

sures that come from immense profits. Violence is when machines and computers, profits and property rights are considered more important than people. Violence is a nation approaching spiritual death, a nation that continues year after year to spend more money on military defense than on programs of social uplift—

Oh my but it does my sorry heart good to read a man like that. Dr. King is one dead man stronger than ten thousand live men. Dr. King I swear he sound just like Uncle Willis used to talk when he get good and righteous.

That first time I see Clete up to Shug's, I tell him what I read about childrens roaming streets, and Dr. King and all. He listen to me careful-like.

Then Cletus he say—Don't matter, though, they done killed the head nigger. Now they got them a plan for us . . . Oh my gawd in heaven, they sure got them a plan.

Slap!

As if she had just drunk a whole pot of Mama's strong coffee, Ruby's head was clear of the fog of passing time and wanton forgetfulness. Suddenly one event connected with another, one person's story to another, all of it constituting an avalanche of meaning.

Daddy . . . Perry . . . the dirt lane . . . real estate . . . mutants, orphans, and misfits . . .

All of it and all of them. *Did Hock know?*

Ruby reached down to the floor beside the bed and collected the Big Chief notebooks in her arms. Then she rose and went to the smaller bedroom, where she put away the notebooks in her suitcase, for safekeeping.

She ran downstairs to the kitchen, her heart in her throat. She took the New Orleans telephone directory out from the cupboard where Mama always kept it and searched for a number.

She would have dialed that number. But an incoming call beat her to the punch.

"What? Hello?"

"Hey now—that you, Ruby?"

"My Gosh! Claude?"

"Yeah, it's me." Claude Bougart paused. He could hear Ruby's strained breathing. "That's some way to answer a telephone. What's got you all jitters, girl?"

"Is my husband with you?"

"What makes you ask?"

"Have you seen him? Please don't fool with me, Claude."

"Well now, earlier this morning we hooked up. I'm looking for him again. Thought he might be back there by now."

"What do you want with him?"

"Ruby, now you just tell him we got us another incident. You tell him—"

"I said don't mess with me." Ruby was shaking but her voice did not betray this. "What have you got?"

"Lot of boys been killed this time."

"You're calling from the scene? You want Hock to come join you?"

"Sound like you been through the drill before."

"I'm a tin wife."

Ruby took some comfort in this crisp back-and-forth with Claude. It was in direct contrast with the vague and roiling discomfort washing over her again. Again her mouth felt sour, her stomach faring no better.

"You remember *Di Moin Qui Vous Laimein?*" Claude asked.

"Tell me who you love."

"Don't you be messing with *me.*"

"Oh, no . . . I don't mean." Ruby touched her forehead, surprised by how warm and moist she was. "Come on now, Claude. I mean *Di Moin,* the old rhythm-and-blues joint up past Nicholls wharf."

"Yeah, that's it. They set up a command post there. Tell your husband it's bad. Tell him I can't afford to be around to make him introductions."

"He's going to understand that?"

"The man ain't slow as most white people I know in my time."

THIRTY-TWO

"Sweet suffering Jesus! Stinks like a pool of goat piss from hell inside of there." The sergeant stopped talking to let fly a big looge of tobacco spit. "Being a distinguished visitor, Detective, we best strap you up with the proper protection."

The sergeant—one Lavond LeMay—was as merry and solicitous as a department store Santa Claus. Which came as no particular surprise to me. Cops in New York are likewise jovial at homicide scenes; the grislier the scene, the giddier the cops.

Two minutes ago I had made the acquaintance of Sergeant Lavond LeMay. That was after I badged my way past the outer line of uniforms at an old juke joint called the *Di Moin* and asked for the command sergeant. A skinny patrolman with his hand down the back of his pants scratching his haunches nodded toward the river, in the general direction of a low cement building inside a small fenced square. He said, "Go see the man over yonder in the panama hat."

After getting the name of the panama owner, my badge and I walked *yonder*—through an opening torn into the fence and through a second line of uniforms, then up to the building itself. I smiled at a middle-aged, softly built man in the kind of three-piece polyester suit available in the plain-clothes cop section of any Sears Roebuck in America, and a floppy white panama that was all his own style. I lied to beat the band.

"Sergeant, it's a pleasure to meet you. I'm Detective Neil Hockaday, a close friend of Alderman Hippocrates Beauregard Giradoux."

"Don't sound like you from around here, friend."

"Actually, no. I'm all the way down from New York City to study your very excellent southern detection methods. Soon as Hippo heard the news flash of this terrible homicide you're investigating—why, he sent me over on the double."

The sergeant looked confused. Either that or his underwear was chafing him.

"Hippo says I got to especially look you up, Sergeant LeMay," I said. "Hippo tells me you're one of his top men."

I waited through a couple of tense seconds. Then Sergeant Lavond LeMay's ashy white face cleared of suspicion, and he said, "Well that's right nice of Hippo. Why'nt you just call me Vonny?"

"Vonny it is then. Call me Hock."

I took hold of the sergeant's hand, gloved in a gauzy fabric, and shook it. Vonny LeMay wore gloves because he was albino fair. His face was round as a silver dollar, and he had silver fuzz for brows over eyes as pale blue as skim milk. The wide-brimmed panama kept his head and face bathed in skin-preserving shade. Vonny was at the center of a gathering herd of New Orleans detectives, all of them white, about a yardstick away from the building doorway. Vonny had one foot propped on top of a wooden crate stenciled U.S. ARMY SURPLUS.

We talked pleasantly for a bit. How long I had been in New Orleans, how I liked it so far, when I was returning to New York—that sort of thing. Conversational foreplay, as I was beginning to learn, was a vital element of Louisiana communication.

Eventually, I told Vonny I wanted a look inside. *Did I?* This was when the sergeant remarked merrily on the foulness of the odor I would encounter, and how I would require proper protection.

Vonny turned his head and spat again, missing one of the other detective's shoes by about an inch.

"Ain't healthy a-tall to be breathing down that kind of gott-damn nigger reek other side of the door," Vonny said. He cast a look around him to make sure there were no black cops in the vicinity, assuming his remark would give no offense to a white man. "Don't you agree?"

"You've been inside yourself, Vonny?"

"Hell no, not me. Nobody gone in 'cept for the fingerprint boys taking a looksee right now."

"Any of them come out yet?"

"Nope."

The air wafting out from that door was truly malodorous, like the worst blast of sewer gas I ever wanted to know. A breeze off the Mississippi, slight as it was, blew the stink up everybody's nose, mine included. I coughed. My eyes smarted, as if somebody had cracked open a cannister of tear gas.

"Well, you know—maybe it don't make no never-mind how your niggers go, life's cheap to them people." Vonny offered something of a sympathetic sigh at what he saw as an unfortunate truth.

Just then, a three-man crew of gasping forensic officers staggered out from the doorway into the open air. They hacked and spit into handkerchiefs until the hankies were so sopped they had to drop them.

"G'wan now, take one of these here," Vonny said, not particularly moved by his colleagues' discomfort. He removed his foot from the crate, pulled off the thin wooden lid, and reached inside. He handed me an oxygen mask.

I slipped olive drab canvas over my head and adjusted the front pieces to fit my face—vinyl goggles, rubber snout.

How could I forget the last time I had occasion to wear such a thing?

Bombs bursting in air . . .

On the ground below the bombs is young Neil Hockaday, special commando of the United States Army—giving proof through the night that our flag was still there and all that crap.

I rise in moonlight from the muck bed of a blue-black river. I have hidden there for hours, submerged in tangled reeds and fetid water, sucking air from the surface through a bamboo shoot, waiting for Charlie. I am equipped to face the foe with a belt-load of murder instruments, courtesy of my government. I am frightened beyond what I ever believed fright to be. I want to scream for my mother, Mairead. But no—I must not make a sound. I must do the duty for which I have been trained. As my Alabama lieutenant has lectured me a thousand times, "Life's cheap to these fuckin' gooks, you got to give them a taste of their own fuckin' throat-slashin' medicine." Here comes Charlie. I swing hard and swift my U.S. Army cutlass machete, whomping it surely and deeply and quietly into the surprised yellow neck of a sloe-eyed Vietnamese. I see as he gasps and dies that he is a boy, another boy. So many are. They tell me that Charlie boy, sinking into the river ooze, is the enemy. Night after night in such moonlit streams where I am waist deep in water thick with silt and fresh blood after doing my duty, I whisper my devotions to the Virgin Mary and Glory Be to the Father. And I ask myself, How in the name of Holiness can somebody called Charlie be my enemy? I decide that anyone who answers is more stupid than myself. Stupidly, I pretend my cutlass is a rosary, and run my fingers up and down the slimy blade. I whisper the devotions all over again, before I resume hiding and breathing through bamboo and waiting for another Charlie. And I beg forgiveness for murderous sin after murderous sin after murderous sin. But I know that if I were God I would never forgive the likes of me.

I hear again what Ruby told me—twenty minutes ago when I walked back into Mama's house and found her at the kitchen with the city telephone directory and some Big Chief notebooks, and her head in her hands. I recognized Ruby's handwriting on the cover of one notebook—the name "Teddy" and a phone number.

"Are you all right?"

"Just dizzy." Ruby pushed aside the directory and notebooks. I poured her a glass of ice water from a pitcher in the refrigerator. Also I soaked a dishtowel in cold water and made a compress. "Daddy . . . Perry . . . the cottage in the dirt lane . . ." Her voice was breathy, as if she had just awakened from a dream. "Mutants, orphans, and misfits . . . All of it and all of them. Don't you see, Hock?"

"I'm beginning to."

"One event connects with another."

"Ruby—?"

She interrupted, to urgently relay Claude's telephone message, about *something bad* I had to go see for myself. She said nothing about my disappearing act that morning.

"You'll need a taxi." Ruby told me to dash out in the street and flag down Huggy Louper before he reached the corner. Which I did. But I told Huggy to keep the engine running while I ran back to the house, worried about Ruby.

"Help me," I said. "Your father grew sick over time from a snake bite, then died—this connects with Perry?"

"I'm not making perfect sense, Hock. Women's intuition, it's like that."

"Nobody should question women's intuition."

The telephone rang.

"It might be Claude again," Ruby said. "Answer it."

It was not Claude. "It's me, keeping in touch," Perry said.

"Hold on, I want you to hear something," I told him. I walked with the phone away from the wall, stretching the cord to the table. I held out the receiver and said to Ruby, "Tell us about your women's intuition."

"Who's us?"

"As if you didn't know. Go on, talk."

"All right. Perry's on to something about that day the

snake got Daddy, he's got all these notebooks full of memories and impressions about the lane off Tchoupitoulas Street, where the family started out." Ruby stopped. I nodded for her to go on. "The notebooks are beautifully written, Hock. You'll see. The stories all connect, from the beginning right up to now—with Perry being hunted for Clete Tyler's murder, and somehow it involves MOMS. Don't ask me how, I just feel it from reading Perry's stories."

I pulled back the receiver and spoke into it. "You getting this?" Perry said, "Ruby thinks I write good?"

I shifted the receiver back to Ruby. "That's how you know what MOMS stands for?" I asked. "From the notebooks?"

"No. Janny broke the news on her television show."

"Your sister knows?"

"She quoted some anonymous City Hall source about its being a mysterious acronym."

"That's all she said about it?"

"Yes, she left the story an open question." An open question, like the expression that played over Ruby's face. "Cletus Tyler's the misfit? Perry's the orphan? Hock—is the killer telling a story?"

"Delivering a message anyway."

Waiting for Charlie . . .

Hot as it was, we paired off in trenches and slept as we could. Our arms and legs were wrapped around another for mutual protection. But there was no sure way to protect against dying alone, not even in crowded trenches covered in jungle timber and leaves.

Many was the time we awoke to find a comrade with his throat hacked open. Just one of us, dead in the trench.

The message was clear. If we stayed where we were, the Cong could get us whenever they pleased, one by one by one.

"The taxi's waiting," Ruby said. "You'd better roll."

"Huggy isn't going anywhere," I told Ruby. Then I spoke into the phone to Perry, "Look—I have to see you, I haven't got much time. We can meet at the shed."

"I left there, I ain't one for gunplay."

"Then where are you?"

"Ain't saying to a po-lice."

"Hold the line." I pressed the telephone receiver against my chest and looked at the notebook with Teddy's name on it. I asked Ruby, "You're planning to see your cousin?"

"Yes."

"Good. I have to get to Perry, but it's hard for him to trust me. Think you and Teddy can get to him?"

"I'm way ahead of you, Hock."

Outside, Huggy leaned on the taxi horn. The urgent sound jump-started my own urgent plan of action. Sometimes the pieces fall into place, quick as honking a horn.

"Slow down," I said to Ruby. "Let's run together. Teddy works at the dog pound, right?"

"Right."

"Before you hook up with him, stop by City Hall. There's something I need you to research."

"What's that?"

"See if any property owners have plans to make promises to the poor lately. Follow me?"

"Follow."

"Teddy's important. He's the choir director, he knows how things go at the church. You're important, too. You know about the stage."

"Hock . . . ?"

I took the phone from my chest and spoke to Perry again. "Believe it or not, pal, you and I are going to have a friendly chat when this is all over."

"What's coming down?"

"Extracurricular justice, like I promised. Be smart and play your part."

I hung up the phone.

"That was Perry?" Ruby asked, as if she had to.

"Later." I looked again at the Big Chief notebook with Teddy's number written down, and memorized it.

"When? Later I'll be someplace else—"

The sound of Huggy Louper's taxi horn interrupted.

"Go on," Ruby said.

"Be careful."

"Same to you."

More horn honking.

"You're sure you're—?"

"Trust me, I'm all right. Go do what you have to do, I'll do what I have to do. Meet me later tonight at a place called Tipitina's, around half-past ten. Any taxi driver will know where to take you."

That was twenty minutes ago.

And now I hear Vonny.

He is complaining again about the smell from the doorway, the smell of burnt flesh. And here I am listening again to a southern voice telling me about life being cheap to some folks, and I have an army surplus oxygen mask strapped over my head. I imagine I look like a Martian.

"Man alive!" Vonny shouts, laughing at the same time. "We going to have to find us a whole gott-damn barrel of Lysol. Here, you going to need these things, too."

Sergeant LeMay leaned over the edge of the army surplus crate as he said this, reaching inside. The crate was a bottomless supply of handy gear for horrible situations. He stood up, smiling with his albino lips. "With this here stuff, you could do some night fishing."

The grainy movie about murky rivers in Vietnam started up in my head again. I shook myself like I was a wet dog, which amused Vonny. I did not want to take what Vonny was holding out for me to take. I did not want to go inside the old power building to see what I imagined I would see. I wanted more than anything to go someplace and sit down in the grass under the warm sun.

I did not want to think about killing . . .

. . . unless it was me killing a pint of Johnnie Walker Red.

The wet dog shook himself again.

Then I pulled on the rubber wading boots Vonny handed

me. After that, matching rubber gloves, up to the elbows. Vonny laughed hard at the Martian from New York City, and handed him a flashlight.

Then I walked through the door.

Black bodies, thin and small and dead, were sprawled crazily over a bullet-scarred cement floor slicked with blood and brains, and the excrement and urine that comes of lightning quick death. The yellow beam of my flashlight fell upon a face I knew.

THIRTY-THREE

"My God, my God—!"

Sister moved quickly from the hand that crept through her clouds, the hand now nudging her bare and lightly perspiring shoulder.

"No—I ain't feeling like it, Minister Zeb! Oh, heavenly Jesus—please, no!"

Sister was now bolt upright in the daybed. She had been sleeping, with her fingers laced across her young brown breasts. She had been dreaming of angels, her favorite dream.

The daybed was set in the shady end of a small back terrace on the attic floor of the church, overlooking the garage. Her private aerie, all draped in cotton mosquito netting the color of eggshells. She thought the nets were beautiful, she thought of them as clouds.

Zeb Tilton did not disturb Sister here, not in her clouds. Well, hardly ever. The only access to the terrace was a long flight of stairs so narrow that Minister Tilton had to scrunch in his fleshy shoulders clear to the top, and Zeb Tilton did not like messing his fine clothes by scraping the dirty walls of an old stairwell. There were plenty of other places he could disturb Sister Constance besides that old terrace.

All the beds in heaven looked the same as her cloudy daybed, Sister imagined. She retreated to it and her terrace in the high heat of the day, after a cool shower bath and talc dusting. There she could lie naked and free, in her beautiful clouds.

Sometimes she would stand at the terrace rail and look down at the concrete drive, and feel the urge to jump to sweet death. She imagined that during her leap she would sprout angel wings, in the final instant before smashing into the ground. She imagined she would soar up into the sky, seen by no eyes but those of God. And with her new strong wings she would dance in the air between earth and heaven, and then finally alight to her rightful place—among her stained glass sisters in the Jesus window.

"No . . . No, I ain't feeling good!" Sister, still in her half-sleep and wishing she could go back to her angel dreams, wrapped her lanky arms across her chest, clasped her shoulders with her long-fingered hands, covering her naked bosoms. "G'wan, go way, leave me be! Maybe I go bleed all over you. You know you don't want that!"

"Hush, girl. Just, please—hush yourself."

"Perry!" Sister recognized his voice. She came fully awake. "What you doing here in the daylight?"

"Don't mean no harm."

"I thought—"

"My Aunt Vi house is no good," Perry said, looking away from the girl's nakedness. "The po-lice no doubt watching the place for me."

Sister thrust herself forward and reached down to the end of the daybed. She picked up her blouse and slipped it over her head while her body was bent low and modest. Perry looked up and saw the back of her neck and the delicate curve of her shoulder blades.

"You got no other place to lie low?"

"Got a little shed I know about off of Chartres Street. Only problem is, couple of friends of mine at Shug's bar up to Jackson Avenue know I know about that shed."

"Talkative kind of friends?"

"I don't want to be taking the chance some barfly going to sing when a cop come round and be giving out free drinks."

"But you say you need something from the house."

"My notebooks. They got to stay put, I guess. But they in good hands."

"What's in them books?"

"Ruminations, observations, cogitations."

"La!"

"Anyhow, the conclusion's something I'm working out in my head, with a little help from an unlikely friend."

"I don't understand."

"You don't got to right away, all you got to do is trust me."

"Why I should do that?"

" 'Cause I got the idea to stay by you, girl. That's why I sneak on back here, try to find some hiding place for myself. I come up this stairway, but I sure don't expect to find you right off like I did. This safe for me up here?"

"Safe as the clouds I guess. Least for today, Perry. After that, I don't know."

"I know this, girl. We going to fix it so Zeb Tilton ain't going to lay even one pudgy finger on you ever again."

"How you going to swing that?"

"Oh, I been thinking. What else I got to do but think?"

"Run?"

"Things work out, I ain't going to be the one running. That's with your help and God willing."

"I'm willing, I know that."

"Good, cause like we say, all hell going to bust loose."

"You making me scared, Perry." Sister got up off the daybed. "If I ain't downstairs Zeb liable to come here looking for me."

"Don't be scared, girl."

"All right," Sister said, heading down the stairs.

But she was scared. She went into Minister Tilton's office and telephoned someone to tell him so.

THIRTY-FOUR

I could not take my eyes from the one face among all the dark, dead faces. This one's eyes were rolled up into his head, unseeing. I had no clear idea how much time had passed since I entered, making the turn from the small hallway entrance to pass into the open, square room. I had no idea how much time was passing as I stared. No more than I knew exactly where I was—New Orleans or New York or moonlit Vietnam, or the River Styx.

I saw that he was a boy. They all were.

But I knew only one of their names—Maybe Richard.

I said aloud my devotionals to the Virgin Mary and Glory Be to the Father.

I heard something. A voice—what? I spun the light around the room. Nobody but me and fifteen corpses.

"You a priest, Mister?"

The voice came from the blooded floor. It was Maybe Richard's voice, what was left of it. The sound of him was less than a whisper, the sound of tissue paper being softly torn. Three other cops, at least, had been in this room. Had no one but me heard a voice hanging on for dear life?

"Hang on, kid," I said, kneeling.

"Long enough for my last rites, Mister Man. That's all the time I got in this world . . . You a priest, right?"

Mister Man. He could not see. How did he know I was white?

"You a damn priest, man, you ought to get on with saying what I got to hear. Oh, man—please . . . ?"

Those would be the last words out of Maybe Richard. This I knew because of the rattle that had now crept into his tissue paper voice. I have heard that sound before, too many times—the sound that comes at the end.

On bended knee I moved in close. The right half of his body was torn open to the bone, from his naked shoulder down to his kneecap. The left side of his railed chest, over his heart, was seared by the brand: MOMS. His New York Yankees caps—my cap—lay beneath his spattered head.

I reached down to lift his head, and replace his Yankees cap. Then I pulled off my gloves.

I touched a thumb to the wet floor, then to Maybe Richard's heart. I made a cross over the ugly brand burned into his chest. I touched my thumb to the floor again, then to Maybe Richard's forehead. I made another cross on his cold, dying skin.

And once more I lied to beat the band.

"You feel the balm of holy water, my son," I said. "You are prepared for extreme unction? Say nothing and I shall take your silence as assent."

Maybe Richard moved his head for the last time, saying nothing.

I said, "Through this holy annointing and His most loving mercy, may the Lord assist you by the grace of the Holy Spirit so that, freed from your sins, He may save you—and in His Goodness raise you up."

When people ask me moral questions, I tell them the truth—I am a cop, not a priest. Once, somebody threw that back in my face by saying, "Either way, living and dying and sinning and saving, that's your bread and butter."

As a sham priest, had I truly lied? It did not matter. Surely for this sin I would know forgiveness.

THIRTY-FIVE

Ava LaRue—dressed in a daytime ensemble of silk brocade sandals, silver and turquoise bracelet, a yellow silk jumpsuit with black tiger stripes that cost two months of a maid's salary at a shop on Rodeo Drive in Hollywood, California—and Ophelia Dabon in her black dress, white apron, and support hose walked into Violet's kitchen. Her back was to them, but Violet knew. The sound of Ophelia's big flat feet on Violet's freshly waxed tile floor was unmistakable, as was the prim shuffle of Miz LaRue.

To Violet's mind, nobody's kitchen needed three women. Furthermore, this was her kitchen—at least when she was working it. Therefore, it was off-limits to these two. There was no real way she could speak her mind on the subject, though. And what good would that do? Ophelia would only give her the evil eye. And the whole house belonged to Miz LaRue, after all.

"Violet, dear? Violet . . . ?" Miz LaRue was smoking one of those oval-shaped cigarettes she bought from a shop on Royal Street that sold French smokes for too much money. The cigarette paper was pale red instead of pure white like a regular American brand. Miz LaRue had her red cigarette wedged into a long black holder made out of tortoiseshell. "Violet—Violet, would you kindly stop?"

"What, Miz LaRue?" Violet turned from the sink, not bothering to cut off the strong rush of water.

"Stop the water, Violet. Why, it sounds like the falls of Iguaçú in here. That's a waterfall in Brazil, dear. Mr. Giradoux and I honeymooned there."

"Yeah, I know they got coffee in Brazil. But how I always did wonder—do they get waterfalls, too? Now I know." Violet left the water running.

Ophelia waddled across the kitchen floor and turned off the tap. Violet cut her a proprietary glare. Ophelia gave the same to Violet, at twice the incandescence—which was close to an evil eye. This made Violet nervous. She put a hand to her throat and pretended Ophelia was someplace else, waxing the parlor furniture or something. Ava LaRue was oblivious to what had passed between her two colored women.

"I'd like you to run a little errand today, Violet." Ava LaRue smiled, as if she were about to present Violet with a great gift. "Out into the countryside."

"Miz LaRue, you sure I'm the one for the job?" Violet did not look over to Ophelia Dabon, though she felt the wattage of her face. "I got all this work piled up on me. I got to prepare for the dinner. There's baking and shopping to do. I got to polish the silvers. Plus I got me a week's worth of your husband laundry. How'm I going to run off to the country and do all that beside?"

"I believe the laundry can wait, dear. And I wouldn't send you terribly far. Just out Metarie way."

"Well, how'm I supposed to get out Metarie way?"

"Matthew is bringing the car around."

"What you need me for in that car? Matthew he already in it, driving. Can't he do the fetching, too?"

"You see, Violet . . . Well, Ophelia tells me it's a woman's place."

Violet had to look at Ophelia this time. She saw a rare smirk on the big woman's lips.

"Woman's place to what?"

Ava LaRue reached into a side pocket of her tiger stripe jumpsuit. She pulled a slip of paper from her pocket and held it out to Violet.

"What's this?" Violet just looked at the paper suspended in the air between Miz LaRue and herself.

"The address of an egg farm. Have Matthew take you there. You ask for a Mr. Fyfe, that's the farmer." Miss LaRue wiggled the slip impatiently. Violet had no choice but to take it. "Here now, I've written it all out. Anything you don't understand, just ask."

"I learnt to read some time ago, Miz LaRue."

"I don't mean—"

"What I'm supposed to fetch by this farmer Fyfe place?"

"A fresh egg, from a black hen."

"Ophelia dream up some new hex for you?"

"Never you mind, dear."

Embarrassed, Ava LaRue puffed strenuously on her red cigarette. Then she turned and stalked out of the kitchen, leaving her colored women to themselves.

"All right," Violet said to Ophelia, "what's going on here?"

"Step one."

"Of what?"

"Mind what you told. Which is never mind."

"You tell me what you going to do with a black hen egg, gal."

"Once you bring back the egg, I going to write down Miz El name on it, only backward. Then you got another little duty to do."

"That'd be what?"

"You got to throw that egg up onto the roof of this house."

"How come me?"

"You the strongest one of us, Vi. Miz El she can't hardly toss nothing high up with them bird arms of hers. And you know I got my bursitis."

"First time I hear about you and bursitis."

"Matthew's waiting. I think he carrying the torch for you, Vi."

"Shoo, you just saying that. Matthew—he say anything?"

"Maybe he say, maybe he need some coaxing to say. Whyn't you get you two eggs out Metarie way, Vi? One for what I do for Miz El, one to make life more charming for you."

Violet looked at the floor. She twisted the toes of her feet, the way she did when she was a teenager. *A man. It'd be good to know a man again. God Almighty, I'm lonesome.*

But then Violet thought about Sunday. A charm spell cast on Matthew, even the start of one, well might interfere with what Minister Tilton had promised to do—call out the spirit of her Willis, her African lion.

Could Zeb Tilton make Violet believe, even for a second, that she was seeing her Willis again? Would Ruby go with her? Neil could come, too. But he was Irish, and probably Catholic. La, what would he think about conjuring up the ghost of Ruby's daddy?

Ophelia was waiting for an answer.

"I bring you one egg today, Ophelia. For Miz LaRue."

"Don't be telling me I never tried helping to charm up your life."

"I won't. I got work to do now, if you don't mind."

"The egg charm it'd work one way for Miz El, the exact opposite way for you, Vi."

"Yeah? Tell me what two things you do."

"Once you toss that egg up to the roof with Miz El name on it, going to make her husband eyes swell up tight. Make his skin prickle like a million crawly ants all over him."

"You do that to old Hippo, I don't care. But why'd you do a mean thing like that to poor Matthew? He a good man. Little slow and quiet, but good."

"Oh, but with your name on a egg and the egg toss up top of where Matthew stay, he going to suddenly have the eye only for you. His skin going to prickle 'til he do something about it. Like slide a big hard piece of it up alongside you, gal. Know what I mean?"

"I ain't dense. You tell me that's step one?"

"Step two only for Miz El, when I need two cock roosters, which I know where to get right here in town. Step one with the black hen egg, that'll do you fine, Vi. Make Matthew fall your way like a bird shot off a telephone line. Don't got to do no more than that for you."

"What you going to do with cock roosters?"

"Going to take the one and bury him up to his neck out by the swimming pool. He be able to see, but he can't move."

"What's the other one do?"

"You never spent a whole lot of time in the country, did you, Vi?"

"Left the country a long time ago for this glamorous big-city life."

Ophelia laughed dryly.

"I let that other cock rooster free," Ophelia said. "Right round where I bury the first one. First cock so damn frustrated his comb fill up with angry blood. Second cock, he don't take kindly to that, since it's like waving a red flag front of a bull."

"Second cock rooster, he attack that poor buried fellow?"

"Peck his damn eyes out."

"La!"

"Cock with no eyes be furious. He got a big old comb of blood now, red as fire engine. That's what I'm after."

"What do you do with the comb?"

"I cuts it off that cock neck. Stick it inside of a frog-leather bag overnight and then take it out before the sun rise next. That comb be all ready for Miz El on Sunday morning."

"What she going to do with it then?"

"Just mind what you told, Vi."

THIRTY-SIX

I stumbled out the doorway and practically fell against Sergeant Vonny LeMay. Not because of a nauseous odor, which I could not detect thanks to the gas mask, but in anticipation of more crude remarks. I fell, hitting the gravel-packed ground smack against the side of my head. I felt a sting in my ear. The lobe was probably cut.

Vonny reached down to help right me, holding out his gauzy hands for me to grab. When he spotted the blood and the mess on my own bare hands, though, he quickly retracted the offer. And so I managed on my own.

"Well, you seen what you wanted?" Vonny asked.

"I saw. Want, I don't know."

A fugitive line of Theodore Roethke's poetry crept into the front of my head. *In a dark time, the eye begins to see.* I firmly believe in Roethke's idea, as both a cop and a regular person with the sense to maintain a healthy respect for cynicism. I have noticed, for instance, that evil in the world is of possibly more use than good. Naturally we require darkness in order to see.

"Them little niggers make us a pretty good mess, hey?" Vonny haw-hawed, then put a handkerchief to his nose and motioned for me to leave my mask on top of the crate and follow him away from the power station building. When we were walking off, he asked, "Ever see anything like it up there to New York?"

"I've seen a lot of messes. What do you do about cleaning up after something like this, Sergeant?"

"Fire department's fixing to drop by with some long hooks. That way we can fish out the slop, cover it up with lime to minimize the stench."

"What about notification?"

"Notify who? Them boys got kin, ain't none of them know about up to now. If it'd be up to me, I'd just torch the whole bunch right on site here. Sounds cold, but it'd save time and money. Like I told you, Hock, life's cheap to these people."

"Yeah, you told me."

Vonny and I walked for a minute without talking.

"Oh, Vonny—I forgot the most important thing."

"Well, what's that?"

"My friend Hippo asked if you'd care to join us for lunch today." Another whopping lie. I looked back toward the power station. A fire truck was slowly making its way up from the road toward the crime site. "But with all this on your plate, I guess the alderman would understand if you had to take a rain check. Too bad for you, Vonny. We've got reservations at the Commander's Palace."

"You do?"

"Well, you know—Hippo does."

"The man has clout."

"That's an interesting word."

"Clout?"

"Look here, Vonny. Do you think you could delegate some responsibility? I just know that Hippo would love to hear about what's happened here direct from your lips." I took a look at my wristwatch. "Got to have your answer now, or I'll be late."

"No problem."

Vonny raised a gloved hand, signaling the same outer line

uniform I had spoken with earlier, the one scratching inside his pants. He was scratching outside his crotch now. He stopped scratching and ran over on the double. Vonny told him to go square his absence with the senior detective.

Then Vonny said to me, "Okay, let's go downtown. We'll take my car. Jeez, I'd like to take a shower." Vonny lifted an arm and tucked his albino face into the pit. "Shit, I believe I can smell them niggers on me."

I put some money into Huggy Louper's shirt pocket when I walked past his taxicab on the way to Vonny's unmarked Chrysler. Huggy was dozing in the driver's seat.

A largely unsmoked cigarette had burned clear down to Huggy's orange fingers. Then it must have been snuffed out by the calluses. The hula dancer on the dashboard shivered daintily in a frisson of air-conditioning. On the other hand, I was growing hot under the collar.

More importantly, I could see in the dark.

THIRTY-SEVEN

"Where we going to do the meet up with Hippo—right down to Commander's Palace?" Vonny LeMay turned the car onto Canal Street at the Moon Walk end.

"I'm supposed to come straight back to his office first," I said. "But if you want, Vonny, you could drop me off at City Hall, then go wait for us to turn up later at the restaurant."

"No, no. That's all right. That's very okay. I don't mind accompanying you up to the Hall."

I figured as much.

"Well, I just thought—you've probably been up there in Hippo's office so many times over the years. I mean, you know—the way Hippo goes on and on about you."

"He talks about me?"

"Sure he does. Just the other day he was telling some people how you were handling . . . well, let's say, the bad element of this fair city. Know what I mean?"

"Niggers."

"What else?"

Every so often I would steal a side glance at Vonny as we crept along through the crush of midday traffic. He had removed his panama, which was sitting on the vinyl seat between us. The material of the hat was straw, bleached down to bone white. Vonny's large bare head was whiter yet. Even the veins running along his skull below a wispy corona of transparent fuzz were white, and I thought it possible that the blood coursing through those veins was as milky as his eyes.

I developed a simple-minded theory that seemed appropriate, given the simple mind sitting next to me. Vonny LeMay despised African-Americans for the understandable reason that every black man, woman, and child had something he never would have—color.

We finally reached Rampart Street. Vonny turned left onto Poydras, the palm-lined thoroughfare where the city's banks and oil companies do business from office silos made with a lot of chrome and mirrored glass, perfect for deflecting intrusions of light. Vonny nosed the Chrysler into a semicircular drive fronting City Hall. He stopped the car at the main door, slipped the automatic transmission into park, and then sniffed his armpits some more.

"Holy shit, I surely do hope Hippo don't smell none of this coon tang. I can't seem to shake it." This Vonny said in the presence of an ancient black man wearing the livery of a car jockey. He had hobbled up to the Chrysler in his orthopedic shoes just as Vonny started sniffing. Vonny sighed now, plopped the panama back on top of his head, and stepped out of the car as the old black fellow held open the door. Vonny badged the car jockey, who was old enough to be his father. Then he patted the Chrysler's hood with a gauze hand and told him, "Keep her right here for us, boy."

These remarks I let pass, like the others. I stepped out from my side of the car and looked up, beholding the seat of government of the city of New Orleans.

I have seen a lot of ugly buildings in my day. Everybody has. Architects are among the worst criminals of modern society. But the centerpiece of New Orleans government was a singular study of repellent design.

The Hall, as Vonny called it, was a low-rise cluster of squatty gray slabs, with windows in thick frames painted in a shade I would call throw-up green. Some of the windows were open, some shut. They all looked burned or broken, even close up.

There was no dome to relieve the flatness of the roofline. No graceful cupolas, no heroic friezes, no inspiring statuary—not a scrap of the Crescent City's trademark iron lace. Out-of-towners would know the New Orleans City Hall was neither a parking garage nor a bankrupt factory with smashed windows solely because of an enormous sign with chipped paint that read simply, CITY HALL.

Inside the hall, the architects vision continued. The lobby had all the atmosphere and amenities of a subway platform, complete with fluorescent lighting that made skin look ill, the bouquet of deceased rodent, and a newsstand over the elevators operated by a sleepy man chewing with his mouth open so everybody on the way upstairs would notice he was enjoying a white bread sandwich with olive-and-pimento-loaf bologna and mayonnaise.

The elevator operator, a flabby white lady with big hair somewhere in her fifties and well settled in a life of occupational redundancy and vending machine snacks, pushed a button that Vonny or I could have pushed for ourselves. This was right after she asked, "What floor you gents want?" To which I had said, "Alderman Giradoux's office, please."

We emerged at the top floor. The first thing anybody sees off the elevator is an open, mahogany-trimmed archway to Hippo's outer office. Vonny was a tool just lying around for using. Maybe I could make Hippo strut and trip . . .

The same as I had in mind for someone else.

Various supplicants—maybe a bodyguard or two—were sitting in the visitors chairs and reading magazines. They were all men, all of them white, all of them wearing sharkskin suits of a type I have beheld only in Bronx mob joints. One guy wore aviator-style sunglasses. This one in the shades gave a little salute of recognition to Sergeant LeMay, who acknowledged the gesture.

"Oh, hello there," I said to the yellow-headed, gum-clacking receptionist. "You're a pretty thing."

"Yeah, I been told that. What do you want?"

"Want to see the good alderman."

"This time of day, you got to have an appointment. You got one?"

"Well, I'll tell you—I was here earlier today to see my old pal Hippo. Detective Neil Hockaday's the name. From New York." I took out my NYPD gold shield and flashed it. Vonny did the same with the local equivalent. "You weren't around, though. I'd have remembered you."

Pretty flipped through her appointments calendar, running a store-bought fingernail from top to bottom of each page. "I don't see no Hockaday from New York."

I turned to Vonny. "Tell Pretty how come we're incognito."

"Oh, sure—yeah." Sergeant LeMay leaned down close enough to smell Pretty's Windsong perfume from the drugstore. He whispered, "It's confidential like. It's about them murders on the TV and all."

"Really?" Pretty was impressed.

"Truly," I assured her.

Vonny puffed out his chest.

"I guess y'all should maybe just go ahead. Nobody in there with Hippo now."

"Like I was hoping," I said.

Check out that office of his, Hock. Look like something from the Huey Long days. Claude had hardly prepared me for the splendor. Many New York politicians of my acquaintance would take one look at the elephant-leg desk and the velvet throne and the potted magnolias and all the booze bottles and flags and framed tributes and devoutly believe they had died and gone to Tammany Heaven.

"Hey now, who in the gott-damn hell let you in?" Hippo

protested, in the process letting fly some warm pieces of his lunch.

The alderman was seated behind his desk wearing a parachute-size napkin tucked into his shirt collar and spooning down a dish of jambalaya as Vonny and I strode across the Oriental rug toward him. The jambalaya smelled good, but I could not imagine it tasting better than Mama's from the other night. Sausage juice covered Hippo's lower lip.

"Alderman, we are here to register complaint about the New Orleans police department," I announced. "Also I want to use your telephone. Just a local call."

"Wait—what the . . . ?" Sergeant LeMay was bewildered beyond finishing his question.

"What's the matter, Vonny?" I asked, turning to him.

"Ain't so, ain't so!" Vonny addressed his denials to Hippo and looked as if he might work up some color yet. Vonny pulled off his panama and wiped his head in exasperation. Also he opened his coat and put his hand on the revolver hanging off his belt.

"I'm telling the truth," I said. "I want to complain about the cops, and I have a call to make."

"Hold on now the both of you!" Hippo's eyes turned to mean slits, like a bulldog protecting a bone. He asked Vonny, "That's your name, is it—Vonny?"

"Sergeant Lavond LeMay." Vonny nodded his paste white head. "Central station detective squad."

"The sarge looks a little peaked, don't you think?" I asked Hippo. "That makes two problems Vonny has with color."

"You talk funny," Hippo said. "You some kind of Yankee?"

"This kind." I laid out my gold shield on Hippo's desk. He picked it up, read it, shoved it back toward me.

"What you doing strayed so far outside your briar patch?"

"My wife—"

"This New York fella he claim he's a old pal of yours, Hippo," said Vonny, interrupting. He was quite excited, which for him was evidenced by a sort of nicotine yellow shade creeping up his neck and through his cheeks. Any other white man would have been purple and scarlet by now. "Tried to get real buddy-buddy with me on a lying basis. Even told me I should call him by his nickname—Hock."

"Hock? As in to cough, to blow chunks?" Hippo asked this with mockery playing across his juicy lips.

"Gott-damn Yankee he tricked me," Vonny said. "Then he used me to get past your receptionist out there."

"Your sergeant's slow, but he catches on," I said to Hippo.

Hippo removed the napkin from his collar and wiped his hands. He cleared away the half-empty jambalaya bowl and folded his flabby arms on the desktop. "Tell me—what's the specific nature of your complaint, Detective Hockaday?"

"Specifically, your cops are pigs."

"Pigs?" Hippo chuckled, making his amusement sound malevolent. "I ain't heard the po-lice called pigs since the days we had all them hairy-headed hippies running wild."

"This guy he's a gott-damn communist hippie *and* a gott-damn lying Yankee!" Vonny turned from Hippo to me. Clutching his revolver, he said, "Tell you what *pig* is, you hippie you. Pig stands for pride, integrity, and guts!"

"Take your hand off the gun and button that coat of yours over your pig gut," I said. "And try to understand something—this is between Hippo and myself now."

"Go ahead, Vonny, relax," Hippo said. "This man ain't going bite us."

Vonny did as he was told.

"Ever since I got here the other day," I said to Hippo, "I have been hearing disturbing things from the mouths of your officers."

"I am a lowly alderman, Detective Hockaday. Po-lice bidness hasn't got anything directly to do with me."

"I hear otherwise."

"Is that so?" Hippo gave me a measured look. If he and I were in the ring, it would have been the kind of look boxers give each other in the early rounds, when they are jabbing and testing.

Giradoux could have thrown me out of his office right then and there, and that was the risk I ran. But I was gambling on his being a fighter, like most long-lasting politicians. No fighter was going to step out of a ring without going some rounds with a challenger.

"Let me just ask you something pertinent," Hippo said. "You care to provide me with a *for instance* in back of what you're allegating here?"

"For instance, Detectives Mueller and Eckles."

"Happens I know those two. Very fine men."

"Couldn't agree more," Vonny said, nodding at Hippo.

I said to Vonny, "Here's what kind of a fair man I am. I am hereby advising you to shut the hell up."

I said to Hippo, "These two fine men of yours came around to my mother-in-law's place the other day and shook her up bad. I don't like that."

"Your mother-in-law's you say? That's right, you did mention something about a wife. So—that's why you here in our beloved city. You married a southern gal. My congratulations, sir. I wonder if I might know her."

"Her and her whole family. Being a figure in the news, her sister is someone you're acquainted with."

Hippo waited for a name, but I decided not to drop one for the time being. He studied me with his dark bulldog eyes. I could see he was adding and subtracting based on what I had said and left unsaid. I figured by now that he knew the game was afoot, that he was engaged in a heavyweight bout, that he had decided against revelations of his own. And that he had decided to play dumb.

"What you're telling me, Detective Hockaday, it's very intriguing." Spoken like a true politician. Hippo had managed to say nothing that would pin him down.

"You're intrigued that I married a southern woman?"

"Maybe you can guess I'm a man of many interests."

"That I heard, too. You'll be interested to know that

Mueller and Eckles—your fine ones—insulted my mother-in-law and my wife and all the rest of us who don't happen to be Kluxers."

"Just what'd they say to set you off?"

"For starters, *Jew* York City."

"Haw!" Vonny chortled. "That's a good one!"

I turned and said to him, "Strike two, Sergeant. Watch your step and mind your mouth."

"Well, let's just pause to analyze what we got here." Hippo tapped fingers on his desk. "You married this gal from a family I know—especially the sister-in-law, on account of I'm in the news somewhat—and now you're telling me that the conduct of a couple of po-lice officers is upsetting to you on the grounds of race."

Hippo stopped tapping, long enough to finish his gumbo. When he was through he wiped his mouth with his huge napkin. "Well now, Detective Hockaday, would your sister-in-law be that good-looking TV news gal, Jan Flagg?"

"That colored one?" Vonny LeMay looked at me, the horrible computation of it all flaming across his colorless face. He turned to Hippo. "Why, that'd mean the Yankee's married to a nigger!"

I did not bother answering the sergeant. Instead, I slammed my right fist square against his breastbone. This is one of the earliest and most useful lessons taught at the New York Police Academy. A person receiving a surprise ramrod punch to the sternum will expel, on reflex, virtually all his breath, rendering him helpless. It works every time. The beauty of such an assault is that the victim is not physically damaged beyond the temporary loss of air. This is because the sternum is designed to stand up to far greater abuse than a human fist can deliver.

Oh sure, it is possible that the breastbone can hurt like hell for a week or two. But this was only a hope as I looked at Sergeant Levond LeMay, crumpled to the floor with one gauzy hand to his heart and the other alternately clutching at his gasping neck and slobbering mouth. His legs were doing pinwheels.

With time standing still for the moment, I thought over something terrible that Ruby had told me during our moody train ride from New York—about the first time she was called *nigger,* as a schoolgirl walking down the street. There are precious few times in anybody's life when perfect justice is served. I looked down at the flailing bigot, Vonny, and knew that his distress came close to being one of those precious moments, lacking only the presence of Ruby to share in the bliss.

Hippo was inspired to rise from his throne. He smoothed his shirt down over his belly and snapped his firehouse suspenders, then walked around the edge of his desk to take inventory of the man who had dropped out of sight.

"Now, I don't know but that was a very poltroonish thing of you to do to poor Vonny," he said to me, lips pursed. He stood close to me, close enough so I could smell Tabasco on his breath.

Vonny stopped pinwheeling as he regained his breath. He reached out for a nearby cuff of Hippo's striped trousers though, like a drowning man grasping after a life preserver. Hippo moved his foot away.

"You got me wrong, Hippo," I said. "If I was a poltroon, I'd do this." Whereupon I kicked Vonny in his side, just below his rib cage so as not to leave a bruise—which is another useful academy lesson that works every time. Vonny lost his breath all over again.

"Vonny," Hippo said, bending slightly from his plentiful waist to be sure he was heard, "don't you think it's time you toddled on out of here? Let me alone for a chin with our distinguished visitor from New York City?"

Sergeant LeMay recovered enough of his dignity to reach for his revolver. I let him pull it out from his belt before kicking the thing out of his hand, not caring this time if I bruised him. The gun went flying from Vonny's hand past the big aldermanic desk to the other side, but not without first discharging and making a rude hole in one of the leaded-glass windows gracing Hippo's Tammany heaven.

"Gott-dammit, Vonny!" Hippo stepped over and gave the fallen sergeant a kick of his own. "Now look what you done."

"Oh—Hippo, you're all right?" Pretty came bustling into the office, hands wild with fright, yellow hair flying. She paid no mind to Vonny pulling himself up from the floor. "Did I just hear what I thought I heard?"

"You surely did, gal." Hippo pointed to the hole in the window. "Look what this moron here done to my office."

"Which moron?" Pretty asked.

"Come on now, that's easy. Which of these here two police officers looks like he's got a head full of room to rent?"

The blonde pointed to Vonny.

"Notice how she didn't hesitate," I said to Vonny. Vonny had learned some sense by now and kept quiet. He rubbed his sore breastbone. I picked his panama up off the floor and handed it to him.

"I'd like you to show this here no-color moron the hell out of my office," Hippo said to Pretty. "Looking at him's giving me the all-over creeps." He walked around back of Vonny and gave him a shove in the general direction of the door while giving his receptionist some further instructions. "Then I'd like for you to locate the damn po-lice commissioner down to whatever whorehouse he's patronizing these days. Get him on the blower. I got a po-lice abuse complaint to pass along to him."

"The Chrysler's down in the driveway waiting for you," I said to Vonny's back. "Later when I'm downstairs myself, I'll be asking the old fellow in the uniform how you treated him—what sort of tip you gave him. Make me proud, Vonny."

"Darling, you best call up a glazier, too," Hippo called after Pretty as she closed the door on us. "Get him over here fast as you can."

Hippo put his hands on his hips, turned, and looked up

at the bullet hole in his window. "Damn, that's not good, not good a-tall."

"That kind of pane in a fancy lead frame like that, it's going to take a real artisan to fix it," I said. "Which is going to cost you plenty."

"Price don't matter. But breaking glass, that's ominous."

"It is?"

"I don't mean just something you drink out of and maybe you so drunk you let it slip out your hand and it smashes to the floor. I'm talking about the window to a man's place of bidness."

Hippo shook his head and rubbed his hands together. His face was flushed and sweaty. So it was not hard to sense that the man was genuinely upset about the broken window, not to mention that he was superstitious. He just stood there staring at the laser of sunlight piercing through into his Tammany heaven.

"Man, I need me a capital-*D* drink," he said.

Hippo hurried over to the office bar. This was a handsome wedge of mahogany with a brass rail in front and a smoky mirror in back. There were glass shelves under the mirror with a stock of everything—including, I noticed, my old friend Mr. Walker's red and black labels. Hippo stepped around to the back of the bar and took down a fifth of Jack Daniel's. The bottle had one of those bartender spouts fitted into the neck. Hippo ripped this out and gurgled the whiskey good and fast into a tumbler.

" 'Scuse me to hell and back." He took a long swallow, then put a pudgy hand to his heart. "What's your poison, Detective Hockaday?"

"Make it seltzer."

"Don't tell me about no soda. Shoo, what about a real drink? We into the P.M. after all."

"I drink with a small *d* these days."

"You're saying you don't stand at the rail no more?"

"It spooks me, Hippo. Like broken glass spooks you."

"Oh, well, you in New Orleans now. Everybody here,

they in a thrall about good luck and bad, voodoo and hoodoo and all. Mumbo-jumbo's bred in the bone down here. Everybody believe in it to some degree or other. Anybody says different's lying."

Hippo looked up at the bullet hole again. Then he took another long swallow of whisky.

"Anyhow, it's a capital-*D* damn shame you don't drink." Hippo reached below the bar and pulled out a small, square bottle half full of something that was a musty gold color and highly tempting. "Shame is I got this real fine old sipping whisky I'd be willing to share. Whisky so good it tastes like little angels pissing on your tongue."

"Thanks, no."

"Say now, what's your roots anyways?" Hippo's eyes slitted. "Irish 'less I'm blind and deaf."

"That's right."

"Always thought Mick blood came half whisky by birth."

"Easy enough mistake when you consider what the Irish call the wonderful stuff."

"What's that?"

"*Uisce beatha.* That's Irish for whisky. It means water of life."

"How about that."

"How about let's talk on the subject of the murders."

"I told you, I'm a lowly alderman."

"Who used to be police commissioner."

"That's just a little tubby boy's dream come true. Nothing like riding through the city on a Saturday night with the siren blazing. I done that once in a while when I was commissioner. Just a career diversion."

"From the law?"

"Law and public service."

"Something else, too. A long time ago, you did some public service in real estate."

"Well, my interest in that sort of thing's all private speculation now."

"Property investments?"

"Craps shoot's more like it."

"One man tosses dice. Sometimes another man dies."

Hippo's eyes narrowed again. He said nothing and tried to act as if he was thinking about nothing beyond how good his whisky tasted. But I could tell he was as rattled by my speculations as he was by the broken windows.

"I never met my father-in-law," I said. "The late Willis Flagg."

"That's too bad. He was a good man."

"He owned some real estate once."

"Come to think, I guess he did. Awful shame he couldn't hang on to that little cottage he had."

"The way I hear, my father-in-law was in over his head. Not to mention he was in the wrong skin at the wrong time. He was just a craps shooter, you could say." Since Hippo was starting to go slurry from alcohol, I decided to press an advantage and let my murky suspicions take a roller-coaster ride. "You play craps, you always lose more than you win. Unless you play by the formula. But Willis Flagg wasn't the type to be playing the formula."

"What you talking about *formula?*"

"Real estate, cops, politics. The usual triple threat. A man who learns all three positions has clout."

"Your mother-in-law Violet tell you that?"

"What makes you think so?"

"Bless her, Violet always exaggerates my power and popularity—'specially if she's having her tea pepped up with something." Hippo laughed. "She don't know it, but I hear her exaggerating like that sometimes in the kitchen—talking to my own wife, I'm telling you."

"The kitchen?"

"Over to my place." Hippo switched from the angel piss, pouring himself another generous Jack Daniel's. His hands shook a little this time. "Ain't it one of my maids been telling tales about me? I naturally figure Violet over Ophelia."

"You got me." I said this quickly, to cover the surprise

of my learning that Mama still worked at the Giradoux house. A holdover from the old days, I supposed, when she worked for Hippo's doctor father.

Not wanting to give Hippo time to imagine other sources—especially Officer Claude Bougart, whose position I saw now more than ever as highly vulnerable—I said as quickly, "You know, Violet speaks very highly of you when she's at home in her own kitchen."

"That pleases me. Violet Flagg's a damn fine woman, fine as any white lady."

"I'm sure that's real high praise, Hippo."

"Well, Vi deserves it." Hippo guzzled about a third of his whisky.

"Oh yes, my mother-in-law is as fine as they come, black or white."

"That's true!"

"I want to shake your hand for saying so." I stepped over and took Hippo's hand, felt how it had gone limp from the booze the way my own hand used to.

"Say, I ain't poured you that fizzy water yet."

"That's okay, Hippo. I'm not thirsty. You keep right on drinking, though."

"I'll just do that." He finished off the Jack Daniel's, and poured himself another.

"You know, there's something that greatly surprises me about you—you being a lawyer and an elected official."

"What's that?"

"You haven't said one word of concern about the way your boys Mueller and Eckles treated as fine a black lady as Violet Flagg. Not to mention how your good old boy Vonny LeMay called Violet Flagg's daughter *nigger* right here in your office. That would be my wife Ruby he called a nigger."

"Does so concern me! It's disgraceful. Didn't you hear me say I was going to pass along your complaint!" Hippo was becoming slightly belligerent, the way drinkers will. He was also slightly nervous, which he tried covering. "By the way, how's that Ruby?"

"Doing fine, thanks. I don't imagine her cousin's doing so well."

"Her cousin?"

"The one you've got on the run—Perry Duclat."

Hippo looked at his wristwatch, a Piaget. Nothing but the best for a lowly alderman. "I'd love to spend the whole rest of the afternoon gassing with you, Detective. But you know, I've got this council meeting before too long."

"You don't want to talk about Perry Duclat?"

"Want's got nothing to do with it. All I know about that boy's his reputation as a thief."

"Boy?"

"Slip of the tongue and memory, Detective Hockaday. Last time I ever seen Perry Duclat is when he was a little shaver. Unlucky kid. Pity the way it turns out for him now—being wanted for murder and all." Hippo shrugged, and drank. "Well, nothing you or me can do about that."

"I think a lot of bad luck never has to happen. I think we let it happen anyway, to some people."

"That badge of yours for real, Hockaday? I never heard any po-lice officer talk like you before."

"Neither have I."

"You after something from me, son, though I can't imagine what. Only know you about as persistent as a dog with two dicks. In time, that gets irritating."

"Maybe I'll just use that phone."

"Surely. In the outside office if you please." I started to leave, and Hippo said, "Like I say, it's a pity about Perry."

"Maybe it's something more than a pity."

Hippo's hand shook so much now that little waves skipped over the surface of the whisky in his glass. He looked up at the hole in the window and grabbed at his heart again, then bolted down the remaining booze. This made no sense to me, since alcohol tends to go through the bloodstream like a carnival ride, making loop-the-loops that cause the heart to pump overtime.

But then a lot of things make no sense since I stopped drinking.

I decided to make my telephone call from somewhere besides City Hall.

THIRTY-EIGHT

I walked past the newsstand guy chewing on the twin of the olive-and-pimento bologna sandwich he was eating earlier and wondered at the vastness of the human capacity for looking at revolting things. I could no more keep my eyes free of that newsy's mulching machine of a mouth than motorists are able to drive by automobile pileups without craning their necks for a look at somebody else's bloody misery. I, of course, am worst of all in this human regard, since I am a cop in the city that never sleeps. I am craning my neck at other people's misery on a twenty-four-hour basis. I even take this terrible habit of mine on the road.

Outside, the sky had gone gray and rumbly and the air had a stillness to it. Mother Nature, hellbat that she is, was up to no good.

I walked up on Canal Street for a while until I was tired of looking at store windows, grown men dressed like teenagers, fat ladies wearing rhinestone T-shirts, and suburban skinheads committing truancy and trying to look menacing.

There was the balance of an afternoon to kill and then an evening before I would see Ruby again. Who knew about Claude? Bougart had arranged things so that he could contact me—period. Under those circumstances, it made sense that I found myself walking along a one-way street.

I bought a copy of the *Times-Picayune* at a stand on Bienville Street, along with the skinny national edition of the *New York Times* to see if there was anything I was missing back home. Such as news about my other police abuse complaint—the one regarding King Kong Kowalski, the one in which Inspector Neglio was supposed to be taking personal interest. I skipped through the *Times* and found no such report. Neglio's concern about rabid cops was proving no keener than Hippo's. The difference between them was that one pushed happy pills when I broached the subject, and the other one pushed booze.

The New York paper I tossed into a trash barrel. I kept the local bugle for its movie listings. A storm was coming, so I decided a movie house would be a good place to stay dry while killing time—and trying to forget the face of Maybe Richard, at least for a few hours.

Huggy was probably irritated with me about leaving him dead-headed back at the power station slaughter, even though I had tucked money into his pocket, so I decided against calling him. I flagged a passing taxi and had him drop me at Joe Never Smile's house on Crozat Street.

I heard the old man and his clumper making their way to the front door.

"Mind if I use your telephone?" I asked Joe when he opened up.

" 'Course not, come on back to the kitchen, sit down awhile."

"How's things going with you and Claude digging around in all this unpleasantness?" We were settled at Joe Never Smile's kitchen table. I had a cup of coffee and a telephone in front of me.

"Joe, everybody says New York is a strange place. But this city, it's something else."

"You learning, son. In New Orleans there's magic in many things, and weirdness in most."

I had one of those jump starts again, this one thanks to Joe Never Smile. So I telephoned Teddy the Torch at the dog pound and laid out the plan.

After leaving Joe's house, I occupied myself at an oyster bar back on Bienville by watching the local artistry of a shucker at work behind the counter who made me a plate of bluepoints. Also I drank a bottle of fake beer.

The *Times-Picayune* movie page carried an ad about a revival house somewhere on Magazine Street called the Blossom Cinema, which was showing a double feature: *They Drive by Night* from 1940 with Ida Lupino, George Raft, Humphrey Bogart, and Ann Sheridan, and *The Little Foxes* from '41 with Bette Davis, Herbert Marshall, and Dan Duryea. Offhand, I could think of no better company that this bill of fare.

I asked the shucker, an amiable gray-haired guy with an ebony face and a starched paper cap, "What bus takes me to Magazine Street?"

"Something a whole lot better than a bus take you down the Garden District way," he said. "Walk back to Canal, catch the St. Charles Avenue streetcar to Napoleon Avenue. Then you only six little blocks away from the Blossom over to Magazine."

And so that was how it happened I was sitting in a window seat of a fine old wooden streetcar. The inside was lined with ribbed maple under a clear stain, and leather straps for the standees. The outside was enameled in yellow and green.

There were clusters of tourists in the car, hanging out the open windows and making videotapes of the mansions along the way. The rest of the crowd were bleary-eyed sheep reading newspapers or Bibles or Grishams, staring at the floor, cooling themselves with cardboard fans, listening to Walkman radios, spacing out.

A twentysomething woman was juggling a canvas tote bag, newspaper, and purse and also trying to apply some powdery makeup to her creamy white nose and cheeks with a brush that could paint a small house. A freckle-faced guy with ginger hair and a poplin suit, about her same age, sat across from her. He stared at her, the way somebody would stare at a museum portrait. The woman picked up on this staring, not kindly.

"What the hell are you looking at?" she said.

"You don't need any makeup at all." He sounded as innocent as a divinity student. "You're so beautiful."

The young woman went crimson. Hostility drained out of her, an emotional boil had been lanced. An old black lady sitting next to her giggled like a kid and stood up. She crossed the narrow aisle and said to the divinity student, "You change places with me, son. G'wan now. Sit down over there where I was, you talk some more to that sweet young thing. I think y'all going to get along fine."

I thought a perverse thought: I like New Orleans, in spite of the mossy heat and palpable sorrow; I like a town where a streetcar carries desire; I like a place where language hangs resplendent in the air, like fresh laundry on the line. I could live here—in the city that Ruby fled.

Napoleon Avenue finally came up and I had to leave the streetcar. I made a tent with the pages of the *Times-Picayune* and covered my head against the rain that had begun splattering down. It was the fat-dropped kind of rain. By the time I had walked the six blocks over to Magazine Street, and despite the sheltering arms of oak bowers along the way, everything from my chest down was drenched.

I stood beneath the Blossom Cinema marquee and shook myself. The newspaper I tossed into the gutter like it was soggy macaroni.

A familiar car pulled up.

The driver leaned across the front seat and rolled down the passenger window, releasing chow mein and cigarette fumes. Claude Bougart, in nice dry civilian clothes, was drinking nice hot coffee from a Styrofoam cup.

"Afternoon, Hock," he said. "How's it going?"

My shoes made squishy noises as I stepped up to Claude's car and leaned into the window.

"What are you doing, following me around?" I asked Claude. I did not feel friendly toward him. If he was tailing me in his car, he at least could have given me a lift from Napoleon Avenue and saved me from a soaking.

"Had to make sure, man."

"Of what?"

"That somebody else ain't after you."

"Who'd want to be?"

"Po-lice grapevine has it that you been doing some powerful riling up since I saw you last."

"That's what they call it?"

"Brother Hockaday, stop a minute, think on the species of po-lice you been around today. Try to read by their dim lights."

"I see what you mean. By the way, where were you?"

"My name's Paul, and it's between y'all."

"Sure, Claude, I get it." I was now feeling even more unfriendly toward Bougart. "You don't want to get involved when a platoon of flatheads straight out of *Deliverance* gets the drop on me. You don't mind it that I'm doing your heavy lifting. But when the shooting starts you'd just as soon be out of town."

"Oh now, I wouldn't say—"

"For the love of Christ, Claude, I'm standing here in the damn rain! You don't even care about that!"

"Aw, man, you got me all wrong." Bougart waved me back, then pushed open the door so I could slide in. Sopping wet clothes would not be the worst things that had sat on that front seat.

Claude handed me a wad of leftover paper napkins from a Pizza Hut box on the dashboard. I used them to dry my face and hands. "I got towels and a duffel bag in the trunk," he said. "Never know when a rain like this'll sneak up on you, catch you unawares. Bag's got sneakers and jeans and a T-shirt. I guess we about the same size more or less."

"More or less." I said that coldly and Claude heard it the same.

"Look, I'm only being careful, okay? Sure you right, Neil, I need you to front me. Right tool for the right job. You get the picture?"

"Do I ever."

"Picture's sharply black and white, you know? Black and white's that double feature you almost saw."

"Almost?"

"We got us more business."

Claude put the car in gear and we drove off.

I changed my mind about liking the city that Ruby had fled.

The news of two more MOMS murders was all over town. Ruby had heard the first report—the slaughter of fifteen black boys living in the old Power & Light substation in back of the *Di Moin*—while she finished scanning through Perry's journals before leaving her mother's house. Then as soon as she reached City Hall, it seemed every radio in every office was turned to news of the butchery in the old dump off Paris Avenue.

In the records room of City Hall, Ruby found the cross-referenced matches she was searching for. It took some serious digging to backlog the personal identities hiding behind innocuous company names, but Ruby was dogged.

She clipped notes into a looseleaf binder she had picked up at the K&B pharmacy on her way downtown, then left City Hall. She needed to walk and think things through. And she was hungry, right then and there in the middle of the day, which for Ruby was somewhat unusual. At home in New York she would have fruit or a croissant in the morning; if she had a business luncheon, it was all she could do to finish half a salad. But here it was only three in the afternoon and she was famished.

With the idea vaguely in mind of a restaurant she used to enjoy almost every day some years ago, Ruby strolled from City Hall across Canal Street and into the Quarter. She found herself on Dumaine Street, where she had briefly lived in a tiny apartment full of big mice. Her halfway house, she called it, halfway between Mama's house and the Big Apple.

Ruby's Dumaine Street days lasted three months, during which time she discovered that it was not possible to earn a living as a nondancing, nonsinging black actress in the New Orleans theatrical world. She made ends meet by dressing herself up every day as Raggedy Ann—complete with rouged cheeks, licorice whip eyelashes, and a fright wig—and serving hamburgers and milkshakes to tourists at a restaurant called Anything Goes. With that theme very much in mind, she ultimately left for New York, where after three months of Manhattan residency she discovered it was not possible to earn a living as a nondancing, nonsinging black actress.

Ruby paused for a moment in front of her halfway house. She looked up at the second-floor balcony, and the shutters that covered the single window of her mousy old flat. She had painted those shutters violet—for Mama—and they were still violet, though faded so badly over time that only Ruby knew their secret color.

She walked on, back along Bourbon Street to Toulouse and a restaurant called the Café de la Paix, the very place she had picked up her croissant habit. She skipped the main door of the restaurant and instead entered a narrow side alley that was full of coffee and pastry smells. The alley opened up to a walled patio in the back, with brick flagstones and tables and chairs in the shade of tulip trees. Ruby ordered a muffeleta sandwich and a tall glass of lemonade. Then when she was still hungry, a dish of butterscotch ice cream with strong coffee.

Things were never rushed at the Court of Three Sisters, especially out on the patio. And so Ruby opened the looseleaf notebook on her table and read over the entries she had made at City Hall—for the third or fourth time, she had lost count. Then she flipped those pages and read over her summary of Perry's journals.

She felt a little disappointed. What would Hock say? At City Hall, she had found what he suspected she would. But what of it? A district attorney could indict a ham sandwich, that was true. But did any of this add up to even a ham sandwich?

Extracurricular justice. What did Hock mean when he said that to Perry on the telephone?

Slap! Maybe a news peg?

Ruby closed her notebook and went to the pay telephone inside the restaurant. "Janny," she said when she reached her sister at WDSU Television, "Mama and I caught your report on Chanel Six this morning. About MOMS and all. I just want to tell you, I'm proud of you. I think you're great."

"That's you, Ruby?"

"Yes, Janny. Now listen. How would you like the follow-up to end all follow-ups?"

THIRTY-NINE

This time it happened near the old railroad tracks at Elysian Fields, where Paris Avenue cuts under the viaduct.

Where Ruby told me the story of a raw December day of 1960—she and Janny and Perry following Mama Violet through the dump, like three ducklings, and Ruby's daddy lying in bed at home, delirious and dying. Mama with much bravery in her face and little in her pocketbook, making her way past jittery tramps and fallen women, picking trash so that Christmas would not be just another day. Mama Violet making a toyland out of a dump, finding a little boy-doll for my Ruby to love . . .

Where twenty black men lay dead.

Their greasy clothes were ripped to shreds by what any cop in the country knows as the work of TEC-9 semiautomatic fire. Rain had washed most of the blood away, but not all. They had been laid on their backs after they died, shirts and coats ripped open to expose their chests. Each had been branded: a mutant, an orphan, a misfit.

Rats and snails and snakes had feasted on the dead men's faces. Stray dogs waited nearby for the rest, teeth bared, howling. New Orleans cops were gathered, too.

I walked through the mud and rain, behind a rise of piled-up garbage bags that hid the corpses from the view of anyone passing along on Paris Avenue. I counted off the bodies. A young fresh-faced cop with rain dripping off his red neck and his hat and shield wrapped in plastic told me I had to leave the area. He smirked at me, and twirled his nightstick, wishing I would make his day.

I do not like cops who smirk. I thought very seriously about dropping Officer Redneck with a well-deserved punch to the middle of his chest, and how such a thing would make my own day for the second time. But then, far off in the distance, where I had left Claude Bougart waiting in his car, I saw somebody waving at me—Claude himself.

"Yes, sir—I'll be moving right along, sir," I told the redneck. I shuffled, he smirked.

When I reached Claude, after losing a shoe in my slog through the mud, I saw that he was not alone. In the car, making a fine mess of the backseat, was a black man maybe thirty years old. He wore denims, sunglasses, and a blue rag around his head. That was all I could see of him through the fat rain, except that he was smoking a cigarette and shaking like a junkie two days into trying to kick.

Claude grabbed my shoulder when I was near enough and shoved me into the front seat of his car.

"Man in back of you, his name's Kenny," Bougart said. I glanced back at Kenny while Bougart ran around the front of the car and jumped back into the driver's seat. Kenny looked away. Claude rubbed spittled rain off his mouth. "This man's a witness."

"Let's get him the hell out of here."

FORTY

"So, what's your husband like?"

"What do you think, Janny?"

"Sort of cute, talks funny."

"Where he's from, they think we talk funny." Ruby looked up at the clock on the wall, the one that read central standard. The other clocks were set for New York time and Los Angeles time—also for London, Moscow, and Tokyo, for what it mattered. "You know, Janny, I haven't got a whole lot more time. You want to go over this again?"

"These are sure interesting in light of these new murders—and where they all just so happen to be." Janice riffled through the pile of photocopied documents that Ruby had brought her. "I can go on air with this much. But what you're concluding from it all—well, I don't know."

"Tell me something you do know, Janny. Where'd you hear about MOMS?"

"I got that from Alderman Giradoux. Hippo called me aside after that press conference of his the other day to give me a police news tip."

Ruby tucked away this information.

"I haven't figured it out about the brandings," Ruby said. "Maybe Hock has."

"Let me know what he thinks, will you?"

"I will."

"Okay, I guess I've got everything here." Janice closed her notebook and stood up from her desk. "I'm thirsty." She stepped over to the little refrigerator in the corner of her cubicle in the WDSU newsroom, opened it, and pulled out two cans of diet Coke.

"Thanks," Ruby said, accepting one.

"I'll whip up something in plenty of time for the eleven o'clock news," Janice said. "Let's talk about your husband some more."

"What can I tell you?"

"I already asked, what's he like?"

"When I first met him, he was living like any other man—like a bear with furniture. But he's trainable."

"You love him a lot?"

"I love him crazy."

"You must. He's not *that* cute. Is he as good a man as daddy?"

"That's going to be hard to answer for a while. It's an easy and natural thing for me to love Daddy—and to respect him objectively as a man. It's so different with a husband. I love my husband, and I respect him, but I'm freshly married. And so in a funny way that I'm just learning about, Hock doesn't measure up to Daddy. Not yet anyway."

"How come?"

"Because I know the transparent devices I used to snare him. I can't imagine Daddy falling for such tricks. But Hock, he doesn't have a clue."

"La, now that's what I call a woman thing."

"I guess so."

"Ruby, can I ask you something else?"

"Okay."

"What's it like being married to a cop?"

"A good cop is a brooder and a dreamer. Hock does both,

all the time. It's catching. I dream about funerals sometimes, the kind where I'm sitting next to the mayor. Every tin wife has that dream."

"So that's what they call it?"

"That's right, tin wife."

Janice said nothing.

Ruby said, "Why do you ask?"

FORTY-ONE

"You got a last name, Kenny?"

"Not that I be telling you. Even a nigger got a right to his privacy."

Kenny had taken a hot shower, and Joe Never Smile had cooked him bacon and eggs. He was now sitting around in a terry cloth robe. But Kenny was still jumpy, especially with me in the picture.

A skel who is jumpy has not yet lost his faculties to booze and drugs and sleeping under the urban stars. Kenny was no exception. Claude was having a hard time getting him to repeat his story, to give up the details he knew he needed. Claude and I knew this drill without having to discuss it. Kenny did, too. We all had our roles: Claude was a good cop, I was the bad cop, Kenny wanted something in return for what he could tell either one of us.

Kenny lit up a cigarette and blew a stream of blue smoke into Claude's face. He curled a hand around the coffee mug in front of him, and repeated himself. "Uh-huh, got a right to my privacy."

"Man got a right to decent air in his own gott-damn house, too," said Joe Never Smile. He took up his cane and gimped over from the stove to the kitchen table where Kenny was sitting and yanked the cigarette from his mouth. "This shit's poison to you and everybody round you. What's the matter with you, fool?"

"I'm cool, that's what. Cool as that humpy Joe Camel. Gimmie that back, old man."

I got up from my place at the table and took the cigarette away from Joe Never Smile. I held it up in front of Kenny. It was still burning.

"You want to smoke, Kenny?" I asked him. He took a swipe at the cigarette, missing the prize. "Then let's be considerate enough to answer Officer Bougart's questions."

"C'mon, man."

"What's the last name?"

"I already told you 'bout my privacy."

I pushed the cigarette into Kenny's coffee mug and fizzled out the burning butt. I let go of the thing and it floated on top of Kenny's coffee.

Kenny protested, "Hey, I ain't got another of those one, man!"

"Say the word, Kenny, and I'll trot out to Claude's car and bring back a whole fresh pack. What brand you smoke, Claude?"

"Pall Mall."

Kenny liked the sound of that. "Name's Kenneth Lambert."

"You live at the dump off Paris Avenue, Kenny?" Claude asked.

"Where's my cigarettes?"

Claude took a red packet of Pall Malls from his shirt pocket and gave them to Kenny, who lit one. Bougart apologized to Joe Never Smile, "I'm hoping you'll be forbearing, sir."

Joe clumped around and grumbled. He went back to his stove and busied himself by wiping the top down with a wet sponge.

"Mr. Lambert, now tell us what you saw this morning," Claude said. "You know, about the three men."

Kenny looked over at me and said, "Saw these three ofays. They were wearing masks."

"What kind of masks?" Claude asked him.

"One he look like a bum. Second ofay he like a Barbary Coast pirate." Kenny sneered at me. "Last one he look just like you."

"What's that supposed to mean?"

"The peckerwood have him lipstick lips and a crown like a queen wear."

"No need to be insulting, Kenny. Unless you want to learn about New York–style cop hell."

"Mr. Lambert, when I happened to spot you, it seemed to me you were running off from all those bodies." Bougart gave me a wink. "Is that because the cops were turning up?"

"Sure that's it."

"Or maybe it was something else," I said. "Maybe you were hustling away what you took off those bodies. Say Kenny, where'd you leave your clothes?"

"Ain't no concern of yours."

"I think it is. I think I'm going to go have a look through your clothes."

"Okay, so you find something ain't mine. So what if I swiped some T-bird wine off a dead guy or something like that. He ain't going to be wanting wine no more."

"Kenny, you fooled me. I thought you were a bright guy. I thought you knew what happens if I find a dead man's stash on you."

"Mr. Lambert, I feel I have to tell you the consequences," Claude said sympathetically. "If we find stolen property in your possession that traces to a murder victim, it means we can close the rap on your head, no problem. That means you wind up in Angola waiting to get a lethal injection. You die like an old cat."

"Living at the dump, that's better than dead?"

"That's right," I said.

I grabbed up Kenny's packet of Pall Malls, took out the nineteen remaining cigarettes, ripped them up and dumped loose tobacco all over Kenny's head. Then I yanked him up from his chair by the collar of his robe. "You're smelling so sexy after your bath I've decided to take you into the other room, Kenny. We're going to play queen for a day."

"You white motherfuck! You crazy?"

"I am stone crazy, Kenny. Beside which I'm horny."

Kenny looked over to Claude, who only raised his eyebrows and said, "Man's from New York, what can I say?" Then Kenny looked over at Joe Never Smile. Joe said nothing, he just crossed himself.

Now it was between Kenny and me.

"Keep off of me, you crazy motherfuck!"

"What else did you see, Kenny?"

"Saw the Jeep they came in, man. But they don't see me 'cause I always sleep off aways by myself." Kenny talked fast. I was choking off his air supply. "Saw them three white motherfucks pile out with they army clothes and they masks on and they take off the license plates before they go run over to the gang of brothers. Next thing, I hear this poppy-pop sound. Then them motherfucks be burning something. That's all I seen."

I jerked Kenny's bathrobe hard. The cigarette went flying from his hand. Joe Never Smile stepped on it. I asked Kenny, "You happen to see a number before they took the plates off the Jeep? Tell me, or I'll lay you out on this table and do you right here in front of everybody."

"Yeah, I seen a number."

Claude put a pad of paper and a ballpoint pen on the table in front of Kenny. I lowered him to his seat.

"Give it up," Claude told him.

We got what we wanted.

"What you going to do with me now?" Kenny wanted to know. He looked at me, then Claude, and back at me again. "You going to toss me back where you find me?"

"Kenny, I'm sorry for your troubles," I said. "If you knew

me better, you'd believe me when I tell you I'm talking straight with you now."

I touched one of Kenny's shoulders, and felt it shiver. In myself, I felt something unfamiliar and wholly unaccountable, a sort of fatherly mood.

"Honest to God," I said, "I'm so damn sorry your life's full of adversity."

"Mister, you don't get it. Niggers like me, we survive adversity. It's contempt that kill us."

Joe Never Smile came up beside me. He put his hand on Kenny's other shoulder and asked him, "You got no place, son?"

"You know I don't."

"I need somebody to carry on with things."

"What things?"

"Jazz funerals. You want to talk about it serious like, you can stay around here. You be my apprentice."

Kenny Lambert, who escaped the branding iron, got what he wanted.

FORTY-TWO

"Now comes the time in the evening where you sing for your supper, Teddy."

"What are you talking about?"

A waiter approached the table to clear away the dishes. Teddy the Torch tinkled the ice in his gin and tonic and brushed a hand through his pomaded hair. The waiter paid him no mind. Teddy pouted.

"You said you're directing the choir over at Zeb Tilton's church, right?"

"That's right. Now, Ruby, you be wanting me to tell tales out of school?"

"If it helps Perry, yes."

"I'd do what I could to help him. Told you how I try getting him a job and all. Sound like you doing some kind of detective work."

"You could say that, Teddy."

"Well, go ahead, little Miss Gumshoe. Your Cousin Teddy ready to sing."

"Over at City Hall, when did you tell Alderman Giradoux

about MOMS—about mutants, orphans, and misfits? Not too many white folks know about it."

"When you think I ever seen Hippo? I'm just working my little job at the dog pound, I don't see no big shots."

"Well then, did you ever mention MOMS to Zeb Tilton?"

"Few months ago Zeb was trying to get some outreach ministry going, yeah. He asked me and some others—that gassy old Miss Hassie Pinkney, too, I think—about the lowest-down types. I mentioned MOMS then. Lot of MOMS hanging around my old haunts in Bourbon Street, you know."

Ruby thought, There's the connection—Tilton to Giradoux. "By the way, what's with Zeb and Sister Constance?"

"Oh, little Connie Ritchie. You remember, she's kin to Hassie. She become one of Zeb's little flower buds."

Ruby knew. She remembered her own baptism, when Minister Tilton placed one hand at the small of her back to lower her into the font and the other hand over her half-grown breasts. She never told Mama, but eventually she told her girlfriends. As it turned out, Ruby did not have the only such experience.

"She's very pretty," Ruby said.

"For a girl. She's the dreamy type, never says much of anything to anybody but Zeb."

"You talk to her?"

"Sometimes. Like this afternoon when she called me. But dearie, you know I don't talk to a lot of girls."

"You prefer talking to boys."

"Stop it, you're racing my heart."

"Why did Connie call you?"

"It was about Perry. He's hiding out there at the church. Sister Connie, she want to know if it's safe with Perry around her."

"Is it?"

"Sure a lot safer than Zeb being around her."

"Does Zeb Tilton know where Perry's hiding?"

"Hell no!"

"Teddy, I need you to do something."

"What's that?"

"Take me to Perry."

"Sure I will. On the way over I'll tell you about the other call I got today about Perry, the one from your hubby."

FORTY-THREE

I used the shower at Joe Never Smile's myself, and spent a good long time in the hot water. Which did not actually make me feel much cleaner, not after what I had been through.

Afterward, I borrowed some more dry things from Claude's duffel bag and an old pair of shoes from Joe Never Smile's closet. Everything fit well enough.

Meanwhile, Claude rang up a friend at a largely black force of cops at the Ninth Ward station house and had him run a check of the license plate number Kenny had provided. I was unsurprised at the resulting identification. Claude asked his pal to run some discreet pass-bys, to make sure the Jeep and its owner were not about to leave town.

At long last, something. Claude was pleased in a private way and said this several times.

Joe Never Smile cooked spaghetti for us all. Nobody wanted meatballs. I myself do not know when I will return to eating red meat.

Around ten o'clock, when I had figured I had to leave to meet Ruby at Tipitina's, wherever that was, I invited Claude to come along. He put up no resistance.

Claude drove us back to where I had been earlier in the day, Napoleon Avenue. Tipitina's turned out to be at the familiar corner of Napoleon and Tchoupitoulas Street—not far from the Blossom Cinema and the dirt lane where Ruby's family had once lived.

"You're going to like this place," Claude said when we were seated.

Maybe I would. The bar held a plaster bust of Professor Longhair, the late great zydeco piano man. And somebody at his old watch was pounding out "Stag-O-Lee" on the keyboards. I asked Claude, "The jazz is good?"

"Oh, man, this here's a shrine."

"Just tell me they don't play Dixieland junk for the tourists."

"Here's where they blow notes so sweet only colored folks in heaven can hear them."

"I don't mean you harm." Ruby took a step toward him, and handed over the journals, then stepped back. "Neither does my husband, neither does Teddy here."

Sister cried softly on the stair step.

"Little girl's a Judas telling y'all where I am so it get to the po-lice before I take care of business," Perry said. "That what she is—Judas!"

"No," Teddy said. "She's only scared. She's trying to help."

"We're all trying to help," Ruby said. "And that includes Officer Claude Bougart."

"Booger, he in on this?"

"He sure is. Look now, I've read your notes. I know where you're going."

"Do you?"

"You were trying to figure out who poisoned Daddy."

"Well, now I know who."

"But it's more than that, Perry. Now it's the murder of Cletus Tyler, and fifteen black boys with nowhere to go, and twenty black men over off Paris Avenue."

"Where Mama Vi took us that Christmas." Perry covered his eyes with his hands.

"It's all about being thrown-away, Perry."

"I been trying to forget, all my life I try . . ."

"But we can't afford to forget." Ruby took Sister's hand. Teddy took the other one, and they pulled her up. Then all three stepped over to the daybed where Perry sat. Ruby said, "Trust my husband's plan. Trust me and Teddy and Sister Connie and Claude. We trust him. Things will start moving in the right direction—come Sunday."

Teddy said, "You better believe I'm getting ideas for one *fab*ulous show."

"Are you with us?" Ruby asked.

"I don't know."

"Oh, Perry, please . . . !" Sister burst into tears, and sobbing spasms, years of anger and guilt vented. "Do it for me! Do it for what that snake lady done to me!"

"Little girl—!"

"I been trying to forgive and forget in the Jesus windows. But I can't. Oh, Jesus help me, I remember!" Sister went into something approaching a trance, which for once was genuine. "The snake got to pay for what she done. She got to pay for Willis Flagg. She got to pay for her lying church tongue, for making that man come after me, spoiling me. For making Daddy do what any daddy have to do, for making Mama so crazy she throw me away to Zeb Tilton!"

FORTY-FOUR

"Maybe I'll open a jazz joint when I get back to New York. I think I'd like that."

"You got time enough to run a club on top of the job?"

"I'm thinking about leaving."

Leaving. It was the first time I had said it, right out loud in a simple, declarative sentence.

"You kidding."

"No, I'm serious."

"Well then—you and me, we in that same boat."

"You know, Claude, I thought I'd be a cop until I croaked."

"There's a bright side for you, Hock."

"What's that?"

"You got a wife." Claude looked past me then and rose from his chair. "At least if you walk off the job, your wife going to be glad."

And there was Ruby. She had Teddy along with her. Claude took Ruby's hands and pulled her toward him. There was an awkward second or two, with poor Claude looking back and forth between Ruby and me. Claude kissed Ruby's cheek.

I stood up and kissed Ruby on the lips. I felt sorry for Claude, but not that sorry.

"Sit down, gentlemen." Ruby looked up at the clock on the wall. In sixteen minutes it would be eleven. "We haven't got much time."

"Time for what?" I asked.

"Just sit down."

Ruby took a seat without answering. Claude and Teddy and I sat down, too. Seeing Ruby take a hand in a criminal case was a first for Claude and Teddy, as was the telepathy that seemed to be working between Ruby and me. And so it was only natural for them to be looking the way they did, like they were out of breath.

"What's your take on the brandings?" Ruby asked me.

"Scare tactic, conveniently diversionary," I said.

"You're reading me, aren't you, Hock?"

"I am."

"Y'all mind letting us in on the ESP?" Teddy asked.

"It's message murder," I said. "Not in the psychopathic sense. In the American-pie greedhead sense. And crude enough for rabid cops to take care of the grunt work. By the way, the Jeep that three-man splatter squad used, it registers to Mueller."

"Mueller's partners on and off duty with Eckles," Claude said. "So that's two of the hitters."

"You said it was a three-man squad," Ruby said.

"The other one's got to be a detective by the name of Vonny LeMay," I told her. "He's got the Mueller and Eckles mind-set, which I saluted by cold-cocking him in Hippo's office. Plus, at the power station, LeMay happens to know it's all black boys inside before anybody from forensics comes out to say so."

"But back to the opening scene of the play," Ruby said. "When did you figure it's a three-man killing crew?"

Claude spilled the inevitable beans. "Well, Hock spotted three men when they tried scaring him off with TEC-9s and—"

"What?" Ruby glared at me. "You were shot?"

"They missed, accidentally on purpose." I could tell I was in for a long talk with Ruby later on that night, the one where she would go on about sitting with the commissioner and the mayor and his wig in a cemetery.

"And then there were three different casing marks found at the power station massacre," Claude said. "So anyhow, we got Mueller dead to rights. We can sweat him and Eckles into giving up LeMay, no problem."

"You mentioned a message," Teddy said.

"Myself, I learned the message in 'Nam," I said. "Let's say you want to take over a village but the locals don't go for the idea. You could just blow them all away, but it wouldn't be efficient."

"There's a better idea?" Teddy asked.

"Just kill a few villagers—throw-aways, let's say. The rest take the hint."

"I see," Teddy said. "And the brandings?"

"That's the diversion here, like Hock says." Claude took over explaining. "The big boys want it to play like a bias crime—the MOMS bit. Like maybe some skinheads doing the city a favor by wiping out disreputable elements. Which everybody knows supposed to mean no-account brothers, and meaning everybody's willing to forgive and forget anything that happen to them—and just move out the way."

Teddy shook his head. "I don't know. Powerful men killing for real estate?"

"Men and real estate, it's the stuff that wars are made of," I said. "You can look it up."

"Can't just look it up," Claude said. "History books 'round here don't tell you the real deal."

"Then here's the short course. Real estate doesn't mean just land and the buildings on it. It's about the type of people on the premises, and in the neighborhood. Which comes down to the question of who has the money and who doesn't."

"But money is restless, like people," Ruby said, adding

to my thesis. "And unless people are shuffled around, real estate just sits there making nobody a profit."

"Buy low, sell high, that gets you the big profits, as everybody knows," I said. "You want to make a killing in real estate, so to speak, one way to do it is you buy cheap in poor neighborhoods—"

"For instance, black neighborhoods," Ruby cut in.

"Right. Then you make sure the neighborhood gets good and run-down. And you get rid of anybody who hasn't already left. After which you develop your empty space into high-rolling casino complexes, say."

"And neighborhoods where white folks aren't afraid to live," Ruby said.

"It takes time," I said. "And manipulation."

"*Manipulation.*" Teddy said this like he was trying to taste the word. "To me that means doing something subtle. But what's happening is . . . Well, murder's so *obvious.*"

"The subtlety comes in who gets it," Claude said. "You want to make sure nobody going to care about who gets it." He stopped and thought a moment, then said to me, "Tell me one thing, though. How you expect to connect up these murders lately with Willis dying all those years ago?"

"That's the point of us all going to church," I said.

And then with Teddy and Ruby nodding their heads, I filled in Claude about the Sunday plan, and finalized assignments. Claude was nodding his head by the time I was through.

"Two things," Ruby said, glancing up at the clock. "First, what about Mama and Janny? Are we going to clue them in?"

"Not necessary," I said. "But just make sure your sister shows up with a camera crew."

"Oh, there's no problem there. Now what about Hippo?"

"In his case, we just let the chips fall."

Ruby stood up. "Right now, gentlemen, come on with me. We're going into the back office for a few minutes. I arranged it with the manager. We have to catch my sister on

TV. She's going to tell everybody what Hock figured—and what I confirmed."

All four of us left the table and resettled ourselves into chairs in the back office. Ruby switched on the eleven o'clock news.

"Janny's looking real nice," Claude said. Janice was sitting next to an anchorman wearing a Gingrich-style helmet of silver hair as the opening credits of the evening news hour rolled. "Yeah, that sister of yours she easy on the eyes."

"You always liked the Flagg women," Ruby said.

"True, true."

The hair helmet spoke.

"Good evening, ladies and gentlemen. Tragically, there are more MOMS murders in the news tonight . . ."

"Oh yeah, like this guy going to lose sleep about it," Teddy said. Ruby hushed him.

"This afternoon, New Orleans police discovered twenty homeless men shot to death, their bodies then mutilated with a branding iron. These latest murders—third in a clearly apparent series of executions—were carried out in a public dumping ground along Paris Avenue. Here with an exclusive report on the possible motives behind these horrifying murders—shocking motives—is Jan Flagg."

Janice Flagg appeared on-screen. "Confidential sources tell us that the three separate sites of the brutal MOMS murders have two respected civic leaders in common—Alderman Hippocrates Beauregard Giradoux, and Minister Zebediah Tilton of the Land of Dreams Tabernacle . . ."

"Go, girl!" Claude said. He apologized for the outburst, never taking his eyes from the television screen.

"The names of the alderman and the minister have been traced through real estate records and tied to prospective multimillion-dollar casino and condominium deals in the near vicinity of all three killing fields . . ."

"I don't believe what I'm hearing!" Claude said.

"We are about to show you news film that is extremely graphic . . ."

Footage of the discovery of Cletus Tyler's mutilated body beneath the levee not far from where we were sitting filled the screen, followed by film of the riverside power station—and finally new film, with Janice doing the voice-over.

"This was the grisly scene this afternoon at the Paris Avenue dump when police discovered the bodies of twenty homeless, as yet unidentified black men. Police officials say the men were probably gunned down as they slept—shot with the so-called street-sweeper, the semiautomatic weapon favored by military commandos and drug dealers . . ."

The news film then dissolved into side-by-side pictures of two smiling men, Hippo Giradoux and Zeb Tilton. The names appeared beneath their faces, as naturally as any prison-processing portrait I have ever seen.

"Damn, she's tearing them *up!*" Claude said. "Hell's nothing but an iceberg now!"

FORTY-FIVE

Sister's eyes were closed. Her delicate face was uptilted to an oval window—her precious stained-glass Jesus. Circled doves formed a plumed halo around the head of the Son of God.

Despite the commotion all around her, Sister betrayed not the slightest facial expression. Sunlight streaked through the windowed eyes of Jesus and shone down upon her.

Then quite suddenly, she was—what? Seized by the spirits? Sister trembled, as in the throes of sexual frenzy. Minister Tilton had told her the first time she knew such a frenzy, *"You just met up with the sweet-assed tremble, my lady-child."*

Then, as suddenly, Sister collapsed into serenity.

Minutes passed. The congregation held its collective breath. Finally, Sister rose from the bench to stand, her body now moving as smoothly as water up a stream. She saw nothing of the people in front of her.

She snapped her neck left and right, tossing back beaded plaits of black hair. Her face glistened with sweat.

Sister raised her hands. Her eyes dropped shut again behind heavy lids. And she chanted:

"Danse Calinda, boudoum, boudoum
Danse Calinda, boudoum, boudoum . . . !"

Then, in great bursts of silver gray mist shooting up from stream jets built into the floorboards for just such very moments of high religious drama, Minister Zebediah Tilton appeared.

Ascending on a hydraulic lift from a pit below the raised altar stage, he was resplendent in a shining black robe, trimmed at the neck and sleeves in sable and covered with gris-gris.

I turned to Ruby and whispered in her ear, "I can tell you now I was worried Tilton might not show."

"Janny got him good with the insinuations on her broadcast. He had to be here. Otherwise he'd be admitting guilt."

"Perry's clued into everything, right? About the Jeep, the gunmen—?"

"Everything. We've got all the angles rounded off. So what do you have to say to me?"

"You've been a very good tin wife."

"Thanks, sexy."

I looked past Ruby, and past Mama sitting on the other side of her. Claude, sitting at the end of the pew, caught my look. I gave him the nod he wanted to see. Claude nodded back, his signal to me that his buddies in the Ninth Ward had made a successful dawn raid on Mueller and his Jeep. I had little doubt that Claude's men had employed unusually persuasive methods to convince Mueller to give up Eckles and LeMay.

Ruby and I turned and nodded at Teddy the Torch, two pews back. He mouthed a response. *Fabulous!*

Minister Tilton beamed at his congregants and then knelt before the altar table as Sister's chanting grew in volume and urgency.

He crossed himself, then again faced his flock. He rapped the floor with a gold-topped ebony cane. And when the worshipers hushed, he reached into his pocket for a silver

Tiffany lighter—to fire the wick of a single candle on the table, shaped like a crucifix, and black as Minister Tilton's robe.

Then he sang, and the dark wattles below his neck quivered to the stamping feet of the worshipers. Minister Tilton's forehead beaded with sweat. He stopped and raised up his hammy arms, commanding his people, "Ladies and gentleman, this *hear*-uh church of ours . . . this *glow*-ree-us Land of Dreams Tabernacle . . . we show an open door to everybody! Yes sir, yes ma'am—yeah, you right, I'm talking about every-*body!* Doubters and pouters, shouters and shiners."

A-men!

"But whosoever shall *be*-uh with us upon this beauty-ful morning . . . Oh La, please—you must understand!"

Understand!

"You all got one big *dew*-tee in common today, don't you know."

"That's right . . . Tell it, brother . . . !"

"You all got to join me, hear-uh? We must lift up our voices all together-uh . . . in a mighty, mighty call—to those whose spirits . . . whose *spirits . . . !"*

Yes, Lord!

"Whose spirits live with the *Lord*-uh!"

Yeah, you right!

Bodies swayed in time with the cadence of Minister Tilton's beseechings, and the oaken pews in the Land of Dreams Tabernacle groaned. And then the mass chanting started, rolling and rolling in throaty waves, pulsating the liquid air.

"Danse Calinda, boudoum, boudoum . . . !"

Three hundred pairs of black hands clapped in syncopation. Three hundred pairs of shoes pounded out the downbeat.

Mama's eyes surged with tears.

She slapped her hands together along with all the others, and beat the floor with her feet every bit as determinedly. She would hear her man. She would believe! And maybe somewhere in all that silver gray steam up on the altar she would even see her Willis, at least in the prism of her tears.

Sister stepped forward to the very front of the altar. Her bare toes inched over the edge. Her arms flapped. She sang:

"Eh! Eh! Bomba, hen! hen!
Canga bafio, te,
Canga moune de le,
Canga do ki la,
Canga li . . . !"

Minister Tilton and the congregation joined this new chant, their massed voices gathering to a storm of pathos and yearning.

"Sis-*tuh!*" shouted Minister Tilton, rapping his cane, addressing his acolyte. "Sister, prepare! Prepare for the dance-uh—the *danse calinda* of your revered-uh *voudou!*"

Sister picked up a leather-bound flask of brandy next to the crucifix candle, opened it, and poured some of the liquor over a sprinkling of brick dust lining a black ceramic bowl. She set down the flask and bowed in the direction of Minister Tilton, then backed away.

Dropping his cane to the misty floor, Minister Tilton picked up the bowl with both hands. A shaft of sunlight glinted off one of his diamond cuff links. He lifted the bowl to his lips, and drank down the gritty mixture of brandy and brick. Slowly, he began rotating his hips and shuffling his feet backward, then forward. His movements accelerated as the congregation lifted their voices again to the *canga,* now minus Sister, whose face was once more lifted to her Jesus window.

Minister Tilton poured the rest of the brandy into the bowl and ignited it with his Tiffany lighter. The bowl flamed up high over the altar table. Minister Tilton passed his hands through the flame, and quickened his dance steps as the *canga* picked up tempo.

"I call out Willis Flagg!" he shouted. *"Eh! Eh! Bomba, hen! hen!* I call out Willis Flagg! *Eh! Eh! Bomba, hen! hen! . . .* Willis Flagg, speak through me . . . !"

Silence, or nearly so, as the congregants waited.

Mama cried softly.

A tall man in a scarlet robe, his head and face concealed by a hood, called from the rear of the church: *"Bomba, hen, hen! . . . Bomba, hen, hen . . . !"*

Minister Tilton was startled.

Grasping the gris-gris in both his hands, as if he sincerely believed in its power, he asked feebly of the man in scarlet rushing toward him, "What—?"

But there was no answer from the man running crazily up the center aisle, whirling and leaping and howling until he reached the altar's edge. Until a thoroughly stunned Minister Tilton tripped over his cane and fell to his knees, and gasped, "No, you mustn't come up—!"

Disobeying, the man vaulted over the railing. He scrambled to the altar stage, then turned to the confused congregation.

He pushed back the hood of his robe and exposed a greased and powdered face with straight, hawkish features, and wavy hair covered in ghostly white powder. Then he undid the laces of his robe, allowing it to slip from his shoulders. Save for a thong covering his groin, and a belted knife at his waist, he was naked. Women screamed, but did not avert their eyes, not even the old ones with the lacy fans and their heads covered in *tignons,* for the figure before them was a perfect masculine beauty.

He raised his hands, clenched in huge brown fists, and cried out over a church fallen to dead quiet:

"I am Willis Flagg! I *am* Willis Flagg!"

And from the pew next to the widow Violet Flagg, a trembling Hassie Pinkney stood up, and shrieked, "Jesus, Mary, Joseph—it's him! Oh La, I can't believe—it's *him . . . !"* The man sitting beside her with the wooden leg tried to comfort her, but his ministrations were of little use. Hassie screamed, over and over, "La, it's him . . . it's *him!*"

The old ladies in *tignons* fainted away. Children squealed. Men stared, gape-mouthed, unable to help the women and the young. The tall, muscular naked man grasped the shoulders of a terrified Zebediah Tilton and lifted him several inches off the floor, then dropped him. Tilton crumpled in a heap.

The man again roared to the congregation, "I, Willis Flagg, have come out!" He then knelt to Minister Tilton, and whispered, "Number's up, chump. We on to you and Hippo and your scam. And I am in control of all these crazy people in your church. You spend all these years riling people up with hoo-doo and voodoo, that's an unwise crime. Because the people you do wrong, they going to rile right back at you. Hear them out there?"

The noise of the church was frightful—the screaming and pounding and shrieking of the Lord's name. The naked man put his lips to Tilton's ear, and growled, "All I got to do is throw you off this altar, tell these good people to tear up your phony ass. You be one dead nigger."

Tilton said something that sounded like a small animal trying to loose himself from a trap.

"We got cops all over the place, by which I mean brothers from the Ninth Ward," the naked man said, still shouting into Tilton's hot ear. "Don't be expecting no politician friends or ofay cops to save you neither. They on their way to jail. Only thing going to save your blubber ass now is you give me straight answers when I ask you. You got that? I think you do."

The naked man stood up. He stripped Tilton's robe of all gris-gris and, with elaborate gestures, dropped them into the bowl of flaming brandy, so that all in the church could see he meant to destroy the minister's control over them.

"Be gone, the imposter's fakery!" the naked man shouted.

He then raised an arm, asking for silence. It took nearly twenty minutes for the crowd to grow quiet to hear anyone on the altar. Slowly, the naked man pointed at Hassie Pinkney in her pew, her hands raised to cover a scared horse face.

"You!" he shouted at Hassie. "You were in league with the imposter cowering at my feet. *You* placed the snake below the steps, where you knew it would strike me. I carried that venom in my body for years after, until it killed me. *You* killed me!"

The naked man used both his hands to pull Tilton to his feet. "And why? Because I threatened the imposter's crimes against us all." Tilton was shoved forward a few steps. "Behold, the imposter! You know he's stolen from all of you—all of you! Be free of him from this day forward!"

Mama sobbed.

"La, gawd—have mercy!" Miss Hassie screamed.

The congregation rose. Men shook their fists at Tilton. Women spit.

"Yes, yes—*you!*" the naked man shouted, jabbing his fingers into Tilton's pudgy back. "You oppressed us and cheated us for so many years—before and since my death!"

Sister seemed to float above the rim of the altar. The congregants became quiet as she pointed to the screaming, trembling Hassie Pinkney.

"You were the one, Auntie," she shouted. "You gave me to the drunken man, to save yourself from being raped! You turned Mama and Daddy against me! You threw me away to Minister Tilton, who has had me in his unholy way!"

Sister stepped back, and the naked man took over.

"But there's more," the naked man said, shoving rudely at Tilton. "Who you been working for, Zeb? Whose hey-boy is you? Tell us now—good and loud!"

"Hippocrates Beauregard Giradoux!" Minister Tilton hollered, his eyes glowing with fear. "Hippo, he done it, not me. Hippo's the devil behind it all!"

"I am not alone," the naked man said. "There are others who were killed! Homeless brothers—boys and men. Tell us, who did the devil Giradoux call on to carry out these murders?"

"The po-lice!"

"Who? Say it loud!"

"Detectives name of Eckles and Mueller and LeMay."

"Say it again, imposter!"

Tilton named the killers, straight into the lens of the television camera advancing up the aisle to catch the confession.

"Eckles . . . Mueller . . . LeMay."

"And what was the purpose of this reign of terror?" The naked man shoved a fist into Tilton's spine. "Tell us!"

"Money!"

"Money, you say! Look out upon the poor people of your congregation . . . Look at their faces, look at all the faces that have known hunger. Imposter! You eat so well a hundred people in this room could have their *Give us this day our daily bread* answered with what you ate this morning! Shame on you—shame!"

The congregation shouted thunderously.

Shame! Shame! Shame!

"And you—Hassie Pinkney! Snake woman!"

"La, mercy! Mercy! Oh La, please!"

"It was you, Hassie Pinkney—you killed me! To keep me from telling the truth I tell today!"

Hassie fell to the floor, gasping and writhing, consumed by her guilt, which took the form of what Charity Hospital would later that Sunday morning diagnose as a massive cerebral hemorrhage.

The naked man used his knife to cut a lock of hair from his head and then held it high over him, so all could see.

"Today, I have destroyed the power of the imposter Zebediah Tilton, who was foolish enough to call me out. I tell you all now—shun him. Let earthly law have its way with him! This hair I hold is the most powerful gris-gris of all, hair from one gone to the beyond. I shall give it to one who lives amongst you—one of the very least of you. I shall plant it in his head this very night as he sleeps—and there it will grow. I shall give the power to a thrown-away child, now a grown man in my own image. That man is Perry Duclat."

And then, the naked man disappeared into the steaming pit below the altar.

Four black policemen, led by Officer Claude Bougart, arrested Zebediah Tilton and read him his rights in accordance with the Miranda law. Janice Tilton and her crew from Channel 6 captured it all on film.

Just before airtime, a visitor was shown to Janice Tilton's cubicle in the WDSU newsroom. He had hobbled in from the corridor and now took a seat across from Janice.

"You might know me," he said. "My name's Newcombe, I live in the cottage your mama and daddy used to own. Next door to Hassie Pinkney, gone to what she got coming."

"How can I help you?"

"I got something I been keeping in trust for a long time. Don't know just what it is, but I always had a bad feeling about it. Hassie, she give it to me."

"Let's see it."

Newcombe reached into the breast pocket of his Sunday suit. He pulled out a flat cardboard box and gave it to Janice. "It's a tape recording," he said. "The old-fashioned kind, not one of them cassettes."

"What's on it?"

"Don't know. Never wanted to hear it. I ain't got a player anyhow."

"Wait here, Mr. Newcombe."

"I ain't got nothing special to do."

Janice got up and took the tape reel to the editing room, where an engineer found a way to play a conversation preserved from way back in 1948.

It was a short conversation. Short and to the point:

Now Sister Hassie, we can't be having hotheads around here like your neighbor Willis to ruin all our church plans. So I'm asking your help . . . What I got to do? . . . The man's a believer in the message of serpents. See to it one of your snakes get to Willis sometime . . .

Janice lay her head on a film cutting table and wept.

FORTY-SIX

In the big house on St. Charles Boulevard, Alderman Hippocrates Beauregard Giradoux awoke in his bed from a fevered sleep. Someone seemed to be calling his name from the sunlit doorway, a woman with a voice that confused him, a voice at once flirtatious and bitter. The drugs he had taken the night before—a fistful of antihistamines, three Klonopin tranquilizers, a Tylenol number 4—had failed to prevent a replay of the past few nights' disturbing vision: a man trying desperately to outrun falling stone slabs taller than himself, unable to lift his feet from a quicksand of broken bodies . . .

This strange-sounding woman, maybe it was only one more nightmare.

"Hippo?"

He raised his head and saw her in the doorway. She glided toward him across the door, her naked body eclipsing the light. He tried to move but could not.

"Hippocrates, my love . . . Hippocrates!"

Now he tried to call out, but his tongue only made dopy noises. She kept floating toward him over the floor, so it appeared, and as she did her voice grew rough and aged and mocking. "Hippocrates, my love," she cawed. *"My love . . . Hah!"*

When he felt hot breath in his face—breath that smelled old, like dried moss on a dead log—he knew the woman was no dream. He knew he was powerless to make her go away by rubbing his eyes, even if he could lift his hands from his sides.

She was now at his canopied bed. His head flopped sideways. He saw the blur of an old woman vaulting from the floor, her witch's figure leaping astride his prone body, her bony legs straddling his corpulent chest. His eyes were tightly closed in fear, but he at last found in himself a defensive movement. He flailed his heavy arms, as if trying to swat away some huge insect.

She squeezed her legs tight against his chest, pinning him to the bed. "Hippo, my darling love . . . *My darling! . . .* Hah!"

Dangling from a silver chain hanging down her veiny white bosom was a scabrous lump of red pulp, something that looked like a rotted bell pepper—waving back and forth crazily from one breast to another as she rode the big man struggling below. She slapped his face. His eyes popped open.

"Look at the cockscomb, my darling!" she cawed, cupping her wrinkled breasts, bouncing them up and down in long, ring-studded fingers. She shimmied over him, smacking his face repeatedly with the blood-swollen flesh of a dead cock rooster.

Hippo grasped wildly at the cockscomb with both hands, but never managed to close his fingers over the thing, to tear it off its chain and cast it away. Instead, a scream coursed up from his heaving chest, through his throat and out his mouth . . .

She would come to describe it as a horrible echo more than a scream. As if the bedroom walls were canyon rock instead of plaster, as if some demon inside her husband was running for his unholy life. She would come to describe the hiss of his dying scream as the sound of chicken thighs sizzling in frying oil. *'Bout the sound he going to make . . . You ain't never going to forget that sound!* And why would she ever want to?

Later that morning, another hospital in New Orleans would make another diagnosis of sudden death, this time cardiac arrest.

When she learned the outcome, Ophelia Dabon expressed the more pungent view of what happened to her employer: "Hex done pulled the heart right outta one evil white man."

FORTY-SEVEN

"Among other things I'll tell you about when I get home, I've been doing a lot of serious thinking down here in New Orleans," I said. I was drinking coffee in Mama's kitchen and talking to Davy Mogaill on the telephone. "About the department, and also about Mogaill and Hockaday, Private Investigations."

"Who're you going to be pleasing, lad? The inspector or myself?"

"It's better we talk when I'm back. I can't hear you so well now anyway." Not with a half-dozen kids running in and out of the kitchen helping themselves to sodas in the refrigerator. Uncle Bud, meanwhile, was padding around in his holiday frock popping open Dixie beer bottles for everybody but me. Mama and the other women were clustered around the stove, debating the finer points of preparing a proper Creole roux and dishing up plates of turkey and sweet peas and yams and white gravied mashed potatoes. Out in the parlor the television set was buzzing with football. I had been sitting there myself a couple of minutes ago with my stomach pooching out over my belt after taking seconds on the turkey and potatoes. "Can you hear me all right, Davy?"

"Aye, I can make out you're in the family way. That's a lucky man, Neil, having folks around you on Thanksgiving Day."

Poor lonesome Davy Mogaill, I thought. I asked him, "What's been happening about King Kong Kowalski?"

"He'd be a man deserving of justice . . ."

Mogaill said something more, but I could not make it out over the Thanksgiving racket. I stuffed my free ear with a finger. "What's that about Kowalski?"

"Enjoy your holiday. But come home soon, lad."

The phone connection to New York broke at Mogaill's end. I thought I heard him laughing before the click that ended our talk. It was just as well. Ruby was calling me from the parlor.

"Come on out here, Hock—you've got to see this!"

"Oh, Ruby just yelling on account that lying mayor coming on the TV again," Mama said as I moved away from the phone. She gave a wicked stirring to something in a pot that steamed her face. "Politicians they just love a big football audience to spread they fertilizer far as they can sling it."

There had been so many City Hall press conferences since Sunday I had lost count. Reporters from all over the state—as well as from New York, Chicago, Los Angeles, and even a correspondent from *Le Monde* of Paris—were likewise encamped at the headquarters of the beleaguered New Orleans Police Department. In responding to the media, the mayor and his police commissioner (and golfing pal) employed every cliché in their respective arsenals.

They were appalled by the scurrilous conduct of the late Alderman Giradoux and his silent partner in the business of real estate speculation and murder, Minister Tilton—who was of course to be prosecuted to the full extent of the law. They pledged a crash program of racial sensitivity training for New Orleans' finest—now cleansed by the removal of Sergeant LeMay and Detectives Mueller and Eckles—as a demonstration of their outrage upon discovering intolerable police practices that of course have no place in the city.

Political hacks use strong words like *appalled* and *scurrilous* and *full extent of the law* and *outrage* and *intolerable* and somehow make it all sound like elevator music. Mama's vocabulary has considerably more vitality, as she was to demonstrate.

"Come out here, Hock," Ruby called again. "Mama, you come, too."

And so we did. A gaggle of reporters had trapped the mayor in the front yard of his Garden District home—among them Janice, who had enjoyed her own fifteen minutes of fame on Tuesday when the *Times-Picayune* proclaimed her a "woman on the move" on the television page. Mama and I entered the parlor just in time to see Janice ask the mayor, "Sir, when will you be replacing the police commissioner with someone more alert to wrongdoers under his command?"

"Well, I'll cross that bridge when I come to it," the mayor said.

Mama said, "Liar means he going to double-cross that bridge if he ever come to it."

"And now let me take this opportunity," the mayor gassed on to the TV cameras, "to wish each and every citizen of New Orleans a happy holiday as we pause to give thanks for the great and gracious bounty that God has seen fit . . ."

Mama flicked off the TV set. "They start jabbering about God, that's it!" Uncle Bud and several others groaned so loud that Perry managed to slip in through the front door, resplendent in new gentleman's clothes, and it was at least two minutes before anybody noticed.

"La, you come back!" Mama finally said, a floured hand thumping over her apron-covered heart. She looked her nephew up and down, from the charcoal gray fedora that matched his flannel suit to the gleaming black of his cap-toe brogans. "Where you grab your fine things?"

Instead of answering, Perry reached inside the breast pocket of his suitcoat and brought out a wallet. He took a hundred dollars in twenties from the wallet and handed the money over to Mama, whose mouth naturally fell open. "I stole this money from you, Aunt Vi. That and more. I'm going to pay you a hundred every week from now on, principal and interest. So now you don't have to be cleaning that Ava LaRue's house anymore."

"You best tell me where this come from." Mama fanned the handful of twenties in Perry's face.

"Well, I'm collecting Zeb's salary, you know. I took me a little advance for the clothes, which anybody in my position's going to need. That's in my pay-back budget. The clothes and what I figure I owe everybody."

"Money s'posed to make things all different with you?"

"To some degree. Actions from now on going to change me more. I'm changing in a big way, too, Aunt Vi. Going to make a good mark by it."

Perry took off his hat. There was a pomade sheen in wavy hair. He crossed the room to where I stood, took my hand, and shook it. It was not hard for him to pick out my face in the crowd. "I want to thank you, man, for being the one who strung it all together."

"Your taking over the church, it wasn't part of my plan," I said. "You were supposed to impersonate Willis Flagg and scare Tilton and Hassie Pinkney into revealing themselves—which I guess you sure did—but the rest of the show, that was your private idea."

"Think I'm doing badly?"

"You're moving fast, Perry. Don't make it fast and loose."

"I'm in a hurry to do right for all concerned."

"How you doing that, Perry?" Mama asked.

"All that property in the lane where my Uncle Willis got stole out of his cottage? I got lawyers working to deed the whole place over to the tenants. We're looking at other properties that way, too."

"What about Constance Ritchie?" Ruby asked.

"I got a counselor and a lawyer working her affairs. So far she want to stay at the church and generally take care of things. That'd be fine, I think. And we going to have a real church . . ." Perry made a little turn, addressing everybody in the room. "Something that support and give back to people. That's the change I promise to make. Now I'm just going to do it, ain't saying no more about it."

"That's good," Bud said. "There's more food in the kitchen, let's eat."

Mama put the hundred dollars in her apron pocket and stepped up to Perry. She touched a cheek and his chin. "La, you look so much like Willis." Her eyes teared over, and she kissed him.

That night, about an hour after the early WDSU news broadcast, Janice came to the house with Claude in tow. I watched out the window as the two of them stepped from Claude's car and walked up to the house, holding hands.

When Ruby and Janice were happily occupied with photo albums—pointing and laughing at each other's growing-up pictures—Claude asked me, "How about we talk outside? Don't want me to be having a lonely smoke, do you?"

Claude lit up a Pall Mall as we stood together outside on Mama's steps in the black night. The two of us big tough cops jumped when a dead branch made a lot of noise falling down from the top of the double oak tree down at the curb.

"Janice and Ruby's father planted that tree," I said.

"It's like he just talked to us now." We were quiet for a while. Then Claude spoke again. "You know I had to put you in front of me, sort of push you into all this to break it up." Rather than looking at me, even in the darkness, he looked straight ahead as he talked. "I got to be straight with you, I didn't care much about maybe you take a bullet for your troubles. Now I want you to know, Detective Hockaday—I'm obliged to you beyond my being able to say so."

"Using me—what was in it for you, Claude?"

"Well, like I say, hell's just another iceberg after all's happened. So that's my sign. I'm staying with the department." Claude threw his cigarette down and stamped it out. "How about you? You staying, or hanging it up?"

"I wish I knew."

Later yet, a black Lincoln pulled up to Mama's house. Miss Ava LaRue's driver, Matthew, had come to deliver a bottle of Dom Pérignon as a gift from Mama's longtime employer.

"No man come to my house on Thanksgiving going to leave hungry," Mama said, accepting the champagne. By that time she had enjoyed a number of lesser intoxicants. Mama grabbed Matthew by the hand, led him to the kitchen, and set him up with a plate. "You ain't going to turn me down, are you, Matthew?"

"I surely am not."

Mama turned her back and whispered, "Thank you, Ophelia."

On Friday, I had Huggy drive me over to Crozat Street so I could say my good-byes to the legend called Joe Never Smile. Then Huggy returned me home, where Ruby had packed our bags and was waiting on the front steps for the ride to the airport.

Then the hard part.

Mama held Ruby tight in her arms and smiled bravely, the way people do when they think they might die and never see anybody again. The two of them made promises to each other. I heard Mama say, "You done all right, girl. I'm proud of you, and if you ever blue you remember I'm right here loving you."

When she broke from Ruby, I took Mama and held her by the shoulders and kissed her lips, and told her she was lovely as spring's first blooms along the cool, blue streams of Galty. Mama said, "I'm going to love you like your own mama and I'm going to nag you, too, Neil. You take care of my girl. Hear?"

Then Mama pushed me away, and said to us both, "Farewells ought to be abrupt. Remembrance is all the fonder that way."

EPILOGUE

"You notice how Janny and Claude were slow-dancing?"

"I noticed."

Ruby lay her head against my shoulder. Below us, as the plane climbed toward cruising level, was Lake Pontchartrain. It was blue, struck in half by a wake of yellow-white sunlight.

"Everything is changed forever for everybody," Ruby said. "Of all people, Perry's going to see to that."

"Change comes every day."

"Not in New Orleans, not in the family. Not until you, Irish."

"I don't know about that. I do know that the rest of the changes coming aren't going to be easy. There's still Tilton to deal with, for instance. Even in prison he's got rights to those properties. Then there's the little matter of Hippo's estate."

"Zeb Tilton will cooperate with property transfers when it's pointed out to him that it's either that or maybe a choice between life in prison or the injection. I suppose that's how Perry's lawyers are going to lay out his options. Wouldn't you say, Hock?"

"Sounds right."

"And I'd certainly say the church members are all behind Perry."

"There's still Ava LaRue. She's Hippo's heir, and I imagine at least some of the estate's tied to Tilton."

"Miss LaRue's a wealthy lady, but I don't think she's the greedy type." Ruby looked out the airplane window for a second or two, taking a couple of deep breaths, as if she were suddenly dizzy. She turned back to me and said, "Even if she was, can't you see Perry's lawyers pointing out the bad percentages of a woman in her position making a profit off a church full of poor black folks?"

"Perry dealing with lawyers, that's hard to compute."

We flew along saying nothing for a while. I read an article in the airline magazine about the carefree life of New Orleans. Also I made a final decision not likely to make for a carefree life back in New York.

"What about you?" Ruby asked. "How's life going to change for you?"

"It won't. I just decided to turn down Davy Mogaill's offer of partnership. I'm staying with the department, King Kong or no. I'll still be pressing my complaint against him, and doing whatever else it takes to get him off the force."

"I bet myself you wouldn't quit, Hock. I just won."

"I have to tell you, for a while there I thought I'd quit."

"Oh, sure. Then what would we do? Move to Coconuts, Florida, with all the rest of the retired New York cops and their tin wives?"

"Not for us, Ruby. I guess I'll be a cop until I croak. If I get to heaven somehow, then I'll retire. The whole idea of heaven is that there isn't a cop in the place."

"So you think when we get home, life's going to be pretty much the same?"

"Pretty much."

"Guess again, Irish." Ruby put both hands on her stomach, which had a rise to it I had not noticed until now. "What would you think about a little Hockaday?"